Thirty Days Has September

THE FIRST TEN DAYS

by

James Strauss

Geneva
Shore
Publishing
GENEVA SHORE PUBLISHING, INC

Geneva
Shore
Publishing

Geneva Shore Publishing, Inc.

www.genevashorereport.com

Cover Art: "Landing Zone" by John O. Wehrle (U.S. Army Combat Art Program)

ISBN-13 978-1-5440502-2-5

dedication

I would like to offer this work as a tribute to all the men who came home only to find a place for themselves on that shiny wall in Washington, D.C. I offer it to their survivors, as well.

contents

author's note

This is a novel. It is peopled with imaginary persons and units and was not written with reference to any person or unit that was part of the Vietnam War. I would also like to apologize to every member of the military who served, and even those who did not but remain vitally interested, for inventing some people places, outfits, and incidents that may appear to have existed but have never really. This novel is, truly, a story.

Thirty Days Has September

THE FIRST TEN DAYS

one

THE FIRST DAY

The door opened. It was a steel door about six inches thick, or so it seemed. It hit with a jarring thud when its heavy flat surface pivoted down and smacked upon the mud. Sunlight shot in like a wave of heat, followed by a wave of real heat, the air-conditioned inside of the armored personnel carrier likely to be my last until my tour was over. I had no weapon, no pack or jungle boots. I was new.

The civilian airliner had landed at Da Nang, offloaded a hundred uniformed men like me and then left without the crew ever getting off. No passengers had been waiting to come aboard. An F-4 Phantom fighter lay burning at the end of the runway. We'd all seen it before we touched down. The flight attendants said it was probably an old plane used to train fire fighting teams.

I hunched over, moving toward the torrid heat and light streaming in through the hole made by the back of the armored personnel carrier falling into the mud. We'd ridden maybe five minutes from the airport. Nobody told us where we were going or what we were doing, so I simply followed the silent procession of men out into the mud, dragging my government flight bag at my side. I was an officer, but I'd taken the single gold bars from my utility jacket after being told by the plane crew that the shiny bars weren't worn in combat areas.

Six of us had climbed into the waiting carrier. There had been other carriers but I had no idea where they'd gone because when I stepped outside, only one remained. A tall Marine staff sergeant stood facing the rear of the vehicle about fifteen feet away, on more solid ground. His boots gleamed in the sun, his spit shine on each perfect. The pleats on his uniform, a short sleeve Class A in khaki, were ironed so starchy sharp they looked dangerous. Unaccountably, he wore a D.I. instructor's flat brimmed hat with a small black leather tassel dangling from its stiff edge. His hands were on his hips, his elbows sticking out looking as sharp as the pleats running up and down the front of his shirt.

"Gentlemen, welcome to the 'Nam," was all he said, waiting a few seconds for his words to sink in before turning and heading off on a path through the thick undergrowth.

It was the first day of my time in Vietnam. I was unafraid, my emotions blocked by wonder. The light, the heat, the thick cloying mud with a burning Phantom sending up tendrils of black smoke snaking across the sky, masked everything else I might be feeling. The plane I'd arrived on was from America and it was gone, America gone with it. I moved along the rough-hewn path, my flight bag knocking into the ends of every hacked off branch. I was nobody. I didn't feel like a Marine officer or even much of a citizen, and I sure wasn't in California anymore. I was a slug moving through a forest that looked like something out of a bad horror film, following an enlisted man I was supposed to out rank but who apparently didn't think so, toward a destination nobody had told me about. I was not disconcerted. It went deeper than that. In only moments, with no warning, I'd become lost in another world that defied the darkest imagination. We came out of the bush to see a wooden structure in the distance.

"Gentlemen, the Da Nang Hilton," the staff sergeant announced, continuing to lead us without pausing or turning.

Just before we came up to the building, he stopped. We stopped behind him in a row, as if we were in a squad he commanded.

"It's got a moat," one of the other men said, pointing at the five-foot-wide stretch of water dug between us and the building. A thick plank extended out over the water to allow access to a ratty five story wooden structure beyond it.

"That's a 'benjo ditch,' not a moat," the staff sergeant indicated. "No bathrooms here, except for the ditch." He stopped and ushered us up, one by one, onto the plank. "They'll come for you when they come for you," he said to our backs, walking away after the last of us crossed.

There was nothing "Marine Corps" about the shanty of an open barracks. No windows or even walls. Wooden pillars held the wooden floors up with a big tin roof covering the whole affair. I saw so many bunks it was impossible to count them from the outside. A corporal sat at an old metal and rubber desk taken from some earlier war supply house. I watched him deal with the officer in front of me, making no attempt to hide his boredom. "File," the corporal said when he finished, holding out his hand toward me. "That's your bunk. Break the rack down and make it with clean stuff in the cabinet down at the end. No lockers. Keep your own stuff close."

There had been no "sir" in any of his delivery to the guy in front of me. There was none to me either.

"Tag," he continued, handing me a metal edged paper tag with the number 26 written on its white surface. "First floor. Officer country. You heard the rest."

I wondered why officers were quartered on the first floor. I presumed, as I made my way to rack number 26, that it was because the benjo ditch aroma would be more available. The rack was filthy when I found it. The place was nearly full with men recently returned from combat patrols or whatever, I presumed. Most were covered with mud. None looked like they'd showered or washed in days or maybe even weeks. I hauled the old sheets to a bin near the end of the narrow row that led to my bunk. I tried to talk to a few of the other officers who lay without sleeping atop their muddy beds. They would only look back at me like I was some specimen on display at a zoo. They would not answer. Not one of them. I finished making my bed, deposited my flight bag under my cot and then huddled with my back against a corner support. The bunks were four high with a slatted ladder going up on one end. The three bunks higher up my tier all sagged with the weight of other officers in them. Their packs simply lay all over in the aisles with junk loosely attached to them. Junk like muddy guns and grenades.

It started to rain. Like the day was not proving bad enough with the smell, the mud, the zombie company and a miserable cot without a mattress as my supposed resting place. There was no pillow either, but there were mosquitoes. Perfect. It was at that moment that I became afraid. I'd never been afraid of anything in Marine training, other than the very likely fact that I might not get through to become a Marine Officer. That I was second in my OCS platoon, and then won The Basic School Military Skills award, only reinforced the fact that I'd found my calling. And here I was, in absolute squalor, trapped in misery with a bunch of other men who'd preceded me and who now appeared all mentally ill. What had happened and where was I really? I'd seen all the war movies through the years and I'd never seen anything like where I was. Nothing close. Those wars and those characters had meaning, relationships, communication and decent clothing. I had shit. Quite literally.

I tried to lay down but could only cower and slap at the mosquitoes. From a bunk above, someone tossed a small clear plastic bottle. It landed on the wooden floor with a small thunk.

"Repellent. Use it and then shut the fuck up," a voice said from above. I leaned over and picked up the container, the voice presumably registering a complaint about my slapping of insects. I rubbed the foul but strangely attractive oil onto all the exposed surfaces of my body and returned to my previous position.

As the sun set out in the rain, I passed the time watching mosquitoes land, but not bite me, as if they sensed a tender morsel nearby but couldn't access it. The repellent didn't repel them at all. It simply made me less edible, which was fine by me. Only a few of the other men had flashlights or bothered to turn them on. I had nothing in my bag except some extra socks, underwear, and a useless change of street clothing. And my hard fought for but now unworn proud gold bars.

I waited. Even though it was still early, I knew there would be no sleep. I recorded each passing moment by reading the luminous dial on my special combat officer's watch I'd bought at the PX stateside for fifteen bucks. At eight o'clock a face appeared before me — a man holding a flashlight so I could see his features.

"Welcome to Vietnam," the face said, its eyes not looking at me. "Chief of Staff will see you now."

Another zombie, I concluded, already getting tired of hearing the welcome phrase.

"What's your rank?" I asked.

"Buck sergeant," the illuminated face replied, staring out into space, waiting.

"Then call me sir," I replied, getting out of the bunk to follow him.

"If you like," the sergeant said, not saying another word — certainly not sir.

My first day in the welcoming 'Nam was over, and my first night about to begin.

two

THE FIRST NIGHT

I followed the buck sergeant down the dark muddy aisle of the Da Nang Hilton, tripping into back packs and other field equipment strewn all over. I'd tucked my flight bag under my bunk, for whatever security that might provide. My watch was my only valuable possession. At some point I knew, since I was a Marine, everything I needed for whatever reason would be assigned to me — if I could just get to the point of distribution where the stuff was issued. The buck sergeant was kind enough to stop, once he was across the plank spanning the benjo ditch, to direct his flashlight back so I could make the crossing in relative safety. Full dark had overcome us, although the light rain continued. The falling drops were more of a sticky mist than real rain and provided no relief at all. In spite of the unending moisture, the sergeant and I walked upon relatively hard ground toward wherever we were going in the dark. The sergeant's flashlight bobbed up, down and all around, revealing nothing. It only took a few minutes for us to arrive at the side of a dimly lit concrete wall.

"Headquarters," the buck sergeant said, turning out his flashlight. "Door's on your right down the wall," he pointed. "Just go in. The others are already there."

I wanted to ask the buck sergeant who the others were but he was no longer there. He moved quieter than I thought possible for a Marine wearing field utilities and combat boots. There had been enough light at the wall to see that he had the new cloth-sided boots, the ones I'd heard about in training with the special triangular metal strips running the length of their soles. "Punji sticks" were a common hazard, or so I'd heard — little pits with sharpened sticks covered in human excrement. Regular boots, especially those like mine that had been regular issue back in WWII, did nothing to stop them. I needed a pair of those boots, a set of jungle utilities, and a gun. But most of all I needed an assignment.

I found the handle to the door and went through into a different world. I actually smiled as the door closed behind me. I felt that all my questions were about to be answered and my problems, solved. I was finally experiencing the real combat conditions that the Marine Corps was all about.

I stood at the end of a short hall in real air-conditioned air. I didn't move, just took in the cold dry feeling. At the end of the hall I saw a water bubbler. I made for it. Hitting the handle, I stuck my face down and let ice cold water pour into my mouth and over my face. I drank until I thought I'd burst.

"Over here," a voice said from behind me.

I let go of the life-giving bubbler and turned in the gently blowing cool air that seemed to emanate out through a set of wide open double doors. I could see Marines inside the room.

"Welcome to the 'Nam," a Marine attendant by the door said.

I nodded. No "sir" here either, but then I wore no rank because I hadn't thought to dig my bars out of my bag in the dark muddy misery surrounding my bunk. I noted that the floor was made of rough dirty concrete, the only dirt visible in the place. A line of concrete extended through the doors leading to what resembled a cartoon illustration balloon on the floor inside the room. A vibrant blue, luscious and thick rug outlined the cartoon balloon area. Five men stood on the dirty concrete, none touching the clean rug. They stood side by side, not at a position of attention but not really at ease either. There was a space at the right end and I guessed it was for me. I walked to where I thought I was supposed to be.

In front of us a raised dais, covered by the same blue rug material, set at least three feet off the floor. A wooden desk rested imposingly atop the dais, with a lectern to its left. A uniformed colonel, wearing short-sleeve Class A attire, stood at the lectern with his hands gripping the top edges, a look of impatience on his face. The other man sat facing sideways behind the desk, his highly polished, black regulation shoes, crossed at the ankles. His ankles sat up on the edge of the same desk. He leaned deeply back into his swivel chair and worked at lighting a long cigar with a Zippo flip-top lighter.

"Glad to see you all could make it," the Colonel said, displeasure evident in his tone and a quick glance toward where I stood. For whatever reason, I was late to an appointment I didn't know I had.

"If I don't miss my guess, you're late…you, person at the end," the Colonel said, staring straight into my eyes. "You don't seem to have a rank, little Marine."

I hadn't been referred to as little anything since I'd been in high school. There, I'd been five-feet tall in my senior year, the smallest male in my graduating class. I'd grown nine inches as a freshman and sophomore in college. Now as tall as three of the other five men standing in the concrete balloon, I couldn't believe what I was hearing. The public disparagement by the Colonel was just the last frosting on a brutally disgusting and bizarre day. I said nothing, however. I'd reply to a direct question but nothing more.

"Move on," the big man at the desk with the lit cigar said. I presumed that he was our regimental commander and I was attending a welcoming briefing before receiving an assignment. The deskman blew smoke rings. Each ring was carefully generated through his pursed lips, and then sent out over his crossed legs and past the tips of his spit polished shoes.

The Colonel went back to talking. He said we'd be given our assignments in the morning, go to supply for our stuff and then be transported out to our waiting units in a matter of days. He talked about military pay currency and why we would be issued some in lieu of U.S. money. I'd never heard of MPC but was surprised that the Marine Corps would give out cash of any kind. The Marine Corps prides itself on being one of the cheapest run outfits in the world. The Colonel launched into a speech which he titled the "Revolutionary Development Doctrine." It was a ten-minute talk about how the U.S. was winning the war by converting enemy soldiers to become allies by joining the South Vietnamese Army. Right after the speech he told us about *Chu Hoi* passes, which we should be aware of because they were free passes to safety being dropped behind enemy lines by air. Any enemy soldier could use one to cross over to the allied side at any time while out in the field. I couldn't believe that I hadn't heard about any of what the Colonel said back in training. Nothing. It was like I was in a different world.

"*Chu Hoi* my ass," the big man sitting at the desk intoned quietly, before blowing little circles of cigar smoke through the big rings he'd already generated.

The Colonel ignored him and finished his introduction. He concluded by telling us that the special photo contour-interval maps we would be getting would all have to be specially marked with magic markers. All north/south coordinate designations sent over the radio combat or artillery net would be referred to by the names of popular toothpastes. All east/west coordinates would be named after different kinds of chewing gum. This last part of the briefing stunned me. How could the enemy fail to quickly find out about such a ridiculously easy and stupid code, and then use it to our disadvantage?

"Questions," the Colonel said, looking up from his notes for the first time since he'd met my eyes at the beginning. He slapped his file closed after only a few seconds, as if the meeting was over.

"That's it, sir," he said, turning to face the back of the man sitting at the desk.

"I have a question," I said into the silence. The lieutenant next to me elbowed me in warning but I ignored him.

"Oh really," the Colonel replied, turning back to the lectern.

"When I was in Quantico they constantly beat into our heads that we were to take care of our men first," I said. The big man slowly brought his feet down from the desk and turned to look at me. I saw the single star on each side of his collar.

I was talking to the division commander. "I arrive here to what?" I continued undaunted. "A muddy concrete walkway leading into a special place in your plush blue rug. An ice water bubbler in the hall. Air conditioning. Electric lighting, for Christ's sake! What's going on here? I'm living in that shithole over there with the rest of these guys. What happened to taking care of your men first?"

Nobody moved. I don't think anyone breathed, least of all me. I could see the Colonel's name tag. It read "Stewart." The General's read "Bonner."

It took half a minute for everyone to recover. The Colonel leaned down and whispered in the General's ear. The General nodded, staring at me with a deadpan expression. The Colonel stood back up.

"The rest of you are dismissed. You can stay," he said, pointing at my chest.

The other men got out of there so quickly it seemed like they simply disappeared. I stood in front the two men, not knowing what to expect.

"You're assigned tonight, right here and right now, so you'll never spend another minute in that 'shithole' over there," the Colonel said, with flecks of spit coming from the sides of his mouth. "You're going to Gulf Company and you're going tonight."

"Get him the fuck out of the General's sight," the Colonel ordered, looking past me at the Staff Sergeant I'd seen when I entered the room. "Get him his field gear, and then get him aboard an airlift right now, General's orders," the Colonel concluded.

"Come on, sir," the Staff Sergeant said, using the word *sir* to me for the first time since I'd been in country. The baleful look on his face scared me more than the instant assignment I'd just been handed. I expected to be assigned and go to the field and into combat, but there was likely to be more to it from looking at the Sergeant's expression.

I followed the Staff Sergeant to a nearby tent at which point everything went like it was supposed to. I got a full pack with everything, a .45 Colt, rations, and even an E-Tool. All by the table of organization book and all crisply delivered. The utilities were Korean War issue but I didn't argue for the new stuff they were all wearing. The old-style combat boots would also have to do.

They wouldn't let me even go back for my flight bag. They said they'd get it for me and hold it for my return, but I knew it was a write-off. I got aboard the waiting Huey. I didn't realize that helicopters flew at night in the war, but, as with almost everything else about Vietnam, I was wrong. I rode in silence except for the ear splitting noise of the chopper's blades and the awful high-pitched whine of it's turbine. Nobody offered me ear muffs or plugs, and it was too loud to ask for anything. There were no doormen and no guns on the doors on the chopper. I was in a "slick," a helicopter used solely for transporting. The crew chief sat directly across from me, staring at nothing in the near darkness, like the zombies I'd never gotten to sleep with in the "shithole."

They'd issued me a waterproof flashlight and there were maps in my pack, but it was too dark and windy to take them out and read them. My combat watch said it was just about midnight. How and where we would land I had no idea.

three

THE SECOND DAY

I could not believe I was flying into my first field experience wearing crummy Korean War utilities. I wished fervently that I'd brought my own from training. At least they would have been green instead of whatever color I now wore. Being colorblind as a Marine Corps Officer wasn't allowed, but then the Navy Corpsman I'd bribed to pass me on the lantern test needed the fifty bucks I'd paid him. Fifty bucks to get into this Catch-22 mess...

The Huey banked sharply and I grabbed for a bit of nylon webbing to avoid falling right out the wide open door. Looking through the big rectangular space to the ground below, I saw how helicopters landed at night. A smoke grenade had been popped below. Obviously the up front chopper crew was in radio communications with the unit below. The smoke from the grenade billowed around while the burning flare of the ignition device turned it into a big glowing lantern. The chopper continued its sharp turn and dropped into the jungle below. Except it wasn't jungle. When we touched down I saw that it was more like great scrub mired in variously hardening chunks of mud. And we didn't actually touch down, either. We hit hard on the skids. At that same instant, the crew chief literally threw me from the machine. I never saw the outside of the Huey. I was too busy pulling my face from the mud and trying to find my pack in the slimy bracken. I heard the chopper pulling away and up at full power, though, and then I heard and felt the incoming fire. Several bursts at a time flew over my head. I stopped trying to find my pack. I stopped trying to get up, instead burrowing back into the mud. I'd never been on the receiving end of a gun before. Not in life before the Marines or in Marine training. Live fire exercises had ended years before I began my service.

The bursts of gunfire were loud cracking sounds, almost loud enough to make my ears ring. But it was the light from the tracer rounds that scared me near to death. The enemy had seen and heard the chopper, I reasoned. They were shooting at the chopper, I argued. Yet the tracers continued to fly right above my head. They looked like fast-moving illuminated beer cans. I knew that each tracer was only one of a three or five bullet string. I wasn't scared. I wasn't terrified. It was something deeper than that — something that wrapped around my insides and then compressed them to the point that I felt like I couldn't breathe. How was it possible that I was lying in the sucking mud during the misting blackness of a night from hell, when only twenty-four hours before I'd been asleep on an Air Force base in California? I was brand new. This couldn't be happening! I knew I was in shock but I didn't know how to get out of it.

The shooting finally stopped. The Huey must have flown out of range, I thought. I worked at crawling. To anywhere but where I was. I didn't care about my pack, my gun or anything else. I knew I had to get out of there, wherever there was. I didn't get three feet before a pair of strong hands grabbed me by the shoulders from above.

"Who in hell are you?" a gruff voice, only inches away, said directly into my left ear.

"Forward Observer..." I answered haltingly, allowing the hands to turn and pull me into a low sitting position. I looked around for more of the flaming beer cans but there were none.

"They flew you in at night? They don't fly anybody in at night, 'specially not lieutenants," the man said, letting go of my shoulders.

"Who are you?" I asked, wanting to lay down and get back into the mud but resisting the impulse.

"Gunnery Sergeant," the voice said. "I *was* the company commander, but you are now... sir." The Gunny stood up and helped pull me into a standing position.

"I can't be the company commander," I said, trying to twist my neck and shake off some leftover hearing issues from the chopper and gunfire. "My MOS is artillery. I'm the forward observer. I didn't even get to check in with my artillery unit. Hell, I don't know who the artillery unit is. I'm here as a forward observer, I'm sure. I can't be a company commander. I just got out of Fort Sill. I'm only a 2nd Lieutenant."

The Gunny hustled me off into the night by one arm, dragging my pack along and acting like he could see in the dark.

"I'll put you on the command net with the six actual back at battalion about the company commander thing if you want."

"Thank you," I breathed, feeling like finally I might be able to talk to someone who would understand.

"Get down and stay down until I come back," the Gunny said. "This hole is designated as the command post."

"There's nobody here," I indicated, being able to establish that even in the dark. "Where are the other officers?"

"There are no other officers," the Gunny replied. "That's why you're the company commander. Wherever you are is the command post. I'll find your radio operators. We have command, artillery and naval gunfire when the navy forward observer is around, which he rarely is."

The Gunny left. I was alone in some old shell hole with my pack. I slid down from the lip until I ran into a small pit of water at the bottom. I searched the small outside pockets of the pack until I found a little bottle of the mosquito repellent I'd gotten some relief from earlier. I slathered the weird smelling liquid all over my bare skin, rubbing right over all the small bumps swelling from previous bites. I pulled my helmet and the liner under it off. It was too hot to wear a helmet. Too hot to wear the body armor I'd been told in training wasn't effective against anything moving faster than a BB. Too hot for a long sleeve utility jacket. I pulled them all off and then layered on more repellent.

The gunny returned with another Marine after only being gone a few minutes.

"Here's Corporal Fessman. The other operator was killed a few days back with the officers, when they met to plan ahead. Fessman can access both nets on his Prick 25."

"Corporal," I said, noting that Fessman also wore only a dark t-shirt, with no helmet or liner on his head. Maybe I was doing some things right.

"Sir," Fessman replied, sliding down the muddy slope to rest next to me, as the Gunny walked away.

"How'd the officers die?" I asked, keeping my voice soft, like the Gunny's and Fessman's own. It was night and an active enemy was very definitely nearby.

"Rather not say, sir," Fessman replied, to my surprise.

Reality was beginning to dawn on me. A reality I didn't want to accept. Was I to be in command of a unit in combat that had killed all of its leaders? That simply could not be. Not in the Marine Corps.

"Get me the six actual," I ordered. The six actual was the commander of any unit, not the radio operator, duty or executive officer.

"Colonel Bennet, make it quick," a voice demanded from the small speaker in Fessman's telephone mic.

"Sir," I said, nervously, "I just got dropped into this company and there are no other officers alive. I'm the forward observer. I'm sure of it. I can't be the company commander. I just got here from the states."

"You're the only officer. You know how this works. Stop calling me for stuff you already know. You're the company commander until I tell you otherwise or you're relieved. Got it?"

I nodded, hesitantly. Fessman poked me. "Got it," I said, handing the mic back to the Lance Corporal.

"Six actual over and out," Fessman transmitted, before clipping the mic to the radio frame he wore on his back. "He's the battalion commander, so you have to call him sir. He doesn't have to use radio etiquette, but we do. And no profanity on the combat net. He gets very upset."

I didn't know what to say. I was out in the mud after almost being shot down and we were talking about swearing over the radio. Nearby gunshots and explosions seemed to come plunging down into the pit we were in. I scrunched even lower into the mud.

"They hit us every night," Fessman said, his voice calm. "They only get guys at the perimeter, and that's mostly with grenades. Except for the mortars, 'cause they come right inside. I don't think they have mortars tonight. They would have fired them first. It's just the way it is."

"Where do we sleep?" I asked.

"Sleep? We don't sleep much, sir. When we get back closer to An Hoa maybe. No sleep here."

"No sleep?" I said, still trying to adjust my ears to the horrid loud noises of incoming fire. "Everyone has to sleep. It's not like it's an option." I pulled my hands into my body, bringing them up to my face. They were shaking. I tried to stop them but I couldn't, which added to my fear, if such a thing was possible.

"You'll see," Fessman said, in his usual matter-of-fact tone.

"How old are you?" I asked, sensing something.

"Seventeen," he replied. "Or at least I will be soon."

"You have to be seventeen to be in the Corps," I said.

"Yeah, I know," Fessman came back.

The hell, I thought. Sixteen. I was serving in combat with a sixteen-year old. A sophomore in high school. How he came to be there didn't matter.

"How'd the officers all die?" I asked him again. "And don't give me that crap about how you would rather not say. We're in this together and I'm the company commander."

"They killed 'em, which was a shame because some of them were okay. I mean in the second set."

"Second set?" I asked, not truly surprised at his answer but not fully understanding either.

"Yeah, that was two weeks ago. They killed the first bunch a month ago. Now nobody will come out here to our unit anymore. Back there they must all know. We only get mistakes or FNGs."

"FNGs?"

"Fucking new guys," Fessman answered. "Like you. No offense, sir."

We waited together for the coming of dawn. The sporadic fire went on through the darkness. Fessman was right. There was to be no sleep. My body vibrated with energy and terror. I was relieved when my hands stopped shaking on their own. I didn't want the men to see me like that. But I couldn't think. My brain would not work right. Every shot in the dark or explosion in the distance blanked me out. The dawn came with the Gunny and some other Marines. The men looked exactly like the ones I'd seen at the Da Nang Hilton.

"Your scout sergeant and Kit Carson Scout," the Gunny said, squatting down to plop a small box next to my side.

The two men squatted down beside him while the Gunny took out some heat tabs and lit them with one flick of a Zippo. He broke the box in half with both hands. An assortment of small cans and green envelopes fell into the mud. "Coffee," he said, holding up one envelope before tearing it open. "No cream or sugar. The guys take those out of the C-Rations before anybody gets them." One of the men squatting down with the Gunny was a buck sergeant while the other was Vietnamese, but wearing old Marine utilities like my own.

"The guys?" I said, in surprise, not really understanding.

The Gunny didn't reply, instead taking his canteen holder apart and pouring the holder full of water.

"Scout Sergeant and Kit Carson Scout? What kind of titles are those," I asked the Gunny. I'd never heard of the either unit designation in training.

"In due time," the Gunny laughed, for the first time.

"I'm an officer," I shot back without thinking, "it doesn't seem like I've got an awful lot of time left."

All four men stared at me with no humor in their expressions.

four

Breakfast in the mud pit was ham and lima beans served with canteen cup holders of instant black coffee. I didn't ask the Gunny why the other men bothered to pull the cream and sugar from incoming C-Rations. It didn't matter. I remained so scared I was unwilling to impart more of my ignorance by asking questions that probably had no rational answers. I crouched and sipped the coffee from my holder. My Scout Sergeant was named Stevens and I found out that his job was to check around the perimeter and with the platoon leaders to keep me informed. My Kit Carson Scout was Nguyen, pronounced "new yen." He wore no rank, although he had on a utility jacket. His job, Fessman said, was mostly to serve as interpreter to members of the local civilian population we might encounter and also to question any prisoners we might take. He didn't speak much English.

"How's he supposed to interpret when he can't even understand me?" I asked quietly.

"That's up to Stevens," Fessman replied, his voice a whisper, as the rest were nearby. "Stevens speaks the gook lingo."

Stevens was supposed to interpret my interpreter. My shoulders sank with the continuing insanity of all of it. I ate a few more spoons of the awful C-Ration fare before looking up at the rising sun, coming up over the lip of the shell crater.

I realized why I was there. I'd dumbly stood and accused my commanding officers of being Marine scum. What could I possibly have expected, other than to be sent to my death? In truth, I would never have expected anything like that before coming out to the field. Suddenly, I was not only willing to believe it but I understood it. Nobody in the rear area wanted to come out to the field and face maiming or death.

The way they prevented that from happening to them was to send new people coming in off of ships and commercial liners. The Marines who occupied rear area positions, by good fortune or because they somehow served in the field long enough to get out, never left the rear area, I was coming to realize. They kept the best of everything that came into the war zone simply because they understood that the best stuff was wasted on people who were going to die anyway.

"How many?" I asked of the Gunny, sitting a few feet away.

"How many what?" he answered, working on his sliced ham and cracker meal.

"How many casualties are we taking a day?" I inquired.

"Eight KIA last night and three WIA. Chopper will be in soon to pick up the body bags and the wounded guys in ponchos. You have to sign off on them."

"Eleven," I concluded, more to myself than to him. "And how many Marines do we have?"

"Reinforced company. Two hundred and twenty-two, including you and the dead and wounded last night."

"Eleven out of two-twenty-two," I said. "So, we're losing about five percent a day," I went on. We have twenty days left, if my calculations are accurate."

"Twenty days for what?" Fessman asked.

"Before we're wounded or dead," I answered, my voice without emotion.

"I've been here for almost two months," Stevens said. "I'm still here," he went on with some enthusiasm. "So what does that mean?"

"Not good," the Gunny said. "You guys scram. I want to talk to the actual."

Fessman, Stevens, and Nguyen moved quickly out of the crater, leaving their stuff behind.

"Don't tell them shit like that," the Gunny said, staring into my eyes. "They're fucked up enough. None of us are going home. Not in one piece, anyway, and there's nothing we can do about it."

"Those guys, and the others, killed the last two sets of officers," I hissed back at him. "What am I supposed to do? Let them kill me too?"

"It wasn't them," The Gunny said wearily, sitting close to me and pulling up his knees. He took out a cigarette. "Funny, we get more cigarettes than we can ever smoke. I wonder if that's because they know back home none of us is going to die of lung cancer."

He offered me one. I shook my head in reply. I'd tried cigarettes in high school. They'd made me sick every time. I was in enough trouble without getting sick to my stomach.

"We've got a race war going on in this unit, but you'll find that out real soon for yourself," the Gunny said, spitting out a bit of tobacco.

"The only way out of here is in a bag or on a medevac. You figured that out. You can do whatever you want for as long as you have left. We're moving out in about an hour."

"Moving out to where?" I asked, surprised. We'd just been under fire. I couldn't imagine going anywhere until a secure passage could be figured out or arranged.

"We move by day and then get hit every night," the gunny said, pulling out a photo grid map layered over in plastic tape. "They don't shoot at us in daytime because hell from the air would drop down on them. It's the way of it out here. We're on what's called Go Noi Island, although it's not. We're trapped by three surrounding swollen rivers about to get more swollen with the monsoons coming. We move inland under our supporting fires, mostly artillery, and retreat toward the ocean under their supporting fires. We've got to get seventeen clicks up the Song Bong River, across from Duc Duc, before dark."

"Who's laid out supporting fires?" I asked, looking down at his nearly unintelligible map, half covered with black magic marker.

"Outside of me, and now you, nobody has or reads a map, much less can call artillery," he said. "Accurate artillery fire might just save your life, although I doubt it."

My stomach would not uncurl. I wasn't sure I could even stand up when the time came. I looked at his map, my own still tucked into my pack. I knew he was right.

Calling artillery was an arcane science passed down by the French from before World War II. A fire direction center in the rear, all the way back at An Hoa, processed calls for fire and then sent the data to the guns so the battery could fire accurately. The language required to be used on the artillery net was as complex as it was inflexible. Call in, using that radio, without the language and knowledge and you wouldn't get anything in return no matter how dire your situation or how badly you needed support. You didn't pick up artillery ability in the field or on the job. You either went to Fort Sill and were trained for six tough weeks or you could forget about artillery support.

"They can't call artillery?" I asked, my voice very soft, almost asking the question to myself. "You can't call it either, can you Gunny?" I asked, looking the man straight in the eyes for the first time.

"In a pinch," the Gunny said, his own tone softening for the first time since I'd been dropped in. He looked away.

"Call Fessman and those other guys back," I said, giving my first order. "Do I call Nguyen a gook too?"

The Gunny got up, climbed to the top edge of the mud pit and gestured before sliding back down. "Nguyen's a scout. He's on our side. Only the NVA are called gooks. Some of the men call all Vietnamese gooks but it's not a good idea. Nguyen's invaluable when we're in contact, which is pretty much every night."

I noticed my hearing improving. The distant ringing was going away. It was a tiny thing but that little fact made me feel a bit better. I grabbed my pack and took out a small stack of folded maps and my compass. I realized I'd need a supply of the plastic tape. Everything around me was wet all the time. I also needed a rubberized flashlight instead of the pitifully cheap metal thing I'd been issued. I found the one-to-twenty-five-thousand quarter map I needed. I realized a second problem about why the unit lacked artillery support, other than the battery I was supposed to be assigned to might have heard about Gulf Company and not wanted to provide any fire. Two-Eleven was the unit, Second Battalion of the Eleventh Field Artillery Regiment. The maps had very few contour intervals on them. There was almost no rising and falling topography high or low enough to merit a twenty-five-meter difference in elevation. I oriented the map north and south. I'd worry about true north, the math calculation closing the difference between grid north (where the map pointed north) and magnetic north (where my compass pointed). The difference was important for accurate fire but not for what I was going to do.

The Gunny was about to put away his map when I stopped him. "Where do you think we are, precisely," I asked,

Fessman, Stevens, and Nguyen assumed their former positions nearby.

"Where do you think we are?" the Gunny replied, surprisingly.

I looked up from the map toward where he sat concentrating over his own. And then it hit me. He didn't know exactly where we were, not for incoming artillery fire purposes, anyway. I let him out.

"We're right here," I reached over and dotted a point on his map above the Song Bong River.

"Yes, I thought so," the Gunny replied, quickly packing his own map away.

I took one more compass reading, re-oriented the map slightly and took bearings on two distant peaks to make certain.

"Give me the arty net, Corporal," I ordered, holding out my hand for the mic.

Fessman handed the instrument over, and then fiddled for a few seconds with the thick radio he'd brought down from his back. The flat bladed antenna was folded back on itself to stick up only four or five feet.

I keyed the mic when Fessman nodded.

"Fire mission, over," I said, pushing the transmit button down with my index finger.

"Fire mission, over," came right back through the little speaker. The words were loud enough for everyone in the crater to hear.

"What are you doing?" the Gunny asked.

I looked at the man coldly, while I held the mic and waited.

"Sir," he finally said. I ignored him.

"Ipana 44565, Wrigley 61238," I instructed, reading the magic marker numbers I'd written to mark out position on the map. The fire direction center (FDC) would not process a fire order without knowing the caller's position for fear of hitting that position. I knew that someone was putting a pin up on a wall map while I waited.

"Ipana 44145, Wrigley 34745," I intoned, still looking at my map.

"Sir?" the Gunny questioned, deep concern beginning to register in his tone.

"One round, whiskey papa, fifty meters, over," I ordered, before handing the mic back to Fessman.

I looked at the Gunny. I'd lied to the fire direction center. I'd stated our coded position on the map incorrectly. I'd placed Gulf Company almost a thousand meters from where it really was. The second set of coordinates were our own.

"Shot, over," came through Fessman's open mic.

I nodded at Fessman, wondering if he had any experience with artillery at all.

He did. "Shot, out," he said into the mic.

"Oh shit," the Gunny wrenched out before going face down in the mud.

"Splash, over," came through the radio. Fessman didn't respond to that because there was no reason. The splash indication was a calculation by the FDC that your fire mission round or rounds were five seconds from impact or detonation.

A huge Fourth of July explosion took place far above all of our heads.

I smiled, I'd gotten the map reading and calculations right.

The forty-six-pound artillery round of white phosphorus had exploded precisely fifty meters over our heads and the phosphorus rained down like a giant fireworks fountain display. The tails of the phosphorus trailed down almost to the ground before going out.

"Holy shit," the Gunny got out, crawling up to his knees. "What in hell did you do that for?"

I didn't reply. I was most pleased. The fifty meters had apparently been sufficient enough to allow all the phosphorus to burn up before impacting down on the Marines of Gulf Company. I smiled openly, not at my success or the fact that I had graphically demonstrated that the unit now not only had artillery support, but someone who could call it accurately on command. I smiled because I didn't give a damn if the Marines below, including myself, were hit or not.

I grabbed my map and began to plot night defensive grid coordinates for our day travel. Those coordinates would prove invaluable if we were hit along the way because they acted as registration points. There would be no need to do any plotting at all if we were close to one of them. I'd be able to call a round to the pre-designated point and then adjust fire accordingly.

I got packed up then and got ready to move.

"If we reach the river can we bathe?" I asked the Gunny.

The man just stared back at me, his expression almost inscrutable except for a very faint look of worry and fear in his eyes.

"Yes sir," Fessman said with open enthusiasm. "The Bong is mostly runoff but it's a lot better than trying to clean up in the rain. We better get to the units and introduce you."

"Oh, I think they all got introduced just now," Stevens said, saying something in Vietnamese to Nguyen that made them both laugh.

The move was unremarkable. The reinforced part of Gulf Company was a machine gun platoon added for security, or whatever. Sixteen M60 machine guns, each manned by four Marines. The gunner did the shooting while the others packed ammo, carried the gun and its parts, and then set it up when it was ready.

Seventeen clicks equal seventeen thousand meters. The clicks were derived by someone with one of those little map distance measuring devices found in training. The machines clicked at the equivalent of a thousand meters on the map. Ten miles, or so, was the distance of the hike. Everything was wet so the company moved mostly atop paddy dike walls. It was lousy cover. In fact, it was no cover at all but the rice paddies were filled with human excrement as fertilizer and nobody wanted to have anything to do with that. It was a long hard hike. I hadn't been in the unit to be there for the last resupply. I had no water in my two canteens, no C-rations, outside of the single box that had been in my pack. I refused to ask for anything from anyone there, however. In a very short period of time I'd found out something about war.

I was at war with everyone and everything from my own men, my commanding officers, the environment, the insect life, the weather, and, finally, the enemy.

five

THE SECOND NIGHT

Night didn't come easily in the 'Nam. The day had been a blessing compared to my first night. Moving seventeen clicks through muddy rice paddies wearing a fifty-pound pack was its own form of misery, but the brutality of Marine training had kicked in and setting one foot in front of the other had become a tweaking exercise of endurance. And I had endurance. What I didn't have any longer was a useless flak jacket or utility coat, and wearing only a Vietnam-issue green t-shirt allowed the shoulder straps of my pack to chaff, cut, and hurt like hell. Being the supposed leader of whatever this Marine Company had morphed into, I knew instinctively that there could be no show of weakness. I hunched and staggered my way through without comment and without water.

We were in the flatlands. From the ocean far away in the unseeable distance to the mountains inland, the land supported subsistence farmers trying to grow rice. Rice and small fish, with inedible fish sauce called *nuoc mam* ("nook mom"), were what indigenous locals ate all of their lives, along with noodles. My concern, with nightfall coming and the inevitability of attack facing us again, was where to set in. The soggy land prevented digging foxholes. The few spotted areas among the paddies of low-hanging jungle seemed to be all that was left. My training told me that those would not work simply because they were the only places to spend the night. The enemy would know that. They would be registered (previously measured for range and declination) for mortar fire, if not heavier stuff.

The unit stopped just before sunset. I'd ended up near the rear for unexplainable reasons. I'd talked to no one during the arduous hike, proceeded by my scouts and followed by Fessman, who somehow managed a full pack and the Prick 25 radio. The Gunny made his way back from the long line of Marines strung along the straight raised berm of the paddy dike. The dikes themselves were all wide enough for two people to pass one another side by side, but that was about it. The slightest misstep and a bath in the awful smelling paddy water would result.

The day itself was okay — dryer with no mist or rain. Although it was at least ninety-eight degrees, that was survivable and there weren't any cloying mosquitoes. Except for a gentle moderating wind, all was quiet except for the radios. Many of the Marines carried small battery-powered radios. The armed forces network put out constant music moderated by a disc jockey I'd never heard of, Brother John. After one day in the bush, I felt I knew him well. Deep voiced, probably black with a slight southern twang, Brother John's signature comment, made between every rock n' roll or country & western song was "This is Brother John, coming to you from Nha Trang in the 'Nam." I didn't know where Nha Trang was but I presumed it was close by. The fact that playing radios in a combat arena might alert any nearby enemy to one's exact location seemed to not matter in this utterly strange war.

Everyone scrunched down on the dike into squatting positions, similar to the ones the local population used to relax. I found it weird to see the Marines all acting like natives while it was obvious they hated the gooks. I squatted. It hurt my knees but I saw the immediate value. The only alternative was to unfold my poncho cover and spread it across the dike or sit with my butt in the mud. Neither of those options worked. I squatted and endured more pain. The Marine Corps was all about pain and the handling of pain. Pain was good. Pain was alive. Pain kept you going.

"Coffee?" the Gunny offered.

I nodded, craving any liquid at all to quench my deep thirst. I laboriously unloaded one of my canteens from its cover and placed the holder atop the mud.

The Gunny half filled my holder with water. "Drink it," he whispered. "They won't notice."

I drank the water as slowly as I could, looking around at the Marines, none of whom would look back at me, except my scouts and Fessman.

The Gunny broke out a chunk of white material. "Comp B," he said with a smile. "Burns hotter than the idiot tabs."

Composition B was the intense plastic high explosive invented after the Korean War. It was extremely stable and could only be exploded using a detonator. I'd never seen it openly burned before and leaned back a bit. The Gunny grinned, pouring water into his own canteen holder.

"Great stuff," he said. "Won't explode. If it did we'd never know. Twenty-six thousand feet per second. Powerful shit to toss down gook tunnels. A lot better than sending Marines down there. But don't let the guys eat it. It's like LSD, except they usually die from the trip, not that most of them care."

I said nothing. I wasn't surprised that the explosive was something more and less than I'd learned in training. There was nothing in the 'Nam that wasn't a surprise. Nothing. But I knew if I could simply keep my mouth shut, I wouldn't reveal my ignorance. The Gunny poured coffee into my holder. I was still thirsty. I drank the hot liquid greedily, not caring if it burned a bit. Pain was good.

"They got the message," the Gunny said, looking at me over the top of his canteen holder. "The arty thing. I suppose you learned about the willy peter all burning up before it hits the ground in Fort Sill."

I remained silent. The "willy peter," or white phosphorus, doesn't always burn up when the shell is exploded that close to the ground. Maybe at a hundred meters. I'd seen it used at Sill, but only in demonstrations. I hadn't cared about it all burning up or not before it came to earth when I called the mission.

"The medevac picked up our casualties but they only dropped more bags," the Gunny said, "Tomorrow's drop will include water, food, and morphine. We need the morphine bad. I hadn't missed the muffled screaming of the night before. It had just added to the symphonic cacophony of horror.

"Why more morphine?" I asked. "Don't the corpsmen have it already?"

The Gunny remained silent for a minute, sipping his coffee.

"You're the company commander," he finally said. "How's this for it being your call? We have three corpsmen. Saunders, Johnson, and Murphy. We get morphine once a week. Saunders and Murphy are out because Johnson used all his in the first couple of days."

"He saw more action?" I asked, since the Gunny didn't go on.

"Nope. He used it on himself. He's an addict, apparently. So what do we do? Can't send him back because they don't take people back. Somebody else would have to come out. That's not happening. Meanwhile, the men have their buddies dying in pain before dawn, waiting for a medevac through the night while they listen to the screams of their friends."

"What's my call?" I replied, trying to wrap my damaged mind around the problem.

"Can't keep him here, can't send him away," the Gunny said. "Gotta have morphine to survive. They can't take him out because the other corpsmen won't help them when they're wounded if they do."

"Dilemma," I stated the obvious.

"Yep," the Gunny replied, "most of this is all of that."

"Where is he?" I asked, finishing my coffee, hoping for a second cup without having to ask.

"I sent him out with the point," the Gunny said. "The river's not far ahead. We'll set up a perimeter for the night once we get down there. He knows he's fucked but I don't know what to do about it."

I presumed the point was a lead scout of some kind. In training we'd moved in unit formation of platoons, squads and fire teams. There had been no point. But then, there'd been no booby traps set into the beautiful pine-studded hills of Virginia, either.

"What am I supposed to do, I mean, as company commander, and all?" I said, hesitantly, accepting another cup of the instant coffee with silent thanks.

"Whatever you do is going to be wrong to somebody here. That's the way it works," the Gunny replied.

"Better you than me, kind of a thing?" I asked, fear returning to my belly to overcome my good sense of keeping silent so as not to show ignorance or to upset.

"If you like," he said, finishing his coffee. "Let me know what's what there. I'll get the unit ready to set in."

"We can't exactly set in where we've been before," I could not stop myself from adding. "It's against all tactical reason."

"You see any place else?" he replied, replacing his canteen on his belt and walking away.

Darkness descended and with it came my fear. When would we be hit, and where, and why didn't anyone around me have an air of expectation or immediacy? Fessman, Stevens, Nguyen, and I moved from the long paddy dike into a bamboo wooded area plush with reeds. The ground seemed solid. Marines spread out around us. I headed toward a small rise near the center of the area.

"Not there, sir," Fessman pointed out in a hushed voice. "They'll register that point for mortar fire, if they haven't already. Go beyond it. It'll be wetter but we're wet anyway.

I did what Fessman suggested, pulling my heavy pack off and laying it down atop some sort of leafy mass of ferns. I unstrapped my poncho cover and spread it next to the pack. Finally, I sat down, exhausted. Nguyen knelt on the edge of the cover and carefully slid a plastic canteen to me. He motioned with his chin for me take it.

"You're tired from lack of water," Stevens said. "Drink the whole thing. We'll have plenty of water in the morning."

I drank the warm water tasting of iodine. I didn't care about the temperature or the taste though. I listened to Brother John from Nha Trang, wondering about the total stupidity of playing tinny music out into the coming night, as if to send a sound beacon out to anyone around. Was there a curfew for playing the music or did it stop when Armed Forces Radio ceased transmission? I wanted to yell "Shut the fuck up" at the top of my voice, but didn't yield to the temptation.

I could call artillery, read a map, and apparently little else to try to prove my worth in a Marine Company gone nuts. The Gunny hadn't even bothered to fill me in on why we ensconced where we were or why we'd been ordered to move there. I pulled out my map and used a grease pencil to write grid coordinates running all around the current position. I waved Fessman over to me and called the battery to register our position at the Fire Direction Center. If I had to call for fire at night, then it would save time not to have to input our own position. I looked down at the map and the ten words and numbers I'd written down around a black point. The information seemed to fly up at me physically. It was inside me. Somehow I memorized the data, the map contours and direction. Surprised, I shut my eyes and it was still all there like it was imprinted on the back of my eyelids.

"Where the hell is the latrine?" I asked, not having eliminated anything from my body all day long.

"E-tool," Steven's said. "Nobody digs a trench on these stops. Just go down by the river and dig a hole. Make sure you're inside the perimeter."

"What's the password?" I asked, unstrapping my E-tool from the back of my pack. "Just in case."

Fessman and Stevens went silent and then stared at me together. Stevens spoke to Nguyen in Vietnamese. The Kit Carson Scout smiled. I looked back at all three of them in the dying light.

"Ah, there's no passwords out here," Stevens said. "Nobody out there speaks American and nobody not American comes through the perimeter in the dark."

Marine training in a lush pine forest set among the rolling hills of Virginia was fast dying inside me. I found a marginally private spot among the bamboo groves to do my business. There was no way I was going down to the river and encounter the perimeter, although the idea of all that potential drinking water crossed my mind. That I could be thirsty in a constantly misting land where the humidity was about the same as pure liquid didn't cross my mind as an analytical problem. It simply was.

My small core group of men had found an area to assemble shelter-halves in a clump, little runnels dug around each one to allow the ever present water to flow anywhere else. I crouched down and set my back under the cover, then fumbled through my pack for writing materials I'd carefully stored in a plastic bag. I wrote my first letter home from in country. I didn't have to lick the envelope to seal it. The weather of Vietnam did that for me.

I waited for the Gunny, my only contact with the Marines around me except for the scout group and radio operator assigned to me. I wasn't a company commander or even a platoon commander. I had no command at all. I was a fucking new guy, a FNG.

six

THE SECOND NIGHT : SECOND PART

The radio music transmissions were supposed to stop at night but it was not full dark when my small team of scouts and radio operator went to work setting up shelter halves around them. I was afraid of the radio transmissions giving our position away. I smelled heavy cigarette smoke wafting in the slow-moving air around me. The air felt like cobwebs passing over my face, as it was so full of heated moisture. I folded my Iwo Jima flag-raising envelope in half and stuck it into my right front thigh pocket. No matter what happened in the night I was determined to make sure that I sent the letter off aboard the resupply chopper supposedly coming in the following morning.

Stevens had a small transistor radio playing the Armed Forces Radio Station. "Ninety-Nine Point Nine FM," the announcer said in a tinny voice, followed by one of Brother John's short baritone comments: "Here's Chicken Man." There was a pause in the transmission. I wanted so badly to order Stevens to turn the damned radio off but I was afraid to order anyone to do anything. And I was afraid of the feeling it gave me to be afraid of doing that.

"Chicken man?" I asked, quietly, instead.

"You'll love this, sir," Fessman said, finally easing the big rectangle of the combat radio from his back.

A hideous laugh came from Stevens' little radio, and then another announcer, obviously pre-recorded, said: "Chicken Man. Benton Harbor, salesman by day, and the world's greatest crime fighter by night, makes his appearance."

I couldn't believe my ears. Chicken Man? The announcer went on to describe how Benton had decided to be a crime fighter and gone to a costume store for a disguise. The store only had a rabbit, a teddy bear and a chicken costume available. Benton tried the rabbit suit on and went outside the store, only to be encountered by a passing citizen. The man kissed him, telling him he was a cute rabbit. Benton went back into the store, took off the rabbit outfit, passed over the teddy bear, and decided on the chicken suit. Chicken Man was born.

I looked at Stevens and Fessman. It was obvious they loved the story and the weirdly and totally out of place character. I presumed the story was funny but somewhere in the last two days and one night I'd lost my sense of humor. I reflected briefly, while Chicken Man fought crime over the radio, about how a person could possibly lose a sense of humor while knowing he'd lost it.

The mosquitoes were back. Armed Forces Radio finally shut down for the night, thankfully. I dug my mosquito repellent out of a pack pocket and slathered it on my arms. Stevens passed me a full pack of unfiltered Camel cigarettes, but I shook my head.

"No, for the mosquitoes," Stevens said, holding the pack out. "You can't put that shit on your face or it'll sting your eyes real bad. Light a cigarette and let if burn under your chin. Does the trick. They send us plenty of cigarettes every morning so you'll never run out. At least a box each."

"Who sends them?" I asked, taking the cigarette pack while Fessman rummaged in his own pack for a lighter.

"Gift packs from home," Stevens replied. "They come with notes inside them from people back home. You never know the people sending them and the notes can say anything. We read them every night we get a chance. Really neat stuff some of the people back home put down."

"Matches don't work in this place," Fessman said, holding out a chrome-plated Zippo lighter.

"Thank you," I said, looking the Lance Corporal in the eyes to communicate my sincerity.

"Oh, that's okay," he answered. "We get a ton of them left over from the dead guys every day."

I stared at the Zippo. Somebody had carved "M.C." carefully into its lower body. I wondered if it was initials or the abbreviation for Marine Corps. "We can't take stuff from the dead," I said, still holding the lighter gently in one hand. "Their stuff has to be bagged tagged and returned home with them," I finished.

"Nah, not here," Stevens said. "Not now. Never seen it. The only stuff that goes home is what you take if you live and what you keep from the body of anyone you kill."

I opened the pack of Camels while I thought. The pack squished in my fingers from the oil content used as the base in the repellent. Would I ever be clean again, I wondered, as I pulled a white tube out, fumbled with it until I got one end in my mouth and the Zippo flipped open. I flicked the small wheel down with my thumb and the lighter flared.

"If you kill somebody you get their stuff?" I asked, lighting the cigarette carefully before pulling it out to hold it under my chin.

"Spoils of war, they call it," Stevens said, lighting a cigarette of his own.

"Wallets, pictures, notes, insignia, belts, knives, and even guns, as long as they're not full auto, get sent with re-supply. They send the stuff to Division where it's stored until we go home, and then they ship it."

I couldn't believe my ears. Why had I heard nothing of the spoils of war? The whole thing sounded like it was a description of what might have happened in war situations hundreds or even thousands of years ago, not the late sixties in the Marine Corps. I had no reason to disbelieve the boys in front of me. They were a mess I realized. Dirty to the bone, nervous as displaced spiders in little ways and looking to be saved. I could see it beyond the surface deadness in their eyes. Could I save them? Would I be the one? Would I get them out of hell? I had just turned twenty-three. Their looks were like knives going straight into what was left of my heart. I'd been there two days, one night and now moving into a second night and already I knew. I couldn't save them. I very probably couldn't save myself.

The Gunny appeared out of nowhere. He knelt on the edge of my poncho, which served as the floor of my half-tent. He took out a canteen and handed it to me.

"Drink that down. Last water until dawn. Pull out your map."

I opened my left thigh pocket and took out my one to twenty-five thousand grid-photo map. The area it covered was about twenty kilometers by twenty. An Hoa, the fire base for artillery and landing strip for small air support was in the lower left hand corner of the paper. I spread the map out as best I could without dropping the cigarette or losing the lighter. The rubberized surface of the poncho cover felt wet but then everything felt wet.

The Gunny knelt and examined the map.

"Night defensive fires?" he asked, noting the grease pencil numbers all around our current position. I hadn't registered our exact location with an artillery round but I was pretty certain. The Gunny took out a small pencil flashlight.

"Here," he said, pointing at the map. "Hill one ten, on this side of the slope heading west into the A Shau Valley. We head on over there tomorrow. Seems like some Army insertion went wrong." He clicked the light off and pulled some stuff from his pack. He lit a fire after plopping some C-Ration cans nearby. "Dinner. Eat if you can. We'll be moving long and hard tomorrow after resupply and medevac."

"Medevac?" I asked, my mind going back to the corpsman problem I'd been given earlier to somehow deal with.

"Yeah, they'll know we're moving out in the morning so they'll hit us tonight. Again. I'll be back."

I moved over to the small fire. I noticed that there were fires all around me and hushed conversations going on but nobody approached. I'd met none of the Marines, had no opportunity to identify or see the non-commissioned officers leading our five platoons and I hadn't been consulted about the coming move on the following day. I presumed that Gulf Company would be assaulting Hill 110, but there'd been no operational planning meeting I'd had any part of.

"When did he get the orders?" I asked Fessman. "Don't we get the command net stuff all the time on your radio?"

"Nah, I don't turn the radio on unless we need to call somebody, sir," he answered, puffing on his own cigarette. "The Gunny has his own radioman. He talks to command as the six."

For the first time I was more angry than I was afraid. In training I'd only had three hours of schooling on how to use the Prick 25 radio but none at all on how to access different commands or even what the language was. I knew the "six actual" of the unit was the commanding officer in person. The "six" referred to someone acting as the commanding officer or for him.

"Turn it on," I ordered. "I want it on all the time. Scroll between the command net and artillery all the time I want to know what's going on and what the Gunny's talking to command about."

"He may not like that," Stevens said.

Fessman handed me a tiny little folding can opener. I opened it and began working slowly around the edges of a can the Gunny had left behind. I had to eat but I wasn't hungry. I needed sleep but I wasn't tired. The Gunny's words "so they'll hit us tonight" reverberated through my brain. It would be my first contact if it happened. I didn't count the horrid weirdness of the night before. That had simply been a confused mess of nightmare oddity. The day's hike had been strange, with little regard for security. We'd taken the high ground all the way without regard to a surrounding enemy. The radios had played and all the Marines had been talking to one another, like we were in training. The night was filled with small fires and hung over with a pall of cigarette smoke to fight off the mosquitoes. There was no hiding the two hundred and seventeen Marines plopped down atop the only high ground around with machine gun snouts sticking out of the brush everywhere.

Hit? Of course we'd be hit, I thought darkly, leaning back into my half a tent, mist starting to fall on the shiny edge of my poncho cover. I ate ham slices that tasted like dull, old spam. I drank down the liquid after, as I had the water in the Gunny's canteen. Water was everywhere but in short supply for drinking.

I didn't sleep. I laid down, my face only inches from the shelter half canvas, listening intently for the enemy through the slight rustle made by water drops running down the outside when enough mist had been collected together to drive them.

We got hit at 2:07 a.m. exactly, according to my combat watch. It started with light machine gun fire going outward from our perimeter I guessed. The sound of the M60s was distinctive, a smooth sort of cracking sound, the bullets going out distinctively from the guns, not like in training. There they'd seemed jarring and staccato in their desire to get out of the barrel in a mass and move downrange. The firing spread all around me, going out into the night. I hugged the poncho cover, rolling onto my face. I had my .45 Colt strapped to my waist but it seemed idiotic to take it out. There were real guns going off all around me.

I didn't look at my watch again. The fire escalated and got much louder. I knew we were taking fire inside the perimeter because tracer bullets began curving over my shelter half. Far enough away to make me shiver but not make me quiver in terror. That started with the explosions. The north side of the perimeter erupted in a series of large explosions.

"Fucking Chi-Com grenades," Fessman shouted, from somewhere nearby. A bigger gun than all the rest opened up and I became terrified. The bigger gun was even slower in delivering its automatic fire but the size of its tracers made them look like express flaming beer barrels going over. It was enemy fire and had to be the 12.6 mm heavy machine gun the enemy used instead of our own Browning .50 caliber. We didn't have a Browning in the company. They were too big and heavy for a ground unit to carry.

What broke me was when the beer barrel trajectories dropped until they were coming in only a few feet over my head. I went blind with their glare and the sound was causing me to lose my hearing when I ran. I'd looked up and out through the bracken to see where the tracers were starting from and it was close. It seemed that they were inside the perimeter. And it was enough. It was too much. I moved rapidly, running fast and staying low. I ran directly toward the paddy dike we'd come in on. And I didn't make it. Just before breaking free of the heavy growth a huge force closed around me and drove me into the mud. When I hit the weight just increased until I was almost submerged in the squishy mess of the paddy dike wall.

"You stay," a voice yelled into my deafened right ear. "You stay until I come back for you. You're the company commander, you don't get to run away."

I knew it was the Gunny's voice but it took me seconds after his leaving for my mind to work well enough to figure it out. The firing continued but more in the distance. Apparently we weren't surrounded. It hadn't occurred to me in my full panic mode to consider that I might be trying to run through my unit's own machine gun fire at the perimeter or why there wouldn't be enemy attackers where I was trying to go.

I waited. I breathed slowly, feeling the mud and muck begin to congeal around me. I was half buried in the stuff but I didn't move. I had nothing. I had no courage, no honor, no nothing. All I had was the Gunny and he'd said wait. I counted breaths. Sixteen to a minute I'd heard somewhere. I did sixteen one thousand times. I was just over three thousand sixteen breath bits when the shooting stopped. Things went quiet, except for some mute screaming in the far distance. I started counting from the beginning but didn't get far. A big hand reached down, grabbed my arm, and eased me gently upward and out of the grip of the mud. The Gunny let go. I sat there, the first light of dawn just barely beginning to make itself felt.

The Gunny smoked a cigarette, squatting like a gook not very far away.

"Your first contact," he said, between slow puffs.

"Yeah," I agreed, shakily, trying to pry loose some of the mud clots that had dried to my clothing.

"This is my third war" the Gunny said, facing toward where the sun would eventually come up. "It's the worst one of all."

I didn't know what to say. I didn't want to say anything. I didn't want to be there. I didn't want to really be anywhere anymore.

"You think you're a coward," the Gunny said with a faint smile on his features, barely visible in the low light. "You think you ran under fire. You think that proves something because of what you've been taught. Well, there's no teaching for this shit. If you tell people later on what it was like they'll think you're nothing but a liar."

I listened intently, trying to grasp what the man was saying, but not quite getting it.

"You're just a kid. You ran because you're an intelligent kid. I was there behind you because I've been in three wars. I knew you'd run. The good ones always run if they have a brain. But you won't have to run again. Next contact you'll stay but you won't be able to say or do anything. Maybe after your fifth contact, or so, you'll be able to talk. Nobody will listen to you. It'll take a few more before that happens, and then you'll be okay. I mean if we get that far. The last part I can't help you with. If you stay here too long and go through too much of this, then you'll get to look forward to the contacts. You won't come back from that and I can't help you with it if it happens. Let's go. Everyone knows you're here, what happened, and nobody gives a shit. We'd all run if there was somewhere to run to."

The Gunny slowly got up and stretched, field stripping his cigarette and fluttering away its small remaining bits. He walked back into the bush we'd come out of.

When I got back to our small command box area my stuff was all packed up and waiting. Fessman, Stevens, and Nguyen made believe I'd never been gone. There was no time to say anything because the sound of a helicopter approaching began to dominate the whole area. The resupply was coming in. I knew from the deep dissonant roar that it was one of the big dual rotor jobs that could haul a lot of stuff. I heard a second machine in the distance.

"The Huey's resupply, if you want to mail your letter home, sir," Fessman said through cupped hands. "The big one's for medevac. We lost a few more than usual. The Gunny's bagging them up and filing the tags."

I looked around but saw no special activity anywhere. In the jungle all sorts of stuff went on only a few feet away that you might never know was happening unless you stepped right into it. The jungle seemed to have a life all of its own. I looked back at my small team and then made my way to the open area near the paddy dikes where I'd spent the night. I headed for the resupply chopper and got my letter off to my wife, or at least placed into the hands of a crewman who looked like he was from a war movie. He stood next to the chopper with his legs spread, the finest new jungle utilities on, and wearing some kind of cowboy cavalry hat folded up on one side in the Australian style. In his hands he balanced a Thompson submachine gun. He looked so wildly out of place in his Hollywood outfit and back home cleanliness I would have laughed at any other time in my life. He took my letter with a grim expression, playing his role to the hilt. I walked away, back toward my team.

As I walked I looked down and saw the imprint my body had left in the mud the night before. I smiled to myself with a twisted bitterness.

seven

THE THIRD DAY

Ham and lima beans. Nobody wanted them so I took all four boxes. It was preferable to the sliced "spam" I'd had before. The boxes had already been picked through for sugar and fake cream packets. I got a carton of cigarettes. Lucky Strike. I sat back against a big bamboo tree, waiting for Gunny's order to move out. I opened the Lucky Strikes and found the hand-written note I'd been told would be there. *What you are doing means so much to my husband and I. He fought in the big war. Here's our address. Come visit when you get back and we'll make our best stew.* It was signed William and Maude Collins, with an address somewhere in Iowa. I wondered if Vietnam would end up being a "little war" later on. I'd have fought in a little war. Not a real one. Certainly not a big one. I folded the piece of notepaper from home and put it in my wallet.

"Don't do that, sir," Fessman whispered in my left ear.

"What?" I replied, surprised.

"Don't save the note," Fessman said, actually holding out his hand. "We're here for a long time. There's going to be a lot of notes. We don't save 'em. It's bad luck. We burn 'em at night, after we read them."

I got my wallet out and gave him the note. The plaintive quality of the way he asked compelled me. He cared about me and my survival. I felt it emanate viscerally from him. Fessman put the note in his pocket, for burning later that night I presumed.

At the chopper I'd also gotten more insect repellent (type II), a brownish-green can of Mennen foot powder, one tooth brush, one tube of Pepsodent, a box of .45 Colt bullets (ball), and a cardboard container without markings about half the size of a shoe box. I put everything except the cardboard box into my pack, wondering why I needed fifty bullets for an automatic I wasn't likely to ever use, what with all the automatic rifles surrounding me. I opened the container and then quickly closed it. It was a box of lead tubes with plastic tip covers. There must have been forty or more of them inside. It was morphine. Ten milligram morphine tubes. The corpsman problem came rushing back at me. What was I going to do? Nobody had said anything once the issue was dumped in my lap. What had the corpsman done the night before with all our "friendly" dead and wounded? I didn't know. Maybe nothing would come of it at all, I thought. The order to move out came down the line. Nobody issued any order that I heard. Everyone just somehow knew and started the process of getting up and going. Fessman and I returned to the other two on my team.

"The leeches, sir," Fessman said, handing me a burning cigarette.

"What leeches?" I replied, looking at the extended cigarette but not taking it.

"From lying in the mud out there last night," he said. "On your neck."

I hurriedly put my hand up to my neck, and then stopped. I felt some rounded growths. Four or five of them. I pulled my hand down. I almost threw up.

"Get them off," I ordered, my voice hoarse.

Fessman approached until he was inches away, bent over and began applying the burning tip of the cigarette to the backs of the leeches. One fell off, and then another. I looked down. Black finger-long things lay squirming on the ground in front of me. I shivered openly. Fessman puffed on the cigarette a few times, and then went back to work. After several minutes he was done.

"When we get set in tonight check the other parts of your body. The heat from the cigarette will make any you have drop off without you having to tear their teeth out. Gasoline works too but they only have that in the rear area and we aren't going there. Still, you'll have scars. Little white round ones."

Stevens began packing up my stuff. I tossed in what I'd gotten from resupply along with the boxes of C-Rations. I held the morphine in my right hand. I had to give it to somebody, but I wasn't sure who. The Gunny would know.

Fessman's Prick 25 radio squawked. He turned away to speak into the small handset. "It's for the six actual," he said, holding out the handset. I just looked back at him.

"That's you, sir," he replied.

I took the handset and pushed the button down.

"Six actual here, over," I said, loudly.

Fessman made his hand go up and down. I got his message to lower my voice.

"Casualty report," a tinny voice said.

I shrugged my shoulders. I had no idea how many we'd lost, in reality. I hadn't seen the bags shipped out or the wounded medevaced. "What do I tell them?" I asked Fessman in a whisper, holding my hand over the microphone part of the handset.

"Make it up," Fessman replied, also in a whisper. "We do it all the time. It's for Battalion daily reports. They don't mean anything. They don't care. They don't check with anybody."

"We can't just flat out lie to Battalion, for Christ's sake," I hissed back.

"They're back there and we're out here," Stevens piped in from behind me. "Fuck 'em."

I looked over my shoulder at him. Nguyen stood next to him, grinning, like he knew what we were talking about. I sighed, loudly. "Eight KIA and four MIA, friendlies," I reported into the handset. "Twenty-seven KIA NVA, no wounded, over."

"Roger," the handset said and then went dead.

I looked down at the ground where the eight squirming leeches were in their last throes. I felt my neck. Blood came back, all over my hand. I looked up at Fessman in surprise. He held out an old t-shirt. I staunched the blood with one hand and, with Stevens help, got into my pack.

Stevens taped his little transistor radio to his shoulder. Brother John announced the first song of the day. "If you hear this song, then you're okay. You'll get back, and there she'll be…" The song "Angel of the Morning" began to play. *There'll be no strings to bind your hands, not if my love can't bind your heart…* We walked back out onto the muddy drying surface of the paddy dikes, all silent and listening.

The song had been the one my wife used to laugh at, and I used to sing, while she waited to deliver our first child back home. In those very last days before I left. A chill went through me in spite of the morning heat. I wasn't going home. I knew I wasn't going home ever again. Wherever I'd landed and however it happened that I'd come there, I'd come to a place that wasn't survivable. I couldn't describe it in my mind in words, but the feeling ran up and down my spine like a brilliant Tesla coil of blazing fire. A coldness radiated out from the fire and ate itself into my body and mind.

The move would be a brutal one, even though the sun came out and a slight breeze blew the cloying misty rain away. The mountains lay ahead of us, with Hill 110 at the top. The company's direction eased toward the west and ever so slowly we left the paddies behind, along with most of the mosquitoes. The brush began to grow thicker and thicker. Plenty of paths penetrated the bracken, bringing about more risk from booby traps. The most common trap, according to Stevens, was a simple "soup grenade." The M26 fragmentation grenade carried by all Marines fit perfectly into a Campbell's soup can with the top cut off. After inserting the grenade into the can, the pin would be pulled. The can would be tied to a tree several feet off the ground with a string or wire running from the top of the grenade to some other tree or bush. Anyone passing on the path would push against the string and the grenade would be pulled from the can. Five seconds later a medevac chopper would have to be called in. If the grenade was American, then a body bag would likely be taken out. If it was Chinese, then injuries might be treated for transport.

The tough part of the hike was enduring the low-level hill climbs leading up the mountain to Hill 110. Training in Virginia, we carried packs weighing twenty-five pounds, one canteen of water, a weapon, and some ammunition. In Vietnam, the packs weighed seventy pounds and were filled with a lot of ammo, food, and as much other junk as could be accommodated for long stays in the field without full relief. We needed four canteens of water, sometimes six. In Virginia, the paths were all hard ground and rock. In Vietnam, even the mountains were made of mud.

I noticed a lot of nasty looks sent my way by Marines I didn't know. Just looks. Nobody outside of the Gunny and my team spoke to me. The Gunny made his way to near the rear of the moving unit by mid-afternoon. We stopped under the trees of the single canopy jungle. The heat-relieving trees were a godsend, as around noon the sun had cooked all metal surfaces to near boiling temperatures.

"I gave a bogus report to battalion," I started out, once I'd dropped my pack and we were crouched to enjoy our explosive-fueled coffee.

"Yeah, I heard," he replied with one of his smiling non-smiles. "The right thing to do. You're learning."

"Really?" I asked. "I presume that most in the company know about last night and aren't too happy. From the looks I'm getting, I mean."

"Oh, they know everything," the Gunny replied, laboriously rolling one of his battered looking little cigarettes. "But it's not what you think. They're mad because they know you can call artillery in and you didn't. Some good guys bought the farm last night. Everything's a trade-off."

"Trade-off for what?" I asked, wondering how I could possibly misinterpret everything every time.

"I left you in the mud so you might live long enough to become a real company commander," the Gunny said.

"Some guys died just for that?" I replied, shocked and hurt a bit.

"Yeah, that was the trade-off and, oh, don't get all teary-eyed," the Gunny said, blowing out a huge lungful of bluish smoke. "I'm in a bad spot here. The worst of my life, and that's saying something. I gotta get out of leading this show and you've gotta get into running it."

"Is Hill 110 defended?" I asked, changing the awful subject.

"Probably," the Gunny replied. "We'll see, and then decide what we're going to do."

"Does that decision involve me," I asked, dreading what he might say in response.

"I'm here to advise you and I hope to keep you alive doing it," the Gunny said, putting out his cigarette by field stripping it while it was still burning. "Anytime you feel you can handle this then just say so and you've got it. You can read a map and god knows you can call artillery. What you're going to do with the doc might determine a lot about the rest of it though."

"No," I replied, instantly, without having to think for one second. "You're doing fine. Just tell me what to do."

"Hill 110, you got it," the Gunny pointed at me with one index finger when he said the words, like the last three were some lyrical mantra. "The doc is an issue you've got to take care of yourself, though. Tonight, when we go down, would be good."

I pulled the cardboard box filled with morphine syrettes from my left thigh pocket and held it out.

"Thought you'd know what to do with these," I said.

"Yeah, I'll dole them out a bit more carefully," the Gunny said. "These are supposed to go directly to the docs, not us. Somebody back there's paying attention."

"You know where we are, exactly?" he asked, holding the morphine box like it contained something much more delicate.

"Yes," I replied. "Nine one nine six seven seven two two one," I read off from memory. "Actually that's a position about a hundred meters off our right flank just up ahead."

"You remember that, just like that, without the map or compass?" he asked.

"Don't need a compass," I replied. "Hill 110 is due west at 4800 mils. North is sixteen hundred mils that way," I pointed with my right index finger. "Then I just memorized the defensive fires I set up."

"Ah, what's a mil?" the Gunny asked.

"Sixty-four hundred in a circle," I described. "Taken from the two radians, as a multiple of pie and then converted to thousands and rounded from 6283 to 6400. Sixty-four hundred mils in a circle. Lot more accurate than degrees."

"Right," the Gunny said, and then quickly departed back toward the point of the company's advance.

"Where is he?" I yelled at his back.

"On the point with the FNGs that just came in," he tossed over his shoulder before disappearing into the jungle.

"How could he not have known all that mil stuff, anyway?" Stevens asked.

I turned to look at him in question before he and Fessman burst out laughing.

The afternoon was a brutal slog ever upward, until going downward every once in a while into a pit of water and more rotten red mud. Even though Hill 110 was only five hundred meters high the hills between Gulf Company and that objective were many and steeply sloped. At the bottom of one of those hills an explosion echoed back to my ears from the point.

"Booby trap," Stevens whispered.

The immediate relief I felt about the possibility that my problem would be taken care of if the doc had set off the booby trap made me feel slightly guilty. I'd heard nothing more about the racial problem the Gunny had mentioned earlier. In fact, I hadn't seen anyone of color since I'd arrived in the unit. Where were they and what was the problem, I wondered.

Gunfire came back from the front of the column. Instantly I recognized incoming small arms fire. Not sixteens, AKs, or the heavy stuff. Something else...

"Arty up," came shouting back to where I was, yelled from man to man.

"Do you suppose that's my new title?" I said to Fessman.

"I'm right behind you," he said, knowing no other answer was necessary.

We hunched over, running up through the path and past a dozen Marines down in the bracken-filled mud. It didn't take long to reach the Gunny. He knelt near two men who lay on their backs. Several other Marines worked over and on them. Everyone stayed as low as possible. There was no more incoming fire.

"Hill 110's hot," the Gunny said. "Last year two Marine units lost their asses on that hill and it's not going to be us this year. Up and to the left a few hundred yards there's some kind of base of fire or nest of VC. That's old U.S. surplus crap shooting at us. We give it out to the RVNs, and it comes right back to us."

"Artillery?" I asked, laying as flat in the mud as I could get without exposing my neck to the horrid leeches.

"That rise just ahead on the left… that's where we're taking some fire from," the Gunny said as he raised one arm and pointed through the jungle toward some invisible position.

I knew the position from the map, relieved to have contour intervals again. My defensive fires had been easily selected. It wasn't likely that enemy forces would choose dips or valleys to observe or fire from. A small hillock, maybe sixty meters high, lay just ahead. A ring of three contour intervals ran around it on the map in my head. A registration point. I smiled my new humorless smile and motioned to Fessman for the handset. He looked at me and clicked the frequency knob around before handing me the set.

After calling for a mission and inputting the coded data, I gave the final order. "Battery of six, H.E., fire for effect."

"Battery of six?" Fessman said, as the radio squawked out "Shot, over."

"Shot out," Fessman said in return, looking at me with a vague frown.

"Splash, over," the machine reported over its small speaker.

"Get as low as you can," I ordered, before following my own advice.

The rounds came in, the first six of them spaced in a circle about a hundred yards in diameter, depending on how the battery was set up in An Hoa.

The forty-six pound rounds, with super quick fuses that blew on contact, exploded with a ground-shaking jungle-swaying intensity. Six more rounds came in six seconds later, exactly as before. And then six more. The rounds kept coming until thirty-six had been expended. Twisted pieces of jungle matter flew over our position and lay hanging everywhere. The air compressed causing a light weather misting just in our part of the jungle. The huge explosions seemed to reverberate long after they had stopped.

"What the fuck was that?" the Gunny yelled too loudly. "You're not supposed to call that shit closer than two hundred meters."

Everyone's hearing had been adjusted, including my own. I scuttled through light bracken moving like a sand crab, more sideways than straight ahead. I reached the Gunny who had his back to me, bending over working on someone.

"The doc?" I asked, hopefully.

"Still with us right here, working on this guy with me."

I looked around the Gunny's body. A corpsman just finished a bandage wrap on the wounded Marine in front of his knees.

"That him?" I asked, thinking it was one of the dumbest questions I'd ever asked. But I had to know.

"Yeah, it's him," the Gunny said. The Corpsman made believe neither of us were right there with him.

"Where are the other corpsmen?" I asked, seeing no one else. The other wounded Marine needed no help. Part of his head was missing.

"Be here in seconds," the Gunny answered. "Why?" he said, his voice still too loud to be normal.

I reached down, pulled out my .45 and pointed it at the Corpsman. "Get up and turn sideways," I said.

"Huh?" he murmured, finally looking directly at me.

"What the fuck?" the Gunny exclaimed, half turning to face me.

"I said get up," I said flatly to the Corpsman, thumbing off the safety of the Colt with a loud click, even to our damaged ears.

The man stood up slowly.

"Sideways," I said, motioning with my automatic.

He slowly turned, a questioning look on his face.

I squeezed the trigger of my Colt slowly and carefully, my aim certain. The gun went off with a bang louder than the artillery shells. The bullet took the Corpsman through the side of his buttocks, and probably out the other side, too, but I didn't see that damage as he was thrown sideways and down. He screamed at the top of his lungs.

"What the fuck have you done?" the Gunny said, his tone one of shock.

My ears rang from the close muzzle blast of the .45. I re-holstered the Colt while the Corpsman continued to roll back and forth on the ground and scream. The other two corpsmen came running up.

"Who's hit?" one of them asked.

I pointed at the Corpsman. Both men went to work on their fallen associate.

"Medevac him," I ordered them both.

The Gunny stared at me as I rose to a standing position I moved back past Fessman, and then crawled forward to the edge of the bracken. The little hill wasn't a hill anymore. The thirty-six rounds had turned it into a ten-foot high plateau of vegetable salad and muck.

"Did you shoot somebody?" Fessman said, close enough to my damaged left ear so I could hear him.

"He got hit," I murmured.

The night was coming and the hill we were supposed to take the next day was occupied. Would we get hit again when it was full dark?

Would I run again?

I didn't know the answer to either question, but I knew I wasn't going to spend another night in the mud with the leeches.

eight

THE THIRD DAY : SECOND PART

I made my way back to the Gunny. The Corpsman lay still, breathing shallowly with a poncho cover wrapped around him. The poncho covers served as our blankets, since they easily separated from the rubber liner. The air mattresses most everyone had, like mine, were filled with holes. They served as immediate ground cover for the hooches thrown up inside the perimeter every night.

"Morphine?" I asked the Gunny.

He briefly turned to stare at me, as he readied the other wounded Marine for storage until the morning's medevac. The wounded FNG to be stored for care by the two remaining corpsmen and the other body bag moved to a nearby clearing to wait. The morphine-addicted Corpsman finally was receiving morphine for the purpose it was intended instead of for escape, I thought, although he was in fact escaping. The corpsmen worked, ignoring my presence. I wondered if there'd be another corpsman on the morning chopper to replace the one we'd lost.

I retreated back toward the area not far from where I'd called in the artillery. There had been no more incoming small arms fire. My mind replayed the cracks the weapons made when they'd gone off outside the perimeter. The Gunny was accurate. Not sixteens or AKs. Different. Like the choppers were different. You didn't have to see the chopper to know what it was. Even the Huey Cobra attack helicopters sounded distinctly different from the supply ones.

Stevens and Nguyen had set up the hooches, mine too. I couldn't remember dropping my pack. In officer candidate school and then the basic school I'd never worked in the field with enlisted men. The work, and obvious care for me the small team exhibited, kept me in a state of disconcerted surprise.

I pulled out a box of "Ham and Mothers," as Fessman called the particular B-2 Meal. "Combat, Individual" was printed on the box. I checked inside and found a pack of sugar and one of cream. I'd thought the boxes had all been gone through, but maybe I was wrong. And then I thought of what might have been done to the food, given that the company had such little regard for officers and absolutely no fear of killing them. I shrugged, reading the little cream container. There was nothing to read out in combat conditions. I was so used to reading. In spite of having no time to do anything but be afraid, fight the awful conditions, and try to survive, I missed reading. The package said that the four grams of powdered cream inside was made by Sanna Dairies in Madison, Wisconsin. For some reason I felt like visiting the company if I ever got back to the world.

"Why do they take the sugar and cream out of the C-Rations?" I asked Stevens, sitting nearby under his own lean-to. "Cut drugs, or something?" I went on, after he didn't reply.

"Hot chocolate," Fessman said.

"What?" I asked, not believing his answer.

"B-3 units," Fessman replied. "The B-3 units have cocoa powder packets instead of the John Wayne crackers you have in the mother box. The cocoa powder tastes a lot better with extra sugar and cream."

"I suppose you got a B-3," I said, tearing open a brown envelope of crackers. The John Wayne crackers, no doubt, but I wasn't going to ask.

"No, sir," Fessman responded, holding up two small discs. "I'm a B-1 man, myself. Pure chocolate. No powder."

I'd never seen C-Rations before, or "Charlie Rats," as Fessman called them. That the codes on the boxes meant something made sense. That there was no training about the subject made no sense at all.

It was closing on full dark. I was eating the ham and limas without shaking, having been supplied a small hand-formed pyramid of the explosives for heating. So far so good. Suddenly I realized I had better use the bathroom, or what passed for one in the field. I put my cans back in my B-2 box, set it aside and grabbed my E-tool, the little folding shovel that was irreplaceable.

"Be careful out there," Stevens whispered to me, as I got ready to go. "Don't go far and stay low. No booby traps in here or we'd have set 'em off already, but there's other stuff."

Other stuff. I was learning about other stuff. During my entire time on the planet I'd never been to a place where I was so disliked so quickly without almost anyone knowing me, or even having met me.

I moved very slowly away from the small fires of my team. I realized immediately that I'd also forgotten to bring the cigarettes and the bad smelling lotion. The mosquitoes were back in full force. I stopped no more than thirty feet deep into the nearby bracken, got down on my knees and quickly dug a calf-deep hole. I set the shovel down, being sure to be as quiet as possible, and then did what I had come there to do. The little pack of toilet paper in the B-1 accessory pack did the job. I covered the mess carefully, and then stopped. The overwhelming aroma of marijuana wafted through the chest-high ferns. A small group of Marines moved in and began setting up not ten feet from my position. For some reason I froze in place, dropping to the prone position near my covered hole.

The Marines started a single large fire, apparently also fueled by the plastic explosives, and then sat around it, working through their own C-Ration boxes.

"What do you think, Jurgens?" one of the Marines said. "This new clown we got."

I held my breath, wondering if they could possibly be talking about me.

"More of the same. Another ring-knocker, most likely," a deeper voice answered.

My mind whirled. Ring-knocker was a derogatory word used to describe a West Point or Naval Academy graduate. I knew it was a phrase also used to describe officers in general. They had to be talking about me.

"So what do we do?" another Marine asked. "Is he going to side with us or them? And does it matter. We're doing fine on our own."

"Yeah, we're doing just great," the deeper voice responded. "Four KIA yesterday alone, not counting the doc, who that asshole took out."

"He needed to go," the one they called Jurgens said, forcefully. "He stole the fucking morphine."

Who were "they," I wondered. The enemy? North Vietnamese Army? The VC? I couldn't figure it out.

"We ain't goin' home, Sarge," the first Marine said.

"Let's just fucking take him out like the rest," another Marine said, his voice low and deep. "Why risk anything? What are they going to do, send some more? We'll take them out too."

"This one's no dummy," Jurgens said. "He can read a map and call artillery pretty damned good, and something had to be done with doc. That was pretty slick."

"We can use the ambush trick. Like with Weathers in First Platoon. We'll just set up an ambush for tomorrow night after we deal with 110. Just like before. We'll give him the wrong location. The Gunny can send him out to check on us and when he walks by we'll let him have it. Hell, remember Weathers? I called him on the net and told him we had activity in our kill zone and he said to open fire."

It seemed that they all laughed together from my perspective a few feet away. I pushed myself down into the wet ferns. They'd just admitted killing an officer, or making him kill himself. If I was discovered I knew I would be dead on the spot.

"The Gunny was pissed about that," Jurgens said, when the laughing died down. "We can't afford to piss off the Gunny. He's all we've got. Do what you gotta do but leave the Gunny out of it. He's kind of soft on the asshole anyway.

"Screw it," the deep voiced Marine said. "That clown is nutty as a fruit cake. He called in that phosphorus round right over our heads. If it'd gone off a little lower, we'd all burned to death. And that little artillery display before, to kill a VC sniper? That was way too close and I think he did it on purpose. He's nuts."

"No Gunny," Jurgens said, flatly. "You can pull the ambush trick tomorrow night but no Gunny."

"What about the radio jockey and Stevens?" deep voice asked.

"Whoever shows up," Jurgens replied. "Fortunes of war. Maybe he'll bring Sugar Daddy along and we can finally finish off that son-of-a-bitch too."

I had to get out of there but I couldn't move. If I moved, the battle-tested Marines nearby, only a few feet from me, would be alerted and then they wouldn't wait for an ambush. I had my .45 but they all had automatic weapons. I felt in my lower back pocket. I'd taken one of the brand new M33 grenades, just to check it out, when I was at the morning chopper. I pulled it out very gently. It was smaller than an orange and perfectly round. The safety pressure lever stuck out and down from the side, almost as big as the device. I thought about pulling the pin and tossing it in among the Marines nearby but I knew I couldn't do it. Maybe they weren't all in on it. Maybe they were kidding and wouldn't go through with it. But I had to get away and I was frightened down to my boots again. My whole body was tensed up. I had the grenade in my right hand but wasn't sure I could control myself to pull the damned pin.

I eased the grenade under me. I'd trained only part of one day with the older M26 model. When the lever, or spoon as it was called, was released, it made a loud mechanical noise when the striker hit to start the fuse. They would know my location instantly when I let the pressure off the spoon, so I did it while I had the grenade under my stomach in the mud. There was almost no sound, my body muffling almost all of the grenade's action.

I rolled over and threw the grenade as far over the group as I could, my whole torso whipping up and then back down. I prayed there was no Marine doing what I was doing in the brush on the far side.

"What the fuck?" came from one of the men just before the five second fuse burned through and the grenade went off.

I vaulted up and ran.

"Grenade!" a Marine screamed, but I was moving low and fast back toward my team's position. I'd thrown the grenade pretty far, and the M33 seemed like it wasn't too big for a grenade, anyway.

When I was within a few meters of my hooch I slowed down, took a few breaths and moved in.

"Incoming?" Stevens asked.

"Didn't sound like it," I responded, as matter-of-factly as I could.

"Maybe a triple play attempt," Fessman added, "since it sounded like it was one of ours. I'd say M33, not 26. Too sharp. That was Comp B."

I was amazed that a seventeen-year-old kid could observe such a thing with great accuracy.

"What's a triple play?" I asked.

"You get three purple hearts awarded here and you get to spend the rest of your tour in Okinawa," Fessman said. "They throw grenades nearby after digging in, usually when there's incoming later in the night. They hold their hands up to get hit by fragments. Three and you're out. Triple play."

I listened to the hubbub in the distance but nobody came in our direction except the Gunny. Moments after I returned he appeared, moving easily and quietly to sit on the edge of my poncho.

"Grenade," he said. "Likely friendly. Don't know. We'll get hit later, of course, but we're in a pretty good position. One KIA and two wounded before the sun goes down though. Not a good omen. The Corpsman's going to live. Thought you might want to know."

"Thank you, Gunny," I responded.

"You did want to know," he came back.

"Of course," I replied, wondering where he was going.

He got to his feet. "I'll be just a few meters over there all night. Tomorrow, before we engage with whatever we have to engage with, I want you to meet somebody. The other problem we got, like the doc, the knuckle-knockers. I'll arrange it."

"What's his name," I asked, before he could walk away into the night.

"Sugar Daddy," he murmured over his shoulder.

nine

THE THIRD NIGHT

Once again, backed into the open-sided "lean-to" my "scout" team had made for me, I took out my writing materials to send another letter home. It was getting too dark to write so I did the best I could since using the flashlight under a hunched-over poncho cover was out of the question in the heat. The night mist had returned with the mosquitoes and I wished for a real thunderstorm like I'd experienced while growing up in the Midwest of the United States.

I wrote furiously about how the Company wasn't a company at all from what I understood one should be. Training had been little preparation with only the physical conditioning, map-reading and artillery school seeming to matter. I wrote of the mystery Marine named "Sugar Daddy" I was about to meet, as if being introduced at some sales conference or maybe a fraternity get-together. And then I stopped. Not because of the diminishing light, but because my wife could not possibly comprehend what I was trying to tell her. Even if she could somehow, did I really want her to know what I was going through? If they killed me, she would think I died in combat bravely, a hero. Instead of whatever the truth really was. Mary could not know, would not know…

I finished the letter without mentioning anything of consequence, focusing on the tropical weather and how much I missed our newborn daughter. I asked her to send me Hoppe's #9 for cleaning my .45, instant creamer for coffee, and a cassette tape of her voice. Some of the Marines in the unit had battery powered cassette tape machines to record or play back messages.

I eased off my leather boots. Because I hadn't gone through combat supply on the way out to the unit, I didn't receive the new cloth-sided jungle boots. The socks with my boots weren't thick enough to handle the moisture or cushion the long hikes. I'd have to send home for more socks. I pulled out my scrunched up utility top, which I'd wear all the time the mosquitoes were so intolerable. The helmet, hot and heavy to wear, provided little protection from anything other than low hanging jungle branches. But I'd wear that, too. I needed to find one of those big rubber bands so I could carry the repellent on the outside of my helmet instead of rummaging in my pack, when I had my pack nearby.

I tried to put Jurgens and the others behind the brush out of my mind. It curdled my stomach to know there were combat Marines in my own unit who not only wanted me dead, but were already devising plans on how to take me out. Maybe someone would shoot me in the buttocks and I'd get to go home like the Corpsman. I tried to laugh at my low humor but couldn't. I must have made some sound because Fessman, folded neatly into his own poncho covered hooch, responded.

"Repeat, sir?" he asked, between large bites of what were supposed to be ham slices.

"Who's Jurgens?" I replied. Maybe a core group in the unit had gone bad. I'd noted from their speech patterns that there were no black Marines that I could tell. Probably a good thing. Without meeting him I presumed Sugar Daddy to be black, just from the exotic nickname.

"Platoon commander of First Platoon," Fessman answered. Barely visible in the waning light, he bit off some more of the ham slice, seeming to avoid my eyes. I stared anyway, waiting.

"Sir?" he asked weakly, putting down his C-Ration tin.

"Jurgens," I said again, without expression.

Fessman fiddled with his ration box in setting it aside. He pulled out a pack of cigarettes and took a moment to light one. I smeared some more of the mosquito crap on and waited patiently.

"He's big and mean. Fair, but mean. The officers before didn't like him because he does with his platoon what he wants, not what he's ordered to do. First Platoon is like a company within the Company, like the other one."

"Other one?" I asked, surprised.

"Sugar Daddy's Platoon Commander of Fourth Platoon. It's all black. They kind of do what they want too."

My mind rocked. How could a five platoon company do anything as a unit if two platoons did whatever they wanted and all the Marines in the other platoons knew it? I watched the drizzle begin to gather in a fold of my rubber poncho and flow into the little channel one of the team had dug around my hooch. The water collected and then began to run toward a little outlet to a hole dug for collection purposes. It reminded me of being home when I lived in Hawaii as a kid, digging castles with walls and motes down near the water. I thought of finding a little stick to float down the channel into the hole but made no move. I knew I wasn't going to run from any enemy fire that night and that thought was a relief. Like the terror of the enemy had been relegated further down inside my being because of a greater terror. Except my growing fear of my fellow Marines was a colder, more angry thing. I wasn't supposed to be afraid of them.

It wasn't supposed to be this way at all.

"Where's First Platoon settled in?" I asked Fessman.

"Why?" a voice whispered out in the night.

I looked away from Fessman into the dark to see a vague shape low to the mud. The shape moved forward until it became the Gunny.

"Getting the lay out of the unit for night defensive fires," I answered, defensively.

"I've only known you for a few hours," the Gunny whispered, taking out his own cigarette pack to light one, "and in that time I've picked up on a few things." He flicked the Zippo and the light from the small fire flared over it. I noted the lettering on it's surface near where the hinged top snapped down. It said "Changjin."

"Gunny," I replied, since he paused longer than I expected.

"You've already got the night defensive fires laid out in spades, and you've no doubt committed them all to memory."

I shifted inside my hooch and searched for my own cigarette pack. After a few seconds I found it. The Gunny's observations made me nervous and I couldn't figure out why. With slightly shaking hands I pulled out a cigarette. The Gunny lit it, the Zippo again making its distinctive little ring when it opened. The light flared. We stared at each other. I didn't know what to say.

"Jurgens runs that platoon," the Gunny said. "Within bounds he does okay. He's got some good buck sergeants running the squads and his fire teams are the best in the Company. When it's all said and done every night we've got the NVA out there in force, not to mention a slew of disorganized local gooks playing at being Viet Cong. We need that platoon. They shoot. They fight. They work."

I listened carefully, wondering what units in the company didn't do the things he so purposefully mentioned.

"What does *Changjin* mean?" I asked him, trying to change the subject.

"*Chosin*," he replied. "It's pronounced *Chosin*."

Every living Marine knew that word. The Frozen Chosin was a legend of the Korean War. A legend among the greatest in Marine

Corps history. Marines trapped on a mountain ridge had fought their way through a killing cold blizzard and twelve divisions of Chinese troops to reach the sea and safety.

"They're going to hit us from either the point or the left flank later on. The right flank's too mushy," the Gunny instructed. "They'll set up a base of fire from high up on the hill to use plunging fire on us while establishing another base of fire on the far side of the right flank swamp. What can artillery do?"

I smiled in the dark, but not in humor. I clutched the letter to my wife, folded into my right front pocket. The Gunny was talking about the kind of war I'd trained so long and hard for. I'd figured out the same likely strategy without even knowing about the swampy mud. I calculated an attack from the left flank simply because the ground sloped gently downward toward our position and had enough scraggly scrub to cover a rapid approach by ground troops.

"Seven registrations on the hill," I answered, needing no reference map or planning materials, as he'd guessed. "Fessman reached 2/13 out of Da Nang. 155s can reach out to the hill from their position. They're good for almost fifteen miles while the 105s at An Hoa are limited to seven. The circular error probability is about the same at our range though, because the 155 round is inherently more stable. The 155s will give us a hundred pounds of throw weight over the forty or so of the 105."

"And that means what exactly?" the Gunny asked.

"I'll start some harassing and interdicting fire in a bit so there won't be anyone crawling about on this side of 110 tonight."

"Did you run into Jurgens?" the Gunny asked, burying the stub of his cigarette in the mud next to my little running moat.

"Why do you ask?" I countered, not knowing where he was going but uncomfortable again with the direction of the conversation.

"Would you mind not dropping anything out of the night onto that platoon?" the Gunny asked. "Could you just leave them to me for a bit?"

I realized that the Gunny was a very bright and sensitive man at that point. He'd picked up on my simple request for the platoon position and then figured out what I might be thinking. What I was thinking.

"What's my nickname, since everyone seems to have one here?" I asked, delaying a response to his question.

"Junior," he answered. "From the initials in your name."

"Fine," I said, although it wasn't fine at all. The derogatory name reduced me to the status of a child. I had a baby face it was true, to the point of embarrassment at times in high school and college, but I knew they didn't give me the nickname because of that fact.

"They haven't made up their minds about you yet, most of the them," the Gunny went on. "Don't make it up for them."

I'd been about to tell the Gunny to handle whatever he thought needed to be handled with First Platoon, as I was not about to tell him what had transpired in the little meeting in the mud on the other side of the bushes. But his comment made me realize something. Whether I lived or died could depend on what the unit thought of me — not that I was going to live anyway — but The Gunny made me even more aware that I did not want to die at the hands of my own men.

"Well?" the Gunny said, still waiting, as he rose to his feet in the dark and stepped out into the fetid mist.

"I'll let you know," I replied, truthfully.

"You might want to dig something shallow if you have to bring fire closer in," the Gunny replied, obviously giving up on his other line of questioning. "I'll be back when the shit hits the fan to check on you. Call the artillery right from here."

As the Gunny walked away, the sound of two sucking plops came from right next to my hooch, "You might need these for later," he said, his voice almost too soft for me to hear.

I reached out and pulled in two round objects. M33 grenades. The new ones, like the one I'd used to give me cover in my escape from the Jurgens group. I wiped them down with my used socks. Smell didn't seem to matter much anymore since everything I ran into, or had near-by, smelled to high heaven of one kind of awful aroma or other. I sat in the dark, wondering if the Gunny knew about my little escape and was resupplying me, or whether he had merely picked up some extra grenades when everyone else had enough. I didn't rate an M16 or a Tommy Gun. The M33s seemed the next best thing since my .45 only held seven in the magazine and one in the chamber. I only kept five in the magazine because my dad had shot the Colt for the U.S. Coast Guard pistol team. He'd taught me years back that the upper right tang at the top of the pistol had a tendency to bend and jam the action of the automatic if seven rounds were loaded and then left to remain in the gun's handle for any period of time.

I agonized for a shower or a bath. Anything to relieve the heat, the itching from the insect bites and the ever present muddy film coating my body, boots and clothing.

"Fessman," I whispered, "Aren't we close to the Bong Song?"

"Yes, sir," he whispered back, the glow of his cigarette tip going on and off like a blinking traffic light.

"Can't we swim in the river?" I asked him. "Can't we bathe in the water there?"

"No, sir," he answered, with no delay at all.

"Why not?" I responded, in frustration.

"You'll see," he said back.

I wondered what arcane rule of engagement required that Marines not swim in the rivers and streams of the country they were supposed to be trying to save. The rivers had to be fresh water, their deep moving waters driven by the rains in the mountains. To have so much water in the area, in the air itself, but not available for drinking or bathing was more than vexing. I determined to swim and bathe in the Bong Song no matter what the rules said, as soon as I could get there.

I didn't think I'd slept but my combat watch said three a.m. when the first incoming mortar rounds sounded in the distance. The distinctive *thoop* of their launch awakened even the most poorly experienced veteran, of which I had to be considered one. At least seven or eight of the loud fear-inducing *thoops* pierced the night, giving us between forty-one and forty-five seconds before impact.

For unprotected troops with no place to hide, the mortar represented a terrible field weapon. Hiding in holes didn't totally work because the rounds came straight down out of the sky, and digging holes in the lowlands of South Vietnam, without supports to hold back the mud, was precarious. You'd have to dig five feet down to harder earth, and there was seldom time when on the move for such protective preparation.

I started the night defense regimen I'd designed earlier. I'd lied about our position earlier when I'd communicated the plan to the batteries, as usual, so there would be no problem pulling fire as close in as it might be needed. The area between our position's perimeter and the steeper rise of Hill 110 was pretty open and bare. Illumination rounds, although difficult to see accurately under because the burning rounds swayed so much in their parachutes, might give any attacking force real pause.

The mortar rounds came in, probably 82 millimeter, but they didn't hit close to where my team lay squeezed down against the mud, tense with anticipation. After I recovered enough to roll back into my hooch, I breathed deeply, covered in even more mud than usual. I wasn't afraid. That thought buoyed me up for almost an hour before the night broke open like a crack in a black granite wall, and terror came rushing through.

ten

THE THIRD NIGHT : SECOND PART

I had heard of the RPG (rocket propelled grenade), the Russian version of America's recoilless rifle. Basically it was a small rocket fired from a shoulder mount. The rocket body, about four inches in diameter, had a warhead about eight inches long. Because the weapon delivered more than two pounds of explosives to any target under two hundred yards away, it had a lot of punch. My first RPG experience came right after the mortars stopped landing in places more distant from my hooch, and small gouging into the earth meant to serve as my foxhole. No self-respecting fox would have considered the mud pit, however.

The RPG came in from the middle of a distant bright flare of explosion not far from the perimeter. The terror of the projectile wasn't in its detonation, which was considerable, but in its exhaust gases. The fiery trace of white hot gas came in not four feet over my head. Later I would swear that I felt the heat of its passing, as unlikely as that was. The detonation took place with a huge roar and the jungle became like day for a few seconds — just long enough to insure that I was night blind after it went off. No more than twenty seconds later, before I could recover, another identical monster blasted through the same air the previous nightmare had occupied. Instead of experiencing incoming tracer fire for the first time, like on the night before, I was experiencing rocket fire directed to explode behind me — as if the enemy knew I was a runner and was taking that possibility off the table. It wasn't until the third rocket went over that I recovered.

The rest of the unit seemed to be engaged in exchanging small arms fire. I turned to Fessman who lay stretched out toward my position, the handset to his radio already extended from his hand out toward my own.

"Fire Mission," I commanded. I rattled off what I thought to be the closest registration position while I clambered over my pack to get at my map and compass. I had everything I needed in my head except for a compass bearing. I needed to do the math between that magnetic bearing and the deviation required for merging grid north (my map's north) to become true north. The guns fired on true north and when changing the position you claimed to need fire for, the calculations had to be accurate. A miss of only a few yards could kill a lot of friendlies, including you. I grease-penciled the numbers and finished the call, then waited past the 'Fire, over" alert. The spotting round came in but I couldn't place where it hit by either sight or sound. I was night blind and the rockets loud exhaust had made me deaf.

"Up fiver-zero, willie-peter, fifty meters air, fire," I ordered. The round would be assured to be farther away than the last one and it would be impossible not to see fifteen pounds of white phosphorus exploding nearly overhead.

The round came in and my call proved accurate. I didn't need to adjust further and fired for effect. I used my favorite 'battery of six' order. The rounds splashed in and the world shook for almost a full minute, with chunks of mud and jungle debris raining down upon us. The impact of the rounds had been closer than I calculated, which either meant that the first round had been off, or that we were closer to being on the gun target line than I thought. Aiming cannons and howitzers was like aiming rifles. The accuracy of direction, or side to side measurements, was easy. The calculation and achievement of range caused the difficulty.

I'd just called in an adjustment of up two hundred and a repeat when the Gunny yelled "Check fire!" only a few feet from me. "You're going to kill us all over a couple of rocket rounds."

"Repeat," I said into the handset, ignoring him.

Thirty-six more rounds came screaming in. Six sets of six, barely six seconds apart. We all hugged the mud. There was no mud or debris from the blasts this time. I'd gotten it right. At near the maximum range for the howitzers, their accuracy faded away. I'd work on doing a better job in the future.

"Shit," the Gunny said, although with all the noise I was nearly deaf again. "You've gone bat shit again. Maybe it's better when you run."

I crawled into my hooch and wrapped the poncho cover tightly around me. I didn't care about the heat and the mosquitoes seemed to have relented. Maybe the artillery was too much for them. I didn't know. I didn't care. I wasn't going anywhere. It felt better to hug myself tightly and close my eyes. The Gunny left without saying another word.

"Call in the H and I," I ordered Fessman, checking myself over for leeches. I'd been in the mud again but apparently escaped the vicious little monsters this time around. I wondered if we would get a replacement for the Corpsman I'd had to send home. We only had two now and I was worried about getting no care if I were injured. I tried to use my wife's go-to-sleep relaxation exercises, but I couldn't use them without thinking about her and I just couldn't have myself thinking about her. I clutched my letter home to my leg. The Gunny had been right in his latest lecture to me in the early morning hours. I may not be running, but I was certainly of no use to anyone. Except for the artillery. I was good at the artillery. I hadn't cared about any of that in training at Fort Sill. My wife had been about to deliver. We had no money. The car would not run. Oklahoma was too hot and we didn't have air-conditioning. I got through the school because General Abrams' (the tank guy) son taught the class, loved Marines (he was Army) and thought I was gifted in map reading and working the FDC. In almost every way artillery was founded on maps and map reading: Where were the guns, exactly, and where was the fire needed, exactly?

But things had changed a bit since Fort Sill, at least for me. Artillery was fast becoming more than a best friend. It was becoming my only friend. I rolled and felt a sharp pain in my right side. My other friends, M33s. In the morning I would find the Bong Song, no matter what, and get clean in it. My socks, my body, my boots and my .45. I imagined the Colt so filled with crud and mud that taking it out might make an enemy laugh himself to death — essentially killing him more effectively than if I shot him. I rummaged in my pack and pulled an envelope from one of my food boxes. I ripped it open with my teeth. Slippery fingers in the jungle weren't meant to open metallic bags. Finding I had an envelope of John Wayne crackers, I laughed to myself. From his films and tough-guy reputation, you'd think John Wayne fought WWII almost by himself. In reality, he avoided fighting in the real war at all costs. I hadn't understood his cowardice but now thought about the possibility of his good sense. I leaned out toward the mist, not hungry but eating the crackers in order to have some normality in my life.

"This outfit have a Starlight scope?" I asked.

"Fourth Platoon," Stevens replied. "They use it to set up their machine guns for fields of fire. It's too big to put on a gun so you can't do much aiming with it. Sees great in the dark though."

We'd had one at O'Bannon Hall, where I'd spent five months in Basic Officer Training. The Starlight scope amplified ambient light dramatically. The inventors had been at the Hall training seminar and said that ground warfare would soon be changed forever because of the technology. Thinking about Presley O'Bannon Hall* drove a small dagger of whatever I had left for emotion up through my spine. I physically jerked before settling down. The memories of sitting in the coffee shop were so vivid, drinking hot coffee without regard for all the cream and sugar I might want. I wanted none back then. I drank it back. That was funny, too, in its way. I didn't want black coffee anymore because I had to drink it that way.

Star Trek had played in the Hall every afternoon, following dinner every evening and before I fell exhausted into my bunk. I wanted to be Captain Kirk. What a commanding figure he was with all the answers for every problem. I remembered the guys who wore red uniforms. They went into the transporter as helpers or assistants on difficult missions to unknown planets. Extraneous, they had no real part to play except to die. They always got killed. Ironically I hadn't become Captain Kirk. I'd become one of the guys wearing a red uniform.

I turned to Stevens, trying to shake off the thought. "Go to the Fourth Platoon and see if you can survey the damage done by the artillery strike."

"Why?" he said without a sir, and in a tone that told me he would evaluate whether it was a good idea to go, and if it involved too much risk.

Anger exploded inside me, but it was too dark for him to read the homicidal thoughts I entertained at that instant. I knew I couldn't threaten to kill him, or really threaten anyone in any way. Provoking such a terminal reaction would be disastrous, to be avoided at all costs. But that didn't make resisting the temptation any easier. ... Close your eyes, I told myself. Breathe in and out. Think about nothing...

"Lieutenant," I heard a voice say. I looked up to see Fessman standing there.

"Did you take your malaria tablet, sir?" he asked.

I understood the basis of his question. Fessman was alluding to the few seconds I'd faded away, trying to get control of myself. "I'm fine," I said. And I actually did need to take my malaria tablet. The awful medication, required to be taken twice daily, gave cramps and diarrhea, and made some people dizzy as hell at times.

"The Starlight," I said. "I'll need two compass points. One from the center of the impact caldera and one from the top of Hill 110." A hint of moon broke through the gravid clouds above, briefly illuminating the landscape — enough for a calculation. With my own bearing from my position combined with what would be brought back, we might survive the night.

"I'll go," Stevens finally decided, with no further hesitation. Before I could respond he headed off toward the hill, Nguyen at his side.

They looked like some sort of dark native ghosts, silent but dangerous as hell. But then, what wasn't dangerous in this cursed place I'd found myself?

I thought about the calculations I'd need to make when they got back. I needed the bearing on the beaten zone the shells had made in order to have a physical registration point in the real world. Given the position I'd called in, and adjusting for the hundred and fifty meters up, or away from what was supposed to be my position, but wasn't really, was vital to calling more artillery. I could adjust from the real registration point because basically the area I'd hit was the only likely area to be used by the NVA in the coming attack. It was dangerous as hell to call artillery from a fake position because the FDC would assume the adjustments were to be made from the "real" announced position. A misplaced "battery of six" would kill or maim everyone in the company, bar none, if delivered to the wrong point. It would be complete lunacy to direct fire on the move from the fake position. Hence the known point to be used as of a deviancy from that "real" position.

I was a fake company commander, operating as a real artillery forward observer, using a fake position to adjust real fire on God knew who or what might happen to come along.

"Fessman, follow them and pace off the distance," I ordered. I would need the exact point Stevens made his observation from to complete my calculations.

"Yes, sir," Fessman responded, distinctly taking long strides when he left. I would be without a radio until he returned but I wasn't planning on calling in artillery until he got back, and there was never any chatter on the combat net. That told me that there was another frequency I wasn't being brought in on yet, but I would have to worry about that at a later time.

Waiting in the darkness, mist and silence that followed, I took out one of the nasty little anti-malarial pills. I wondered if they really worked. The pill was bitter as hell so I gobbled down my remaining John Wayne crackers. When I got to the bottom of the tin foil back I found another little bag, heavier than it should be. I used my teeth to tear it open only to discover a cheese spread for the crackers I'd already eaten. Cheese Whiz. I sucked it down in one big gulp. It tasted awful but felt like home.

The moon broke through the clouds. It was half full. I wondered if my wife could see it where she was in San Francisco, which I calculated to be seven thousand six hundred and forty-two miles from where I lay. It would be daylight there. Sometimes the moon was visible in daylight but it would be unlikely that she'd be looking up at it in the mid-afternoon hours. I knew I wasn't a hero and not much of a patriot at that moment because I would have accepted a bad conduct discharge from the Marine Corps if I could have shot up to that moon and then back down to the street just outside of our apartment in Daly City, only a mile or two from the Ferlinghetti's City Lights Bookstore at the Haight and Ashbury Street intersection. The Corps could process my paperwork while I waited, seated just inside the Red Victorian Café.

A wraith appeared out of the dark, moving smoothly by, leaning as he passed.

"Where is everyone?" the Gunny asked, slowing to a stop.

"Needed some bearings," I replied, knowing the answer would sound idiotic under the circumstances.

"Hope we don't get hit until they come back," the Gunny replied, putting one knee down on the exposed wet portion of the poncho cover. He wore his own poncho, which covered all of his upper body but made him sparkling visible in the night.

I didn't reply, wanting to ask questions about where he would position himself in order to command the defense. Why I wasn't allowed to hear what transpired over the combat net. Was he doing something about my upcoming date with death from First Platoon. But I kept my silence.

"You just stay here and stay down," he said, before rising to his feet. "If they hit us, and they have to hit us before dawn, then depend on the machine guns and what you can drop on their heads with the artillery. We're down on sixty millimeters ammo so the mortars aren't going to do much in return fire. I'll come get you when it's over, or at dawn if they come through clean."

"Anything you want me to do?" I asked, wondering why I asked as soon as the words were out.

"Don't get hit," he said, with a fake laugh, "and pray. Pray for no joy in the valley tonight." And then he was gone.

I waited, taking another cigarette out to supposedly ward off the mosquitoes, although the mosquitoes hadn't come back. I'd seen plenty of amulets on the men. Special pins, bracelets and necklaces. I'd majored in anthropology, the cultural park. The amulets were for luck or to influence the gods. It was common in lower social orders for the men going on the hunt or into combat to gird themselves with everything at their disposal before the actual event or challenge. All I had was my cigarette.

My team came back silently, the only noise of their approach being a slight squishing of the mud out from under their boots. I would prepare a simple artillery defense based upon complex but very effective calculations. I puffed on the cigarette to keep the fake mosquitoes away and I silently prayed that there would be no joy in the valley this night.

eleven

THE THIRD NIGHT : THIRD PART

They came before dawn. How they came was impossible to imagine. An entire reinforced Marine company, dug into low scrub with marginal cover, waited for them just where they hit. The company used the Starlight scope. The base of fire predicted to be launched from Hill 110 itself, beyond the marshy land on the right flank, was never proven to have occurred. But it didn't matter much because the firing outward from the Marine perimeter was so overwhelming that nothing could be heard or seen anyway.

I was not terrified. Not in the beginning. I was analytical. Stevens and Nguyen ran back and forth from and to the nearby perimeter giving short verbal reports after each trip. Fessman wanted to know why I didn't move close to the perimeter to be able to direct fire by sight, but I ignored him. Directing fire was extremely difficult when you were dead, but I didn't say that. If someone had put a gun to my head I still wouldn't have gone into that maelstrom of flashes, painful explosions and obvious physical carnage. The Gunny had been right. I wasn't running but I wasn't exactly functional communication-wise either.

I called in night defensive coordinates on any presumed bases of fire on Hill 110. The sound of 155mm rounds slamming into the muck and then heaving great chunks of it into the air overrode the shattering staccato blasts from nearby machine guns and grenade explosions. I called for a variety of fuse detonations. Super quick high explosive, radar sensing variable time, and even some time delay bunker busting stuff. The H.E. provided penetrating blast waves and ground shrapnel, the variable time rained shrapnel down from above, and the busters served to cave in any and all tunnels dug under the cloying mud. The 155s went to work on the right flank to my preset coordinates while I used Stevens and Nguyen as my quasi-forward observers to guide the 105 fire back on and across the devastated lowland spread of the presumed attack area.

There was no real organization to it all. I could not make out artillery from grenade blasts. The illumination rounds acted like strobe lights to make the whole scene of combat seem like a weird Hollywood horror set. Flashes on and off everywhere from every direction, deafening sounds making hearing anything almost impossible, debris, condensed mist and micro-fragments of mud raining down on everything. I pushed backwards, ever deeper into the crease of my poncho cover, Fessman jammed into the same space with me.

I worked the radio back and forth to 2/11, Battery D — my battery. Russ was the commo officer at the FDC dedicated to the company's little battle. Russ and I had been together in the Basic School back at Presley O'Bannon Hall, in Quantico. His last name wasn't close to mine so, among two-hundred and fifty-eight men in the class, we didn't bunk together or really get to know one another. He was new in country like me, but, apparently, hadn't pissed off the commanding general on his first night. Russ was a bright and caring kind of guy, or at least I got that impression from our radio traffic. He kept asking how I really was. I never answered but kept trying to sound better, wondering what it was about my radio transmissions that made him ask. After a directing a couple of hundred rounds at my instructions, he said something that told me how smart he was, as well.

"From our calculations it appears that your own position isn't where you've registered it to be."

Fessman looked at me. His big round eyes got bigger and rounder, standing out in the dark from his mud-blackened face. I hit the transmit button.

"We're right where I say we are," I sent back. If the battery check-fired, or stopped firing, for the safety of the Marines in our unit then the whole unit could be lost.

There appeared to be a full scale attack going on, although I could see nothing. If our position was in question, even our precarious condition would be ignored and the battery would stop firing until the FDC could confirm the proper position of our unit.

"This may be a check-fire situation," Russ said, and then, "Sorry."

"Sorry?" I transmitted back, my hand almost crushing the green plastic of the handset. "You tell those assholes in the FDC that if they check fire and I'm still alive, I'm slogging twelve thousand meters back there and I'm going to kill every fucking one of them."

The radio remained silent for several seconds.

"The artillery net is no place for foul language," Russ sent back. "The six actual is on site at the battery. And he knows where you are."

I couldn't believe the words coming into one of my bad ears. I held the handset out away from me like it had somehow become the handset to a child's toy phone. I pushed the button. "Please tell the six actual for me, on behalf of the whole company, to go fuck himself!" I screamed. Would it really be any worse if the six actual fired artillery at us because I'd threatened them? I rested the handset down on my poncho cover for a few seconds. I tried my wife's breathing exercises but I could not get myself back under control. I hadn't made the threat lightly, and maybe Russ hadn't either. I would go back there and shoot the bastards if they let the company die out here in the wet misery and mud.

"Did we lose fire support?" Fessman said, leaning so close to me that our foreheads almost touched.

I snapped out of my towering anger and back into the aching misery of our situation. Fessman was right. Screw the emotion. Screw the battery and the FDC. Fuck the six actual at the battery. Did we still have life-saving artillery support?

"Fire mission, over" I said, pushing the arty transmit button down.

"Fire mission, over," came right back.

"You still there Russ?" I asked, in relief. We had artillery.

"You still there?" he asked back, emphasizing the "you." We were going to be okay, maybe.

I went on, laying fire back and forth across the beaten area of the attack grounds, adjusting without observation the 155s, marginally out and around from the registration points I'd had them fire on. The 155 FDC officer didn't seem to care where we were or our situation. The 155s simply fired where they were called to fire. Maybe it was because they were so far away, I thought later. If I was in deep shit again, I'd use the 155s if they were in range. The trouble with artillery was range.

Once we moved beyond Hill 110 into the A Shau Valley, the VO-SOD (valley of the shadow of death), we'd have no artillery at all. Only air, and air was fast, inaccurate as hell and could only stay on station for short periods of time. There also wasn't enough of it to go around. When you needed air everybody around needed it, too. And then there was the resentment. The air crews were up there in the cool rushing air in almost complete safety, while we were dying in heated misery a few thousand feet below them. Hating air was automatic, except for the Hueys and the crews in them. They were okay — all that according to Stevens and Fessman. I couldn't seem to catch up with anything as we sat waiting for the dawn. It was like history going too fast and only being able to catch a snippet here and snippet there.

The attack was over. The firing had gone from constant and intense to lightly sporadic, and then nothing. The Gunny came to inform us that the company lost eight more KIA, and we had six wounded awaiting evacuation. Three of the dead had been killed by friendly artillery shrapnel, all of them from First Platoon. He said that most in the company thought I'd saved everyone, except for a few who knew and liked the dead Marines. A couple of NVA kills were confirmed outside the perimeter, with body parts totaling probably thirty more, but those could not be confirmed on the daily report, because of the rules. The artillery beaten zone was a charnel house of human destruction, even by only the briefest inspections before dawn, according to the Gunny.

The Gunny came to sit on a small section of my hooch that wasn't wet. The drizzle had abated only minutes earlier. Dawn was in the air even if the sun hadn't yet risen above the horizon. The light would come from over the ocean, illuminating the Philippines before it crossed the nearly one thousand miles of South China Sea to reach Da Nang.

"You did okay, this time around," he said, taking out a cigarette.

Fessman eased back toward his own hooch, while Stevens and Nguyen remained invisible in the darkness, although I felt them there and paying attention. The company was like a small mid-western town where everyone paid attention to the smallest detail of words and actions while making believe they weren't at all.

"I had my radio operator come up on the combat net, but it's not the net I was looking for," I said matter-of-factly. "You mind giving him the right frequency so I don't have to spend hours trying them all?"

"You're not ready yet," the Gunny replied.

I noted that he'd only used the word "sir" once before, and that was right after I'd called in the first spotting round of white phosphorus. Was I going to have to somehow earn the right to be company commander by passing tests I didn't know were tests? I said nothing because there wasn't much I could think of for an answer that wouldn't make me look weaker, and even more cowardly than I had already demonstrated.

"First Platoon's gonna be a problem," the Gunny said, puffing on his cigarette and then spitting little chunks of tobacco into my small moat. "Jurgens, Harrington, Boaz, and Nim called themselves 'The Four Horsemen,' like from the old movie. And now Harrington and Boaz are bagged and going out on resupply. That's not going down well. The fact that they died from artillery you called in, I mean."

"Maybe they can change their name to 'The Deadly Duo,'" I replied, without thinking. I heard Stevens muffle a laugh in the darkness just beyond where the Gunny and I sat.

The Gunny ignored my comment. "You know what I mean."

"I presume you're telling me this to either warn me or let me know I've got to do something, or both?" I asked.

"Just letting you know," he replied.

I thought for a moment about what the man was really telling me. I was supposed to understand that First Platoon was even more likely to kill me than before, but I was to do nothing about it. Maybe the problem would simply go away after we took Hill 110.

"Stevens, get over here," I said, raising my voice a bit.

Stevens rushed past Fessman's hooch to stand waiting at the edge of my moat.

"I need a position and bearings on where First Platoon is down for the remainder of the night," I ordered.

"You can't do that," the Gunny said, rising to his feet and motioning Stevens back with his left hand. Stevens didn't budge, waiting for me to confirm my order. Or so I presumed.

"They won't fire on our position," the Gunny said, emphatically. "Artillery doesn't do that, ever. It's part of our rules of engagement."

I looked at Fessman, who'd approached to stand on the edge of my poncho cover. His eyes were big and round, like before. I said nothing to the Gunny, just letting the time run until dawn. The Gunny had just revealed that he didn't know about our real position in relationship to the battery, or probably anywhere or anyone else, for that matter. I wasn't going to tell him otherwise. I had no intention of calling in a mission on First Platoon, except deep down in the confines of my darkest emotions. But I would have to do something. Something would either come up or I would be dead. I was going to be dead anyway and I knew it in my bones. The NVA were well-equipped, supported and tenacious in numbers. The Marines around me were the same.

"What's the battle plan for tomorrow?" I asked the Gunny, changing the subject. First Platoon was now my problem and I understood that. "And when's the CP meeting scheduled with platoon commanders before we cross the line of departure?"

"Dawn," the Gunny answered. "We can meet right here, if that's okay with you, and then I'll see if Sugar Daddy can make it."

If it was okay with me… Like I was anybody at all, except the guy hiding in his hooch after running away, who happened to be able to call effective artillery. I wasn't even allowed to listen in on the combat net, much less issue any orders. And then there was the matter of First Platoon and Sugar Daddy. The company had a whole platoon of black Marines and I had not seen even one. How was that possible, I wondered? And why was I meeting Sugar Daddy? What was his role? How could I avoid telling him that we didn't have black units in the Corps and that he had to disburse them into the other platoons? I didn't even know his rank, not that rank seemed to be that important in the company I'd been dropped into.

"I'll be back," the Gunny said, tossing his cigarette into my little moat without field stripping it or even making any effort to put it out.

When he was gone Stevens leaned forward. Only when he whispered and I understood him did I realize that my hearing was coming back.

"You still want the data on First Platoon?" he asked.

"Fuckin' A," I replied.

Stevens and Nguyen went back to their hooches to get ready, or so I thought until a few seconds later. Stevens pointed at me and Nguyen stepped forward with both hands held out. I looked down but it was still dark and I couldn't see or imagine what he might have. When he noted that fact, Nguyen took a small object out of his right palm and held it up. I squinted to make out a black bracelet composed of some kind of strands. Nguyen motioned toward my right arm. When I brought it up he reached over gently and held my wrist. Slowly, he expanded the bracelet with both hands and then slid the thing up over my hand and onto my wrist. He tightened it by sliding something.

"Montagnard," Stevens said. "The bracelet will protect you. It's only given to great warriors of his tribe. He's not Vietnamese."

"Great warriors," I whispered to myself, trying to figure out how the thing adjusted. I wondered how the great warrior with Stevens could so mistake what I was?

"What is he if he's not Vietnamese?" I asked, shaking the bracelet. It would take some getting used to but I could not take it off, I was certain, without hurting the man's feelings.

"Montagnard, of course, sir. The mountain people." Stevens said. "We're now in his area of operations."

I nodded toward the Montagnard, not knowing what else to do. I now had my first real amulet against the forces of evil, other than a Lucky Strike. The whole thing had to be hilariously funny but I couldn't find the humor in it anywhere. I pushed back into the poncho cover, ate some more crackers and waited for what dawn had to bring.

Where was John Wayne when I needed him?

THE FOURTH DAY

ove child, never meant to be. Love child, always second best." Brother John, on Armed Forces Radio, presaged the lyrics in his deep baritone voice. A different voice introduced John without actually introducing him. Was John really in Nha Trang, spinning a platter with the latest Supremes' song on it? The song was as far and distant from the coming dawn as I was from any kind of reality that I wanted to be a part of. I got up, although I could not remember sleeping like I'd been so accustomed to doing back home. I'd merely missed a few hours somewhere. I didn't feel like I'd slept or was waking up. The sounds of morning gentled their way into my recovered ear canals. I knew I needed some kind of ear plugs for night combat or I was going to go deaf, but then when I thought about it further, I realized that I'd be deaf anyway with the plugs in and I could not afford to be deaf in combat any more than I already was when the firing began.

I poured water into my helmet, setting the liner aside until later. I shaved carefully with no mirror and a mechanically operated double-edged razor. The edge was brand new but not sharp. I worked at it intently, trying to forget where I was. I took off my utility top and washed under my arms for no good reason I could think of. I brushed my teeth, spit out the water and was done. I got dressed for the coming day, put my helmet together, strapping the rubber band Fessman had given me around it. Now I had repellent right there at any time anywhere. My utility top still had some wrinkled starch left in it which had nicely absorbed now blackened sweat marks. Shirts or tops were not called that in training. They were called blouses, but I could never think of them that way. Folding up the bottoms of pants, called trousers, at the bottom was called blousing too, for whatever reason.

The day was going to be partly cloudy with the sun soon coming up over the top of Hill 110, our target or objective. I had now seen the hill that had become famous a year before for some attack that had been punishing on some other unit.

I stood up, got my gear together as best I could, and went to work brewing some instant coffee in my canteen cup holder. I was out of cream and sugar again.

But maybe there were packets in one of the Ham and Mothers I'd have for breakfast. The Gunny came out of the heavy brush nearby as I ignited some Comp B. A big, black Marine wearing a bush hat followed him. Bush hats were flattened, soft things that would also look right at home on some sailor's head off the cost of Maine, except this Marine's was green. The black Marine wore no rank, which I was now accustomed to. He also wore a utility top, but with the sleeves cut off all the way up to his armpits. His boots were the jungle boots issued back at Battalion, if I ever got back to Battalion. The most distinctive feature of the Marine was his purple sunglasses. Big twinkling lenses surrounded by gold frames.

"Sugar Daddy, I presume," I said, looking up but making no attempt to move from my crouch over the small fire.

The Gunny squatted down, as did the big Marine.

"You'd be Junior," the man said with a giant smile, revealing snow white teeth except for one centrally located shiny gold one.

I made no move on the outside at the use of the nickname, glad I'd already heard it. I brewed the coffee, stirring slowly until it was hot enough.

"Some coffee, Gunny?" I asked, looking the Gunny straight in the eyes. I noticed that Fessman, Stevens, and Nguyen had retreated into the background completely.

"Bracelet," Sugar Daddy said, pointing at my right wrist. "Don't give those to nobody. Elephant stuff. Big mojo."

His voice was as deep and beautiful as Brother John's, I noted. I drank some coffee, wondering if I was supposed to say something, complain, question or whatever. I could think of nothing that wouldn't create instant conflict. If there's anything I'd learned at lightening speed, it was that training and experience were no help at all. I didn't know anything relevant except what I was learning day by day, as long as I lasted.

"I'm platoon commander," Sugar Daddy finally said into the silence.

"Yes," I answered, drinking more coffee, but not tasting a thing. For some reason this meeting was vitally important, but I didn't know why. I waited some more.

"Unit's doing fine," Sugar Daddy said.

Fine. The Company was losing five percent of its strength per day, and that was just the dead. There were no officers. There'd been no way to call in accurate artillery or even read a map before I showed up. And evidently there were as many deaths caused by friendly fire as from the enemy. The Company was doing fine? What did he mean?

"Why are we here?" I finally asked, deciding to show my ignorance.

The Gunny refused to look at me, instead taking out his K-Bar and poking around at the remains of my little fire. Sugar Daddy took out a cigarette and lit it. It was no ordinary cigarette. It was pungent smelling marijuana or maybe something stronger. He blew the smoke gently across the fire. I didn't blink or cough.

"Tom says things can stay the same," Sugar Daddy intoned, blowing more smoke, as if to accentuate his message.

"Who's Tom?" I asked, surprised.

The Gunny waved one hand upward a bit. I realized that Tom was the Gunny's first name.

"Okay," I replied, drinking some more coffee.

"Okay?" Sugar Daddy asked. "What's okay mean?"

I drank more coffee, thinking about the fact that there was no safe or comfortable place the conversation could go. I was living in some anthropology experiment where the apes had been replaced by Marines. Different sized and different colored, but apes nevertheless. Sugar Daddy was applying his somehow attained Alpha Male status and I was supposed to either meet him right now in combat or demonstrate that he was the alpha and I was a lower class male.

"Benton Harbor," I said, putting my coffee down and looking as far into the distance as the jungle would allow. "Do you know where Benton Harbor is?" I asked.

"What's he talking about?" Sugar Daddy asked the Gunny after almost a full minute of silence.

"I don't know," the Gunny answered, finally looking up at me. He frowned but said nothing more.

"Well, I don't give a shit about no Benton Harbor or any of that," Sugar Daddy said, forcefully. "I'm running the Platoon and if you've got questions about that you can ask them here and now or forget it."

I took the few seconds I had to think about how out of control and totally lost a Marine company had to be to have come to such a desolate unruly place where every vestige of the training and spirit of the Corps had been lost. Marine training had forged me from a middle class kid doing okay in school and sports to a physical specimen acing every test they could throw at me. I was a Marine through and through and I knew down in my bones that another dead Marine officer was going to be of use to no one and nobody, especially me. I was probably dead anyway but I deserved to be killed by the enemy, not my own.

"Okay," I said again, this time looking at the man's purple sunglass lenses. "What position does your platoon hold in the company? Where are you bivouacked from here, grid-wise?"

The Gunny jerked his head up and I felt someone hidden in the jungle behind my hooch inhale sharply. I knew it had to be Fessman.

"We're done here," the Gunny said, getting to his feet. "We've got a meeting to decide about Hill 110, medevac coming in and resupply. Let's move on back to our units."

"Three days in-country and he's nuts," Sugar Daddy said to the Gunny in a loud whisper, intended for my ears I was certain. He stood slowly. "He's your problem unless he becomes my problem," he said, speaking in full volume.

"The fourth day," I said, not moving or looking at either one of them. "It's my fourth day in-country."

They walked off without anybody saying anything further. I listened to their boots making sucking sounds in the mud until they disappeared into the lower jungle ferns and fronds. When they were gone my team reappeared out from the same undergrowth.

I pulled back into my hooch, thinking about resupply, clutching my letter home and wondering about the battle for Hill 110. Only five hundred meters high, the small hillock or mountain was nearly conical with no good approach to taking it, except by direct frontal attack after an artillery and/or air attack. Machines guns, which the NVA had plenty of, made frontal attacks in modern combat about as attractive as a fur covered apple. Why was it called Hill 110, when the contour on the top read 1004? It should be Hill 1004.

I thought about the earlier meeting. It had been a high threat meeting without there being any threat issued directly. I could not meet the threat directly and I could not shrink away from it. So I'd gone sideways. But I had to respond or I would become prey, which I was a bit already anyway.

Chicken Man blasted out from Stevens' shoulder-mounted radio.

"Benton Harbor," Fessman said, in obvious surprise. "That's the secret name of Chicken Man. That's why you asked Sugar Daddy about that place?"

"It's a place, too," Stevens answered. "In Michigan. There was a big anti-war riot there a couple of years ago."

"Stevens, go on over to where that guy's platoon is and bring back some bearings," I ordered "It's almost light. Should be easy. Pace off the distance there and back."

"If I go over there, sir, and you drop some artillery on them, then every time I show my face in the Company they'll think I'm getting their location for you."

"You've taken my order wrong, Stevens," I replied calmly. "It's good to know where your people are if you're company commander. That's it. So, don't go. Send our Kit Carson Scout. Why do I have the feeling that he'll have no problem at all registering where that shadow of a real Marine platoon is set up?"

Stevens spoke softly to Nguyen. The small Montagnard seemed to disappear after the conversation.

"Where are those guys in First Platoon from?" I asked the remaining two members of my makeshift team.

"What do you mean?" Fessman asked back.

"Please tell me that those guys aren't a bunch of crackers from the South." I'd heard the talking through the bushes the night before. The accents had all been Southern. If the blacks had all pulled together into one platoon and the white southerner Marines were in another platoon, then the war going on inside the Company might be explained.

"What part of the country?" I said.

"Oklahoma, Texas, places like that, mostly," Fessman answered hesitantly.

Some things were becoming clear to me, not that knowing what was actually going on would do much to forestall my death. Two sets of officers before me had totally failed, and they must have had a pretty good idea before they bought it, or so I thought until I saw the Gunny coming back.

The light was just enough of a glimmer for me to be able to spot him easing from the nearby jungle growth. Five other Marines, all in different states of uniform repair or disrepair, followed him. Some wore utility blouses, some not. Some helmets, some not. I guessed the first man behind the Gunny to be Jurgens. Big and hard-boned looking, he lunged forward more than he walked. The other three, all Caucasians, were nondescript. And then there was Sugar Daddy, who hung back until everyone else gathered before my hooch. I watched them approach, having no idea how the planning for the assault would go. I was mentally prepared with as much training material as the Corps had provided me back in Quantico. The five paragraph order was standard fare for planning an assault. SMEAC was the memory aid acronym: situation, mission, execution, administration/logistics, and command/communications. It was simple stuff but every area had to be covered before more complex acronyms could be brought into play. My right hand remained inside my pocket clutching the letter to my wife, the most important part of my day. My link to home. I wondered if the same Hollywood Tommy gun guy would be there at the resupply chopper to accept it from me. I also wondered, if the rear area was run anything like what I'd discovered in the field, whether my letters would ever reach the continental United States at all.

The other Marines, who I presumed to be sergeants, squatted in the mud facing the Gunny, sideways to me. I got the message. I also wondered where the Company paperwork was stored and moved. Even in the field a clerk is assigned to keep the records, write letters regarding casualties and keep track of supplies and personnel. Where was that clerk and where were the records? I took out a small square of plastic and wrote the number "1" on it, and looked up at the men gathered before me.

"We're not attacking," the Gunny stated, shaking his head. The other Marines all nodded their heads. "If we were attacking, we'd just do it without all the mumbo jumbo you learned in Quantico."

I looked the Gunny straight in the eyes. It was the first time I sensed true resentment in anything he'd said to me. I could not afford to lose the Gunny. He was really all I had. I put my plastic sheet and grease pencil back in my pack as I thought furiously about the situation. We were ordered by Battalion to attack Hill 110. We were going to disobey a direct order in combat, if they had their way, an order I was responsible for obeying. The penalty for such disobedience was clear, and it included punishment up to my execution. I waited. It took about half a minute for the Gunny to go on.

"If we take that hill or even try it, then we're going to get the same medicine the last outfit got and they lost about a quarter of their men." The Gunny stopped to let that message sink in before continuing.

"Nobody back there gives a damn about that hill or what might be on it. They're just moving us around. So we sit here, call in some fire and probably take some, but go nowhere. You call Battalion and let them know we took the hill by late in the day. Then we wait."

"For what?" I asked, giving no indication about whether I approved of the treasonous plan or not.

"Until they order us to move out and on to another position."

"What happens when we don't have any casualties or need resupply on top of the hill, or even gunship support?" I asked, wondering how many times this same scene had played out with this group of Marines.

"They won't care," the Gunny replied. "We'll tell them we took the hill unopposed."

"And if the other companies on our flanks run into the NVA occupying that hill?" I inquired, rummaging behind me for my canteen holder.

"That's their problem, Junior," Jurgens answered, his tone acidic.

I noted that none of the Marines attending the meeting appeared to be armed. Although it was almost dawn and we were seldom hit during daylight hours, I still thought it unusual that anyone in a combat situation would go anywhere at all, including inside our own perimeter, without a weapon.

Making like I was going to tear another packet of instant coffee open with both hands, I let my right drop to my side and remove my Colt from it's holster.

I brought the automatic up and pointed it slightly downward at the space right in front of and between the men. The men froze in their positions, not appearing to blink or breathe.

I moved the safety lever on the back left side of the weapon down. The click of it disengaging sounded like a gunshot in the silence. I looked around at every member of the group, each of whom stared back at me without expression or movement.

"You guys shouldn't move about in the field without being armed," I said, not moving the Colt from where I held it. "Always keep one in the chamber with the hammer back and the safety on," I went on.

Nguyen came silently out of the jungle behind the group. He blended in so well with the foliage I was reminded of an American Indian in the old west. He held an M16 before him, slightly angled down, but its intent was plain. I wasn't alone in whatever might happen. My heart and intense loyalty went out to him across the short distance.

"Okay," I said. "We'll play this one your way. You're dismissed."

The Gunny stayed while the rest slowly backed off and then were gone. "You can't beat them all, sir," the Gunny said.

I re-engaged the safety on the .45 and returned it to my holster. "Coffee?" I asked, hoping he'd say no because my hands were shaking too hard to make any. I pushed them down into my thighs so he wouldn't notice. If I smiled any more I'd have smiled on the inside. The Gunny called me 'sir' for only the second time since I'd met him. It was a tiny little thing but it was all I had to hold on to.

thirteen

THE FOURTH DAY : SECOND PART

I sat in my hooch, waiting for the sound of choppers distant in the air. I thought about all of what had gone before, since I'd arrived. It felt terrible to know I would have to sit and wait for orders to move from Hill 110, which we would not be taking, in direct violation of orders. My very first orders in combat. My only decision was to go along. To stay alive. The platoon commanders did not gather in front of me like they had to give me the message. The Gunny could have done that quite easily. No, they'd met in the mud right in front of me to send me a different message. Don't screw with them or get dead. Go along to get along and even then get dead. And then there was the enemy. I had yet to review our own dead or even the wounded. I felt that the Gunny was waiting for my maturation, my coming of age, my ability to handle even more bad news. I had to admit he was right. I wasn't ready for more bad news. I was scrunched backed into my poncho cover, like it was my blanket at my parents' place at home. And I could no more stay there than I had been able to in that home. I knew I was supposed to review the carnage I'd called in on the enemy. I knew there was a vital, hard and tough enemy too. How could the Company not be united to fight that enemy? I didn't know. I wasn't going out to count the dead or try to put body parts together. I had no interest whatsoever.

I'd seen the tracers from the enemy and fired out at them in the night before dawn. I'd seen them the night before. They were so impressive, possibly their effect increased by the density of the fetid hot air. Tracers were death. And tracers might be life. I would ask at resupply, not that I was being given an opportunity yet to actually order supplies. My primary mission was to mail my letter. My first objective to accomplish my mission was tracers and my second was to order size eight jungle boots. It made no sense but the plan seemed sensible to me.

"Fessman, up," I commanded.

Fessman almost literally jumped to the opening of my hooch. "Sir," he said. He made me feel like a Marine officer and I was thankful, although I showed nothing.

"Who orders the ordinance for the company at resupply every morning?" I asked him.

"The Gunny," Fessman said, right back.

"Is it verbal or does he use a requisition form?" I continued.

"Requisition form," Fessman answered.

"Get me one," I ordered, not knowing if he would be able to accomplish that part of the objective to accomplish a mission that had no relationship to tracers at all.

"I think Stevens can get one," Fessman deferred.

"Have him do so, then," I said, becoming a bit irritated.

"He's a sergeant and I'm a corporal," Fessman replied. "I can't order him."

"You've got to be kidding me," I said, amazed. "Someone is actually mentioning rank in this bunch of fucked up, misfit, asshole Marines?" I let some of the acid that had brewing deep inside my belly for three days and nights come spewing out in my tone and words. "And then the rank is supposed to mean something?" I would have laughed when I finished. It was funny. I knew that but I could no longer laugh. Laughing was for another life.

"What are we going to do all day since we have to sit here and make believe we're taking Hill 110?" I asked.

"I think we'll do all the things that make it look and sound like we're taking the hill," Stevens said.

I peeked out from under my poncho cover. Stevens was squatted down, no doubt tracked down and brought back by Fessman.

"You want a requisition form?" he asked.

"Roger that," I replied, rolling out of my hooch. It was dawn. It was time for coffee and a shave and some useless but necessary deodorant.

"What do you want to requisition?" he asked.

I filled my helmet with water from one of my full canteens, thanking the great helicopter god of resupply for fresh water almost every day. My Scout Sergeant did not have the faith and confidence of his non-English speaking counterpart. I glanced at my bracelet, and then looked around to see if I could find the Montagnard. Something moved in the jungle. I saw him. He looked back at me, invisible to everyone else. I knew he'd moved in response to my looking for him. How he knew to move was beyond me. The more I learned of the enigmatic silent man the more I liked him.

"I want tracers," I said, guiding my Gillette around my cheeks and chin, dipping the difficult to hold little tool occasionally in my helmet water.

"They don't make tracers for the .45," he replied. "Too short range."

I wondered if he was making a joke. I stopped shaving and looked into his eyes. He was serious. That was funny too. I thought about laughing. Of course they didn't make tracers for the Colt. I didn't laugh, funny as it was.

"I want tracers for the M16s. In fact, I want all tracers. No more ball ammo. Just tracers. It's going to work."

"What's going to work?" Stevens asked after a minute or so of thought.

"You afraid of tracers?" I asked him.

"Yes, everyone's afraid of tracers."

"Right," I said, putting a stick of Old Spice deodorant up under each of my arms. I loved the smell of the Old Spice until I put it on. I smelled like shit. I smelled like Vietnam all gooey with Old Spice deodorant.

"We're going to light up the enemy at every opportunity and scare the shit out of them. Usually tracers are one of every three to five regular ball rounds. We'll use tracers for all the rounds. That way the enemy will think that our rate of fire has increased tremendously. And they'll keep their scared little heads down so we can kill them in their holes. And I'll be able to see where inside the unit that every 5.56 millimeter goes."

"I've never heard of this," Stevens replied, surprise in his tone. "I don't think anybody's ever heard of it. We don't even requisition any tracers for our M16s. The tracers we use are all 7.62 fired from the M60 machine guns.

"I'll check with the Gunny," he said, finally, when I didn't reply.

"No, you'll get me a requisition form like I ordered you, or you can walk the point next time we move."

"The point?" Stevens said, real fear in his voice. "You'd put me at the point?" his voice began to rise.

I realized I'd gone a bit overboard.

"Just kidding, Stevens. Just get me the form."

Stevens rushed off, to be replaced by Fessman, who squatted in the same spot as the Scout Sergeant had occupied. I thought of cokes in a coke machine, for some reason. I also thought that I had to get control of myself. I hadn't been kidding with Stevens. I was fighting for my life, but I'd already learned that you don't threaten men with guns in combat zones. Period. Ever. Shoot, bomb, drop artillery on them, but never threaten. A threat took power form the person threatening and gave it to the person threatened. What might happen next was up to the person threatened. And that's the last thing I wanted. I could not build trust and loyalty by demanding it. I remembered the best training officer I'd had at Quantico. A funny guy who said things like "Irish Pennants" for loose threads, and "Troub City" for a difficult circumstance. He'd one day told us what real leadership was. I hadn't really internalized what he said but I never forgot the words: *Leadership is getting people to do what you want them to do because they want to do it.* I was finally coming to understand those words, and just how complex an undertaking it is to lead men in combat.

I knew it was likely that the rear area would have plenty of tracers for the M16s simply because they weren't commonly used. The Marines in my company fired mostly in jungle terrain, not across open fields of fire. In truth, I knew the idea of using all tracers hadn't come to me on my own. A few years earlier I'd read a book about German SS soldiers who'd been allowed into the Foreign Legion to get away from being prosecuted as war criminals. Those Nazi troops had ended up fighting in Vietnam. The all tracer idea was from them. Whether it worked or not I was about to find out. At the very least, using only tracer rounds might cut down on many of the casualties I now knew we were taking from friendly fire.

I finished my morning preparations for the day by taking a malaria pill, eating a bag of dry cocoa, and brewing a canteen holder of coffee.

The Gunny appeared in the jungle undergrowth, shadowed by Nguyen. I wondered if the Gunny knew he was there. The scout looked at me from under a palm frond of some species I didn't know. He didn't wink but I got the feeling of a wink from the strange silent man.

The Gunny pulled his canteen out and went to work building a small fire to make his coffee since my own had quickly burned out. The Composition B burned very hot but also very fast. He didn't say anything while he worked.

I waited, knowing why he was there. Stevens was undoubtedly staying out of it.

"Tracers?" the Gunny said, sipping his hot brew, not looking directly at me.

I knew he was going to nix the idea if he could. I just felt it in my bones.

"Brilliant," he said. "You've been here what? Three days and a wake up, and you come up with that one. It might just help. These weathered Marines aren't going to like revealing where they are when they shoot, though," he added.

"Won't," I answered, speaking to his conjectured concern. "The 16 tracers don't ignite until they're fifty feet from the tip of the barrel. And most of the fire going on, I notice, is in the crap we're in right now. They're not going to like it when everyone knows who's shooting who in the company though, that's for certain."

"Okay, I'll give your scout a form," the Gunny relented.

"No, you'll order the tracers for us yourself," I countered.

The Gunny put down his canteen holder, took out a pack of Camels, and then took his time getting one carefully out after tamping the pack down against his boot top for almost a minute. He lit one up and blew the smoke toward the position Nguyen had held moments earlier.

"Tell you what, sir," he blew another big puff, "I'll tell the guys that I agree with you and we'll take less fire from the NVA because of the tracers scaring them off, if you place the order yourself."

I stared at the side of the Gunny's hard face until he finally turned to look back at me.

"That's how its played when you're in your third war?" I said.

"Re-supply will be at our little makeshift landing zone in a few minutes. The dead and wounded go out at the same time. Gunships can only be spared for one run so it's going to get a bit busy."

"Then you better get me the form," I replied, knowing I had no choice. The Gunny was riding the middle all the way, stuck between the wants and desires of the errant Marines, the obvious race war going on, and me, the supposed representative of the outside world.

Stevens appeared out of the bush, like he was following a Hollywood script. He carried a form in his hand, as he walked up.

The chopper came in from high up, dropping into the small cut away zone the Marines had cleared. Two Huey gunships orbited around the big twin rotor CH-46 as it came down. The gunships, from my position below, looked like predatory and fast-moving cobra snakes.

The wind from the landing 46 battered the remaining foliage on the ground until it beat those of us waiting half to death. Debris that had been chopped out took to the air in twin whirlwinds, striking down on everyone and everything below. There was no "Cisco Kid" commando in Hollywood attire to great me this time. I gave my letter home and the ammunition request form to a crew chief who looked tattered, battered and tired beyond the point of exhaustion. There was not one phony aspect to the man's appearance or behavior. We didn't speak. He took the letter and the requisition and stuffed them in one pocket of his utility trousers before going to work to wave aboard some of my company's men assigned to unload the supplies. The wounded went in sacked up in ponchos like living burritos. They were unloaded gently onto waiting gurneys attached to the insides of the big chopper. Several medical personnel were there to receive them. The dead were dragged aboard in body bags, black in color and unmarked. The crew chief was handed a small cloth sack I presumed to be the dog tags of the fallen.

I stood watching the whole operation, wanting to see the Marines we'd lost but not wanting to make a thing of it at that time. The noise was daunting and a bit overwhelming. The chopper's rotors never stopped turning, although they'd slowed considerably from the landing. The gunships rotated close in, sounding like hunting banshees, their rotor blades making the distinctive Huey *whup-whup-whup*, but the sounds much closer spaced than regular Hueys. I'd never seen the Huey Cobra helicopters before. In training we'd used the old Sea Knight helicopters for transport and only heard about the ferocious Huey gunships.

The dirt and heat was oppressive. I crouched down to await the supply choppers departure so I could glean what I could from the supplies unloaded. The crew chief walked as far toward me as his communications cord would allow, and then waved me toward him. I scrabbled a few feet toward him, wondering what he wanted.

"What size boots?" he asked, yelling the question between cupped hands to penetrate the sound and short distance between us.

"Eight," I yelled back, and then held up two hands with eight fingers extended.

He nodded, taking out a pencil and scribbling briefly.

"My name?" I asked, wondering how they'd know to get the boots to me.

"Junior," he answered, giving me a thumb's up before walking to the rear of the chopper and climbing in the fast closing opening.

I watched the chopper pull up, dive its nose down and then pull away sharply into a curving departure making it look like it had to crash, but it didn't. In seconds all the choppers disappeared. I went for the supplies. I was Junior, I thought to myself. Not Lieutenant Junior or Junior, Sir. I didn't like it at all, but I took some satisfaction in at least being something, and I was not yet in one of those black body bags.

fourteen

THE FOURTH DAY : THIRD PART

On the second day there was no meeting to plan the fake attack on Hill 110.

The Gunny drifted by when the big Double Trouble CH46 lifted off from resupply, loaded with body bags, the wounded, and one Marine who'd served out his time. Actually, he was six days short of the thirteen months, but he was called back to be processed out, whatever arcane procedure that might be. When I asked the Gunny about how someone ended up out with us to finish his tour, since most knew that if you lasted six months you got to go to the rear, he shrugged and said it was the luck of the draw. When I stared back at him with one raised eyebrow he relented.

"Pissed somebody off, like you," he said, squatting down to brew some coffee and to drop off a large unmarked cardboard box. "Start the attack fire with artillery and then cut it back after a few hours," he instructed. "That'll give us enough time to take the hill."

"And then we wait," I responded. "We wait for orders to move on or for me to be transported to Okinawa for a general court martial." The Gunny looked up at me, hesitating for a few seconds while stirring the instant coffee mix into his canteen holder. From behind me I heard suppressed laughing. Fessman, nearby, joined in. Pretty soon the Gunny was laughing too. The laughing grew louder. I just sat there looking around in wonder.

"That's good," the Gunny said, putting his coffee down to wipe his yes. "That's really good, Junior, like you're going to Okinawa?" Things settled down to the way they were after a few minutes.

"What's so funny?" I finally asked. "You're not getting out of here to go to Okinawa or anyplace else," the Gunny said, matter-of-factly. "None of us are. Magnussen got out because he was only here a week. Someone sent him in to kill him. We kept him off the perimeter and well back from point. He made it. We're not making it."

"Why him and not the rest of us?" I asked, my tone dark and negative.

"Because you're the Company commander," the Gunny replied. "Here, these are for you, and the problems that come with them." He pushed the box across my tiny moat and onto the edge of my poncho cover. I took the box and pried open the paper sealed top. The box was filled with the distinctive plastic mosquito repellent bottles. According to a white slip glued to the back of the cover there were sixty of them.

"I've already got plenty," I said, my voice questioning.

"There's something about that stuff you don't know," The Gunny said. "If you take half a bottle, put it on your feet and wear clean socks for a day or two, then your feet break out and infection sets in so bad you can't walk anymore."

I peered closely at the side of the bottle. The ingredients listed a whole load of chemicals I'd never heard of or seen written anywhere.

"And this has to do with me how?" I asked, although in the back of my mind I was already thinking about pouring half a bottle in each of my socks.

"Got three cases this morning," the Gunny said. "If we medevac them because they can't walk then the whole company will be pouring that crap on their feet until they get out too. We can't medevac them and they can't function in the field."

"And this has to do with me how?" I repeated, although this time my tone was low and sad.

"You're the company commander," the Gunny concluded.

"So," I said, pausing to catch my breath. "I get to mount the phony attack that I can't get court martialed for and then handle the problem of three Marines who can't be taken out of the field but can't stay in the field either. And the day is just beginning." By the time I finished, my tone was acidic. The Gunny had also referred to me as "Junior" and I didn't like that one bit either. I hated him but I couldn't hate him because he'd saved my life, and was likely to do so again if I was to have any chance of making it. I hated it all. The Marines, the mud, the bugs, the bug spray, the C-Rations, the battalion, and even the country that had lied so knowingly and awfully in throwing me away in hell. I felt paralyzed with hate. Too frozen to even speak further.

The Gunny watched me closely, nudging the steaming mud in front of him to put the remains of the composition B explosive out.

"Not quite," he said so low it was almost a whisper.

"Not quite what," I forced out.

"Zero," the Gunny replied. "Lance Corporal Zero. He's a problem. I can't fit him anywhere."

"Fit?" I asked, incredulously. "How can a Lance Corporal be out of place in any Marine company, for Christ's sake?" I asked, feeling like I was reaching the end of whatever tether I had left. The Gunny didn't reply, probably gauging the level of my emotion. I was angrier than I'd ever been in my life, it was true, but not with a heated anger. My anger was cold and seething and the more horrible for it. I could not truly express it at all, except by nuance.

"Okay, so tell me," I began, my voice flat and level. "What color are the Marines with the athlete's foot problem?"

"Good guess," the Gunny replied. "All white. Cracker white. The black Marines don't do the foot thing. They lay down and won't fight or fire back at night so we can't put them on perimeter. It's different."

"And the corpsmen are all white, am I right there too?" I asked.

"They marked them for medevac but we can't do it," the Gunny said, putting his canteen rig back together, and then motioned to someone waiting behind the heavy brush. A big, black Marine came forth and walked over to the Gunny and squatted down next to him.

"This the guy?" the man who was obviously Zero, I asked.

"He can't go out by medevac and he can't stay here," I said, no question in my voice. "He can't be with the crackers and he can't be with the blacks for some reason." Both Marines looked at me like I was something less than an intelligent human. Neither said "no shit," which I was somehow thankful for.

"He won't lay down and wants to do what he's supposed to do as a Marine. And the whites will have something happen to him if I assign one knuckle-knocker to them."

"Finally, an easy one," I said to the Gunny with a cold unfeeling smile, having seen the procedure of knuckle-knocking many of the blacks did when they ran into one another, but not understanding it all except the obvious fact that it was so visibly and totally anti-white.

"He's now a scout working for my scout sergeant," I ordered. "And I presume the repellent is for me to decide whether it gets distributed or not. It can't be distributed without Marines putting it in their socks so they can't walk. It has to be distributed because without it the mosquitoes will drive anyone totally insane, not that they aren't already. So hand it out."

"What about the three?" the Gunny asked. "You'll be running up against our three corpsmen if you don't let them leave and you may need a corpsman yourself at some time." The Gunny finished and lingered a bit before getting up and walking away without the answer I didn't have for him. I not only didn't know what to do I didn't want to know that I didn't know. The Gunny had summed it up nicely. The decision was impossible. I couldn't shoot them all in the butt. We had to keep them in the company somehow and the Gunny didn't want to be denied help if he was wounded by going against the corpsmen.

"They call you Junior?" the big black corporal asked.

"You report to Stevens back there behind me somewhere," I said, pointing beyond the raised edge of my poncho cover where I couldn't see. "You don't have to call me anything."

I knew my last sentence didn't mean anything either but I couldn't think of anything intelligent to say. I didn't want to tell anyone in the entire unit to call me sir. The sun would go down and everything would descend into the real jungle of the night and there were no "sirs" living in that jungle night. There were not supposed to be any factions in a Marine unit, other than the "factions" of platoons, squads, and fire teams. My company, if I was to call it that, was divided and sub-divided into tribal groups based upon function, experience, race, and quite possibly religion. There were those who apparently wouldn't fight at all and those who'd fight but use every crooked device possible to get out of the fight. I gestured for Fessman and then called in the strike upon Hill 110. Hours of 105 and 155 artillery dropped onto every aspect of the hill. Using high-arc indirect fire I even rained shells down on the backside of the hill.

The Gunny came back when the earth-shaking and noise came to an end. He brewed another cup in front of me, saying nothing.

"We won?" I asked him.

"I sent the message to Battalion," he answered.

"But that's not all of it, is it," I said, reading his worried expression.

"No," he came right back. "Lima Company on our flank has a couple of 81mm mortars. Battalion's sending them over with a squad to support our defense of the hill."

I laughed out loud. "This just gets better and better. I suppose we have to do a casualty report. Should we make up KIA and WIA reports and then wait for the night for our guys to kill one another?"

The Gunny said nothing. "How do we handle the Lima problem," I asked him. "Fire mission while they're on the way?"

The Gunny stared, his eyes getting wider. "You're kidding, right?"

I just looked back at him, realizing I really didn't give a damn whether the Marine Corps might have one little mortar squad or another go missing or not.

"Get a grip," the Gunny finally said. "I'll handle it. I'll talk to them."

"Big of you," I answered, sarcastically. "I'll lay here and worry about going to Okinawa." I regretted the words when I said them. The Gunny was doing his best in an insane situation. "Sorry," I got out, standing to face him. "Don't worry about those guys…or yourself either. No fire mission."

The Gunny exhaled loudly, turning away. "Just don't tell me shit like that anymore."

He walked off into the jungle. I looked at my growing tribe of scouts, all crouching over their own cooking fire behind my poncho liner half-tent. I didn't understand what the Gunny's last comment meant. I didn't understand the blacks, the whites, the corpsmen, trouble with the repellent or any of it. I also didn't understand why I was supposed to understand any of it. I had no training at all, really, only in artillery and map reading. I wished that I had the old Waffen SS field manual I'd read so many years ago, about the Germans who had to fight the Vietnamese before me. Night would be coming and my tracers would not be in until the following dawn if resupply went then. I laid down, wondering what the Gunny was going to do with the Lima Marines, opening a can of Ham and Mothers and taking out the stuff I needed to write my third letter home. A third letter about the pleasing fauna, lovely flora, and acceptably comfortable weather.

fifteen

THE FOURTH NIGHT

Once the artillery barrage of Hill 110 was over, the surrounding low growth jungle area subsided into a windy silence.

The hot air wafted like blown cobwebs sweeping slowly back and forth across the face and body of anyone standing. I lay in my hooch, waiting. The night was coming and my fear was rising once again. I hated that the Gunny was right and that I was starting to get used to being terrified to death, not that the terror lessened. It didn't. Somehow I could maintain control while going through it. Maybe, for the first time, when the sun went fully down, the terror would not be as bad as it had been every night before. It was only my fourth night but thinking back to the airliner ride into Da Nang was like mentally going back a year in relative time. The only good thing about the night was the coming of the next day, if I lived. Resupply, with tracers. Another day closer to getting a letter from home, or even a package or tape. Anything. Home was in the music from the radios and from the notes in the cigarette cartons. And the letter hastily written to Mary in my front pocket. That was it.

"Stevens, front," I ordered, leaning out toward my little dry moat. There was a scurrying sound before my three scouts appeared before me, each looking compliant and ready for whatever I might order. They resembled the Marines in combat I'd been led to believe I'd be leading. But in only four days and nights I knew better. They were each independent thinking machines making decisions based upon their own survival strategies. How to get them to do what I wanted or needed them to do because they wanted to do it occupied much of my thinking.

"Stevens, go on over to First Platoon and tell the commander of that unit that he's going to have his men carry the Marines who can't walk when we leave here," I ordered.

"The Gunny's not going to like that," Stevens replied, not moving an inch. I was ready for his response, however, so I showed none of the mild exasperation I felt at not being instantly obeyed. My mission was to lead to the extent that I survived, nothing more and nothing less. I too had quickly become an independent thinking machine dedicated to my own survival strategy. The other Marines in my unit kept their strategies secret, for the most part, unless they were dumb enough to frag or injure themselves to the point of attempting to get out. I had to go along to get along. I had to keep my own secrets, even from the Gunny.

"Then tell the Gunny on your way, but don't come back here until you've told Jurgens what I ordered," I said, my voice going soft and casual. Stevens still made no move, as he considered his options, not wanting to be the bearer of bad news to racially volatile First Platoon's command post. Mentally, my right hand slid marginally closer to the butt of my .45, but physically I made no move. I could not openly threaten any of the men under my command, not with full darkness on the way. My mind worked as if on two levels, one deadly lethal and wanting to kill anything that was the slightest threat to my potential survival, and the other totally shocked at being able to think such awful and foreign thoughts about any other human being without hesitation or regret. Stevens stared into my eyes. My eyes did not blink as I looked back. I tried to soften my facial features while we stared back and forth, so the man would not understand the battle going on in my mind. Suddenly, Stevens got to his feet, motioned to Nguyen and was gone. The last glance he'd given me told me I'd succeeded somewhat. He hadn't picked up on my conflict although his frown indicated he wasn't happy with my leadership decision. Nobody was being evacuated, not without having their ass literally shot off. Zero moved to join the departed scouts.

"Stay," I ordered, before the man got fully underway.

"Why do they call you Zero?" I asked, as he settled his huge bulk back down in front of me.

"Wrestling," he replied, looking wistfully after Stevens and Nguyen. "I wrestled at 285, what they used to call Heavy Weight. But I was so big they said I was off the chart so they called me Zero. My wife lives in Japan."

I looked over at the giant child. The wife comment came out of nowhere so I pursued it.

"What's her name and where does she live?" I asked, not really caring but trying to come to grips with what I had to deal with in the man and why he would not participate in whatever was going on in Fourth Platoon.

"Yokosuka," he replied. "Namika."

I frowned. Which one was the place and which one was the name? I didn't know and didn't want to embarrass myself by asking.

"I'm a Private," Zero went on. "A Marine Private. Is Scout a higher rank than Private?"

"You have to be a Corporal," I answered, having no idea.

"So I can't really be a Scout?" he asked, his voice disappointed.

"You're now a Corporal," I answered, wondering if I was being funny or serious with myself, much less the Marine in front of me. "Combat promotion. The needs of the unit. Heroism in being real when everything and everyone else is shit," I finished, no humor in my tone.

"Thank you, sir," Zero said, rising to his feet and coming to attention. I looked up at the man mountain.

"What are you doing?" I asked, a bit befuddled.

"The ceremony," he said, staring straight ahead, his facial expression as rigid as his body. I rubbed my face with one hand, feeling the oozing remainder of repellent oil from the night before. I was down the rabbit hole but Alice's Wonderland was a whole lot more sane than where I had landed. I stood up.

"You are now officially a Corporal in the United States Marine Corps." I saluted him, even though I wasn't wearing any cover. He saluted back.

"When you find the company clerk, if we have a company clerk, then report yourself in on the daily," I ordered before returning to my hooch. The new corporal saluted again and then moved back to where his own hooch was under construction near where the other departed scouts had their stuff. I thought about the big man. He was the first Marine I liked, other than the boy Marine Fessman was, since I'd landed in country. And he called me sir. I had the feeling that he'd always call me sir, no matter what, and the thought was somehow comforting. I gestured to Fessman by holding out my right hand. In seconds the radio handset was plopped into it.

"Rittenhouse, sir," Fessman said. I looked at him in surprise. "Rittenhouse, the company clerk. We have one. I can get him."

"No, later," I said. "I've got to set up night defensive fires for the hill we aren't going to be on. I silently wondered what the battery FDC might think if and when we got hit later in the night. All of the fire I'd be calling would form around a small perimeter circle some distance from the hill that I'd preprogrammed defensive fires earlier. They were cool, dry, just out of Fort Sill and not dummies in the Fire Direction Center. They'd figure things out if we needed too much help and then check fire. The Gunny and the Company was playing an extremely dangerous game I was being required to try to work them around and through without them being aware of what I was doing.

Trying to talk artillery ballistics to someone who'd not been trained in it was almost useless. The detail was everything. Back at the Battery, when their rounds started going out charge six and seven they had to begin calculating for the earth's curvature and even its rotation. The density of air the shells would be moving through was vital and the shells went up thousands and thousands of feet through different densities. The Company wasn't playing chess, it was playing dice, with every night being another throw. I finished setting up my layered defense with both the 105 battery and that of the 155s closer to Da Nang, knowing the 155s would be much bigger rounds but less accurate because we were out near the edge of their effective range.

The Gunny appeared, bringing with him somehow a cloud of the evening mosquitoes. I reached for the repellent bottle held to the side of my helmet by the big rubber band Fessman had found for me earlier. The Gunny squatted down but made no move to make coffee or be social in any way. I slathered bug juice on my face and neck, and then my hands and wrists. I put the bottle back where it belonged and waited.

"That's a bizarre solution and not really a solution at all," the Gunny began. "That just means we'll have to deal with them later on or other problems because of them."

"So, Jurgens is unhappy over there in First Platoon," I said, without making the sentence a question.

"As you knew," the Gunny answered. "I don't know what you've got against him, anyway, but there's something between you. He's probably going to kill those kids. You know that."

"Couldn't ship 'em out and couldn't keep 'em here," I intoned, ignoring the Jurgens thing. I realized how hard it was to hide anything in such an emotionally charged environment. Everyone was watching and judging everyone else while lying about watching and judging. I felt absolutely nothing for the 'kids' who'd damaged their own feet in an attempt to get out of the same hell I'd have done anything myself to get out of.

"He may not do it," the Gunny mused. "Jurgens just may leave them behind for us to deal with when we pull out of here. If we pull out of here."

"Then he can lead the way in the taking of Hill 110," I replied. "I'm playing along with this charade, as is everyone else. I presume you've got Lima Company's 81s under control. If somebody wants to break ranks, then up they go and we all assault that hill or call Battalion and tell Bennett we're refusing to attack because we're a bunch of chicken shits."

"Well, mister new tough guy, what if Jurgens simply decides to take you out?" the Gunny asked, his voice little above a hissed whisper. I looked over at Fessman, who all of sudden was drifting outward into deeper vegetation.

"First Platoon is registered," I replied. "Are they coming now?" I picked up the handset to the Prick 25 Fessman had shed and left lying on my poncho liner."

"Jesus Christ," the Gunny swore, raising his voice. "No. I don't know. This whole thing is fucked. Leave it alone. I'm trying to help you. I'm trying to help all of us."

I heard the sound of mortars leaving their tubes and flinched.

"Outgoing," the Gunny said, getting control of himself. "The 81s are firing around the hill we just took, to make it look good. Lima's okay."

"Thanks, Gunny," I said, softly.

"For what?" he answered.

"For everything," I said, being careful not to sound paternalistic or commanding, but trying not to sound weak either. "This is impossible and you're doing the best anybody could."

"Shit," he said, forcefully, and got to his feet. "They're going to fire down on us tonight because we're sitting targets and they know it. Use that underground crap you called in before when it starts. I think it shakes them down to their little gook asses."

He disappeared into the brush without further comment. Fessman reappeared, as if by magic, as Stevens and Nguyen returned to report back. They both squatted down before me but neither said anything. I gave Nguyen one slight head nod, motioning toward behind me. He moved quickly and silently, like he was made of liquid, and disappeared behind me. I faced Stevens, wanting a cup of coffee, but it was too late in the waning day to light anything.

The radio on Stevens' shoulder was turned way down but I heard the announcement by Brother John that the next song would be the last until the morning. The song began to play. *I know you want to leave me but I refuse to let you go...* came across the short distance between us. I thought about the lyrics of the song and my wife, and Stevens and the Gunny. It was like God was talking to me. *Please don't you leave me, girl, don't you go.* I needed these men and yet the circumstances of my needing and the circumstances of their own seemed so divergent. How could it ever be possible to bring them together? I had my third letter in my pocket. How many letters would I get off before there would be no more letters?

"Call the other guys," I said to Stevens, as there was no point in discussing what he'd been ordered to do, what the result was or even how the Gunny had become involved. I waited while I heard the hustle and bustle behind me meant they were coming. My scout team. In the Basic School, one night a week, each platoon got together to play a game before calling it a day. The game was "What now, Lieutenant?" The phrase driving the game was "Any decision is better than no decision." Decisions were supposed to be what lieutenants did. A problem would be trotted out by a trainer. A problem impossible to solve. Like the Lieutenant and his unit had to get across a bottomless chasm where there was no bridge or rope, or they'd die where they were. A few pieces of junk, like stakes, hooks, some fishing poles and a few planks too short to do the job would be provided to be used in solving the problem. The trainer would make sure everyone understood the problem and the only tools. Then he would point at one lieutenant, of those gathered before him, and say: "What now, Lieutenant?"

My team squatted down before me, except for Fessman who sat next to me in radio cord distance. Stevens, Nguyen and Zero. I thought about how much fun it would be to describe where we were and what our situation was and ask the "What now, Lieutenant" question. But I was the lieutenant and the problem was worse than some chasm or canyon that could not be crossed. I lit a cigarette, ostensibly to let the smoke drift over my face, before talking, but really to delay for a few seconds.

"Things are going to heat up tonight and there's no predicting what's going to happen. We'll get hit with whatever they've got up on that hill because they think we're going to attack at dawn anyway. I'll use arty to suppress what I can. First Platoon isn't happy with me and there's nothing I can do about it. So, we may have visitors from them, as well. I want you guys to move to another location until dawn. Leave the radio here so I can call in the night fire."

I looked at them through the smoke and in the waning light. They were good men, all four of them. God hadn't been fair to them. I was going to be.

"I registered First Platoon earlier," Stevens said. "I've got friends there. Are you going to call it in if they come in the night?"

I stared back at the ambivalent sergeant, torn between his friends, being a stand-up Marine and trying to stay alive.

"I don't know," I answered, truthfully. The nine-digit grid coordinates of First Platoon's position were at the forefront of my memory. I could even see the code conversion on the map, burned into my mind like blackened letters burned into a wood board.

"Does it have to be this way?" Fessman asked, his voice a whisper from my right. I puffed on the cigarette without inhaling. I didn't want to go into a coughing fit in front of these men.

"One night when I was thirteen years old, my uncle, who was in the Army and had fought from Normandy all the way across Europe, took me up into the attic of his house. He opened a big wooden box and showed me his souvenirs from the war. Daggers, helmets, and even an old non-functional Luger impressed me mightily. I could tell my uncle was drunk. He smiled at my enjoyment until I asked him a question. I don't know where the question came from. It just blurted out. 'What was the worst thing you had to do in the war?' I asked.

"Uncle Jim's smile disappeared, like it had never been on his face. He stared at me so furiously I became slightly afraid to be up there in the old attic with him alone. He took a long time to answer, but he finally did. 'The worst thing was killing the young officers assigned to us. I was the senior sergeant. It was my job to get rid of the officers who might get us killed.'"

I looked at the men in front of me, and then over at Fessman. I puffed on my cigarette some more, even though there were no mosquitoes.

"I never believed his story and we never spoke again of the war he was in," I said. "He died years back. It wasn't until four days ago that I found out Uncle Jim had told me the truth that night in the attic."

I looked from one Marine to another, waiting until I thought they might have had enough time to absorb what I'd said, before I went on.

"I don't make the rules out here and neither do you. This was all like this when we got here. We're here and we're trying to go back home, just like Uncle Jim. We'll do what we have to do to accomplish that, all of us together or each of us alone. Now, go find another place for the night and return at dawn, if there's anything to return to. No matter what, I hope you make it home."

Like that they were gone in the night, none of them even stopping to pick up gear or equipment. I had the radio, some C-Rations, clean clear water, and the radio. I was surprised to find I wasn't terrified. I wasn't afraid. I wasn't anything.

sixteen

THE FOURTH NIGHT : SECOND PART

They came back like they left, only slight movements of the near-by undergrowth giving any evidence of their reappearance. Like wraiths just outside the area of my hooch, they moved to where they were already dug in, although it was mostly useless to dig holes in mud that slowly filled back in without anything to reinforce or hold it out of the excavated area. I felt them more than saw them and it gave me a feeling of unaccountable warmth inside my very being. Warmth where I didn't think I could feel warmth anymore. Fessman slipped across the mist laden outer layer of my strewn out rubber poncho. He pulled the Prick 25 radio slowly from under the cover I'd shoved it for protection from the elements. The mist and rain, Vietnam's only and nearly ever-present elements anything could be done about. The heat was un-remitting and nothing was to be done about that except when gaining altitude in mountainous regions.

"We're staying, sir," Fessman whispered, since I had not moved or given any indication I knew they were back and about our small area.

I didn't reply, wondering once more about the mindset of the men I was among and how nothing in life had prepared me to under-stand or deal with whatever it might be at any given time. A shiver of fear went through me. It was a shiver because I might live and therefore feared I might die. Knowing you are going to die takes almost all the fear away. The unknown disappears and the process of dying isn't nearly as fearful of worrying about the prospect of dying. I might live, at least through the night, and that scared me deeply all over again.

"Corporal Zero," Fessman said, softly, "he says we live with you, which isn't likely, or we die without you, which is almost certainly. So, we're staying and if they come in the night they have to come for all of us."

I remained silent. I had no ready answer. I was reminded of war movies back from WWII when such whispers bound warrior Ameri-cans together against advancing Germans. How unreal it was to have my small tribe of Marines banded together to face the prospect of an attack by other Marines.

Suddenly, the Gunny appeared from nowhere to squat down just outside my flowing little moat.

"It's me," he whispered unnecessarily, like who else would it have been. The list of visitors I received was short, indeed.

Without saying anything further he unstrapped his pack and began settling into the small area between my own hooch and the nearby bracken. Two other Marines soon joined him. After only a few moments of work, getting his own hooch set up, he squatted before me again.

"Rittenhouse and Pilson, Company Clerk and my radio operator," he said, glancing to his right. "We'll set up here if you don't mind."

I would have smiled if I really smiled anymore. Like my permission was needed for much of anything. And, it was rather apparent, the three of them were settling in for the night anyway.

"Come to protect me?" I asked, sounding confident while feeling anything but on the inside.

"It might be a difficult night," he responded, after a moment of reflection. "You registered First Platoon's position. No, I don't think they know that, if you're wondering whether they'll move or not. There's probably only one position our 105s probably won't rain down on tonight so we came here."

It should have been funny. I was afraid of what Jurgens might do while the Gunny was afraid of what I might do. Fourth Platoon was no doubt worried about what the crackers would do. The enemy outside the perimeter could strike at any moment but they'd be striking a force more divided and afraid of one another than it was of them. And I was back to being afraid of all of them. And the Gunny was wrong, although I was not going to tell him so. I had registered my own position and I had no reservations about calling fire down on it whatever, that I could think of, other than that I would miss not getting off a fourth and final letter home.

I heard the crackle, pop, and hiss of the real command radio across the short distance to where Pilson, the other radioman, was getting set up to support the Gunny. He came scrabbling across the top of the mud, holding out a handset identical to the one Fessman was constantly sticking in front of me.

"They want you, Gunny, the six actual," he said, holding the mic out toward the Gunny's right shoulder.

The Gunny took the mic, looking at me for a few seconds before saying anything.

"They think I'm you," he said, waiting to answer the call.

"I guess, in a manner of speaking, you are me," I replied, feeling relieved that he'd at least waited for my permission to pass himself off as me. I wondered, if I ever transmitted on the command net again, whether the operators at the battalion end would recognize the differences in our voices.

"Six actual, over," the Gunny transmitted.

"Casualty report," came right back through the little speaker on Pilson's back.

We hadn't lost any personnel or taken any casualties in the attack because there had been no attack. Battalion knew the hill was occupied and fully expected that the Company's losses would be substantial in taking it, or at least I thought they presumed that. I knew for certain that they wanted low Marine casualties and high enemy casualties for their daily reports.

The Gunny cupped the mic to his chest, thinking.

"When does Rittenhouse send in his dailies?" I asked, in the silence.

"Every morning, just after dawn," the Gunny said, his eyebrows going up.

"Tell them the situation is fluid, the hill taken, but a firm perimeter is still being put in place to repulse counter attacks," I said, reciting training material and language learned in the Basic School back at Quantico. "Casualty report will be filed with the daily in the morning."

The Gunny repeated what I told him word for word

"Roger that, over," came back, after only a few seconds. "The actual says nice work."

The Gunny went back to building his hooch and getting out of the rain.

"Fessman, have Zero come over here," I ordered.

Seconds later the giant of a man appeared, the moonlight gleaming off his black skin. He wore only the green undershirt. I wondered if he was impervious to the awful onslaught of the nightly mosquito attacks.

"Sir," he said, squatting down, his comment sounding not like a question but more as a request for orders.

"You backed me," I said, looking into the black pools where his eyes were supposed to be. "I back you."

"Sir?" he asked, a tone of surprise in his voice.

"You heard me," I answered. "Dismissed."

The man scurried away, no doubt getting under his own poncho to get away from the cloying misty rain.

"The best combat promotion I've ever made," I whispered to myself, in some twisted attempt to find any humor within me. I wasn't even sure I could make battle field promotions at all. I'd heard of such things but presumed them to be the province of generals or admirals, and not lowly make-believe lieutenants.

"Fessman," I whispered, knowing the Child-Marine would appear in seconds like some sort of magical ghost. And he did.

"Sir?" he inquired, ready with the radio handset extended.

"Not yet," I said. "I need a rubber band, but a smaller one. Where do you get rubber bands out here, anyway?" I asked.

"Rittenhouse, sir," he replied. "Company Clerk. I'll get one. What do you need it for, I mean, if I may ask, sir?"

"Cover my flashlight lens so I can write something," I said. "I can punch a hole in a piece of paper and see good enough. In fact, get Rittenhouse over here."

Rittenhouse did not come because the night exploded with incoming fire. Small arms tracers began to arc from the mountain down into the Company area, effectively making it a beaten zone. I cringed. The whole team cringed. Even digging in would have been of little help unless digging deep down below the heavy layer of jungle mud and tough interlacing roots. I could not call fire on the hill because our company was universally known to have taken it earlier in the day. There would be no suppressing artillery fire and air did not fly at night, unless it was to dump officers like me into hell.

I crawled the few feet over to the Gunny's hooch.

"What's our plan?" I asked, wondering if there was any plan at all, other than to exchange small arms fire with the NVA occupying the hill.

"Nothing," the Gunny said, sitting up calmly and eating from a C-Ration can. "We don't return fire. They kinda know where we are but not really in detail, otherwise they wouldn't be lighting up the areas we're not at. All we can do is wait until morning. At least we know they're on that hill in force. We'd have lost half the company trying to take it. Tonight we'll lose some but nothing like that."

I heard the distinctive *thwup* of mortar rounds leaving their tubes. I went flat, face down into the mud at the Gunny's feet.

"Outgoing," he said, lighting a cigarette and looking down at me.

I knew he was trying not to laugh at my appearance. How I had gone from being the cutting edge of a wired-together, highly-trained Marine Officer to the piece of muddy flotsam laying at the Gunny's feet was beyond understanding or accurate description. I plucked myself out of the mud.

"The 81s stayed for the night," the Gunny said, as the big mortar rounds impacted on the hill and things got quiet again.

"Variable time fuses on those things. The shrap will keep their heads down for awhile, but they couldn't haul too much ammo on their backs alone."

"So, we just wait?" I asked, feeling stupid.

"Sometimes God means it that way," the Gunny said, making me wonder if his being Spanish also meant he was Catholic, like me. "We do nothing but wait."

"And pray?" I asked, looking for a hint at his background.

"Sure, if you feel lucky," he said back, giving me nothing.

"We wait for the Red Ball," he went on, taking in a double lungful of smoke, and then blowing it out slowly.

I noticed that the mist had relented. It was only oven hot, not wet oven hot. I wondered how I'd get my new layer of mud off. I didn't want to use my precious half-canteen of drinking water. I lived for my coffee moments where I could read the cigarette box notes from home. The last one I'd read had promised a farm breakfast of fresh eggs and salted bacon slabs from a farm couple in Iowa. I'd saved that one in my wallet with the address. H54 Nodaway, Iowa was the address. The Mulberrys. I would go and visit them for breakfast I promised myself, if I ever got back.

"What's a red ball?" I asked, hoping I was not simply revealing more of my endless ignorance.

"Sometimes the medevac chopper is so filled with wounded that the fuselage bleeds red," the Gunny answered, no derisive inflection in his tone. "Called the Red Ball. If the chopper comes in and leaves under fire, it does it real fast. That's called the Red Ball Express."

I thought about the lucky ones. Aboard the Red Ball Express. I then thought about how bizarre it was to think about being shot as being lucky. I crawled on all fours back to my hooch to wait out the night. To make it from one bout of incoming fire to another, with the 81s providing the only release from the noise and paralyzing fear. And the cries of the wounded. No wounded yet. No cries. I girded myself to wait. No heavy machine guns or mortars on the hill or they'd have opened up already. That kind of "good news" in combat was as bizarre to think about as hoping to get aboard the Red Ball Express.

I did pray but I didn't feel lucky. I prayed that Jurgens' men would not be sent to kill me in the night, and if they were sent they'd be put off by the Gunny being nearby, or maybe not able to find me in the muck of the night.

seventeen

THE FIFTH DAY

No light meant it wasn't yet morning. Not even moonlight under the broken bamboo and soggy brush that cascaded down and over almost everything under it. I lay there, disturbed by the fact that I'd lost the ability to determine if I was asleep or awake. Had I slept or been awake for the whole night? Humans had to sleep. I'd read somewhere that the world's record for going without sleep was only four or five days — about the same time I'd been in country. I didn't feel rested or experience any of the relief I would have felt if I'd actually slept. It seemed that the night had been filled with one volley of green tracers after another plunging down on our position from the side of the untaken hill, followed by mortar rounds sent back by Lima Company's on-loan mortar team.

For some reason the mosquitoes had let up. Had they taken in enough of the repellent to cause them to go soggy and inert? I wondered. I thought about the jungles of Vietnam — how they were nothing like I'd been led to expect from Tarzan and other Saturday morning shows from my youth. There was no "triple canopy" stuff, rising hundreds of feet into the air, with vines and liana strung everywhere. Tarzan would have had to walk like the rest of us in the lowlands of Vietnam, where lush green shoulder high brush and bamboo groves were interspersed with only an occasional large cypress, and there was plenty of mud everywhere. Reed clumps permeated every open area and allowed for hooches to be inhabitable with the monsoons approaching. The reeds could be easily cut and then laid under ponchos or the few air mattresses that weren't filled with holes. I had no mattress since I'd never made it to supply.

My letter home was ready to go although I wasn't sure I should send it. My wife was back home in San Francisco, waiting. My parents were in Florida doing whatever they were doing, what with my dad being a warrant officer in the Coast Guard. My brother was an army officer tanker serving in the Big Red One down South in a place called Bien Hoa. My letter detailed what was to be done when I didn't come home.

Ever. There was the government life insurance, the six month's pay, a small private policy with a company called Mass Mutual, and the pay I was owed but hadn't been paid out yet. My list to Mary was eleven items long. I couldn't believe that everything I had ever had could be easily described in eleven entries, wherein about six of them were rather meaningless. What to do with my Ace Double Science Fiction collection of books seemed idiotic. Would my wife react badly or understand that she had to do certain stuff without me in order to take care of herself and the baby? Would the contents of the letter be too much for her emotionally?

Dim first light allowed me to see the ground around me but not much farther. As the mist slowly lifted, I could make out where the incoming bouts of small arms fire had died out. The enemy entrenched on the sides of Hill 110 were probably wondering why no artillery had been dumped on them, I thought with a frown. The whole idea of making believe we'd taken a hill, lying to Command and then trying to survive nearby was so unlike any Marine operation that it was simply too much to take in. I wondered if I was a better more experienced officer whether I would have been able to actually command the unit and effectively take the required objective.

I struggled up and got my stuff together to make coffee. The Gunny came over, Pilson crawling behind him. Fessman appeared at my shoulder with Zero and Stevens not far behind. Only Nguyen hung back, barely visible behind everyone, his gleaming black eyes meeting mine. It was like seeing a leopard in the bush and like a leopard he disappeared after only a few seconds.

"Your nickname's not Zero anymore," I said to him, and the group in general. "It's Zippo, like the lighter. Every time someone calls you Zero you correct him, and so will everyone else. Zero is a put down and you don't have to take that here or anywhere." I looked around but no one met my eyes except Fessman. He smiled. My first commands to the unit were about seemingly nonsense items, but where was I to start? I wasn't even the real six actual.

"How many?" I asked the Gunny, over the too-hot lip of my canteen holder, the liquid slightly burning my lips.

"Six and three," he answered, making his own fixings.

Stevens, Zippo, and Fessman munched on crackers from the C-Rations issued the day before. I accepted a cracker. Fessman handed me a tin of Peanut Butter (fortified) from somewhere in Georgia. I wondered what "fortified" meant, but gouged some of the stuff onto my cracker without comment. I took a few seconds to eat the whole cracker down. The peanut butter was some of the best I'd ever had in my life, although I knew some of the flavor might be enhanced by where I was and what was happening. The stuff was called Cinderella. I also wondered about why it had any name at all once packaged inside one of the rather anonymous looking ration tins.

"Six KIA and three wounded," I noted, trying to get my tongue straight after clearing the peanut butter from my mouth. "All by small arm injuries I would presume. And why are there always more killed than injured. That doesn't seem right."

"The way it is," the Gunny replied, his tone revealing a little exasperation.

"I'd like to see the bodies before they go on the chopper," I responded.

"Sealed up, tagged, and clipped," the Gunny came right back. "Tomorrow, if we have any, maybe."

I stared at him until he focused his eyes on mine. I waited, neither of us taking in any of our cooling coffee. I didn't know what I was after but I knew I could not go on as the fucking new guy who does nothing, yet doesn't get sent out to be the point. The dead and wounded were my men, my responsibility, and there wasn't much getting around that. Why there was any discussion about it at all surprised me. Not totally, because of the friendly fire casualties I knew we were enduring, but there was something more. I felt it.

"Fine," the Gunny said, putting his coffee down and reaching into one of his cargo pockets on the outside of his right leg. I thought he was going for a cigarette but he wasn't. He pulled out a small rubber-banded white paper package and held it out toward me with is left hand. With his right he picked up his coffee. It was his turn to wait.

I stared at the package. I'd gotten through the night frightened but not terrified. I'd gotten rid of the shakes. I wasn't used to the dirt, grime and smell, but I had a feeling I was never going to get used to those. While I stared at the unwavering package held out before me, I vowed to never ever start another day, if I made it back to the real world, without taking a hot shower. The thought of such a shower made my mind waver a bit. Enough to make the Gunny comment.

"Well?" he said. "You wanted this." He shoved the package out a few more inches.

I took it into my right hand. The package was about the size of a child's fist. My peanut butter fingers, undercoated with layers of grimy bug juice and dirt, made smudges on the outside of the paper. I looked over at the Gunny, who seemed positively clean and crisp compared to the rest of us. I wondered how he did it but brought my mind back to the package without asking him anything.

"What's inside?" I asked, my eyes going back and forth between the Gunny's and the package.

He didn't reply. I noticed that the tableau had become frozen. Nobody was moving, eating or even breathing around me. They were all waiting. I looked over the Gunny's shoulder, past Pilson, his radioman. Nguyen's eyes looked out from low down inside a nearby bamboo grove. His head slowly nodded. I looked back down at the package and then back, but the inscrutable Montagnard was gone.

I slowly removed the two rubber bands, being careful not to break them. I set them gently down on my poncho cover. I unwrapped the paper. Nine morphine curettes fell into the palm of my right hand. I struggled a bit to hold them without dropping any. I looked closely. Each small lead curette was partially covered by a white label. Written in red on each were the words: "solution of morphine ½ grain .5cc"

"Morphine," I said, feeling rather stupid. "Morphine, like with the corpsman." I'd never seen morphine in any container before. I was surprised that the most effective and wonderful painkiller on earth came in such small packages. Each curette was no bigger than my little finger. I worked to get the package back together while my mind went into overdrive. What did the morphine, intended to be carried and applied by the corpsmen alone, have to do with being now in my possession and somehow associated with the dead and wounded?

I looked up when I was done, not sure whether I should hand the package back or hold on to it as I was seemingly intended to do. I noticed it was lighter around me. The resupply would be coming and it was an important one. The Gunny looked around at the Marines surrounding us. They all got up and left, as if he'd given them an order. But nobody had spoken. In seconds we were alone, only the faint chatter of birds starting their day sounding in the distance.

"What's the mystery?" I asked.

The Gunny said nothing.

"What is it, God damn it, Gunny?" my voice rising slightly.

"When they're hit bad enough and no medevac can come in because of the night or weather, then you have to do something," he said, like saying the words was difficult for him.

"Yes?" I replied, not getting what he might be talking about.

"Company commander. It's part of the CO's job," the Gunny went on. "It was my job. Now it's yours. I don't know what to say about it. You'll know when it's the right time."

"What?" I said, stated in more of a demanding tone than a question.

"When they're too badly wounded to make it through the night you punch in three curettes, unless the Marine is really big, then it may take four," the Gunny said back, forcefully.

I looked down at the package. I got it suddenly. My hand opened and the package fell down to the poncho cover, resting against the side of my old leather combat boot.

"You've got to be kidding me," I finally said, in a whisper. "What in hell is this? Where is this? I'm supposed to what? Kill one of my men? Make the decision that he can't make based on what? I'm the company commander, not God."

"I did it last night," the Gunny replied, his voice so sad sounding I didn't know what to say back.

"Did it?" I uttered, not knowing why I said the words because I understood all too well what he'd done. "How did you know?" I asked, for no reason I could think of, my mind in complete turmoil. I couldn't believe we were having the discussion at all. I'd shot the Corpsman. I'd called in artillery dangerously close. I'd even targeted First Platoon and thought about dropping a battery of six down upon them, but the thought of injecting of an overdose of morphine into the agonized body of a living Marine kid hit me hard.

"Do the men know?" I asked.

"Please," the Gunny answered, his voice almost a snarl. "The corpsmen tell you when it's okay to do it. The men know. You think they want to hear one of their friends scream, cry, and talk about his family while he's dying through the night? You think they want him crying and attracting more fire that might kill them?"

I looked around. There was no one, not even Nguyen nearly invisible in the brush. No wonder, I thought to myself. No wonder no one was around. Who wanted a part of this? Maybe they'd go home one day. Maybe I'd go home one day. How was I going to tell anyone about this? What kind of war story would this be, and how many of them would there be? I thought of my Uncle Jim in that attic and I pitied him. He'd probably never told a soul on earth about what he'd done. Only a teen-age kid in an attic once. Was that going to be me someday? Telling some kid in an attic about killing my own men to stop their suffering, to keep them quiet, to make an absolutely unbelievable and hellishly unexplainable situation somehow limp along and work?

"I don't think I can do it," I finally said, staring down at the deadly package.

"You ran from combat that first night," the Gunny said, softly. "You haven't run since. You learn out here or you die. You can do it. I did it. You have to do it. I had to do it."

"Like we're going to live anyway?" I said, shaking my head slowly, my tone bitter.

"I can't fault your logic there," the Gunny replied. "Pick up the package. It's your package. You're the company commander. You want-ed to know. Now you know."

I picked up the package. The Gunny was wrong. I'd pick up the package and carry it with me, but I wouldn't use it. I couldn't use it.

"What were his injuries?" I said, more to cover the fact that I was not going to use the morphine than because I wanted to know.

"Private First Class Thomas Haxton from Toledo, Ohio. His dad's running a coal hauler out of there back and forth to Taconite, Minnesota. He had three brothers and a sister. One of the grenades you might have heard in the night landed in his shallow hole. He was blown in half. Everything from his belly button on down was there but not connected anymore. He couldn't live. He couldn't really be alive, but he was. He told me about his family, what he wanted to be, his girlfriend and even his dog. It's a —."

"Stop," I said, raising my left hand palm up. "Please." My first emotion since landing at Da Nang coursed through me. Tears ran down my face. I was glad it wasn't lighter yet. The Gunny could see them but maybe nobody else around. And then I felt worse. I realized I wasn't crying for Haxton; I was crying for me. I was feeling sorry for myself while my men were dying like flies all around me.

"What was I supposed to do?" the Gunny asked.

I looked him the eyes. He hadn't asked the question rhetorically, I saw. He was really waiting for some sort of answer from me. From me. I gripped the package in my right hand so tightly I was afraid morphine would squirt out all over. I brushed my face with my left hand as best

I could. I felt a slight breeze. The resupply chopper would be coming in real soon. The medevac would be going out with the bodies and the wounded. A slight breeze swept some fresher air across my face and body. I was alive. Somehow still alive. The Gunny in front of me was alive too. And waiting.

"You did the right thing," I said, forcing my voice to be flat and sincere. "You did the only thing. Nobody's coming for us. You gifted Haxton out like a Marine instead of a weeping child."

The Gunny's shoulders slumped slightly. "Thank you, sir," he said, his voice almost a whisper.

It was only the second sir I'd managed to collect from him and it was one I would rather not have had.

eighteen

THE FIFTH DAY : SECOND PART

Hill 110 lay quiet in the distance. I realized for the first time that I lacked a forward observer's most important tool: a pair of binoculars. The Army had Leica German range-estimating binoculars back at Fort Sill, but any pair at all would be better than bare eyes. I lay prone on a bed of dry reeds, astounded that anything in the pre-monsoon lowlands could actually be dry. The sun beating down, even in the early morning hours, was hot and relentless. No mosquitoes though, and I wasn't about to overlook that blessing. Little bumps still dotted my wrists, face, and neck, only the daily ration of anti-malaria pills probably keeping me alive.

My memorized artillery registrations were only approximations when it came to the hill itself, since I'd not been able to adjust fire on it since before the company supposedly took it. I'd be firing on it intensely, however, once we got the order to move on, if for no other reason than I felt bad about disobeying orders in a cowardly way and also guilty about what another unsuspecting outfit might come upon, thinking the hill was subdued and clear prior to their encountering it.

I felt the low drumming beat of distant chopper blades well before I could hear them through the air. I made my way toward the landing zone with Fessman at my side. Everywhere I went my team went, straggling behind except for Fessman who hovered only feet away no matter where I was. We reached the cleared area in minutes, my right hand clutching the letter I'd written in the dark.

Two Huey Cobra gunships swept in from opposite directions, diving in low and then swooping back up and around. It was like watching big sharks hunting above from the bottom of a huge fish tank. Two transport Hueys followed, both sinking slowly down from higher altitudes without encountering any enemy fire. I stood with one hand guarding my eyes and the other securing my helmet against the wind from the rotors. Would there be an officer with the air crew? A real Marine officer — not one like me. A captain or a first lieutenant. Maybe an officer transferred from another field unit who knew about all the stuff.

The real stuff. I looked down at the fat little packet in my trouser pocket, bulging slightly outward. Morphine. I could give it to a more senior officer. Almost any officer in the entire Marine Corps would be senior to me. Maybe I could pass it over to him and then disappear, like every member of my team had done when the Gunny gave it to me, even Fessman. I didn't blame the men. What kind of upstanding disciplined Marine would want to be a part of anything like the morphine thing? Their instant departure revealed the fact that they all knew, however. They all knew. The Gunny had taken out Haxton during the night. If he'd lived, would there be some investigation back home in twenty or thirty years? Would some aging veteran talk? Haxton's family would sure never forget his dying, or the manner of his dying, if they knew it.

The lead supply chopper dived in nose down before jerking up and plopping down forty yards away. The wind almost blew me over. I forced my eyelids to squint down to the thinnest of slits, leaning into the prop wash. The macho man from days before, with the great outfit and the Thompson, stepped out to stand guard. Other Marines began dragging boxes of stuff out the side door of the Huey, the boxes thudding down soundlessly below the unrelenting roar of rotor blades still spinning at near flying speed. I rushed forward, nearly arriving at macho man's side too late. I handed him my letter home and a short folded note requesting a set of binoculars from supply. He stuck both items into his own pocket with the hand not holding the Thompson. He turned around to grab something while I admired the wonderfully machined weapon slung from his shoulder. It gleamed with a layer of thin oil. The gun looked like it had never been fired. The man turned back and handed me a pair of jungle boots. I gathered them in with both hands, unable to speak or be heard. I thanked him with my eyes. Then he was gone, back inside the helicopter. He waved one hand downward several times before I got it. I threw myself onto a clump of reeds as the chopper's engine spooled up to maximum and the Huey lifted out under emergency power. The powerful rotor pulled up little spalls of mud and splattered them all over everything. I crawled away, back to where Fessman waited, wisely distant from the chopper's landing position. The second chopper came in at the same place. It brought replacements and prepared to lift out the casualties and body bags.

No officer. I could tell immediately. Six men clambered out of the hole in the side of the Huey, then ran awkwardly, dragging their huge packs with them as they fought to get as far from the down-blast of the chopper's rotors as they could. I knew they'd be covered with the same layer of speckled mud that adorned every part of my body. I looked down and realized that in only five days I looked exactly like the vacant-eyed deadly silent men I'd circulated among at the Da Nang Hilton. A young square-headed Marine with a clipboard stood just beyond the effects of the helicopter's artificial hurricane winds, waving to the new guys who all changed directions to arrive in front of him.

The second chopper, stuffed with bodies, pulled up from the LZ and backed away before diving down slightly and flying off. The two hovering shark-like Cobras made one more curving pass over the company before disappearing. They hadn't drawn any fire. Marines loved and hated the choppers. They were the company lifeline and if you were hit they could save your life, but on the other side of it they drew death dealing fire almost whenever they showed up, and they were grossly undependable. Not the aircraft, but the crews. Some crews came any time you needed them and would endure heavy fire to save the wounded. Other crews would simply wave off if things seemed too hot in the LZ they were supposed to land on. Huey Cobra gunships were exceptions. They never landed and drew little fire simply because even the NVA were not often stupid enough to get their specialized sort of terminal attention. There just weren't enough of them around, from what I'd seen so far.

"You'd be Rittenhouse?" I asked, reaching the stocky blond man working on the clip board held before him.

"That's right," he replied, not looking up, while he checked off any number of things for each Marine coming in.

"You do the paperwork on the dead and injured?" I asked.

Rittenhouse stopped what he was doing and looked over at me. "Yeah, I do, and on everything else in this unit, too."

I saw him look at the jungle boots tucked under my arm.

"Don't have a record of those coming in," he said, making no move to write anything down, however. "And I don't remember you coming in, either."

I liked Rittenhouse right off the bat. It was like I'd finally landed in the middle of the unit I was supposed to be in. Rittenhouse waited, not turning back to his charges, just like he would have back home. He wouldn't turn until he was ordered or dismissed.

"As you were, take care of the men," I said. "And assign them to Fourth Platoon. I don't care where the men we lost were from."

"Can't do that sir," Rittenhouse said.

I just stood there staring at him, wanting to say the words "Say again?" but holding myself back.

"The dead and injured were from First Platoon and Fourth Platoon, it's true, but these men, well, none of them can go into the Fourth." Rittenhouse returned to a squirming sort of attention after he was done talking.

"Because they're Caucasian and the Gunny said so?" I asked, speaking slower and softer than I had before.

"Yes, sir," Rittenhouse replied.

I noted that the squared-away, bright Marine in front of me was a corporal. Talent didn't always get a high rank in the Corps. I was willing to bet, in having listened to the man for only a few seconds and watching his comportment, that he was at least a high school graduate and most probably had some or all of college too.

"Let me guess, Corporal," I asked, sidestepping the authority issue. "Three of the them were from First Platoon and the rest from Fourth."

"Did you read the tags, sir?" Rittenhouse shot back. "I think it I got it all right."

"Three of them had foot infections, did they not?" I asked, not really expecting an answer.

"You'd have to ask the medics, sir," Rittenhouse replied, looking down at this clipboard and moving around in such a way that it was apparent he wanted to get back to checking in the new guys.

I wondered about Private First Class Thomas Haxton. Which among the casualties was he? Why had I been unable to counsel the Gunny in his obvious grief over what he'd done? What he'd had to do. Awful thoughts would not stop once they started running through my mind. What was Haxton's dog's name? What kind of dog was he? What difference did it make whether First Platoon had killed the malingerers rather than carry them or simply shot them in the ass, like I'd done to the corpsman? Haxton would get a Purple Heart, but that was it.

"How do you put somebody in for a medal?" I asked Rittenhouse, wondering why that hadn't been covered in training either.

"You put him in the dailies, along with a citation draft, sir," Rittenhouse said, still working with the new guys. "Division edits and rewrites it if they approve the medal. What medal? For what?" he finally asked, this time turning with a questioning look on his face.

"Bronze star for valor in the taking of Hill 110," I said, thinking that I would normally be laughing inside but couldn't quite do it. I knew I couldn't laugh out loud either. That had gone away. How can a person lose the power to laugh, I thought, growing slightly fearful. What was happening to me?

"But we didn't take the hill, sir," Rittenhouse said.

"We were ordered to take the hill," I said back, my voice low and hard. "We told Battalion we took the hill and soon we'll be leaving the hill we didn't take but said we took. And Haxton gets the only real thing in the whole deal. At least his parents and siblings do. Write it up and send it in."

"I don't know what to say, sir," Rittenhouse replied, shrugging his shoulders, the new guys having moved on.

"Figure it out, Corporal," I ordered. "He died attacking the hill with his fire team, the rest of the Marines on that chopper died with him in the attack. Put that in your dailies."

"What about the new guys?" he replied, after going silent for a full minute, while making some notes on his clipboard.

"What do you mean?" I said, in surprise. "What do you usually do with them?"

"Assign them to platoons where the platoon leaders put them in squads and fire teams. But these are P-1 T.O. special guys, sir."

"Would you mind a little English, Corporal?" I said, frustrated.

"Ah, they're Project One Hundred Thousand, Table of Organization exceptions, sir," he replied, waiting for me to respond.

I felt angry at being so very ignorant about everything, and my facial expression must have shown it.

"Project One Hundred Thousand is Secretary McNamara's program to help young guys succeed in the Corps, sir," Rittenhouse said, like he was a schoolteacher and I was a dumb kid in the front row.

I just looked back at him with a waiting blank stare.

"They can't read or write, sir," the corporal said, his voice little more than a whisper. "And they are slow, if you know what I mean, sir."

I stood in shock. I'd never heard of the program, and I was taken totally aback by the blatant insanity of providing damaged, untrained and unschooled young men help by sending them to a ground unit in Vietnam in full on combat.

"They can't read an ammo or C-Ration box, sir. They can't read or understand a map. They can't..." Rittenhouse went on but I stopped hearing him.

I plopped myself onto a clump of dry reeds and began pulling my boots off.

I moved as fast as possible. I was determined to die in my new combat jungle boots and not my old cast off Korean war specials. I rushed because I wasn't sure, in the world I'd landed, that I would live long enough to get the boots on. I made it, heaving the old boots off into the bracken and standing up.

"Much better," I breathed out.

"Sir?" Rittenhouse said, having talked almost the whole time I was working.

"Sir, what?" I answered.

"What do I do with these men?" he asked, tapping his clipboard with a long yellow pencil. I noted that he carried a spare tucked in above his right ear. The pencils were razor sharp. I wondered where he got pencils sharpened in a combat zone.

"Pair them up," I said, inventing as I went along. "They've all got to be privates, right? So, pair them with Marines of higher rank and then make the ranking Marines responsible for them. We can't have them wandering about on their own. In fact, put them all in Fourth Platoon. Sugar Daddy can teach them all to knuckle-knock, or whatever those guys do instead of saluting."

"This isn't going to be good, sir," Rittenhouse said. "There's going to be trouble."

"Trouble?" I shot back. "Oh, we're not in trouble here. How many wars are we fighting? The real one with the NVA? The fake one against Hill 110, or maybe the crackers against the blacks in First and Fourth platoons, and I don't even have a clue about the others. Trouble, you say? Come again?"

Rittenhouse looked down at his clipboard. I breathed in and out deeply. Here was a kid trying his heart out to be a real company clerk in a Marine outfit that had become as phony as a three-dollar bill. It wasn't his fault. I knew I was extremely fatigued and the knowledge that I was the least informed person in the company bothered me deeply. And yet, every time I found out something vital and new it was equally awful and about as far from what the Marine Corps was supposed to be about as was possible.

"Ignore that last, Corporal," I said. "We're probably set in for the day so the Gunny and Sugar Daddy will no doubt be taking this up with me sooner rather than later. Did the tracers come in? What about food and water?"

"Yes, sir," he replied, turning and walking back toward the LZ. "Five gallons of water for you sir. You can have your men hold the big bottle up and sort of take a shower. You need a shower, sir. The Gunny ordered it special for you."

"Who would have thought?" I said. "How nice. Not that I need a shower that badly." I grimaced at the thought of how bad my physical well-being had suffered since arriving in country. I was one muddy stinking mass of ambient oils, stickers, blood and mud. My leech bites were infected and my socks had dissolved when I'd taken off my old boots. How could my socks dissolve in only four days, I wondered in amazement.

"Got any extra socks, Corporal?" I asked Rittenhouse.

"No sir, socks are in short supply here. Gotta requisition from Supply."

"Get me a hundred pair," I replied. "White, fluffy, and new."

"I'll get right on that, sir," he answered. "Four pairs of white athletic socks."

I watched the kid write it down. I knew I'd changed because the kid was as old as I was but that's not how I saw him, or anyone around me. I was growing older and older by the second.

I spent the next few hours moving from re-supply to different parts of the company, trying to find out who was who and where they all fit in, however they fit in. My scout team and Fessman followed, carrying boxes of tracers. I retrieved eight AK-47 rifles. The rules of engagement did not allow for the use of enemy weapons by Marines. In my case, I wanted no ammunition shortage problems and I wanted to be able to see where the Company's rounds were going at night.

We returned to our hooch area just after mid-day, the heat building toward furnace conditions. Even with no mist, the moisture in the air was palpable. Everything felt greasy instead of wet. I saw the Gunny hunkered down for coffee between our poncho-liner tents. At least he hadn't moved away from me yet, I thought with relief. He wasn't alone. Sugar Daddy squatted to his left. The only good news was the clean looking big plastic container of water sitting up under my poncho liner. I knew that after dealing with the Gunny and Sugar Daddy, I would need the full five gallons for a deep, cleansing shower.

nineteen

The Gunny and Sugar Daddy looked at me when I approached, but neither man stood up. I hadn't expected them to. I was becoming fully adjusted to life beyond Marine training and stateside barracks behavior. I dumped my supply of C-Rations, and other stuff I'd gotten from the re-supply piles, on my poncho liner before turning to squat down and join them.

"Fourth Platoon has a problem with the new guys," the Gunny began, his coffee steaming up out of his canteen holder held right next to the dying chunk of composition B he'd used to heat it.

I looked around. Once again Fessman, Stevens, Zippo, and Nguyen had somehow managed to blend back into the jungle, taking Pilson, the Gunny's radio operator, with them. Both Prick 25 radios left behind continued to comment and hiss meaningless transmissions through their small speakers.

"The FNGs can't read or write, and that's a problem," I said, taking my time in pulling my own canteen holder out from under my small stack of junk at the poncho's edge.

"Fourth Platoon's all black," the Gunny said, looking directly at me, a bit of anger making its way to the edge of his facial expression.

"That's another problem," I replied, "but the times they are a-changing."

"Funny," Sugar Daddy noted, speaking for the first time.

"Things have worked that way for some time," the Gunny said, looking away to cover his growing frustration.

"Yeah, I noticed how they've been working. What's our body count going to be tonight? We lost seven last night and we didn't even attack the hill."

"Under your orders," Sugar Daddy said, his eyes invisible behind his gold-rimmed purple sun glasses.

"Beside the point," the Gunny cut in quickly.

"The point's that those white, honky motherfuckers aren't coming to my platoon at all," Sugar Daddy spit out, his voice low and challenging.

"I don't see how we're going to avoid that, Daddy," I replied, not meaning to bait the man but not really caring, either.

"It's Sugar Daddy, not Daddy," he replied, his voice more heated. His body started rocking slightly back and forth. "And we can avoid it if you're not here anymore."

I stared across the six or seven feet of space between our positions. I took everything in, from the mud on the Gunny's boots to the nearly invisible face of Nguyen in the low jungle growth. My holster had no cover, mounted down low on my right hip. The .45 canted backwards from my squatting position with the safety off. With a round in the chamber, all I had to do was cock the hammer back as I drew and the Colt would be out and ready. I slowly put my canteen holder down in the mud and eased my right hand down to my side. I smiled as nicely as I could while I did it.

"Take it back," the Gunny said softly.

I didn't move, my entire body beginning to relax, my right hand feeling like it was hot and tingling.

"What?" Sugar Daddy said, looking back and forth between the Gunny and me.

"The threat," the Gunny said, almost imperceptibly, moving a little back and away. "Don't threaten him. Take it back."

I stared at Sugar Daddy, the embodiment of everything that was wrong about Vietnam, the Marine Corps in Vietnam, and my being forced to endure both. I knew Sugar Daddy had to die. I felt it in my very core. There was no better time. None.

"Okay," Sugar Daddy finally forced out. "We'll sort it out some other way."

"You heard him," the Gunny said, still inching away, "no threat. We'll work it out."

The words "work it out" reverberated back and forth in my mind. Where in hell was "work it out" in any Marine manual of operations or organization? Work what out? The horror of the whole nightmare? A Marine Corps company that thought it was living out Golding's *Lord of the Flies*? A murderous race war going on inside the cover of a merciless guerrilla war? A bunch of brain damaged kids who couldn't read or write wandering about a combat zone, and we were supposed to help them! Work it out my ass...

"I think I'm going back to my unit," Sugar Daddy said into the silence that had begun to stretch from seconds into minutes.

"Wait for a bit" the Gunny said to me, his voice soft and convincing. "Let it go. Just this one time. Let it go, for me."

"Let what go?" Sugar Daddy asked, looking from the Gunny to me and back.

"Shut the fuck up," the Gunny hissed, without turning to him, his eyes locked with my own.

I could not go against the Gunny. Seeing the doubt in his eyes surprised me. Didn't he know how I felt? I thought about Fourth Platoon's position. I'd registered it earlier in my tour of the area. Could I overlook the killing of so many of his men simply to assure that Sugar Daddy didn't shoot me after dark, or find some way to have his men "ambush" me in the future? I decided that I could. I eased back and started breathing normally again, realizing that I hadn't been. My hand still rested on the warmly satisfying butt of the Colt.

The Gunny turned to Sugar Daddy. "Take the new guys for now and we'll talk about this at our next position," he ordered.

Sugar Daddy frowned, removed his specially made and flattened bush hat, fanned himself with it, and then slowly stood up.

"I'm not afraid of him," he said, talking to the Gunny and ignoring me. "Officers come and go out here, none of them lasting very long." With that he tossed the remains of his own coffee into the jungle not far from where Nguyen lurked, and walked away.

"I'll handle him," the Gunny said, staring after the disappearing Marine who looked more like a character out of some eighteenth century poem than a modern combat outfit.

"What's his rank," I asked, looking in the same direction.

"Buck sergeant," the Gunny replied. "Can you believe we're reduced to running platoons with buck sergeants?"

"Stay away from his area," I said, knowing I'd made a mistake in not killing him on the spot, and wondering how long it would take to rectify that mistake.

It was coming down to who was going to kill me first, Jurgens or Daddy, or some of their Marines. It was as if the North Vietnamese Army wasn't even playing in the same ball game.

"So, we're moving out?" I asked, having caught the inflection in his nuanced exchange with Sugar Daddy.

"Yeah, looks that way. We're headed into the A Shau at first light."

I waited out the day in my hooch, Fessman nearby, finally able or willing to access the real combat net frequency. I waited for the order to move on. The Gunny talked back and forth with Battalion Command, and the fiction of our taking Hill 110 would go on until we moved out in the morning. Rittenhouse transmitted the fiction of the number of enemy killed in action by the company. There were no wounded, of course, because there were no casualties at all, and a wounded enemy might have to be turned over to be taken for "retraining" in the rear. I lay back under the poncho cover, the sun making it too hot to be exposed directly to its rays. I kept my helmet, with the cloying fiberglass undercover, on my head, along with my long sleeved utility blouse. I hated the bugs more than the heat. I hated the leeches more than the bugs. And I hated being afraid all the time more than any of it.

I thought about macho man back at the re-supply LZ earlier. He looked so much like I wanted to be. Solid, steadfast, clean and ready for anything. We'd only exchanged looks, because of the noise of the rotor blades. He'd twice stood tall under them while I'd pitifully crouched before him. But he'd brought my boots special. Somehow, he'd read the manifest and seen the request. He'd had to go to Supply and get the right size, and then carry the pair, especially aboard the chopper, separate from everything else. Why had he done that seemingly tiny chore himself? It was a thought that would have made me smile in my former life. I wanted to grow up to be just like macho man. He was real, living a real life, moving back and forth across a death strewn battlefield, taking it all in without having to be terminally afraid or attacked by bugs, leeches and mud, or even other Marines. Maybe he took some incoming up there in the cool air, but I wasn't sure. When his time was up he'd go home with tons of war stories and war souvenirs, like my uncle in WWII had done. I'd be dead. Maybe I was the only emotional connection he gave into, between our distinctly separate and different worlds.

Stevens and Fessman held the heavy five-gallon plastic bottle high in the air for my shower as I stripped and washed my entire body under it's splashing flow. Fessman contributed an unopened brown box that said "soap, surgical" on the outside. It was a substitute for something else but the printing about whatever it substituted for had worn off the box. It was strong stuff and I relished in its nasty cleansing aroma.

I used up the whole five gallons, the last to wash my feet. Water filled my little moat when I was done. I dressed, wondering if I'd ever wear clean clothes again. Maybe I could get Rittenhouse to requisition the new jungle utilities later in the day for next resupply. Nobody around in the unit had them yet.

Unbelievably refreshed, I started my next letter home, writing the same mundane stuff to my wife as I did to my parents. There was nothing in either one about Sugar Daddy, or any of that. Two letters. Both free. No need of stamps that wouldn't have worked in the moisture-laden heat anyway. I could write all I wanted. I saved a nickel every time I mailed a letter, the thought somehow comforting. I wrote about my new boots. They weren't really new. Macho man had gotten them from somewhere strange in Supply, or maybe not there at all. Used boots in Vietnam. I pictured a little stand set up in the rear and staffed by some capitalistic Vietnamese urchins with a homemade crooked sign: "Qualidy Used Combat Boots." Used boots were better, though. Perfectly broken in and conforming to my feet like glue, since I didn't have any more socks. Tons of green socks in training but none to be found in Vietnam.

The Gunny returned as the day came to a close. I presumed he'd spent plenty of time discussing Fourth platoon with Buck sergeant Daddy, or whatever his real name was. I realized that Rittenhouse would know, but then, it didn't really matter. We only needed real names for body bags and medevac.

"Where does Rittenhouse set up?" I asked Fessman, wondering why his hooch wasn't near that of the Gunny and Pilson.

"Wherever the LZ is," Fessman replied. "He checks everything in and out, including whatever we're short on. Then he has to dispose of what's left behind whenever we move."

I was familiar with the logistics of combat units in action. That part had been in the Quantico training courses, although only at the platoon and squad level. Supply was a constant prodigious undertaking. Ammo, batteries, medical supplies, food, water, tools, explosives, flares, grenades, clothing, boots, and what they called "sundries." The sundries came in sealed packs to everyone every day. Soap, toothpaste, shaving cream, throw away razor and cigarettes, came in a sundry pack. I hadn't gotten my first sundry pack yet because Battalion had taken longer than usual to find out I was assigned to it.

Jurgens showed up, looking uncomfortable as he approached, probably because Nguyen was unaccountably right behind him and making no secret of it.

I stopped what I was doing and stood up. The Gunny sidled across the short distance between us.

Jurgens looked back and forth at both of us, and then squatted down without comment. I went down with him, the Gunny following suit. Nguyen stayed behind the man, but only a few feet away. I frowned at my Kit Carson Scout, but he gave me no expression back. The man was as inscrutable as was most of his language.

"First Platoon wants to set up an ambush along our course of travel on into the Oh Shit Valley tonight," Jurgens said.

He used a stick he'd brought along to draw a crude mud map of the company's presumed path of travel. I wondered if the pasted together part time replacement for a real platoon commander had a real map. The one to twenty-five thousand quarter maps issued were inlaid with satellite photo enhancement and gave a pretty good representation of the area, albeit without many contour intervals for positive position placement.

"Why?" I asked, fully recalling every word of the conversation I'd overheard in the bush earlier.

"Why what?" Jurgens said, looking over at the Gunny for some explanation.

The Gunny remained quiet, making believe he was studying the few lines Jurgens had drawn in the mud.

"Why are you here in front of me about it?" I rephrased my simple question.

"Because..." Jurgens replied, obviously becoming flustered, "the rules of engagement say that we have to clear all ambush set ups with the CO, that's why."

"Gunny, you want to handle this little operation?" I said, looking the Gunny straight in the eyes. I knew the Gunny could not be a part of the little deadly game being played in front of me, but I didn't know if he knew and was simply avoiding or ignoring it.

The Gunny didn't answer, as if he were trying to make believe he wasn't there. This told me he had an inkling of what was going on, and I wasn't comfortable with that revelation at all. I fought to control my temper. Why was it that every time I faced any of my noncoms, other than the Gunny, my right hand started to tingle and my whole being began to shift its attention to the Colt on my waist. I resisted the temptation to rest my hand on the weapon for reassurance, and preparation.

"Setting ambushes is a command authority thing," Jurgens said. "It's in *The Rules of Engagement*."

The Rules of Engagement, I thought… The six-inch book that sat on its own pedestal back at Bonner's Division office. Like a valuable old Bible, only the head preacher was supposed to read it, although everyone in the 'flock' was subject to it.

"What's the difference between killing and murdering?" I asked him.

"What?" Jurgens replied, a strange expression on his face.

"Killing is terminating human life while you're obeying society's rules, where murdering is termination outside those rules," I informed him.

"What are you talking about?" Jurgens asked, obviously baffled.

"Last night," I shot back, staring right into him. "You lost three men last night. The guys with the foot problems. It's all there, the difference between killing and murder. Rules of Engagement."

"Are you accusing me of something here?" Jurgens asked.

"You can set up your ambush," I said, ignoring the man's question. "I'll send the scout team here to check the position. You might want to stay in position because I'll work the artillery night defensive fires around your unit, in case things go the wrong way. We've got to make sure the artillery comes down exactly where its intended to come down."

"We don't need any artillery at all," Jurgens responded, "It's just a simple roadside ambush."

"It's my job to make sure the men are as secure as we can make them, like you took care of your platoon last night," I replied, my voice going lower by the word.

"You sent them back to the platoon, not me," Jurgens forced out.

"And I lay down the registrations and fire of the artillery to take care of the company," I responded. "Rules of engagement, as you say."

"What do you say?" Jurgens asked, turning slightly to face the Gunny.

The Gunny looked back at him and then over at me, his expression flat, unreadable and as inscrutable as Nguyen's.

"I think in some circumstances, a man's got to do what he thinks is best," he finally said after a minute had gone by.

Jurgens stood, messing up his little makeshift map in the mud with a stick.

"I hope the ambush goes well tonight," I said, getting to my feet. "I'll be up checking out the position. Tell your men not to shoot me by mistake. I'll be sure to do the same thing for them with the 105 registrations."

Jurgens turned and walked away, looking at first like he might walk right through Nguyen, who gave him no ground at all. After he eased around the Montagnard, Jurgens disappeared into the jungle. Nguyen nodded to me ever so slightly and I nodded back, not having any idea why. Nguyen then went off in the same direction as Jurgens. I stood thinking how I had a thousand times more confidence in a foreign scout who didn't speak English than I did in one of my own Marine platoon commanders. It wasn't right but I didn't know how to fix it.

"You're playing with fire," the Gunny said, staying squatted down and working to get out a cigarette and light it.

I hunkered back down to join him.

"You think so, Gunny?" I replied. "And here I thought we were playing with high explosives, grenades, machine guns, and a bunch of damaged children."

twenty

THE FIFTH NIGHT

The sun was low enough to allow for some cooler air to flow among the bamboo and cypress jammed jungle around me. Low enough to allow the mosquitoes to begin to form their more than annoying small clouds, as if they possessed group minds in search of evil-conceived targets of evening opportunity. I rubbed the never-ending supply of repellent I carried all over my exposed parts, still trying to get used to the strange smell. It was like my freshman year in college when I learned to accommodate the lousy taste of beer before coming to like it. Maybe the repellent would work that way, too.

"Chickenman" played on Fessman's small radio. Chickenman had boarded a jet liner in mid-air on his way to Minneapolis to be the guest speaker at a chicken and egg convention. I didn't find the plot funny except for the part where Chickenman presents his Chickenman identity card to the stewardess to get her to let him on-board.

"What kind of super hero shows an identity card?" I asked absently of Fessman, sitting right next to me.

"I wonder if Chickenman wears dog tags," was his response.

I looked up from working on my letter home — the follow-up to the one I'd written the day before telling my wife I would not be coming home. Chickenman was a welcome interruption, revealing the rather obvious fact that Fessman hadn't even heard my question. It reminded me of the exchange I'd had earlier with Sugar Daddy. Only the Gunny had figured out that I was going to shoot the man right where he squatted. Sugar Daddy hadn't had a clue. He hadn't picked up on a thing, like Fessman with the Chickenman question. Maybe under extreme tension, anger, despair and fear, people didn't really understand much of what's said to, or around them.

"Chickenman wears dog tags," I answered. "He's Army, so of course he wears dog tags."

"Army?" Fessman replied, looking over at me intently.

"Yeah," I said. "No Marine would ever wear feathers."

"Hmmm," was Fessman's only reply.

I wrote to my wife about the possibility that the company would come together and I would be alright. I wrote about the Gunny being the wonderful father figure I sort of believed him to be. I wrote of Fessman, Stevens and Zippo, hoping that she would not take the previous day's letter too seriously, although I was glad I'd written about the things she'd have to do. That I wasn't coming home, that part, would only reveal itself on a later day.

Brother John came on, from Nha Trang, with the final musical piece of the day. Fessman's tinny radio pumped out a song called "Holy Moly" by Quicksilver. Brother John, announcing the title in his comforting baritone, sounded better than the song itself.

I finished my letter and then thought about the coming of night. The night before I'd lain in fear of Jurgens and his angry Marines coming to do me in, while I'd also twisted and shuddered from the plunging small arms fire intermittently raining down from high positions on Hill 110. What had changed? Now fear chilled me to the bone that Sugar Daddy and his Marines would come in the night to take care of what Jurgens' men had failed to do, although First Platoon was obviously not out of the 'kill the lieutenant' game with its ambush plan. I could think of no other reason for the ambush. The only road leading between the peaks and running half the length of the A Shau valley was Highway 49, but that road ran directly inland of Hue, many miles to the north. With no road, where was the ambush supposed to be set up? In spite of what I'd said about sending my scouts to check out positioning, I couldn't. I wasn't going to risk them getting caught in the net Jurgens intended to pull over me.

I got up and walked toward the Gunny's hooch. The Gunny would know what to do. He came out from under his poncho cover upon my approach. I waved off Fessman, ever attached to my right shoulder. He backed off, but not far. I straightened my shoulders. A very few of the Marines around me were caring and protective, while almost all of the others were uncaring or murderous. It wasn't right but it was the way it was.

I'd brought a block of the Composition B. I tore off a chunk, lit it with safety matches from a sundries pack, and settled down to heat the water I carried in my canteen cup holder. The Gunny sat on the end of his poncho. I noted that his exposed skin didn't seem to be sodden with repellent, like mine. A crazy thought flashed through my mind about the possibility that his being Hispanic gave him some sort of extra protection.

"The ambush," I finally said, since he obviously wasn't going to mention it.

"First Platoon," he replied, answering without telling me anything.

"Yes, First Platoon," I said. "What happened a while ago, with the ambush that killed First Platoon's lieutenant?"

"Who told you about that?" the Gunny asked back, confirming everything I didn't really want to know was true. The discussion back in the bush hadn't been my imagination, or slanted the wrong way.

"What was the lieutenant's name?" I asked, trying to draw him out.

"Harrison," the Gunny replied. "I'll join you." He moved over to his pack and combat rig to get his own cup and coffee. I knew he was stalling for time, so I just waited, stirring my own coffee, which was more than hot enough.

"Was he a good man?" I asked, when he got settled in. I pulled my cup aside so he could use the still-burning explosive.

"Yeah, he was okay," he answered. "Like you. He could read a map and call artillery."

"So, what happened?" I said, going for broke.

The Gunny made his coffee, ignoring the question. I waited.

"You think they're connected?" he finally got out.

"There's no road," I informed him. "There's probably a path not far from here leading up between the peaks. The last time they pulled this stunt there was a road. Jurgens didn't know he was giving anything away when he mentioned it."

"That's it?" the Gunny replied, taking a sip of his steaming coffee before going on. "You figured all that out from his using that one word?"

I didn't reply. There seemed no need to. I might have shared the story I'd overheard in the bush with the Gunny but what was the point? Nobody in the entire company was coming clean about anything, at least not where I was concerned.

"What are you going to do?" he finally asked.

"Oh," I said, pausing, and then faking a laugh. "I'm just going to slither around in the mud tonight wondering if I'll somehow end up inside an ambush intended to kill me, or maybe run into one or two of Sugar Daddy's Marines trying to cut my throat sometime before dawn."

"That's not what I meant," the Gunny said, "and you know it."

"For one thing," I said, thinking while I talked, "I've got to move us off that hill to some supposed nearby position so we can suppress fire that's going to come down from there again. And this is our second day in this position. They haven't been asleep up there."

"Heavy machine gun," he replied. "Yeah, I was thinking about that, and maybe RPGs and some other junk too. We could move out."

"Can't move out until they tell us," I said, pulling out a map from inside my right chest pocket. I unfolded it. "Here's where we are, exactly. The river is there, at our back, too deep to cross. Hill 110 is right here, and there's only steep paths on each side of it starting the climb necessary to reach the A Shau."

I pointed at each place.

"There's not only no place to go but there's also the fact that the NVA commander's probably going to figure out we're headed into the valley. Those paths will be littered with booby traps when we start the climb tomorrow."

"Okay," the Gunny finally said, after staring at the map for a few minutes. "What are you going to do?"

He'd returned to his earlier question. He'd told me about Harrison. I owed him something for that, although not the whole truth. Nobody was owed that where I was.

"I can't call artillery on our own position because the battery won't fire, and in order to fire on the hill, I've got to report our new position as being right where we are, so you can stop worrying about that being an option."

"This can't work for long like that," the Gunny replied, dumping the remnants of his coffee onto the still burning explosive. The coffee had no effect, however, and the Comp B burned on. "It won't work if everyone in the company's afraid of being killed by artillery or in some other manner."

The Gunny stared at me intently. "By you."

The Gunny raised his voice in saying the last sentence. Fessman openly laughed. I turned to glare at him. He immediately retreated back to Stevens' hooch, where Zippo and Nguyen sat working on their short-timer's calendars. Almost universally distributed and carefully maintained by nearly everyone in the company, the calendars were all similar in one respect — each had a full page frontal nude drawing of a woman, her body divided up into 395 tiny blank pieces, all numbered. The number one was always printed on the small triangle of the bottom of the figure's pubic region. One day and a wake up, when that box was filled in, was all you had left in the 'Nam, given that tours were all thirteen months long.

"I'm going to suppose that the men here were all frightened to death of the other sets of officers who served here before me and went home in body bags." I stared at the Gunny after falling silent.

"There's that, but still…" he commented.

"Those officers are all dead, but here you are," I said. I realized my error when his expression changed. "I'm sorry, I didn't mean that to come out that way,"

I followed up at once. I needed the Gunny desperately. I couldn't hold him to any moral standard because there were no moral standards where we'd found ourselves. That the Gunny was still alive after surviving with the company in continuous combat for over a month was surprising, no matter how he accomplished it.

His features softened following my apology. "So what about Jurgens and Sugar Daddy, and all of that?"

"I think we may have bigger problems tonight if they've brought in heavy stuff up on that hill, and then there's the trail we've got to climb up tomorrow. We don't have many 81 millimeters rounds left. I've got to suppress fire all through the night and then put one round every fifty meters up that trail until we're out of range of the battery. But that part's for the morning, if you're still worried about First Platoon's ambush."

"There's no ambush," the Gunny said, his voice dropping to just above a whisper.

"True," I replied.

The ambush was a façade to be used only as a device to lure me into some killing ground. It wouldn't take much of the night for Jurgens to figure out that a repeat of the Harrison murder wasn't going to work.

"So, what about First and Fourth in the night then?" he went on.

"I need the Starlight scope," I said. I'd thought of telling him he could move his hooch further away but bit my tongue in time. It would have been a snotty emotional comment. And, I didn't want him to move away.

"For what? The damned thing's near useless," he replied. "We can see them running around like wild chickens across the barnyard but can't use the scope to aim or shoot them. By the time we look up from the thing our night vision's gone and so are they. And it doesn't magnify anything either, so anybody more than a hundred yards away is invisible."

"I don't need it for range."

"Then what," he asked.

"All of that, as you said," I replied.

"Rittenhouse's been hauling it around on his back," the Gunny mused, almost to himself. "He'll be happy to part with it. Maybe your scout team can hump it from here on. That Zippo's huge. Useless, but huge."

Zippo was perfect for my needs, however. I could not use pre-registered fire to protect us from a heavy machine gun position on the hill. The NVA regulars weren't stupid or inexperienced. They'd been fighting for longer than I'd been in the Corps. They'd simply move under fire. Which meant the artillery rounds had to move, too. I would have to adjust fire and I could only do that from moving positions close to the base of the mountain. I needed to see where the artillery rounds I called in were impacting. I'd need Zippo to haul the stuff, Stevens to be the lookout, Fessman on the radio, and Nguyen for the other stuff. The other stuff being those Marines from First and Fourth who would be out hunting for me while I was trying to save them from the NVA.

I moved back to my hooch in the waning light, darkness closing in on me. I'd never been afraid of the dark growing up but now it terrified me. I promised myself that if I lived, I'd never spend another night without light. I couldn't help but wonder what my great Fort Sill instructors would have thought about the real job of an artillery forward observer in the combat world I'd dropped into. Of course they'd have trouble believing it. I sat with my envelope home, wondering if this would be my last letter telling Mary everything was going to be okay.

twenty-one

THE FIFTH NIGHT : SECOND PART

Zippo didn't get back from retrieving the Starlight scope from Rittenhouse until full dark. There'd been no fire from the hill. I'd registered our new position but not ordered a fire mission. I knew it wouldn't be long. I wasn't afraid of taking fire from a heavy machine gun nearly as much as I was from the prospect of the NVA attacking and penetrating our lines, or what might come of the obvious threat from First and Fourth platoons internally. By the time I moved to Zippo's hooch to try out the scope, I realized my shaking hands were back. Longer than an M16, the scope weighed twice as much. It was like handling a thick length of sewer pipe with a big rubber grommet on one end. The night mist returned, combining with my repellent soaked hands to make the black metal hopelessly slippery. Handling the ungainly scope, in conjunction with my shaking, was nearly impossible. The case for it had to be bigger than Fessman's radio. I wondered if the thing was worth the effort until Stevens flipped a switch and I pushed my eye into the rubber grommet and stared into the lens. A strange whirring sound came from the device. Strange but reassuring.

Green light everywhere. Shadows of green light in the distance. I knew I was seeing things in the dark that were impossible for a human eye to detect, but I couldn't make them out. Everything moved too much and the scope seemed to be slowing things down. If I moved the scope at all it seemed to take part of a second for the green scene to catch up.

"You've got to prop it up on something," Stevens said. "It came with a tripod but that got lost somewhere."

I laid down on Zippo's poncho cover and propped the "sewer pipe" across the back of his pack. I pulled the scope and pack closer, and then stared at the jungle not far away. I knew it wasn't far away because I'd seen it during the day, but I also knew because I was seeing it at night. The view was astounding. The wind wafted across the tips of different kinds of jungle growth. I watched, feeling like I was hypnotized. I could even see the moisture falling and blowing around in the air. It looked like rolling green mist. I watched the Gunny light a cigarette in his hooch twenty yards away. His lighter flared briefly, like a street light burning out. I saw every green feature of the Gunny's face. Gazing through the scope took some of my fear away, and I didn't want to stop looking through it.

"It works best across cleared areas," Stevens said, "and tracers coming in make it impossible to see anything because it takes a while for the tubes, or whatever, to recover from bright lights."

I pulled away from the addictive device. I noted that my hands had stopped shaking.

"What case does it come in?" I asked, wondering how much space on Zippo's back it would take. I'd already decided that I never wanted the scope far from me at night if I could help it.

"Case?" Stevens said, "It straps to the outside of a pack with a sock on each end."

"No case," I replied, shaking my head. "Lost somewhere, no doubt. Let's move out," I ordered. "We're headed straight for the perimeter just short of the hill. Maybe we can use the scope to find the best way through the muck."

"There's a path not far from here," Fessman pointed out, getting strapped into his radio rig.

Nguyen leaned out of the dark and whispered to Stevens.

"No path," Stevens said. "We'll break some trail south and come around along the western perimeter," he went on. "Wouldn't want to run into an ambush," he finished.

I wasn't sure about whether my team was looking out for me or for themselves, or both. But I appreciated it.

"When we get set in to observe, I want the scope out and operational, pointing behind us," I ordered.

My team had picked up on the phony ambush routine, or seen it before, so I fully expected they'd understand what I was trying to do.

"Everyone's got tracers now, sir," Fessman said, standing nearby and ready to go. "The scope doesn't work around tracers."

"I'm not worried about anyone shooting," I replied. "At least not until they find us. I want to see them coming first."

Zippo carefully slipped two socks on the ends of the Starlight scope and slipped it over his shoulder. He'd found a rifle sling from somewhere. The heavy scope was like an invisible twig on his broad back. I noted that he carried a mostly empty pack in his right hand.

We didn't wear packs inside the wire, especially when we expected to engage the enemy. Without a deep foxhole to dive down into the only protection available from some threats was the ability to move.

Creeping through the brush was hard work, even with Stevens and Nguyen breaking trail in front of me. Fessman and Zippo followed up. If visible in daylight, I'm sure we resembled hunched over dirty lobsters as we crept around and then straight up to the perimeter.

"Who the fuck is at our six?" came back from up ahead.

We automatically slunk down into the mud on our hands and knees.

"Arty up," Stevens half-whispered toward whoever manned the perimeter ahead of us.

"What do you think this is?" the voice hissed back. "Fucking officer country?"

I listened to the exchange, knowing that I was crazy and not caring. I wanted to take out an M33 grenade and lob it forward. That would take care of the problem. A craven need building inside me to do something about the flagrant insubordination and the lack of one shred of respect toward me was a basal force driving my emotions. I knew it, and what remained of my sanity made me hang on. Instead of replying or taking action I simply waited in silence. My normal role.

A form appeared from out of the nearly invisible mist.

"Over here," the voice said.

The form moved back the way it'd come, and then away when Stevens and Nguyen settled in, their bodies pressed up against a beaten down hillock of reeds.

I joined them, pulling out my map and my taped up flashlight with the small hole in the center of its lens.

"Who was that?" I asked, unfolding the map and looking out to see what I could see of the hill in the dark, which was mostly nothing.

"O'Brien, Second Platoon," Stevens said.

I recorded the name into my memory for no good reason.

"The handset," I ordered softly, holding my right hand out behind me.

The handset magically entered my open hand.

"Fire mission, over," I said, knowing Fessman would already have changed the frequency to the artillery net.

I put one round of white phosphorus above what I thought was midway up the near side of the hill. I used a super quick fuse since I didn't care if anybody on the ground was injured or killed. Seconds later the shell exploded, briefly showering part of the hill with flaming particles of the horrible burning substance. For some reason wooden bullets, like the Japanese had used on some of the islands of the WWII campaign, were banned by the Geneva Convention, but not the use of much more horrible napalm and white phosphorus.

The flash of light was enough to let me see the whole hill but gone so quickly I couldn't adjust any fire using it. I called in for a battery of three using illumination rounds.

"Your position is on the gulf tango line," came back over the radio instead of "shot, over." "Calculating casing and base impacts now. Are you in contact?"

"Negative on contact," I sent back.

"What did they mean, sir?" Fessman asked, when I handed the handset back.

I wasn't intending to fire high explosives until incoming fire began. I wanted to have the layout and plenty of potential targets of opportunity, however, when that happened. I had not thought about the company's position on the gun target line. That meant that the guns were directly to our rear and had to fire over our heads to reach Hill 110. Since we weren't at the extended maximum range of the howitzers, that wasn't much of a problem for regular rounds, but illumination ammo came apart in mid-air a good distance from the target. Where the canister and baseplate holding the parachuted flares landed was sometimes life or death information.

I explained the delay as briefly as I could to the team. The fire direction center was busily calculating where each piece of every round was going to fall. They would not fire if any of those pieces were likely to impact on our position, unless we were in contact and absolutely had to have the light.

Minutes later, Fessman answered the shot and splash warnings. The rounds came screaming in, distinctive pops coming down from on high when the shells opened to permit the flares to complete their travel and rain down on the target. The *whup-whup-whup* of the canisters sailing on through the air could be heard after the illumination rounds lit up the scene like an old black and white television screen.

I studied the hill intently, making notations on my map, but I didn't have long to work. The illume rounds were still up there doing their thing when the heavy machine gun opened up. Green tracers began stitching back and forth along the perimeter line. The company had set in earlier, leaving one rounding curve of reed covered hillocks to be the natural perimeter between the company and the hill.

I burrowed into the mud. The giant fast-moving beer cans of green light fired by the gun blasted by. Terror swept through me, only relieved by the fact that I knew I had a twenty-foot thick berm of mud between the gun and me. That relief was short-lived, as a couple of lower rounds exited the berm right next to where I lay cowering. The fifty caliber bullets could go right through twenty feet of mud. That just couldn't be, I thought, my memory of the weapons underrated capability in combat slowly returning. The .50 armor-piercing rounds would go through up to five inches of steel. Twenty feet of mud was no problem.

The machine gun stopped firing. I peeked out but the illumination rounds had burned out so I couldn't see anything to adjust fire on. I shrunk back down, slowly realizing my mistake. I had illuminated the entire area between the hill and our own position. The gunners on the hill had taken advantage of the light to register their machine gun so it could accurately deliver fire all along our perimeter without the need to see the target. My own Army training methodology had been used to good effect. On me. "You're not in Fort Sill anymore, Dorothy," I intoned under my breath to myself.

"Why are their tracers green?" I asked Fessman in a whisper, just to make human contact. My hands were shaking badly again, but they only did it if they had nothing to do. I folded my map and then opened it again, and again, and again.

"Ours are all red," he answered, also whispering.

I waited, but after a few seconds knew that that was all the answer I was going to get. It was a physics problem and Fessman was seventeen. Physics was still ahead of him if he went on in school. I also knew that the color had something to do with the composition of the material used in the tip of the round. Magnesium burned red in a lab using a Bunsen Burner. I couldn't remember what burned green. Copper. But copper wasn't a material that would ignite on its own and trace across the sky. I knew I was thinking about the composition of tracers because I was so afraid. "Displacement activity" it was called in anthropology. Anything to avoid facing the threat directly.

I forced myself to rise a few inches and look over the edge of the berm again.

"Assholes," I breathed. "Fire your chicken shit little machine gun. I have artillery. Big boom."

I somehow felt better and my hands stopped shaking in saying the words, even under my breath. I also wanted the binoculars badly. It was hard to feel like a real forward observer without them. They also would help penetrate the darkness. Not like the magic of the Starlight scope, but some.

I saw the machine gun open up again only because my head was up high enough over the berm. I ducked down, but I had an idea where the things were up on the hill, at least approximately. My mind had also recorded a second series of flaming bullets coming by me, from not thirty yards forward of our position.

I hunched back down. I wanted to say something to Fessman but couldn't get anything out. Artillery. I couldn't call artillery. The battery wouldn't fire this close and they knew where we were now. Thoughts bounced around in my head as the perimeter Marines opened up with their own machine guns and M16s. Somebody else had seen them coming. Grenade. I had two M33 grenades. I pulled one out, held the perfectly round little spewer of death and pulled the pin. And I lay there frozen. The spoon of the grenade was depressed with the death grip of my right hand wrapped tightly around it. In that position I'd become frozen, unable to get the grenade out with my body lying face down, the M33 and my fist crushed between my chest and the mud under me.

I breathed deeply in and out, trying to get control of myself. My ears rang from the nearby gunfire. After a while the shooting stopped and a silence fell over the whole battlefield.

"Fessman," I finally grunted out, the side of my face in the mud.

"Sir?" Fessman said back, leaning down close to be able to make out my words.

"I've got a grenade under me and I pulled the pin," I got out, my voice hoarse from fear and pressure. I still imagined the enemy racing up and over the small berm to bayonet me from above.

I felt someone else move up to my right side.

"Forget the pin," Stevens said. "Just roll over and throw the grenade as far as you can out there. We'll back up." I heard Stevens slither away.

I had control of my breathing. Could I simply roll to my left side and toss the grenade over the berm without killing myself or any other

Marines? And what must my team think of the stupid predicament I'd put myself in?

I rolled and threw the baseball size grenade, all in one motion, like I'd been taught in explosives ordinance disposal training back in Quantico. The spoon audibly clicked as it flipped itself away from the round body of the grenade. It was gone. Five seconds later there was a sharp crack as it exploded.

I edged my way back up on the side of the berm and turned, sensing movement.

"Fire mission?" Fessman said, pressing the radio handset into my hand.

It took only a moment to call in the topmost registration numbers back to the battery. I called for a zone fire mission after the single adjusting round landed just where I'd calculated. The battery then dropped six rounds on the point I'd chosen and six more on four other points forming the end of an imaginary X calculated by the FDC.

We set in to wait. If and when the fifty caliber opened up again, I would call for either a repeat of the same barrage or move the initiation point around until it was close to where a new position for the gun had been found. Ammunition, like for the 81s on loan from Lima Company, was limited in the field but there was no end to the amount of artillery that could be called throughout the night. The only real limiter was demand from other units in contact, if there were any.

Things remained quiet for some time. Nobody moved about at all but nobody fell asleep either. I patiently marked where the Hill 110 rounds had impacted on my map. When I was done with that I started counting. One one thousand, two one thousand, and so on. If I could count the long night away — if I could just live until morning — I might have another day. I figured I would probably be on a hundred and forty thousand or so, before first light.

"We've got company coming," Zippo said, his nearby voice low and his words slow.

I moved backwards and down from the berm, and then crawled across the mud flat to join him. Fessman trailed behind while Stevens and Nguyen were already next to Zippo when we arrived.

"What have we got?" I whispered.

"Some of my old friends from the Fourth," Zippo said, moving aside from the Starlight scope so I could stare through the green lens.

twenty-two

THE FIFTH NIGHT : THIRD PART

The NVA Russian-made fifty caliber opened up, and the heavy green "flying lantern" tracers tore through the thick air over our heads. I popped my head up for a micro-second to confirm that they'd moved the weapon lower down on the mountain's front slope. I adjusted my plan for an in depth response, this time for thirty-six rounds on each of the four points of the zone "X" I'd recorded earlier. It was a simple "drop two hundred, repeat in depth" mission, but I had bigger problems closer in than that. Instead of reaching for Fessman's handset I crawled up next to Zippo.

"Get the Starlight out," I ordered.

"How you think I see 'em," he whispered back.

"Where is the damned thing?" I asked, unable to see the black instrument in the dark.

"I'm slipping it on my back," Zippo replied, continuing to whisper, although the Marines or NVA approaching had to know exactly where we were anyway.

I got hold of the slippery scope lying across Zippo's right shoulder, then eased myself half way up onto his broad back. I stuck my left eye onto the rubber mount and my world turned green. I blinked, and then looked out into the night. I pulled back and blinked. The scope was an all or nothing night device, and I realized my night vision was shot. If you used it, then one eye would be night blind for some time and, since human eyes acted in sympathy for the most part, that meant night blindness. The bright green vista revealed by the scope drew me back. I used the focus knob to sharpen the flat area between our position at the back of the berm and the area out to the forested jungle. The scope moved slowly up and down, distracting me.

"Hold still," I ordered Zippo.

"I gotta breathe," he replied.

"No, you don't," Fessman whispered, from behind us. "We don't stop them right now, whoever they are, and they'll kill us all. No witnesses."

The scope stopped moving as Zippo held his breath. What looked like three blobs of mud moved slowly across the open grassy field. One would move and then another, and then the third. "Fire and maneuver," the movement was called in combat. Here we had a similar situation, without the "fire." The three blobs had worked together in the past, I realized. They did what they were doing too well and too soundlessly. With all the mud and no head gear, we couldn't tell if the slowly moving blobs were Marines or the enemy. I breathed deeply in and out, Zippo still holding his own. It didn't matter who they were. They weren't moving toward us to share rations, warn us, or to give us a message. They could only have one intent, and that made them the enemy, regardless of their originating outfit.

I'd briefly examined the scope earlier and it didn't have an attachment for any rifle in our company. The bottom screw holes on the device's one flat side would probably allow it to be mounted on a sniper rifle, but I hadn't seen any snipers since I'd joined the company. If snipers had been attached to our unit, they no doubt would have taken the scope to use on their own. Rittenhouse wouldn't have had to pack it.

"Breathe," I ordered Zippo, speaking very quietly into his right ear, the scope sticking out over his big burly shoulder.

I eased my .45 from my holster and brought it up. With no way to slave the automatic to the scope, in order to fire I'd have to parallel the scope with the short barrel of the gun. With one eye looking through the scope and the other out to steady the Colt, I'd have to accurately get the rounds down range with my night vision shot — a task unlikely to have positive results. But there was no other option.

"Stop breathing," I commanded, and Zippo stopped moving.

I stared through the reticle of the scope with my left eye and brought the Colt up experimentally, to see what it would be like. Then I lowered the gun and re-inserted it back into the holster. We'd have to wait. In order for it to work, the blobs needed to be almost upon us, or I could call in an illumination round to light up the area. That would mean the blobs would be able to see us, too. And then there was the Battery problem. The Battery wouldn't fire that close in upon our position anyway. I started to think of the three moving blobs as a puzzle.

"Breathe," I ordered Zippo.

I still had unused pieces of my sundries pack in my leg pocket, jammed in with the killing morphine. I rummaged in the pocket, nervous about waiting for the mud blobs to get closer. I found what was looking for: a small box of Chiclets chewing gum. I threw the little tabs into my mouth and discarded the box. I chewed rapidly, waiting for the gum to soften before removing the wet mass from my mouth. I pulled it into three parts and leaned onto Zippo's back again.

"For your right ear," I said, before sticking half the wet mass into his right ear canal.

The .45 going off so close to his ear would deafen him, possibly for life, without some sort of ear plug. I stuck the other two smaller wads into my own ears.

"Stop breathing," I instructed, leaning onto him, jamming my left eye into the rubber grommet and then pulling my Colt out again.

I clicked the safety off, the sound much louder than I intended. The three approaching blobs froze. I waited, gauging the distance at about fifteen feet. I wondered how long Zippo could hold his breath. I knew the blobs were not going to back up so it was a matter of time before they moved again.

I raised the .45. I didn't want to hold it up for too long since it was a heavy piece and accuracy diminished rapidly when muscle tension began to give way. I'd been raised with a similar Colt, although highly accurized. I was an expert on the Marine Corps course, but even better than that range test had called for. Even un-accurized, the weapon was plenty accurate at fifteen feet. The longer I could wait, the less would be my chances of missing.

I steadied on the first hump, my sight going back and forth from focusing through the scope to lining up the gun. The humps moved. The Colt was no doubt sighted in for twenty-five yards, I thought, which would be standard sighting from the factory. I'd have to hold a bit low since they were closer than that. I aimed, if I could call it that, just short of the first advancing hump. I squeezed slowly, not knowing when the heavy trigger would release the sear, just as I'd been long taught to do. And then Zippo breathed and the gun exploded.

"Shit," I whispered, wondering if I should squeeze off another round. I stared through the scope, but it was moving up and down with Zippo's breathing, screwing up the scene.

My Colt was down to five rounds. I'd kept one in the chamber and five in the magazine, even though the magazine held seven. Dad had taught me that loading seven might cause the upper tang on the magazine to bend, making the normally dependable automatic a one shot device.

The humps didn't make a sound that I could hear with the gum stuck in my ears. The Colt going off had been loud anyway, but not ear-destroying loud. The humps did not move. Zippo took a deep breath and held it. The scope steadied. The two humps behind the leading one began moving in toward the front blob. Even with Zippo's jarring breath, I knew I must have gotten some kind of hit.

Then I realized that I was adjusting fire, and it was just like calling in artillery. I'd used the first round for a spotting round and it had been dead on. I held the .45 up again, just as before, then gently eased it left a little bit and at about the same angle the first shot had gone off at.

"Left five feet," I whispered to myself. The Colt exploded again. This time I kept my left eye right in the rubber grommet. The left hump stopped.

"Right ten feet," I instructed myself. The gun went off again.

Zippo took a breath and I briefly lost the scene.

Just at that instant the heavy machine gun on the hillside opened up again, raking green fire over our heads. This time the flaming bullets raced lower than the last. The berm was not going to stop the horrid gun from killing us. Moving the machine gun up there after the last artillery barrage must have been difficult for the NVA, I knew, but I was also certain that the gunners would get in the groove soon and home in. The company had nothing of size except the 81 millimeter mortars to retaliate with, and their ammo was expended until the morning re-supply. I reached back for Fessman's handset and wonderfully it filled my hand.

"Fire mission, over," I said, and called the mission in from memory, thinking about the fire I'd adjusted with the smaller hand howitzer a few seconds earlier. I set down the handset and, not waiting for the rounds to land, turned my attention back to the three humps.

"Stop breathing," I ordered Zippo, and then used my left eye to look through the Starlight scope at my three targets, hopefully still out there in the mud.

They hadn't moved. That was either good or bad I decided, with nothing yet to be done about it. The green tracers started up, but only about ten rounds came out of the heavy machine gun before the assorted forty-six-pound variety of high explosive, variable-time and concrete-busting rounds started to tear Hill 110 apart. The artillery fire went on and on. The ground shaking thunder and cracking atmospheric noise of well over a hundred rounds pouring onto the mountain drew and held every bit of attention on the battlefield. And then it was over.

Distant cries of seeming protest came across the stilled misty air from the mountain. The enemy would not be destroyed by carpets of artillery fire, no matter how dense those might be, I knew. The enemy soldiers, used to being out-gunned and out-numbered in every area, were dug in deep. But anyone near the surface had paid a price, those bodies and souls still alive, but quite possibly wishing they weren't, broadcasting some of that price.

I thought of calling in a carpet of variable-timed white phosphorus, just to keep the underground enemy from coming up for awhile, but I had other business to conduct first.

"Nguyen," I whispered to Fessman, more as an order than a request for his presence.

The small enigmatic Montagnard appeared in the dark without having to be summoned further.

I nodded my head over in the direction where I knew the three humps of the enemy lay, glancing through the eyepiece of the Starlight to make sure nothing had changed. It hadn't. The shapes were in the same places as when I'd looked before.

I crawled away from Zippo's side and Fessman crawled with me. I gripped him by the shoulder.

"You stay close," I said, probably whispering louder than I thought because of the gum I'd left in my ears. "I'm going out there to check them out. I'm not going to lie here all night watching through that damned scope. Stay behind me, but not too far behind, in case that fifty opens up again."

I drew myself slowly across the mud and reeds toward where I'd last placed the three humps. Without the scope, a flashlight or overhead illumination rounds, I couldn't see much of anything in the dark, and none of those three choices were available. I felt Nguyen move in front, angling me off a bit to the right. I guessed the Montagnard to be a lot more capable in the dark than I was, particularly since we'd reached the base of the mountains and were fighting virtually in his back yard. I could barely see the bottoms of his boots in front of me, but that was enough. When we got closer I could see the mildest reflection of the moon's small sliver coming over at me from the three unmoving lumps to my left. About ten feet from the leading hump, I stopped to lay down for a few seconds. Nguyen continued to crawl or slide across the mud until he was beyond the forms.

"Are they ours?" Fessman said, from behind me.

I eased the Colt from my holster, hoping that the mud hadn't jammed the gun beyond use.

"Are they wounded?" Fessman asked.

Taking great care, I brought the .45 up to make sure the barrel pointed parallel to the mud. I held it with the butt resting lightly on the ground's gooey surface. I fired three timed rounds, each about three seconds apart, and each into the center of mass of each hump, as best I could gauge. There was no movement.

"They're the enemy," I said, answering Fessman and re-holstering the empty Colt." And they're not wounded."

I rolled to one side on the muddy surface and turned around to begin crawling back to our original position. I had another magazine for the Colt buried in one of my back pockets. Only five rounds in that magazine. I eased over the mud, moving as fast as I could. I had to get out of the open area and back to some semblance of cover before reloading the Colt. For a few moments, getting the Colt reloaded was the only thing on my mind.

Somehow, Nguyen was already back when I slithered up to the raised mound we'd departed from. Fessman came behind. I reloaded carefully, slowly and quietly. I'd killed my first three men in combat. I felt nothing at all. I tried to think about caring but couldn't. All that mattered was to have the Colt ready again, as quickly as possible, and then adjust fire onto the hill when and if the hill demanded to be struck again.

Zippo lay where I'd left him, still pointing at the unmoving forms with the heavy Starlight scope stretched across his back.

"Can I breathe now?" he asked.

I realized he was making a joke, and also that it wasn't a bad one, but I couldn't smile, much less laugh out loud.

"You can breathe, and then mount that thing on top of a pack or something so we can scan the area until it's light. Do we have extra batteries, and how long can we keep it on without burning them up?"

"Rittenhouse thinks of everything, sir," Fessman replied. "I've got the batteries with my extra radio ones. They're not heavy and they last for about twenty hours if you leave the thing on."

"Were those guys from my old platoon?" Zippo asked, working in the dark to fold something to rest the scope on.

"I don't know," I said. "Likely we'll know everything when the sun comes up."

I'd lay two more zone adjustments down on Hill 110 before that dawn. Once again, I had no recollection of sleeping, although I experienced moments, or even longer periods of time, where I wasn't fully conscious. The battlefield grew quiet before the coming of that dawn, to the point where the four of us decided to move slowly back to where we'd located our hooches. If Nguyen hadn't been a part of our team, we'd have needed the scope for the return trip.

I laid down on my dry poncho liner to wait for the dawn. My hand slipped down to the hump resting uncomfortably in my right thigh pocket. I prayed there would be no wounded requiring that kind of pain-relieving morphine between now and then. I thought about meeting the re-supply chopper, mailing my letter home and counting the bodies when the time came. There was little doubt in my mind as to what kind of enemy I'd been forced to make my first kills in combat, and I didn't want to add any more. I worked the small wads I'd fashioned for ear plugs out of my ears. I'd need to be able to hear in order to listen to both the Gunny and Sugar Daddy after the sun came up. I didn't have to be a rocket scientist to know that there would be plenty of recriminations in the morning. I lay with my right hand caressing my reloaded Colt, my left squeezing my letter to be mailed home for all it was worth.

twenty-three

THE SIXTH DAY

Full dawn would not come. I lay there, looking at my little Fessman-dug moat. The mist had stayed all night, which I now knew to be the precursor to the monsoon season. It could get worse. It would get worse. Just how in hell God would figure out a way to make it worse, I didn't know. Only that it would definitely get worse. If I hadn't lost my sense of humor I would have laughed. How about keeping every little bit of "Dante's Inferno" the way it was written while adding pouring rain for twenty-four hours a day? I'd read in college that the highest suicide rate ever experienced fully by any organized body of humans occurred in India after the British took over the tea plantations up north there. It had rained for two hundred and twelve days and nights straight. Fifteen percent of the entire occupying British force committed suicide before the rain let up. Many of the dead were the wives of the English officers.

I rubbed my face with both hands, the repellent oil now a part of my skin structure so it felt like rubbing a soft lubricated pumpkin. I knew why morbid thoughts dominated my mind. I'd just killed three men up close. I hadn't seen their faces, but guessed they were black Marines sent on a mission to kill me. They'd crawled across the mud flat, probably scared to death, and they'd died the way they feared they might. Killed by an insanely frightened lieutenant who didn't know, or couldn't figure out, what else to do. The fact that I didn't care enough also concerned me. I couldn't reach any center of my soul where guilt, sorrow or contrition should be. It reminded me of being a kid again after confession at the Catholic Church. As soon as I'd confessed my sins, then repeated the appropriate Our Fathers and Hail Marys, that was it. Done. Sins forgotten. I knew I should feel bad. Now there was no confession. No forgiving Catholic priest smiling wisely down upon me, assigning punishment prayers. Just me, the bugs, the mud and my .45.

"Fuck," I whispered to myself.

Tomorrow, if it would only come, would probably be the last time I saw the light of day. I doubted even the Gunny could save me from the two opposing factions, both now committed to making sure my existence on the planet was over. I tossed and turned about killing the men and whatever feelings I should have had, but didn't. When I stopped thrashing about, my thoughts congealed back into my own personal world of terror. Thoughts of what discoveries the morning would certainly bring faded to backstage as a plan began to hatch itself in my mind. I grabbed my flashlight with it's little hole cover in place, took my one-to-twenty-five-thousand photo map from my pocket and crawled out of my hooch.

The Gunny slept. I laid down next to him in the mist, guarding my paper-holed flashlight and map. I marveled at the man's ability to seemingly sleep so comfortably. I waited, staring, my unending patience fueled by terror. My hands did not shake, however, and for that I was thankful. Maybe I'd been there long enough to get used to it — a thought as awful as the terror itself.

The Gunny's eyes opened. Through the darkness I could only make out the whites of his eyes, blinking rapidly. His head turned fully to look at me, only inches away. He said something but I couldn't understand him.

"Shit," I intoned, "The gum." I stuck my flashlight and map under the Gunny's poncho while I worked my fingers in and out of both ears. I still had the chewing gum embedded from last night.

"What in hell do you people want?" he whispered, sticking his head out into the mist.

People? I wondered, before hearing little sounds I hadn't been able to pick up with the gum stuck in my ears. I turned to take in Fessman at my right shoulder, Zippo and Stevens just beyond my left, and Nguyen barely visible behind them. I turned back to the Gunny, not having any better idea of what the others were doing there than he did.

"I've got a plan," I said, my voice soft, as I unfolded and spread out my map on a part of his dry poncho liner. "They have to know we're pulling out of here. They have to figure that we'll either head back into the Go Noi or we'll climb up into the mountains overlooking the A Shau. Because of the river, there's only two ways out. By now they'll have mined and booby-trapped both of our options."

I used my black grease pencil to roughly outline the depression we'd be forced to follow up into the A Shau after sunrise.

"Fifteen clicks," I pointed out. "Fifteen thousand meters, divided by five hundred meter increments. I adjust one round onto the path every five hundred meters, which will take about a hundred rounds from the battery to perform, given adjusting fire."

I stopped and looked the Gunny in the eyes.

"Yeah, so?" he answered.

"Sympathetic detonation," I said, sounding enthusiastic, I hoped. "One forty-six-pound round will go off on the path and the blast wave, using a concrete-piercing fuse, will set off any booby trap or mine within fifty meters. All the way up the path."

"Like a mine-clearing operation using explosives," the Gunny mused, leaning further forward to study the map. "Like they use with those long lines of explosives on the tanks. Okay, sounds good. Why are you telling me now?"

"There were some casualties during the night and tempers are probably going to run high," I said, folding up my map and turning the flashlight off.

"That was your Colt firing last night?" the Gunny asked, although I knew it wasn't a question.

Although it had only been six days, I'd become pretty adept at identifying every weapon fired by its distinct sound. The .45 made a very distinctive barking sound when it went off, not like the crack of a 16 or the longer thunder of a .50. The Gunny could not have missed the different sound in the night from such a close position.

"There's likely to be trouble," I replied, avoiding answering his question directly.

"And this is your plan to take care of that?" he went on. "Without you to call in this shit tomorrow, the company suffers from booby-trap casualties. So everyone needs you."

"Something like that," I agreed, surprised he'd caught on so fast.

"Might work," he said, after almost a full minute to think. "But what are you going to do when we get to the A Shau tomorrow night?"

"Tomorrow night," I repeated flatly, without adding anything more.

Another full minute went by. I felt my scout team behind me, totally silent but totally all there, waiting. I wondered if the Gunny had modified what he was saying to me because of their presence, although I'd never know the answer.

"Bird-in-the-hand kind of a thing, or tit-for-tat or something," the Gunny said.

I didn't respond, except for getting my stuff together to crawl back to my own hooch. When I got back out into the mist, the Gunny called out once more from behind me.

"How many?" he asked.

"How many what?" I threw back over my shoulder, moving away.

"God damn it," he said, but he let it go.

Back under my own poncho I asked Stevens, "Who's on the scope?"

The three of them knelt a few inches out from my moat, dawn not far off. I shivered at the thought.

"Well?" I asked.

"Nobody coming now," Stevens finally replied. "Too late in the morning, so we quit watching to save the batteries. They will only sneak around in the night."

"We all sneak around in the night, if you haven't noticed, sergeant," I answered. "Go do what you guys do before we move out. You make up your mind," I finished, pointing at Stevens.

"About what?" he asked, in a tone of complete surprise.

"You know damn well what," I replied, wondering what I might do with a scout sergeant who wouldn't back me. But I couldn't think about it further. I had to get my mind ready for Sugar Daddy, Jurgens, the Gunny, the complex artillery fire I'd have to put together under the most difficult of terrain, and the rest of what was likely to come. I hadn't mentioned to the Gunny that we were running out from under our supporting firebase. The 155 battery could reach all the way into the A Shau but not very far into it. By the time we got to the top of the ridge overlooking the valley, we'd be just beyond safe 105 range, even at maximum charge for those howitzers. And the rapid response multiple-round-firing 105s meant just about everything to my staying alive. The Marines around me only whispered when they spoke of the A Shau, like it was some sort of special hell compared to the regular hell we were already in.

I laid on my back in my hooch and my mind went blank for what I thought was a few seconds, but when I opened my eyes there was light. Morning had opened at the first light, as the song lyrics went. I reached my hand inside my front pocket to squeeze my letter home. It was there, but I wouldn't breath easier until I turned it over.

Sugar Daddy and several of the men from Fourth Platoon already squatted by the side of the muddy path that ran between the Gunny's and my hooch. I hadn't heard them come up, or noticed The Gunny leave. Only Fessman sat nearby, waiting for me to arise.

My right hand moved slightly to glide over the comforting outside edges of the .45's butt.

"Truce," Sugar Daddy said, extending one hand out toward me, the other gripping a canteen holder, as if the three of them had simply been passing through and stopped to heat up some coffee.

I had five rounds. I knew a single round in the center of mass, from close range, would take down the largest of humans, even if only for a few seconds or moments. The other two would take side torso shots but that would leave me with only two rounds left, and that wasn't enough for the three finishing head shots I would need.

I got to my knees, leaving my hand on the butt of the .45, and then crawled forward to the edge of my poncho cover. I estimated the Marines to be ten feet away. If I got closer, I could take them all with head shots and have two more extra rounds left over. I liked that thought. I rose up and walked to where they squatted before squatting down a little distance off. They all had their hands occupied with canteen holders held over burning composition B explosive chunks.

Advantage in, I thought, my hand on the butt of my Colt. The automatic was off of safe with a full magazine, but no round in the chamber. I regretted that I had not been paranoid enough to properly reload when I'd gotten back to my hooch. I'd never make that mistake again, I knew.

It would take me a full two seconds to pull the .45, operate the slide with my other hand, and then squeeze off the first round. Two seconds — a long time in a gun fight — even if the other men facing me had their automatic weapons decked, butt down on the surface of the mud. It might take them a full second to figure out exactly what was happening, and then maybe a second or more to get into action. Risky? Most certainly, but a risk I felt well worth it to take.

I knelt on my right knee instead of squatting. Drawing it would be faster and the gun, less likely to catch on anything as it came out and I put it into action. I glanced behind me briefly to make sure Fessman wasn't in the line of fire, or any of the rest of my team. It was clear. I was clear.

The Gunny came walking out of the jungle growth just behind Sugar Daddy and his two accompanying Marines. He moved up behind Sugar Daddy. I could not shoot without fear of hitting him, either by mistake or because a .45 slug at close range doesn't tend to stop when it hits a human body, not even one of Sugar Daddy's size and not even it it's a head shot.

"Truce, you said?" he asked of Sugar Daddy, finally moving to one side and settling down to squat between the platoon leader and the Marine to his left.

I made no move to do anything, frozen in position, waiting for just the right moment.

"Did I hear you say truce?" the Gunny asked again, since Sugar Daddy simply concentrated on reheating his coffee over the burning explosive.

"Some of my people bought it last night," Sugar Daddy said, his eyes unreadable behind his purple sun glasses, impenetrable to normal light.

I looked at the three men from Fourth Platoon with disgust, but showed nothing in my facial features. The Marines embodied everything that could go wrong with the Corps. They didn't obey orders or follow traditions. They dressed the way they felt like in what appeared to be Halloween costumes. Personalized smashed flat hats of some sort, gold chains they'd found somewhere, with strange pendants hanging from them. None of them wore Marine utility attire except for their trousers.

"So I heard," the Gunny replied. "Rittenhouse and I'll be doing the paperwork to send them home. That .50 took out a few more in the other platoons, as well."

"My guys were shot with a big caliber side arm," Sugar Daddy said, taking his right finger from his canteen holder and pointing at my side. "Like the one Junior there wears. You can't mistake them big holes. Each one got a round in the head at close range and then again in the body."

I would have shot the man then and there if I'd thought to load a round into the chamber before they'd appeared. I waited instead, for a better moment, hoping the Gunny would move away.

"They were good Marines," the Gunny said. "And it's not likely that Junior here has enough experience or guts to shoot anyone. Not yet, anyway, so maybe the .50 on the hill is a more likely cause."

"That fucking green shitting thing tears a man to pieces and you know it, and not like any sidearm does," Sugar Daddy replied.

"You said something about a truce as I walked up," the Gunny lied.

I knew the Gunny had to have been waiting in the bush and heard the first exchange, or more likely was behind the whole meeting. I wondered why he hadn't been in his hooch when they showed up. I also wondered if, when I killed all three of them, the Gunny and my scout team might think it was because Sugar Daddy called me Junior. Not that I would change my mind, I concluded, as I'd already learned that respect didn't matter at all if you simply killed what didn't respect you.

"Truce," the Gunny repeated, watching me instead of them.

The man was prescient in some way, I realized, or he could read minds. I did not want him interfering or getting in the line of fire for what was going to go down, so I slightly shook my head without looking into his eyes, refusing to take my focus away from the three targets.

"Junior here's obviously a racist, like those clowns in First Platoon," Sugar Daddy said, his two Marine buddies nodding, as if their leader's speech was prearranged. "But it don't matter out here 'cause, except for that artillery stuff, he don't mean shit." The two men with him grunted while continuing to nod. "Leave us be and we'll leave him be. Just like before they sent him in."

"Deal," the Gunny said, extending his right hand out toward Sugar Daddy.

I could not believe my ears. I stared at the Gunny's outstretched hand like it was some sort of alien artifact. That the black platoon wanted to go on like before was befuddling enough, what with a nightly KIA rate between the warring platoons greater than anything the NVA was inflicting, but that the Gunny, a long-time veteran of three wars, readily agreed and then shook hands with a lower enlisted man, as if they'd just negotiated some minor business deal, was astounding. My mind reeled in shock.

After the Gunny and Sugar Daddy shook hands, everyone stood up as if by an unheard unseen command — everyone except for me. I knelt there with one knee sunk in the mud like an idiot. Frozen in place, I gripped the butt of my Colt while life seemed to go on around me. The three black Marines walked back into the bush. The gunny pulled out his canteen, poured some water into the holder and started preparations to make some coffee, ignoring me entirely.

"Deal?" I hissed across the space between us.

"Good morning, lieutenant," he replied, not looking at me, making believe the fixing of his coffee took all of his attention.

A minute went by. I finally stood up shakily and then hunkered down across from him. I took out my own canteen, hoping he had enough coffee for both of us because I was out and it would be an hour before resupply arrived.

"You sold me on the artillery magic," the Gunny finally said, getting his explosives lit. "You're going to pull that off later this morning and I've seen what you can do. Booby traps are the worst we face out here. I don't care if I get killed nearly so much as going home without my arms or legs, or even my balls."

He tossed a brown foil container of coffee to me, as if to punctuate his last sentence.

"And so you made a deal with that black devil in my name?" I said, my anger evident, but accepting the foil coffee.

"In your name?" the Gunny said back, his anger meeting my own in the space over the fire between us. "Your name is Junior, if you didn't notice. And you weren't going to get all three of them. They're better than that. They've been out here for a while. They were locked and loaded and casually ready. And they know about you."

He stopped talking to take a sip of his coffee, looking over the lip of his canteen holder. Our eyes met for the first time in the early dawn's dim light.

"If I live," the Gunny said, "which seems a pretty big if just now, I'll be damned if I'll go home to a dishonorable discharge, or worse."

I sat staring into the man's coal black eyes, some sense of reason returning. Getting ready to kill Sugar Daddy and his men had consumed my mind like the focused blaze of an acetylene torch. The flame was gone but the heat remained, like a hazy red fog. A small tremor ran through my hand, the canteen holder I gripped shaking a tiny bit. The Gunny's gaze flicked toward my hand, and then quickly back into my eyes. I knew that he knew I was not quite right.

"So what are we supposed to do with his 'deal' you've made for all of us?" I asked, partly to understand what was going on and partly to cover my shaking.

"Tomorrow night," the Gunny said, and then sipped again, his eyes never leaving my own.

"Tomorrow night?" I replied, not understanding.

"You said that last night, about what we'd do when we got to the A Shau."

"It's today with this 'deal' and we won't get to the valley until late," I said, starting to understand.

"So that would make it tonight, instead of tomorrow," the Gunny replied.

I slowly removed my right hand from its death grip on the butt of my Colt. I moved my canteen holder with my coffee in it to that hand while slowly reaching into my left pocket with the other. I clutched the letter, but not so hard as to crush it completely. It represented the only sanity left in my life. I'd get it on that coming chopper and then start another letter. The Gunny was telling me what I'd told him, and he'd already known. We were living from one day into the night following that day, and the days and nights were divided into segments without titles or names. We could only live from one segment to another, and we would do anything and say anything to make it through and on into the next segment.

"Binoculars," I said, thinking out loud. "I need them…and tracers. We need more tracers. They're working I think."

"Tracers," the Gunny repeated. "Do they make those for .45 automatics too?"

twenty-four

THE SIXTH DAY : SECOND PART

If you go chasing rabbits and you know you're going to fall, tell 'em a hookah-smoking caterpillar has given you the call… played on Stevens' little shoulder-mounted radio. As usual, Brother John's fatherly deep-throated introduction made me feel better just hearing it. Fessman had the same transistor rig stuck in his helmet band and as I listened to the apropos lyrics, Fessman and Stevens got onto the subject of how stereo radio worked. Fessman argued that if a person stood between their two radios, listening to the same transmission over the Armed Forces Radio Network received by both, then the listener would be hearing the song in stereo. Stevens argued that the song had to be sent over the airwaves in separate frequencies from different positions around the singer for that to be the case. I saw where the discussion was going and decided not to step between them to be a part of it.

"Stevens is right," I said, my tone decisive, I hoped.

"See, I told you," Stevens said, the dialogue of both men giving away their young ages.

I got out of my hooch and stretched, more to cover my examination of everything around me than out of a need to flex my muscles. I'd killed three men. Three young and frightened men. And I'd done it without one speck of resistance from my internal moral code. *When the White Knight is talking backwards* came through the little radios, and the lyrics seemed to describe my life and how it had all changed to run quickly and violently right off the rails.

I could hear the choppers in the distance. Heading for the landing zone I hurried through the brush, concerned that if the choppers landed in the same place again as before, the spot might have been preregistered by an enemy very diligent about doing such things. But I could not stop myself from going anyway, even if the zone took fire. I had to mail the letter and nothing else had any real importance. There would be no mail coming to me. My wife was not the writing type and my genetic family, a "lifer" Coast Guard family, wouldn't be writing either. Mary would send a package with the things I'd asked for earlier, but that would be it.

The utility Huey dropped out of the air, both of the usual supporting Cobras flitting about hungrily, waiting for something to chew up and spit out. This time there were three gunships, however, instead of the normal two.

"They always fly in pairs," Fessman said from behind me, the whine and roar of the chopper blades not close enough to cut off conversation completely. "Wonder what happened to the other one?" he went on, until the roar of another helicopter swept across the landing zone in front of us.

The fourth Cobra opened up on the relatively bare and muddy ground of the landing zone, its nearly flat surface covered with shredded bamboo stands, pieces of small ferns, and broken reeds. The gunship opened up with twin pylon-mounted mini-guns. We stood there, neither Fessman nor I having time to get to any real cover. All we could do was hunch over from the intense wind and the screaming fiery roar of the rotary cannons strafing the zone. And then the thing was gone, seeming to flow over the edge of the landing zone, disappearing into some unseeable valley.

I pulled my hands down from my ears, knowing they would ring for the remainder of the day. If I could have called in a fire mission on a moving gunship at that moment, I would have done so. I knew, even with what little experience I had, that the gunship was showing off and trying out its brand new weapons. I'd heard of the rotary cannon, scaled down to fire 7.62mm NATO rifle rounds, but had never heard or seen one in real life. It was bad enough to be nearby when those exotic weapons went off. I could only imagine what it was like to be in front of them taking fire. How the Vietnamese had been able to resist, fight back, and even pull ahead of some U.S. combat units was almost impossible to conceive. The enemy had almost nothing in the way of truly modern or quality arms, yet it persisted to the point where American casualties were in three figures each and every day of the conflict.

Zippo, Stevens, and Nguyen stood roughly back from where Fessman and I waited. I wondered if they were waiting for anything in particular from the resupply, or was it that the small scout team had, for whatever reason, become a tribe within our bigger tribe that wasn't a tribe at all.

The Huey sat nearly still on the two skids running the length of he aircraft, the pitch of its blades reduced to zero, although they whirled around at high speed. Macho Man appeared, jumping down from the craft's open side door past a gunner moving the barrel of his M60 machine gun back and forth across the scene in front of him. Macho Man carried his precious Tommy Gun slung over his left shoulder. In his right hand he held a black leather package. I approached, automatically ducking down under blades that whirled safely at least six feet over my head. The man held out the package, which from its shape could only be a set of binoculars. I smiled and took the package, handing over my letter home at the same time. Macho man didn't smile back. Instead his eyes swept the landing zone looking for potential trouble spots that might call for him to use the Tommy gun that appeared to have never been fired. I instinctively knew that he could not smile for fear that such a human reaction breaking across his combat charade might spread like a terminal crack running through safety glass.

I retreated out from under the chopper to let others approach and do the actual work of unloading supplies. I watched the scene, with the swooping gunships flying and all the men running around below. Jungle bracken wafted upward, sucked into the sky, and then whirled about by the powerful blades of the helicopters. I watched the boxes of tracer ammo being unloaded. Soon tracers would be all the rounds left in the unit and then there would be no more secret shooting in the night, or so I hoped. Unless it was with Colt .45s, I thought, remembering the question the Gunny had asked in humor. Tearing my eyes from the wildly active but strangely hypnotic scene in front of me, I opened the binocular box. I pulled out huge binoculars manufactured by Nippon Kogaku, an outfit I'd never heard of. The field of view, at 7.3 degrees, was good and 7X50 power was okay, too. They lacked caps, a strap, and they had no range estimator, like the expensive Leicas the Army used, but they would do.

The replacements piled off the chopper as I approached. I hadn't given them a second look since I now knew there would be no officer among them. All FNGs. They'd be assigned by the Gunny. Hopefully, there'd be no more of McNamara's *Project 100,000 Marines*. We had three. I had no idea what the allotment might be for disbursing the non-reading undereducated privates. As usual, with resupply, all anyone could do was requisition and then hope. The Gunny appeared with a line of Marines behind him carrying body bags. It took three men to a bag. Bodies were heavier and harder to transport in the field than any-body might guess. They didn't cover that in training, either. I watched the moving bags while slowly grinding my teeth. Training made Ma-rines look and act like they were ready for combat. It did almost nothing to prepare them for real combat, however, and not one person back in the real world had ever bothered to mention that.

I went over to the Gunny, leaving Fessman and the rest of the team to meet with Rittenhouse and scavenge what they could from the supply load.

"You shouldn't be here," he said, as I walked up.

"We're not taking any fire," I responded, thinking he was con-cerned for my well-being.

"Sugar Daddy's platoon is going to be right behind me and they've taken your involvement last night a bit personally," the Gun-ny said, pointing toward a spot he wanted the body bags placed. "Shit, where the hell are they going?" he went on, leaning around and looking upward before putting one hand up to shelter his eyes from the morn-ing sun.

The gunships had climbed to altitude and were quickly becom-ing invisible in the distance.

"What do you mean?" I asked. "Where do they usually go?"

"You gotta get the hell out of here," the Gunny said, heading for the crew working at getting the supplies unloaded.

"I don't see anybody from Fourth Platoon," I murmured to his departing back.

The Gunny turned his head and yelled. "The gunships are gone."

My team ran by me, back the way they'd come, with Fessman saying "Come on, sir, we're going to need you" as they passed.

"What for?" I shouted at their fast departing backs, starting to lope after them until some sounds hit me like thudding drum beats. The extremely distinctive sounds that could only be one thing on earth. The sounds of mortar charges going off and launching their killing loads high into the air. Forty seconds, on average, before impact. I ran like hell, shouts of "Incoming!" behind me.

In seconds I made it back to the area of our hooches. Fessman waited on my poncho cover, his radio already on the ground with the handset held out toward me.

"Where?" I said, grasping the black plastic tube in my right hand.

"I don't know," he answered. "With mortars we never really know. They don't smoke and they move them all the time."

My team looked up at me from their sitting and squatting positions nearby. They looked at me like I would know. I took the handset, having no clue as to where to direct the fire.

"Fire mission, over," I said, knowing Russ would be all over my call. I thought for the three seconds it took for him to come back.

"Contact fire. Repeat last zone then repeat right three hundred, up three hundred, left six hundred, down three, and give me H.E. super quick with confirm reception, over," I finished.

And then I waited. I ordered a lot of ordinance covering a lot of real estate. Were others commandeering the fire? Was I ordering too much for supply to handle? Did I need to intersperse fuses? While I waited the incoming mortar rounds impacted in and around the LZ behind us. Every explosion made all of us wince, although none were close to our position. I wondered if the Gunny had made it out, or the men hauling bodies and after the supplies. I hadn't even gotten resupplied with water or food, much less anything else. I thought about the water and food and then felt bad because I cared more about losing those than losing the Marines, and I knew it.

"Shot, over," came through the tiny speaker on the Prick 25 in Russ's voice. So much for confirmation, I thought. I'd laid out fire all around the mountain, figuring that the cover of the wooded region just distant from our position would be the likely launch point rather than the flatland more visible from the air. I had two more areas to take out if the mortars fired again, but I would wait.

"Splash, over," came in just when the mortars stopped exploding.

The sound of the express train rounds came first and then the real explosions began. They seemed to go on forever, but in the distance, like the artillery in some war movie. Unlike in a movie, where the sound of the rounds was instant with the appearance of a blast, in real life when you called artillery the sounds came back so late that the whole battle scene became eerie and off-worldly. If I'd been positioned to adjust fire at the perimeter, I'd have experienced that but I wasn't on the line and wasn't going near there either.

The artillery fire stopped and everything grew quiet. We all sat unmoving. First the mortar round sounds coming in one side and then the artillery from the other was mind-numbing. There would be no ground attack. The NVA did not attack in daylight unless it was a sniper delay team or sappers laying booby traps along any suspected avenues of travel.

The Gunny appeared out of the jungle, with Pilson, his radioman, right on his shoulder. The Gunny stooped to drop a five-gallon plastic bottle of water while Pilson unloaded two armfuls of C-Ration boxes. Stevens and Zippo moved in to get everything while the Gunny and I squatted to make coffee. Nguyen remained hidden, but there somewhere, I was certain.

"Good morning," the Gunny said, with one of his super-rare smiles.

"Thanks," I replied. "For the warning back there."

"Chopper made it out, but they blew the hell out of six casualties," he said, taking out his fixings.

"Six?" I replied, in shock. "We lost six in the attack?"

"Nah, they blew the hell out of the body bags," he replied. "The three wounded made it out on the chopper though."

"Six?" I said, still shocked. "We lost six last night, then?" All I could really think about was the three I'd been responsible for.

"Machine guns are a bitch on the ground, and then there's the other troubles," the Gunny replied.

I thought about the "other troubles" and then the landing zone being ripped up by mortars. I thought about Macho Man. Maybe he wasn't fighting on the ground in combat but he sure had to be taking some fire in that Huey coming in and out of hot landing zones. Maybe his gunfighter rig, however affected, wasn't so out of place after all. Was it easier to stay in the shit or be able to fly out every day but then have to fly back the next, day in and day out.

"Binoculars?" the Gunny said, waving one hand toward the case I still carried in my hand.

"Artillery," I answered, not knowing what he was getting at.

"We're always too close," he said. "Where you gonna look with them?"

"A Shau," I replied.

"Maybe so, but up there we're out of range for calling fire."

"Beyond maximum effective range," I said. "Not beyond maximum range."

"What's the difference?" he asked.

"About five miles with the 105s," I replied. "The Fire Direction Center doesn't want to fire beyond 18,000 yards but I can get them to fire out to 23,000 in a pinch and from what I hear we're always going to be in a pinch up there."

"Artillery's never fired over the lip up there before," the Gunny concluded, taking a sip of his hot coffee.

I looked through the wavering heat waves the burning composition created, with no smoke. The Gunny wavered a bit in front of me.

"We've never had you before to call fire, right?" he said. "Is that what you're saying?"

"What time do we cross the line of departure?" I asked back. Ignoring the question, I thought about how I would get over to the southern perimeter to begin calling the fire mission I'd designed earlier to clear our path of booby traps.

"You'll have plenty of time," the Gunny said knowingly, smiling his strange smile again. "Last night they got a pallet of Tiger Piss in here somehow. Most of the guys got shit-faced. Strong beer. They're all moving pretty slow for a bit."

"Just great," I responded, with my voice gaining strength as I talked. "You let them drink? Out here? In this shit? With everything on the line every minute of every day?"

"Let them?" the Gunny shot back. "Hell, I drank with them."

"At least you're here and not hung over," I said, exasperated and relieved at the same time.

"That's because I didn't stop," the Gunny said, drinking more coffee.

"You didn't stop?" I said, my tone one of apprehensive surprise.

"Nah, I'm shit-faced right now. Still."

I put one hand on my forehead, set my old binoculars down and tried to phrase some question to the Gunny that made sense.

"So how are you going to lead this company up that path to the A Shau today, if your drunk as a skunk?"

"I'm not," the Gunny smiled his drunk smile. "You are. You're the company commander."

That he'd said those words in front of other Marines was important to me. He'd not go so far as to call me sir, and I didn't miss that, either. He'd been absolutely correct when he said that I was completely incapable of being the commanding officer only days earlier, and I felt he was still correct about that. But with everything else I was coming to understand about the situation, nothing followed any preset plan and day to day, hour to hour and even minute to minute survival was everything. Somehow I was supposed to get everyone to do what I wanted them to do, and absolutely no one wanted to do it. What now, lieutenant, indeed?

"Tell me something," I said, wondering if he'd tell me the truth since he was drunk. "Do we ever really kill any of the enemy, or is that all about as real as the hill we didn't take?"

twenty-five

THE SIXTH DAY : THIRD PART

My scout team took apart my hooch and packed me out while I went forward to the perimeter to lay in the defensive fire up and down the area of our travel. By the time I laid down on a poncho cover provided by one of the Marines on the line, the sun was fast rising over the jungle.

"Do your thing, Junior," the Marine said. I saw Fessman wince and frown at the man, but I did not react at all.

I laid down and brought the binoculars from their case. The path leading up into the A Shau Valley was thousands of meters long and, the start of it hidden in the jungle brush and low-lying trees. The cleft between the peaks leading up to the ridge that stood up over the valley could be viewed for almost half its distance. I focused in and studied the terrain. Even though the glasses didn't give me much more to work with in terms of adjusting fire, having them made me feel better. With range always the hardest thing, by far, to attempt to gauge, not having to adjust the glasses on a single point made things easier. In single target firing, over and under fire had to be used to "home in" on the target. Creeping up on the target shot by shot had been the norm in early artillery, but range had proven so difficult to judge that the French were the first to dump the creeping system, followed by everyone else prior to WWII. Shooting over and under the target and then splitting the distance was faster and used fewer rounds.

I called Russ and revealed my plan in detail, hoping that the battery would have plenty of concrete-piercing and high explosive shells on hand. I asked for a lot of artillery support that wouldn't be going elsewhere, but I needed it badly for my own survival. The Marine's comment, even though he used my disparaging nickname, had been revealing. I seemed to have developed a reputation for my ability to call in artillery for anything necessary to protect the unit. That in doing so I, first and foremost, managed to protect myself in several different ways, didn't appear to matter much, if at all.

"Got it all dialed in?" a voice from behind my back said. I didn't have to turn to recognize the Gunny.

"Roger that," I replied, having received an assent from the battery that it could and would do the job.

Russ had wanted to know what was going on but I didn't have any way to explain things to him because of the open nature of the radio system. Any Prick 25 radio could receive the transmissions. We didn't have encryption, although that had been discussed for years by the Defense Department.

Having the enemy hear anything didn't frighten me nearly as much as what higher ups might think about what I might say.

"When?" I asked, wondering just how drunk the Gunny was.

"Probably kick off in an hour or so," he replied.

"Guantanamera" began to play over Fessman's little radio. The words weren't what I remember from the Seekers song, since they were in Spanish.

"That's a cool song," Fessman said, "but what does it mean?"

"Cuban," the Gunny responded, before I could say anything. "It's a song about the Cuban revolution."

If memory served me from a college discussion, the lyrics told of a lost or unreturned love from a peasant girl, but I said nothing. I'd never been sure about the lyrics, anyway, even though I loved the song.

"I'm going to walk a running series of zone fires up the path all the way to the top just before we start, and then as we move up," I said, pulling my glasses down and turning to face the Gunny. "What about flank security?"

"That's a laugh," the Gunny replied, laughing out loud. "Hill 110 is on our left flank full of the NVA we didn't clear out or kill, and the other hill is unknown. What do you recommend?"

"How about sending First Platoon out on patrol along the flank of Hill 110 and then Fourth Platoon up the other hill?"

The Gunny laughed some more, my attempt at humor weak, but my meaning reaching him in spite of his inebriated state.

"Variable Time," I said, swinging my glasses back up to examine the hillsides bordering the path. "The 155s can reach out this far and if we keep the V.T. stuff up a bit on both sides, we can rain down shrapnel kind of at will. We can't neutralize booby traps that don't operate off of detonation, so we have to watch out for them. Other than that, the biggest fear ought to be the big bore machine gun. If they get that set up on the left flank, then they could play hell back and forth across our strung out line."

I leaned down to check my map, noting that I didn't have a map for the A Shau Valley or even the ridge area where we were supposed to end up.

"How long will it take the company to hump the distance?" I asked the Gunny.

"About four hours, give or take," he said.

I grimaced. Even being inexperienced I knew that the trip would probably take much more time, particularly since it was likely we'd be hit in some fashion and have to set in along the trail. Medevac among the bigger thicker forest was out of the question, which meant any wounded or dead had to be hauled along. To be caught trying to move the last few thousand meters in the dark was too horrid to even consider.

"I'll need to be up near the point to call fire," I said, although deep down I didn't want to be anywhere near the point.

"Not likely," the Gunny said, to my great relief. "You bring up the rear with the feckless Fourth. I'll be up there. It's my place. If we need you, we'll call you."

Stevens, Zippo, and Nguyen joined us, all three wearing heavy combat packs with Zippo dragging mine along in one hand without it touching the mud.

"I'll hump it up the path, sir," he said, setting the pack next to me in case I wanted anything from it, although he didn't comment on that.

"Nobody wants to go up there," the Gunny said.

I put down my binoculars, turned and went to work lighting a chunk of the explosives in the mud.

"The A Shau is that bad," I replied, wondering what he was getting at. "I've heard stories."

"It's a shit hole, one big, long, and beautiful shit hole," the Gunny said, "but that's not the problem."

I tore open a great envelope of coffee and poured the small amount into my canteen cover. Somewhere in my pack I had sugar and cream packages but I didn't know where. Nguyen slipped to my side and stuck two packages of each into one gaping empty pocket sticking out from my chest. The pockets were only usable if you didn't wear the flak jacket that wasn't a flak jacket. The jacket didn't stop high velocity bullets or even hand grenade or rocket fragments. I'd never been issued one since I'd come to the field direct and I wasn't going to try to find one. It was simply too hot and the loads we packed, too heavy.

"Artillery," I said, after a few minutes, reaching for my hot coffee. I'd put my packets in with the coffee powder so I wouldn't have to stir. The Marines around me had K-Bar knives, giant Bowie knives, but I hadn't been issued one of those either.

The Gunny nodded, looking away, his squat so deep and native that he would have looked Vietnamese if he weren't so big.

"Me?" I said, finally connecting the little dots he'd laid out in front of me.

I would have smiled a real smile if I could have. The Marines in the company were afraid of me. It was the first good news I'd heard since the battery had gone along with all my zone fire orders. Admittedly, not too many forward observers called for concrete piercing fuses. They'd have a lot of those laying around, but still.

"I can't call in any fire missions on the company location just now," I said. "The battery knows where we are and they won't shoot."

"God damn it, it's talk like that they're afraid of…that I'm afraid of," the Gunny replied, his tone a plaintive one.

"Oh?" I answered, surprised. "They didn't want to take Hill 110, either."

"And they didn't," the Gunny shot right back.

"Anybody mention anything to them about our flanking companies and the rest of the battalion, not to mention Regiment and Division?" I asked, my voice low but my tone scathing. "They just think we're going to be left on our own to do what we want and move where we want out here?"

I held out my hand behind me and Fessman filled it with the radio handset. I looked first at it and then at the Gunny.

"Fire mission, over," I said into the handset, to begin the series of zone fires that would guide the company up the path and into the dreaded A Shau Valley.

Pilson handed the Gunny the command net handset, but I couldn't hear what he said. The company left as one, with Marines filing by headed toward the break between the two hills. I watched the move begin, wondering how it all seemed to happen automatically without the substitute platoon commanders yelling orders like would have been heard in training.

The rounds began impacting up and down the sides of the hills in another awesome display of distant firepower. I could not see the impacts but could certainly hear and feel the ground waves from their explosions. My plan was nothing new. I'd read of that in the German SS book, just like the tracers. The Germans had been nearly as good at possessing outstanding artillery guns as they were using them. Nobody on earth in the modern era, however, could match the power and precision of American artillery, and the American stuff had one other advantage: the supply of shells seemed endless.

I waited for most of the Marines to pass us by, the Gunny departing with Pilson, not saying a word when he left. They fell in easily with the Fourth Platoon, all black except for the few replacements I'd attached to it. I didn't see them and wondered if Sugar Daddy had used the same solution to his additive problem that Jurgens had. Sugar Daddy appeared near the rear of his platoon, slowly walking by but not stopping as he passed.

"You keep that shit away from us," he said, pointing at Fessman for some reason, like the artillery came out of Fessman's radio.

My scout team picked up the rear. In training the rear guard was important to a unit moving in combat, but not in Vietnam. For some reason the Vietnamese almost never attacked from the rear, probably because all movements of American troops, barring special ambushes or recon patrols, took place in the daytime.

The artillery barrage continued up in the valley, splintering the wooded forest on both sides of the path and turning it into timber charnel houses. Craters from the concrete-piercing pocketed the area. Cordite, the smell of exploded munitions, clung to everything and a very thin layer of smoke floated up from the bottom of one hole and over to fill another. With the sounds of artillery becoming more distant, I moved around the blasted tree stumps, careful not to touch them, the shattered wood edges looking razor sharp.

The sound of the heavy machine gun firing came at nearly the same time as the call "Arty up!" echoed from Marine to Marine down the line.

"Come on," I said to my team, breaking into a loping run through the broken forest where the central path, no longer visible, had to be. I ran for several minutes without looking back, unsure whether at least Fessman followed me. I could use Pilson's Prick 25 command rig to reach the battery but it would be so much better to have Fessman. The big green tracers became visible as the gun fired from high up on the side of Hill 110. Firing in five shot volleys meant that the invisible bullets, without tracer heads, probably numbered about twelve or fifteen more.

The gunners up on the side of the hill could see that I was the only thing visible and moving, every marine I passed either lying behind fallen trees or pressed hard into the forest surface. The tracers came screaming by me, some so close that I thought I could feel their heat. Instead of dropping for cover I increased my speed. Suddenly I found myself face down on the forest floor.

"Stay the fuck down! Without artillery we're dead men," the Gunny hissed into my ear.

I looked around. The tracers continued, hunting the bracken for Marines and occasionally finding one, if the screams coming from the bracken were any indication.

Fessman crawled up, the handset pushed out in front of him. I pulled out my binoculars before grabbing the plastic implement and shoving it under one arm. I leaned into the side of a fallen tree trunk, focusing in on the hill. Two thousand meters, I guessed, because I could actually see the gun and crew. It was as if the artillery before, and now the clearing operation, had made no impact on them at all. Four men seemed to man the gun, one doing the shooting and the three others supplying the ammo. I found it hard to see actual movements but I knew exactly what they were doing because the tracers, before they ignited, left the end of the barrel with a series of yellow flames, almost like a toy flame thrower if ever one existed.

"In contact, break zone and fire mission, over," I said into the handset.

I wanted the 105 battery because the 155s would be in defilade from the side of the hill I wanted to target. They wouldn't be able to get down on the hill where I needed fire. I called for one round up over the very apex of the peak. I had that grid and code memorized. The round came in less than two minutes later, dead on target. The white phosphorus, or Willy Peter, exploded like a chunk of giant fireworks and then showered its burning contents down into a big beautiful fountain.

I dropped three hundred, hoping to establish a point between the machine gun and me. This time I asked for H.E. Due to my proximity, it would be easier for me to see the impact, even in the cloying clutter of the forest. The round came in about a hundred yards below the gun and I smiled a cold smile. The gun crew had stopped firing and started to pack up, but not soon enough.

"Battery of six," I called, "up one hundred and fire for effect." Russ had been waiting at the FDC and alerted the gun crews. The first six rounds came in only seconds later. Then six more and so on, until 36 rounds shredded the small area, where the gun once sat. It was impossible, even with the binoculars, to see if there had been a gun there, or any humans nearby.

The Gunny crawled over. "Jesus Christ, you blew the living shit out of them and you only called in two rounds. Wow. I'm putting you in for a medal for that run. That was classic." He got up and took off toward the front of the path where he'd obviously been before the unit got hit. I lay there breathing hard.

"A medal," Fessman said, more to himself than me.

From behind him jubilant laughter came from the rest of the team. I would have joined them if I'd been able to laugh anymore. A medal. What use was a medal to a bunch of dead men?

I listened to the sounds of wounded men being cared for and shushed by their friends. My hand edged down and over the bulge in my trouser pocket.

THE SIXTH NIGHT

Booby traps that weren't made with detonators or explosives subject to sympathetic detonation couldn't be destroyed, disabled, or damaged by the rolling artillery barrage I'd designed, and that the battery had applied so effectively. The machine gun had caused significant casualties before the artillery had blown it and its emplacement to hell. And now three lowly punji pits, along with one sniper, had brought the company to a dead stop. Punji pits were made by digging a shallow hole and then inserting sharpened up-pointing sticks into the mud at the bottom of the little pits. The sharpened sticks layered in human feces, and generally barbed as well, penetrated the bottom of any Marine's boot unfortunate enough to plunge through the disguised hole covering. I'd heard rumors that the newest issue of jungle boots had a triangular aluminum bar built into the soles that made them punji pit proof, but nobody had seen or been issued such a set in the company.

The Gunny called me up to the point in order to attempt to deal with the sniper. The company came to a halt as the sunset. The evening mist and the lugging of casualties, along with packs and the other equipment necessary to operate a reinforced Marine company, had already slowed our progress to a snail's pace before the sniper showed up and stopped it completely. As I moved forward the going became more difficult. Walking became climbing and the mist on the forest floor made the strewn plant life and blown-apart wood pieces as slippery as the mud. I labored toward the point, with Fessman cursing behind me as he carried the twenty-pound radio with extra batteries. It didn't take a genius to figure out that the company itself would never make the ridge before dark. The Marines I climbed around to get to the point were all digging in and setting up for a night that had not come yet.

I finally arrived near where the Gunny lay talking on the radio, Pilson not far away with his Prick 25. Each platoon had small radios called "sixes" leftover from the Korean War. Most didn't work at all unless the operators could see one another. They looked like giant bent bananas, green in color. A Marine with one of the six radios talked on it.

I presumed him to be the acting platoon commander, probably talking to one of the other platoons over the limited range radio.

A shot rang out from somewhere in front of us and everyone ducked down, even though anyone I could see already squatted, or lay under or behind, some sort of cover.

"Anybody hit?" the Gunny yelled.

No answer. I reached for the artillery net handset and Fessman complied instantly. I really appreciated his ability to sense my needs from a single gesture.

"Fire mission, over," I sent.

"A lotta good artillery's going to do when you can't see shit," the guy with the six radio said.

"This sniper hitting anything?" I asked, surprised by the sniper's last shot being placed to hit no one in particular.

"He's a lousy shot," the Gunny replied. "Hasn't hit shit but we can't move past him until we take him out. They're probably stalling us so they can set up an ambush ahead. Can't flank him successfully because of the size of the clearing in front of us. If we'd taken Hill 110…" his voice trailed off.

"In contact, one round Whiskey Papa," I said into the handset, and then read off my second to last zone fire coordinate key, with code from memory.

"Your position?" Russ asked, his voice coming over the little speaker built into the top of the Prick 25.

I hastily calculated where we were likely to be, and although the body of the company lay strewn behind me for nearly a thousand meters, the battery only ever asked for one grid coordinate. The FDC would approximate "check fire" radius using its own numbers and approximations. I could have taken a bearing on Hill 110, visible on our left flank across the valley, but after my run through fire, however inadvertent it had been, I was in a wild guessing mood. I gave the battery a number and seconds later the Willy Peter lit up over the top of the path about a thousand meters in front of us.

"Told you," the six radio man said, as the sniper fired another round into the jungle bracken somewhere nearby.

I motioned for Stevens to come, as the scout team had followed me in my move forward.

"Watch the trees up ahead," I said. "We have visibility for about a thousand meters. The sniper's using an AK that's well beyond its effective range, and he's probably using metal sights. Spot the muzzle flash when he fires again."

"But when's he going to fire?" Stevens asked.

"The muzzle velocity of his rifle should be about six to seven hundred meters a second," I said. "He's such a shitty shot because he's using shitty equipment. If I walk slowly and turn then he's got to figure out where I'm going to be a second and a half or so before I get there. Watch the tree line."

I stood up, handing the handset back to Fessman, and walked forward toward a thick-trunked tree. I abruptly stopped, turned, and then went back the other way. A bullet seemed to whisper past the back of my head, the sound of the shot coming out of the barrel arriving a few seconds later. I dropped to the jungle floor.

"You hit?" Fessman yelled.

"You get his position?" I asked back.

"Yeah," Stevens said. "He's about two fingers to the left of the smoke from that last shell and maybe a bit forward."

I grabbed the radio handset and called it in, dropping fifty meters and shifting the fire of the spotting round two hundred meters left, figuring that a finger held up translated to about a hundred meters at a distance of a thousand. I called in a battery of six.

After the "shot, over" came through the speaker, I yelled for everyone to get down. "These are going to hit hard and close!" I covered my ears with both hands.

The battery of six came in, wave after deadly wave, the nearer rounds impacting, by less than five hundred meters, the relatively open area between our position and the forward tree line where the sniper lay. Peeking over the edge of the fallen tree after the "splash" transmission, I saw the white blossom of a shock wave rushing outward and at me. I scrunched down to take the shock, but too late. The blast threw me a good ten feet backwards. Nobody moved to help me as the other six round impacts came down in waves with only seconds between them.

"You all right, sir?" a voice I knew had to be Fessman's said from a distance. Only Fessman called me sir.

I'd dropped my hands when the last of the rounds impacted.

"No more sniper," the Gunny said, "and you are battier than bat shit," he finished. "You never ever stand in front of a sniper," he continued. "Not ever."

"He wasn't a sniper," I defended. "He was just the delaying action. We can move now."

In spite of holding my hands over my ears, they still rang, and my head felt like a big giant marshmallow from the shock wave of the round I'd been stupid enough to stick my head up to see. But I knew that I'd never ever forget what the white rolling shock wave looked like as it crushed the water out of the air in its passage.

"White water," I said, a bit giddy to be alive. "It's white water, like in the waves."

"Water, give him some water," the Gunny ordered, pointing at Zippo.

I lay on my back, not wanting any water but figuring it was better that they thought I needed some than for them to really understand what I wanted to say. My mind would not come back from Sandy Beach on Oahu in the Hawaiian Islands. I wondered, if I made it home and back to that particular beach, whether I'd ever swim there and not see the white rushing aura of that artillery round's expanding halo.

The man with the six radio walked by my prone figure, glancing down as he passed.

"You one crazy motherfucking dude, Junior... but you're our crazy motherfucking dude."

I wasn't sure whether what he said was a compliment or an insult, or an insult inside a compliment. I sat up. No incoming that I could hear. The Gunny squatted down beside me to make coffee. I moved to join him, although I didn't have my pack. I knew Zippo or Stevens must have it somewhere but I wasn't going to ask.

"We can move forward," I said, the Gunny sensing my predicament with the coffee and handing me a spare envelope.

I heated my water, sharing the burning explosive with the Gunny. I read the coffee envelope. Made by the Coca-Cola Company, which seemed strange. Then the Gunny came up with a package of sugar. I didn't know if California produced sugar but if I ever got home, I determined to support Dole, the only sugar producer left in Hawaii.

"We're setting in," the Gunny said, confirming my previous thoughts about the Marines digging in further down the path. "The open area out here can serve as a landing zone in the morning. Find a place a bit back down from here. The perimeter will run along the edge of this clearing and First Platoon will be on watch. They may attack across there tonight because they've had long enough and besides, the A Shau Valley is Indian country."

I mixed the coffee and sugar and then drank the result, which seemed too wonderful to be what it was. I emptied the canteen holder and replaced it on my belt. Having my canteen full of water made me happy, too, although I realized that I was experiencing some kind of high from almost being dead but still alive and relatively unhurt.

When I was done I got up and moved down the path. I had no good reason to be alive. None of the danger I'd been in since I arrived lessened one bit, but I could not keep a certain bounce from my step.

My team struggled to keep up until I stopped about a hundred and fifty meters back the way we'd come. A small hill not far from the main course of travel looked like a perfect place to set up the Starlight scope. I worked through wet messy undergrowth to climb to the top, thinking one man could view the small area around us quite easily. The flattened top of the hill would accommodate all five of our hooches.

I wondered who would be coming in the night, this night? The platoon of small-minded country racists or the platoon of angry black combat avoiders who still seemed to fight quite a bit, as long as it was inside the company. The platoon commanders were successful tribal leaders in the company, as was the Gunny. But I was not. I had no real place unless I could find a place, and the only thing I had to offer were my services. Those services had been badly needed, but mostly ignored or underplayed, before my arrival. Would I have enough to offer? Would I have enough to offer in time?

Fessman joined me on the hill, dragging my pack up and turning on his little transistor radio. Brother John came on immediately with his last offering of the day. Some sort of Native American Apache War Chant, he said. *Hena hawaya yo, hen na yo, hey ya hey ya a* accompanied by beating drums with the same lyrics repeating over and over again. I had no idea what they meant but for the moment, I felt like an Apache sitting on a mountain top of the American Southwest so many years in the past. I thought about moving from the Go Noi Island area, called Arizona Territory by the men around me, and then on up to the A Shau, which they called Indian country. The Apache War Chant seemed most appropriate, indeed, and I wondered how Brother John, down country somewhere in a place called Na Trang, could know that.

twenty-seven

The rain came and the smell came with it. The temperature dropped, our altitude reducing the steam heat to an oily cloying mass of moving air that felt so intensely like spider webs that I constantly brushed my hands across my face to get rid of them. It was full dark and Stevens manned the Starlight scope, relieving Zippo from scope tripod duty because the team had fashioned our half full packs into a sort of raised mound for the Starlight.

"What in hell is that smell?" I asked no one in particular. "It's like the mosquito stuff, but worse."

"It's snowing," Stevens whispered, looking through the scope.

I moved to his side, all of our ponchos and whatever bound together to form a lumpy inadequate roof against the rain. The Gunny had returned with Pilson. They'd set up a few feet further down the small slope, close enough to overhear the rest of us.

"Rain looks like snow in the Starlight scope," he said, not bothering to whisper. "It's because of the way it magnifies light. There's three intensifiers in that thing. Each one adds fake photons to the real ones until it looks like there's more light than there really is. And that smell is something called 'Agent Orange.' Don't know what's in it but that's why the clearing is there — why all this is somewhat clear. Without spraying every couple of weeks, this place would be impenetrable jungle."

"Is it dangerous?" Fessman asked.

The Gunny laughed first, and then the others. I stayed silent. It was funny. Was the stuff dangerous? We had all been sent out to die, and dying we were. What possible greater danger could some oily crap sprayed from the air be to us?

"Oh," Fessman said after a few seconds, finally getting it.

"The only good thing is that the gooks don't like it," the Gunny said. "They don't like storms either because they can't hear. They don't like the rain for the same reason. And they don't like the night even if they have to fight in it all the time or be chopped to ribbons. Get some sleep if you can. I don't think those clowns from the First and Fourth are coming in the rain, but Charlie probably will."

"I thought you said they don't like the night, the rain, or that oily stuff," I replied.

"They don't," the Gunny said. "But they're also tough as hell and they're not killing one another to stay alive, they're killing us."

Nobody laughed, although I saw the analytical humor in the Gunny's remark. Killing to stay alive. That was funny, too, in a way. A stand-up comedian would be able to make something out it after the war.

I crawled back to my hooch, or what part of the big hooch we'd jammed together belonged to me. I took out my flashlight and wrote a letter to my wife. I started it out with killing to stay alive, but then ran into trouble when I could not give her a rendition of what had happened earlier. She was smart. After a bit my descriptions of the fauna and flora were going to tip her off that I wasn't telling her anything at all. I wrote of the men around me. Real Marines who acted more like shape-shifting pirates, with a good bit of Peter Lorre and Burt Lancaster thrown in. Difficult men to predict and nearly inscrutably impossible to form any kind of relationship with. Dying together was not a group thing. It was a bunch of lonely men moving in mass who found it impossible to share anything, especially death.

The Gunny came across the little distance between us, his bare torso turning shiny in the pouring rain. He scrunched in beside me.

"Who you writing to?" he asked, sitting his butt next to me, with his knees drawn up and his big solid arms wrapped around them.

I finished the letter, folded it into an envelope and turned off my flashlight. I tucked the letter in with the morphine packet. I didn't want to share my wife with anyone, not anyone in the company I no longer hated, but certainly didn't love, either. I didn't answer the Gunny's question. I knew he didn't care about who I wrote to, or what I wrote. I wondered if he'd not come to sit with me so he would not have to be alone.

"The 81s are gone," the Gunny indicated, after he realized I wasn't going to answer the question he probably knew the answer to, anyway. "We got two 60mm mortars on the last resupply with some ammo. They're okay but they won't drop stuff down through this kind of heavy cover. The new super-quick fuses are just too sensitive."

I knew the Gunny made sense. The 105 fuses were the same way but the huge size of the rounds made them effective, even if they went off up in the tops of the trees. Shrapnel moving at about twenty-thousand feet per second showered anything underneath. The 60 millimeters rounds only weighed a couple of pounds, however, most of that weight in the shell casing itself. They would be effective targeting the open area between the company position and across to the ridge tree line. But not at night. The rounds gave off too little indication of where they went off to be adjusted effectively in the dark, not to mention in heavy rain.

"Are they coming?" I asked, finally saying something.

"Is who coming?" he asked back

"Across that mud flat. Will they attack tonight?" I repeated, knowing that he had understood me the first time.

"That's the question," the Gunny answered. "It's perfect. We're out here near the very edge of our artillery, it's raining like hell and dark as a cesspit. Night vision is all but useless and so is air illumination. Yeah, I think they'll come and that will be almost as big a problem as what's going to happen in the morning."

The Gunny was right. I couldn't call for illumination because the battery knew where we were, right on the gun target line. They wouldn't fire. With the tree line so close, we couldn't get them to fire high explosives or white phosphorus unless we were in direct contact.

"What's the tomorrow trouble?" I asked, wondering how our rotten exposure in an unfortified position could get any worse.

"Tomorrow we have to cross that open area to get to the valley," the Gunny replied. "The last time we were up here we took a lot of casualties in exactly the same place. There's no way around it. We don't usually come into contact during the daytime hours but they've had a lot time to get ready, and that ridge is snaked through with spider holes, tunnels and underground hideaways. Indian country."

The Gunny eased out of my hooch area and slid across the mud back to his own. In spite of the pounding rain, enough moonlight streamed through the black clouds to see shadows moving. I ordered Fessman to let me know if the Starlight scope showed anything before laying back myself, the rain making everything wet even though it didn't come down directly on me.

I didn't remember sleeping but what seemed like a few minutes turned into three hours, according to my illuminated combat watch face. I must have slept but didn't have time to think about it. We were in contact. Strafing fire, probably to make sure nobody in the company got any sleep, came out of the opposing tree line in multiple bursts. The good news: It was AK and not heavy machine gun fire. I pulled myself out from under my poncho cover to find that the rain had stopped. The smell of mud, mosquito repellent and the oily mess of the Agent Orange cleared area permeated everything. I breathed lightly, trying to avoid taking in a lot of air. A dumb idea that couldn't possibly work, but it made me feel better. I crawled up the small incline to find Fessman and the rest of the team gathered together with the scope, but they weren't using it. They stared out into the night directly in front of them, toward where the tree line had to be in the distance. I could see occasional muzzle flashes, followed by the whine of bullets passing overhead. We couldn't overcome the urge to duck every time.

All of a sudden the company's perimeter defense opened up. Five M60 7.62 caliber machine guns and about twenty or thirty M16s began to fire into the tree line. It looked like someone pouring an avalanche of white Christmas tree lights across the open area. An avalanche that seemed to rush right into the opposing line of forest. What an unbelievable show!

"The tracers," I breathed out. The machine guns had tracer bullets loaded into their belts fairly sparsely, at one tracer and then four regular rounds, and then another tracer. The M-60 tracers came out as yellow glowing objects while the M-16s burned white. And then everything stopped as fast as it had started leaving a strange silence. The faint ringing in my ears returned from the close distance of the guns and the volume of fire they'd put out.

"How do you like them apples, Charlie?" a voice cried out into the night.

I waited, but couldn't detect any further fire. I dreaded calling artillery so near to the end of our circular area of probability, or in other words, the maximum effective range of the guns. Being on the slope of a mountainside, as well as directly on the gun target line, made range estimations very difficult. The word difficult likely having a lot of blood and gore attached to it if fire had to be called.

I settled back into my hooch. With no more fire from the tree line, I tried to imagine the enemy commander attempting to figure out where all the machine gun fire came from. I knew it would take him a while to figure out that the company had fired all tracers, possibly explaining the silence.

The Gunny scurried up behind me.

"What have we got through the scope?" he asked. "It's stopped raining," he went on, as if to indicate that the rain being past would bring on the expected attack.

Stevens swept the scope across what he could see of the clearing and then slowly brought it around to cover the broken forest area between our position and the rest of our unit.

"We've got company coming in," he whispered.

"Shit," I whispered back, not liking the direction the scope pointed. I gently moved him away from the reticle and pressed my right eye into the rubber cup. The world turned green. In the distance I could see three figures approaching, each wearing a rain-shiny rubber poncho. I knew Jurgens led from his size and his strange John Wayne kind of rolling gate.

"First Platoon," I said, back to the Gunny, "but coming in vertical and seemingly in the open."

"Welcoming party?" Zippo asked, the first words he'd spoken in some time.

"Okay," I replied. "Fessman, you're with me at my hooch. You other three make yourself scarce and take your weapons off full auto. Don't shoot everyone in the dark if things go south. Shoot the right ones. Take your time and lay back, and pay attention to Kit Carson there – this is his kind of shit."

"They're not coming to fight," the Gunny said, Zippo, Nguyen and Stevens ignoring him and fading into the night on my orders. "They're coming to talk, although I don't have any idea about what. I'm staying right here with you."

"Thanks," I replied, relieved to have the Gunny at my side but having no reservations at all that Jurgens would take both of us out if he felt threatened. And he wasn't coming alone.

They didn't come in out of the night trying to hide anything. All three Marines moved out of the brush, making no attempt to hide their sucking footsteps or quiet the swishing and crackling undergrowth. I smelled them before I could see them and I hated the fact that I was beginning to be able to smell human beings around me so well that I could tell their identity by their particular smell. And then they emerged out of the dark and into the relative light of our small clearing at the bottom of the swell we inhabited. The two Marines stopped behind him as Jurgens moved forward and squatted down just outside my part of the combined hooch area. The Gunny and I stood to meet him, before squatting down ourselves.

"Fuck this shit," Jurgens said, without preamble. "We're not going out there tomorrow. We're not leading the company and taking all the hits anymore. Send the other platoons. We're going to sit back and lounge around like Fourth Platoon does all the time. It's our god damned turn."

"We can't just stay here," I replied.

"Who the fuck is talking to you, Junior," Jurgens shot back.

I hadn't thought about my Colt but my hand had. It rested on the butt of the weapon making me feel better. I knew in my center of centers that I could not continue to survive under the current circumstance of being prey for any and all would be authority figures in the company.

"So," I said, as casually as I could, the Gunny remaining silent, "What we've got here is a bunch of 'shake-n-bake' noncoms who've taken over a Marine company and are going to decide to do whatever it is they want to do even if the whole outfit gets killed," I said, looking through the gloom behind the men to see if my team was in place to back my play.

"Who gives a shit what you have to say. You've been here less than a week," Jurgens answered. "The only reason we've not had our ass shot off tonight is the Gunny's decision to go to all tracers. You don't learn that shit from books."

My eyes flicked over and back at the Gunny's. I couldn't see well enough to make out his eyes in detail, but I got enough to guess that he looked away in another direction. He'd taken my idea, actually the German's from the book, and he'd made it his own. I'd have worn a real smile if I could smile anymore. The Gunny had to survive, too.

I made a decision. I reached my Colt .45 hand back and held it out toward where I knew Fessman had to be behind me. The handset filled my hand in seconds. I pulled it up to my face, hit the transmit and said: "Fire mission, over," hoping Russ was up and waiting. I shifted the handset to my left hand and let my right naturally fall back to the automatic.

"Fire mission," came right back, the small speaker sounding like it was a home stereo boom box in the silence of the night around us.

"What's he doing?" Jurgens said to the Gunny, half climbing to his feet.

"I don't know," the Gunny answered.

"Where are you directing fire?" the Gunny asked me.

I reached into my front trouser pocket, the one without the morphine pack, and pulled out my folded map. I made a show of unfolding it, and then taking out my rubber UDT flashlight with the paper over the front light. The little brilliant hole lit up part of the map.

"One round —," I began, before the Gunny cut me off.

"Stop," he said, moving to my side and gripping my right bicep with one of his powerful hands. "Don't. Let's talk this through."

I turned off the flashlight, rested it atop the map and looked over at Jurgens. My right hand automatically returned to the butt of the Colt.

"He's calling that shit on my platoon, right now, I fucking know it," Jurgens said, pointing down at me.

He stood fully erect. Both of the Marines with him stood with their M16s roughly pointing in my direction. I saw Nguyen's eyes behind them in the gloom. I would probably not survive the coming confrontation I knew, but they would not either, and what did it all matter anyway.

"Tell him you'll lead the crossing in the morning," the Gunny said, his grip on my arm not lessening at all. "We don't' have anybody else. Sugar Daddy's platoon is useless and the other two are disorganized messes. You've built the only effective combat platoon we have. But if your guys won't go then nothing matters anymore. They're better off dead here than lying in that mud out there for the NVA to come finish off."

"Comm check," came out over the radio, as I'd stopped transmitting in the middle of a fire mission.

I stared into Jurgens' eyes, the whites of them and the surrounding tissue making them fully visible even in the low light. I held no animosity for the man. I wasn't angry. I truly did not care whether he died or not or whether I died or not, except I could not shake the literal terror of having to go through the process.

"Comm check," Russ said through the speaker, his voice as uncaring and unemotional as my own.

I waited. If I drew and shot the men, then who would lead First Platoon? And then where would we be?

"Alright," Jurgens said, finally. "Tell him to check fire."

"Just get back to your men and be ready at first light," the Gunny said, his grip on my arm finally starting to loosen. "I don't tell him anything. He's the company fucking commander."

"I don't care what he thinks he is, he's nuttier than a fucking fruitcake," Jurgens said, suddenly turning and walking off into the bush, his two Marine guards disappearing with him. My team came in a few seconds later.

"Do you really have to check fire?" the Gunny asked, letting my arm go. "I thought you said they wouldn't fire on us because they know our position."

"True," I said. "That grid number is at the top of Hill 110."

"So you were bluffing?" the Gunny said, getting to his feet and exhaling deeply.

"About the artillery," I said, my hand still gripping my .45. "Thanks for calling me the company commander."

"Did I actually say that?" the Gunny said, moving back to his own hooch and slipping inside.

"Check fire," I said into the handset.

twenty-eight

THE SEVENTH DAY

Fessman whispered into my left ear before first light. I blinked rapidly, once again not aware of having slept, but nothing could explain the passage of time from one waking moment to the next. I shook my head. Maybe I did sleep. If so, then it didn't resemble, even remotely, the sleep I'd enjoyed all of my life up until one week ago. I eased up to near vertical position and rubbed my mosquito bitten repellent covered face. I brought my hands down, wondering when we would have enough water for me to take another jungle shower. Maybe it would pour rain again and I could run around in the mud naked, scrubbing madly with one of the small white bars of sundry pack soap.

Fessman knelt only inches away, already wearing the Prick 25 on his back, its flat field antenna folded over several times looking like a sheaf of palm blades. The shadows moved around me. I hated the moving shadows. Anything could come out of them or be them. Light was my friend and darkness, a tool of the enemy. I looked around me until I could get my bearings and overcome the night terrors. I breathed deeply in and out. The darkness had one good feature: nobody could see that I was too afraid to be an officer, much less a company commander.

"On the seventh day God rested," I whispered, my left hand going to my thigh pocket to feel my letter home.

"Sir?"

I could make out Fessman's young face hanging in the air only a few feet in front of me, his eyes big, round and somehow still filled with innocence.

"On the seventh day God created Fessman."

"Oh, okay, sir" he replied.

I liked being called sir, even if my radioman was the only one who would use the word.

"Army's coming in, sir," Fessman whispered, as if warning me of the arrival of some devilish witch.

"What army?"

"On the net. I can get Army command," Fessman replied. "I can hear the 101st on their frequency, if nothing else is going on."

I pictured Fessman up all night listening to whatever he could find on the small powerful radio that didn't work nearly as well as the little transistors most of the men carried. That a multi-thousand-dollar radio rig, big as a suitcase, could be outperformed by a tiny cheap transistor job confounded me. The little radios invariably picked up both Da Nang transmissions and Brother John's down in Nha Trang, hundreds of miles away.

"What army's coming?" I asked with a frown.

"The 101st Screaming Eagles Army Airborne are on our right flank, over the hill on the other side, I think," Fessman replied. "The Army guy running that company over there's coming to see you, or the Gunny, or somebody here."

I didn't know what to say. A real officer, even if from a different service, coming here? That was big news to me. Would he know what was going on? Did he have similar problems? Did his company suffer horrid casualties? Were racial problems plaguing his unit, too? Did he carry morphine?

"Do we need to acknowledge, or what?" I asked,

"No, sir, I don't think so," Fessman replied. "Razzy, the radio guy over there, said his CO was coming over the hill at first light. I said it was okay, sir."

"You said it was okay," I replied. "God has spoken. Well, somebody ought to alert the perimeter. Isn't there a pass code or secret sign to get through the line?"

Fessman started to laugh, but stopped when I glared at him.

"No, sir, no sign. It's kinda easy to spot the gooks when you can see them at all, and so far none have tried to get inside the perimeter by asking."

Another combat joke, I presumed, at my expense. I decided to get ready for the big event. I shaved, using the last of my water supply. The choppers were due in just after dawn, although if the open poisoned area was hot they probably would not land. I didn't care. There was no point in saving for a future, even one that appeared just up ahead in the day, when moment by moment there seemed so little chance of survival. Water would be a problem for later in the day, since nobody I'd seen had humped the big plastic containers up the trail. The coming dawn and crossing the clearing without being killed were problems that had to be handled much sooner than water issues.

The Gunny came across the mud mess between our hooches. Reverting to ape-hood, I smelled him before I could really see him. I hated the smelling. Soon I would be swinging from the low-hanging branches nearby.

"We've got a problem," he began, squatting down and lighting a block of explosives with his Zippo.

I waited, but he said nothing more. Finally, I squatted down, tossing a packet of the Coca Cola coffee to him. I'd dug through the pack and found my small supply.

"Thank you," The Gunny said formally, as if we were in some mess hall back in America.

When I couldn't wait any longer to for him to tell me about this new problem, I spoke up. "Fessman heard that the Army on our flank is sending somebody over to see us at first light."

"That's great news," the Gunny replied, his tone suddenly one of excitement. The first excitement I'd heard in his voice since I'd jumped from the chopper a week before. "They'll bring hot food. They always bring hot food. The men will go nuts. The Screaming Eagles. Great name for an outfit, isn't it, even if it's Army? Do you think eagles really scream in the wild?"

I sat on the edge of my poncho cover, a bit befuddled. The Gunny's enthusiasm seemed so out of place. We had to cross almost a quarter mile of flat muddy open area where the enemy had to be encamped on the other side after dawn. We had no water to speak of, unless somebody had worked to haul it up, and our artillery was all but useless as an effective accurate means of fire support. We were about to get shot to pieces, and the Gunny was excited about maybe getting a hot meal. I decided to shut up and wait, sloshing what water I had left around in my canteen cover over the Gunny's fire.

I thought about crossing the flat open area, wondering about the chances of the letter in my pocket ever making it home? In Basic School, one of the best training officers had said, "Take care of the big things and the little things will go to shit." I didn't really understand what he'd meant at the time, and I wasn't entirely sure now, but the letter in my pocket was a big thing. The little things would have to dribble on down or take care of themselves, unless the choppers didn't show up.

"We got a blooper problem," the Gunny finally said, sipping his steamy brew. How he drank it so boiling hot I had no idea but, it impressed me.

"Blooper?" I asked, knowing I should know but obviously didn't.

"M79 thing," he said.

The M79 was a grenade launcher. A 40-millimeter, shotgun-like weapon, that shoots spin-armed "balls" or small grenades. The weapons were issued one to a squad, which meant that the company had a bunch of them. I hadn't noticed any Marines carrying them. In the Basic School they'd shown us the weapon and then demonstrated it but, since we were officers, we didn't get to fire it because, well, we were officers. Some Marines thought the weapon was terrific and others found it an underpowered, slow-reloading and heavy piece of crap. It was hard to justify a grenade thrower used in a jungle where bamboo and other heavy growth were seldom more than a few yards away, and the "blooper" round, named that because of it's strange blooping sound when it launched, didn't arm itself until it was thirty meters from the end of the tube.

"We out of blooper ammo?" I asked, trying to prompt the Gunny to explain his situation.

"Nah, one of the guys from Fourth Platoon fired some rounds last night and a Marine from First Platoon got hit."

I wanted to scream "No shit!" in the darkness around me. Bloopers did not have tracers that I knew of, so there was no way to know where rounds fired came from, or went. The race war inside the regular war went on, no matter what plans I implemented to stop it.

"Wounded or dead?" I asked, sipping my own tepid coffee.

"Sort of wounded," the Gunny replied. I couldn't see his shoulders actually move but I would have bet that he had shrugged when he said the words.

"Sort of ?" I asked, in surprise. "How in hell does someone get sort of wounded out here?

"Well, it seems that the round went through the air, probably armed itself, and when it came down it hit this guy's soft tissue just above his collar bone, and then entered the area around his lung or somehow got down into his abdomen. That's where the round is now. Inside him. The Marine seems fine though, except for some bleeding and breathing shit, but he's got that live round in there."

"I'd say he meets whatever standard we have for being wounded."

"That's funny, right?" the Gunny replied.

"I don't see the problem," I said, ignoring his comment. "Medevac him and let the aid station work it out. Since they were shooting at each other inside the perimeter, it's likely the damned thing never got far enough to arm, anyway."

"The problem is that medevac won't come if he has this live round in him. If it goes off in the chopper, then everyone aboard's dead."

"Screw it," I said. "Don't tell 'em. This is a game of risk. Lousy risk. They signed on just like we did."

"Pilson told them when he called for the chopper," the Gunny murmured softly so Fessman, sitting by like a bird of prey, didn't hear. "Even the resupply won't come," he finished, his voice trailing off. He took another swig of his coffee.

So here it is again, I thought. The company commander, but not the company commander. I get the ability to make the wrong decision handed to me, and if I'm wrong, I'm "that crazy fucker," but if I'm right, then somebody else gets the credit. I only get to make decisions that have no solutions. We had to have medevac and resupply. What was the alternative? None. We needed water, ammo, food, and more. Even the gunships would provide invaluable help by strafing the tree line before we crossed, unless they didn't come because the other choppers wouldn't. I clutched the morphine package in my other thigh pocket, massaging it gently. Was I supposed to kill the Marine with morphine to save the unit? Leave him behind? Take a K-Bar and cut the big round out of him? What?

"It gets worse," the Gunny went on. "Jurgens wants to take his platoon and carry the man all the way back to the aid station. If he does that, then we won't have our best platoon at point to get us across that open area or available to us as we cross down into the A Shau."

I just sat there thinking about the problem and drinking my coffee. I wondered if the Basic School ever offered to teach young officers how to handle problems like this, instead of how to cross a radioactive bridge or raging river with no bridge. Once, in a college poker game I'd been forced to play in, that I didn't want to play in because I had so little money, I'd bought the same kind of cards used to play. I made up a 'cold deck' by stacking the cards, kept the deck under my right thigh and then substituted that deck with the one I'd just shuffled, dealt and won the hand and was able to quit. The situation I faced was much the same, with no acceptable solution that had odds either way too high to gamble. How could I cheat my way through?

I knew when to expect first light because Brother John, three hundred miles away down in Na Trang, told me with his first daily broadcast: "This is brother John, coming at you with Otis Redding from Na Trang." The song began to play. *Sittin' in the mornin' sun, I'll be sittin' when the evenin' comes, watching the ships roll in and then I watch 'em roll away again…*

What I would give, if I had anything to give, to be sitting on the dock of any bay anywhere in the world and watch ships roll in. It would have been more appropriate if John had started the day out with a "Chickenman" episode.

"They're here, sir," Fessman said.

"They radio in?" I asked, presuming he was talking about the Army visit.

"No, sir, listen."

I picked up the sound of laughing and talking around me. An uncommon sound. A group of men came out of the waning darkness and jungle bracken, the mud-sucking sounds of their boots preceding them.

"Six actual?" the leading man asked, holding out one hand.

I looked at the Gunny. He shrugged but said nothing.

I climbed to my feet and faced the man. I noticed that he was clean, wearing a set of the new jungle utilities I'd only heard about, along with the duty flak jacket none of our Marines wore. A small group of men behind him brought forth a few big green canisters, which they plopped down in the mud next to where the Gunny squatted.

"Hot spaghetti and ice cream," the man said, still holding out his right hand. "We gave out the rest back there to your men."

I shook with my own repellent and Agent Orange smeared hand, feeling like an alley vagrant in comparison to the picture perfect officer in front of me. He wore double black bars on his helmet and on each shoulder of his green flack jacket.

"Captain Dennis Morgan, at your service," he smiled. "West Point, Class of '66. How can I help you guys? It's always good to have you Marines taking care of the flank. Where are the other officers?"

I sat back down on the edge of my poncho cover and motioned for the captain to do the same, wondering if he would because of his pristine condition.

The captain sat immediately, to my surprise. The Gunny and the rest of my scout team went at the canisters without comment, the captain's men standing back to get out of the way.

"Thank you, sir," I said, automatically.

"Sir? What's your rank?"

"Second lieutenant, sir," I replied, looking away.

"Stop calling me sir. We're out in the field. I'm commanding Echo Company, 101st. What happened to the other officers?"

I thought about his comment and his question. Maybe it was okay for my Marines not to call me sir. We were in the field. The other officers didn't matter, so I set that part of his question aside without answering. Maybe the captain could help with something other than food.

"I heard that your choppers are piloted by young warrant officers," I said.

"Crazy fuckers, every one," the captain said, with a laugh like he was proud of their insanity. I noticed his gold Academy ring, worn where other men wore wedding rings. "Ring knockers" the rest of us non-academy officers had called them in Basic School. "Why do you ask?"

"We're headed into the A Shau and we gotta get across the clearing, sir. Our air won't come in. I'm at the end of range from the An Hoa battery for supporting fire. The Cobras won't be here to strafe the tree line if the Hueys don't come in."

The captain lost his smile and stared at me. I wondered what he saw. I knew what he saw. A ragamuffin officer covered in stinking oils and probably smelling like a cape buffalo straight from a wallow, and a second lieutenant to boot. The captain looked away without replying.

"Why no air support?" he asked.

I told him the blooper story.

"Larsen, get over here," he yelled to the side when I finished. "Give me that," he ordered, holding his hand out. Larsen, coming in out of the dark, proved to be the radio operator. He gave the captain his handset.

"When do you want them to come?" he asked.

"They're coming?" I asked, incredulous.

"Are you kidding me?" the captain exclaimed. "To be a part of a story like the blooper thing? This is *Stars and Stripes* kind of shit. You want a Cobra dustoff and supplies, too? What do you need on the resupply ship?"

I sat stunned. This was the Army? The Army that was supposed to hate the Marine Corps? Was nothing in the world the way I thought?

"Water, food, and some 60 millimeters ammo for the crossing would be good, maybe in an hour?" the Gunny piped in, talking between big bites of spaghetti he'd loaded into his cleaned out canteen holder.

"What's a grid number where you want them down," the captain said, dangling the mic from his hand and flipping it around like it was a ball at the end of a piece of string.

"They'll take the Marine with the round in him?" I asked, just to make sure he'd fully understood what I'd told him.

"Hell, if he was going to blow up he'd have blown up already. That's American ordinance he has inside him, not that Chinese shit."

I gave him a grid number from memory, as I'd laid out fire for our attack across the open area earlier in the night.

"Okay," the captain said, waiting to hear back from whoever he called for air support. "I'll give your radioman the frequency for the Americal Division. They've got some of those M102 lightweight 105s on top of Cunningham peak a few miles down the A Shau. Dropped 'em in by helicopter a few months back. I'm sure they'll be happy to fire for you guys. Gotta air drop ammo though, so you might have to use them sparingly."

I sat in front of the man in wonder. A real company commander. Fessman's radio began to squeak out another song that seemed so appropriate for the coming of the light and maybe the possibility of living through the day.

"Fighting soldiers from the sky, fearless men who jump and die. Men who mean just what they say, the brave men of the Green Beret."

The 101st weren't Green Berets but they sure seemed like it.

twenty-nine

THE SEVENTH DAY : SECOND PART

You want wet or *lurps*," Captain Morgan said, holding the radio handset to his right ear.

"What are lurps?" I asked, vaguely having heard the word but not understanding what it meant.

"Long range patrol rations," he responded. "They're dried. Lightweight. Just put water in, heat, and there you go."

"Okay, lurps then," I said, wondering about what the "u" might stand for but not enough to ask.

I watched him call it in. It would be good to lessen the load in all of our packs if the mountain we were climbing was any indication of how tough it would be to scale the cliffs of the coming A Shau Valley.

"Water," the Gunny whispered to me. "A gallon weighs eight pounds."

We'd been hauling almost all of our own water between air drops. I hadn't thought about that. Were C-Rations heavier than lurps, after adding water? I was willing to bet that the whole thing was a wash, just like everything else I'd so far discovered in Vietnam. For every First Platoon there was a Fourth Platoon.

"You have any racial problems in your company?" I asked the captain, my own problems on my mind. And then, suddenly, even before he answered, I knew I'd made a mistake asking.

I felt both the Gunny and Fessman shrink back from where we stood. The light was good enough to see the captain's full face and read his expression. Or the lack of it. His facial features instantly changed from the smiling Army ambassador of good will into one of the Washington Monument stone things.

"Okay then, lieutenant, your medevac, resupply, and dust-off will roll in fifty minutes," he said, hesitating, making a show of looking at his watch. "Just give the hot chow container vats to the Huey crew. Good luck."

He smiled again, but not like the smiles he'd graced us with before. He held out his hand, again, a strange gesture because we should have been saluting for any kind of greeting. He was a captain and I was a second lieutenant.

I shook his dry, crisply powerful hand with my small, oily one, and like wisps in the night, he and his radioman were gone, slipping away into the still dark jungle. I squatted back down, reached over and loaded some of the spaghetti into my unwashed canteen holder.

"Try this," Fessman said. Grabbing some metal implement, he scooped into the other container and dumped a big white glob onto the top of my spaghetti.

I stared down. Ice cream. Fessman had dumped a load of ice cream on the still warm spaghetti and it was melting away. I exhaled deeply, took my dirty metal spoon, cleaned by rubbing it with my oily hand, and dug in. After a few seconds I could only smile and dig ever deeper into the red, white, and whatever mess he'd piled into my holder.

"Told you," Fessman laughed.

It felt like home. Hot spaghetti and ice cold vanilla ice cream. Mixing it didn't matter. It wasn't canned ham and lima beans put together in rusting old tin cans during the Korean war. I regretted asking the question about the racial thing. I could have talked to the captain all day long about so many things but I'd driven him away.

"Where do you get those big black rank markers the captain wore?" I asked the Gunny, between massive mouthfuls of the food.

"I'll take care of that," the Gunny said, between spoonfuls from his own canteen holder. "Sugar Daddy said his platoon won't cross the open area, that there's no reason to go into the A Shau. He says we can just wait here, like we did below Hill 110."

I stopped eating. My shoulders slumped a little. I chewed on what I had in my mouth, my mind racing. I was still a Marine. We were all still Marines, animal and jungle Marines, but Marines nevertheless. As long as I breathed, I knew in my heart that I would never go around a Hill 110 again. Not in the jungle, Vietnam, any war, or even back home.

The Gunny stared at me over his food, his spoon paused in mid-air. I could not hear Fessman breathing near my right ear, or the soft gentle sounds the other scout team members usually made nearby. I said nothing. I looked intently into the Gunny's eyes, not really waiting so much as not having any reply to make.

"Yeah, I kinda thought so," the Gunny finally said. "Me neither."

He went back to eating while I tried to figure out what his laconic phrases really meant. The sounds and Fessman's nervous breathing came back.

"Fessman," I began, but he'd already held it out right in front of my face. "Americal?" I asked.

Fessman nodded. "We're Tango Tango Deuce, and I think the officer there is Lieutenant Howell but they call him Lieutenant Howler, because he's kind of loud."

"Why deuce and not delta?" I asked, delta being the proper alpha-numeric for the letter "d," but he didn't answer. I went on, "Since you've been gossiping a bit, can you tell me if they've been in contact with Captain Morgan and his company?" I held the mic in one hand and my canteen holder in the other, sipping from it between phrases.

"Who?" Fessman asked, looking befuddled.

"Army artillery," I replied.

"I don't think so, not that I've overheard," Fessman said.

I turned back to the Gunny. "I'm going to register our current position as a night defensive fire location. Hopefully they don't know at Bravo Battery where we are. Once we clear here and get across onto the ridge overlooking the A Shau, I'll zone fire this whole area. The battery back at An Hoa, the 155s and the Army outfit, if they'll fire for us. Whoever stays back here can either run all the way back down and across the Go Noi to be court-martialled, or be shot or die right here."

"Kinda thought," the Gunny said, after scooping more ice cream into his mouth. "The knuckle-knocker's won't fight."

"Crap," I replied angrily. "Jurgens and First Platoon won't lead the attack and that threat came first. It's not totally about race. It's about who the hell is commanding this outfit and, if that isn't you or me, then we're all dead anyway. It's just a matter of mathematics and time."

"Want me to give him the bad news?" the Gunny replied, not sure whether he was talking about Jurgens, Sugar Daddy, or both of them.

"I don't really give a shit right now, Gunny, whether they stay or leave with us. In fact, if I could order it, which we both know I can't, I'd order First and Fourth to squat right here. They can both meet their maker on their own terms. I'm sure they'll have an appropriate nickname for him, too. I want to see the kid with the blooper round in him."

"That shouldn't be a problem," the Gunny said, washing his canteen holder out with what was left of his own water. "Nobody'll get within ten meters of him."

The Gunny handed me my helmet, which I hadn't seen him take. I looked at the front of the green-side-out cloth cover. The Gunny had used a magic marker to color in a single large black bar on the front. Underneath, in smaller letters, he'd printed "Junior."

I put my canteen holder down on the poncho liner and accepted my helmet back.

"That's so everyone will know your rank," the Gunny said, no expression on his face.

"A junior lieutenant," Fessman said, with a laugh. "Second Lieutenant, junior lieutenant."

I glanced at my radio operator. He stopped laughing. I put the helmet on, realizing I really didn't give a damn anymore about what anyone called me. The difference one week made.

I called the registration mission in to Bravo Battery of the Americal outfit. Using the Tango Tango Deuce identifier was laborious compared to simply directing Russ to fire at my own battery. I hoped using the Army battery would be somewhere close to being as effective as my own had been. I registered the tree line on the opposite side of the Agent Orange oily open area, as well. I had to use Russ very sparingly because of our position on the gun target line, and being at the end of charge seven (maximum) range inaccuracies.

The Gunny guided Fessman and me back through the jungle to a position not far from where I'd killed the three enemy approaching in the night. It disturbed me that only hours later, I didn't have much memory of the when and where of the event. The first men I'd killed, and I couldn't remember them well. Not what I'd been led to believe from friends, family, movies, television and even the higher officers at The Basic School. I wondered if I'd recall the incident in more detail later on.

We came upon another of the strange small clearings that appeared like some kind of tiny oasis in the heavier wooded mountain jungle. A Marine lay on his back with one of the company corpsmen bending over him. I squatted down next to the corpsman, meaning to ask how his patient was doing but the wounded man spoke before I could.

"The crazy lieutenant," he said, his voice a raspy whisper.

I leaned back a few inches, surprised to identify the Marine from the sniper incident.

"Don't worry lieutenant, I'm not going to explode, or anything," the Marine continued, laughing gently.

I could see that his throat was wrapped in combat bandages, like the rest of his torso. I couldn't tell where the M79 round had gone in and, short of an X-ray, nobody would be able to figure out exactly where it had come to rest until they cut him open, if he made it that far.

"You'll be on the medevac in a few minutes," I said, recovering.

For some reason I felt close to the man, and a regret I'd not experienced since before arriving in county. Outside of the mixed acceptance I'd received from my scout team, the first platoon grunt had been the first, and possibly only, man to find my presence in the company acceptable at all.

"Doc told me," the wounded man said, "the Army guys are coming, thanks to the Gunny. Stick with him, sir, and you'll be okay."

I gripped the Marine's hand and wished him well back home. I stood looking down at him and thought about my own situation. If the chopper didn't blow up and they got that grenade out of him, he'd be out of Vietnam and back in the world, while I'd remain behind or be dead. All I had to get me through was a completely broken down and dysfunctional company, my small strange scout team and the Gunny. First the tracers, and now the Army warrant officers coming in at the Army captain's orders. The Gunny had done magnificent work, I thought grimly. I'd spoken to my own battalion commander exactly once since I'd been here, the XO never, and I had no idea what the other Marine Companies around us had in the way of orders.

I moved to the position I'd occupied to call in fire the night before, hoping to find the Army's Bravo Battery at least the equivalent of the Marine outfit firing for me out of An Hoa. Stevens, Zippo and Nguyen came out of the jungle behind Fessman and me, as I prepared once again to rain down hell on the tree line across from our position. Knowing they had my back made a big difference, with Jurgens and Sugar Daddy still seething and convinced that my removal from life would improve their situations.

The very edge of the sun rose above the jungle horizon. In the far distance I could hear the familiar sound of Huey chopper blades, but the sound of the coming medevac and resupply seemed different from before. The choppers sounded more like a flock of Huey bees than the distinct whooping of blades I'd become used to. The reason for that became apparent only a few minutes later. Three utility Hueys came up into view along the open area that flowed north from our position. Above them flew five Huey Cobra attack helicopters. The attack helicopters swooped ahead of the regular Huey delivery birds, a sight to behold. Black instead of Marine Corps green, they had giant shark's teeth painted on their noses and looked ferocious. Three came in low and two wound back and forth above the three. Without taking any fire, they opened up on the jungle behind our opposing tree line.

The utility choppers landed in a clump close to one another, and the crews went to work. I realized we weren't going to need any artillery support. The Cobras were tearing up the same area I would have called fire into, and the artillery rounds would have endangered the choppers themselves, anyway. The Marine with the grenade was whisked aboard one of the machines while boxes and bags were dumped from the other two. Three body bags went aboard the chopper that took the wounded Marine.

I looked at the black bags being loaded aboard like stiff bundles of covered fire wood. I could not dredge up any emotion at all.

"They put on quite some show," a voice behind me said.

I put down my Japanese binoculars, having checked the cock-pits of the Hueys to assure myself that the pilots really were little more than kids. With helmets on and through the low light penetrating the windshields, I couldn't make out much but their laughing smiles. They had to be what they'd been described to be, I knew. I turned to find the Gunny and Pilson behind me. The tone of the Gunny's voice hadn't been positive, but I ignored it. The Army was doing the Marine Corps a big favor, not in simply providing a vital medevac our own service would not provide, but in supporting our coming high risk crossing of the Agent Orange sodden expanse of open ground.

In what seemed like only seconds the Hueys pulled out, leaving two stacks of supplies behind. I waved at the choppers, although I could only see the machine gunners stationed just inside the wide open sides of the machines. The one Marine who'd said I was "his crazy fucker" was going home, leaving me in hell with a bunch of Marines, most of whom probably felt they'd be a lot better off if I'd been on that chopper carrying a grenade in my chest.

Full dawn lit the open area as I studied it, slowly sweeping the tree line back and forth. In spite of the volume of rocket and rotary ma-chine gun fire it absorbed only moments before, it looked untouched, except for a few lingering wisps of rising smoke. There had been no en-emy firing when the choppers were so highly exposed. I pictured the NVA forces lying in wait, crouched down inside their fabled, but as yet unseen, tunnels and underground quarters. They'd be waiting for the real enemy that they had to know would come. Waiting for us.

thirty

There was nothing to be done until crossing the open area in front of us was imminent, except get hold of some of the rations and water. My letter home was in my pocket, forgotten for the first time, my full attention and following thought process had been unable to refocus after the three body bags were loaded into the choppers. I'd forgotten to mail my letter home. Belatedly, I wondered if it mattered. Would Marine mail get through the Army system and make it all the way home or would it be discarded into some holding or dead-end bin? Before I could get my things together enough to get ready for the coming mad dash to the distant tree line Nguyen showed up, lugging one of the white plastic bottles of water and some big green envelopes stuffed into his utility pockets. He dropped his load with a thud, and then several of the packets. We exchanged glances but neither of us spoke. For some reason the Kit Carson Scout communicated more loyalty and respect in utter silence than any of the others in my small team, with the possible exception of Fessman, could do in speaking.

I picked up one of the thick green envelopes. "Food Pack, Long Range Patrol Ration" was printed in black letters on the deep green background. I held food packet number two, which was labeled "Chili Con Carne." The bag had been made by a bag company in Rochester, New York. If the food was any good, I mused to myself, I would put that place on my places to visit if I got back to the world. I refilled my two canteens with Fessman's help, the big plastic bottle being heavy, slippery and cumbersome to handle. The instructions on the package said I had to heat three quarters of my canteen holder with hot water, so I poured that too. One pound of water, or thereabouts, I recalled from my conversation with the Gunny earlier.

I waited for the water to heat over my explosive little fire, poured the contents of the bag into my canteen holder and then began to eat with my single combination fork and spoon. The chili tasted like nothing I'd ever tasted before. I looked around to see if any of the rest of my team were eating it, but they were taken up with heating and eating whatever they had. All the food kind of looked and smelled alike. I went on eating, reading the back of the envelope to pass the time. Two thousand calories were supposedly being transferred from the tasteless bag contents to my body, but it seemed like a whole lot less. I looked around for the Gunny, but he had not returned from his mission to talk to both Jurgens and Sugar Daddy about the coming move.

I took out my government-issue black ballpoint and wrote another letter to my wife. How I had forgotten to mail the one in my pocket was bothering me more than I could explain to myself. Was I becoming lost down the rabbit hole I'd fallen into to the point where I was losing perspective about what was important and what was not? I tried to write, but could not. What was I going to write? One of those existential tomes I'd read by the great philosophers in college but never really understood. Nihilism? I was living it. Abandonment? Right here with me like a cloying mosquito-bitten friend. I could write none of it. My wife had to be tired of reading about what Fessman looked like, what Stevens was up to and why I had scouts who never scouted anything, anyway. I could write her that they were scouting all night long to make sure none of my Marines, with some good cause, were coming through the mud and mess to kill me. I grimaced, pen in hand. My hand was not shaking though. Terror was becoming the dark moving creature that accompanied me everywhere but no longer lived deep inside whatever core I still had left. Terror was the NVA ready to kill me in the crossing of that open area. Terror was First Platoon. Terror was Fourth Platoon. Terror was a crazy M79 grenade launcher who shot anything that moved, or didn't move.

I wrote: "The weather is cooler up here at this higher altitude. I'm going to this lovely valley inland called the A Shau. I'm not sure you can even find the place on a map in the library back there. I don't know how far it is or what the weather will be like there. I ate chili today and it was pretty good." I thought for a moment, looking over at my child-radioman. "Fessman says hello." I signed the letter and put it in one of the little blue-colored envelopes with the shape of the country on it. No matter where terror was around me I swore I would not forget to mail my letter home again. I had only Mary and Julie no matter how few days I had left. I had something. I jammed the envelope down into the pocket that held the other one, checking to make sure it was still there.

The Gunny came loping back to his hooch, moving faster than I'd ever seen him move before. As he passed by my small mud area he tossed a packet onto the only dry part of my poncho cover.

I was about to ignore the package and crawl over to the Gunny's hooch when the edge of a map stuck out of the side of the clear plastic bag. I stopped, grabbed the bag and tore it open. Half a dozen one to twenty-five thousand contour interval maps fell out. Relief flooded through me. I could not call artillery without a map. Without an accurate map of any area all I could do was adjust fire from the gun target line or simply guess at where we might be. Both of those methods were eventually terminal in result. It only took me seconds to orient myself on one the maps. I looked up to where the berm we would have to go over to cross the open area was located. We weren't even close to the A Shau Valley. It wasn't even on the map, although I knew the direction where it had to be. I hunted through the others until I found it. I'd thought we were moving a few thousand meters to the valley but our move was going to be whole lot longer than that, as the A Shau was a good twenty thousand meters ahead and the terrain was all mountainous with poor cover and little concealment.

"Death march," I whispered to myself. Where would our supporting fires come from? Cunningham fire base was on the edge of the valley firing away in our direction. Calling them was almost as bad, for accuracy purposes, as calling back to my own battery, although we would be slowly getting closer to the Americal the more we traveled. There had been no geography classes at The Basic School in Quantico. The first Vietnam map I'd seen had been examined in country a week ago. I wondered why they had taught us so little, even though they all had to know exactly where we were going. Almost all, I reflected. The senator's son had not gone with us. On the last day of TBS Major Kramer had announced the occupational specialties we were to be assigned. That's where I'd been assigned to artillery and ordered to Fort Sill. Sam had been the only officer to get a really different and weird specialty. He was to become a reporter for the Stars and Stripes and be sent to Korea. He'd been mortified by the public announcement, made by the heartless major in front of all 246 of the rest of us going to Vietnam. Sam had broken down and cried. I'd felt so sorry for him. Until now. I now knew I'd change places with him in an instant and I would not care who I had to cry in front of to get the assignment. I folded up my maps and stuck the mass into my morphine pocket. I never had to check the morphine. I knew it was there waiting, and it knew I was there too, waiting. I crawled over to the Gunny who was making his usual canteen holder of coffee.

"When do we kick off?" I asked, making no move to get my own canteen holder out.

The Gunny didn't reply, so I waited, my ability to squat for long periods, without pain in my ankles or knees surprising me.

"They'll go," the Gunny said, getting right to the point without my asking. "Some of them have been to the A Shau before. They call it the Ah Shit Valley. I've been there too and I call it something else. The Valley of No Joy. The Valley of No Return."

"But you came back," I said, wondering if I sounded stupid.

The Gunny sipped coffee and then smiled one of his uncommon smiles. For the first time I realized he had wrinkles on his face. The Gunny was old.

"I didn't come back," he said, slowly, looking far beyond me over my shoulder. His expression was dead, once the smile faded from his lips.

I almost gave in to a powerful temptation to turn and see what he might be seeing behind me. But I didn't.

"This isn't me," the Gunny said, and I could tell there was absolutely no humor in his tone. "This is just the Gunny you see sitting here with you. That other Gunny is never coming back."

"What does battalion say?" I asked, changing the subject as fast as I could. I thought of asking about being brought in on all command communications but afraid of the expression the man still wore on his aging face. I couldn't believe I'd missed the fact that he was so old. I knew he had to be at least thirty-five or forty. My shoulders slumped. I would never see twenty-three, much less forty.

"You're the Gunny to me," I finally said, not knowing how to make him feel any better.

"Are you the same man you were a week ago?" he asked, after a few seconds.

I didn't know how to answer his question. My left hand reached down to clutch my letters home. My wife had to think I was the same person. My daughter could never know because she was too young to have known me before I left. If somehow I lived after Vietnam, I would try to make sure no one would know. I realized, coming to my feet slowly and starting to back away, that I did not know who I was or what I had been before. It hadn't been important to be anyone before. I was just me. The Gunny was telling me that I wasn't me anymore and that I never would be again. The Valley of No Joy. The words would not leave me. How had someone thought them up and put them together? It was an awful expression and for the first time I began to dread going to the A Shau.

"The problem is that nobody wants to go," the Gunny continued, like I was still squatting next to him. "Once we start," he went on, waving the hand not holding the canteen holder toward the open area, "we can't come back here."

"Gunny," I said, knowing that my voice sounded a bit wheedling and weak, "there's no place to come back to. All we have is the Marine Corps. Where's Gulf Company and Echo? Are they coming? And if they're coming then battalion command must be coming too." I hated having to ask but even in the asking I felt better than where the discussion had been going before.

"I know," the Gunny replied. "They're not stupid, you know. They just don't want to die and the Marine Corps isn't keeping them alive or giving a shit if they die, and they damn well know it. Command will command from the rear. This is the 'Nam, not some movie."

The Gunny wasn't telling me anything and he was all I had. Whatever he was not telling me I didn't need to know, and I had to think that way to survive until the night. He was old. He had to know.

"I can use our battery for another five thousand meters or so up the trail, just like before, but the accuracy's going to suffer and we are on the GT line," I said.

Then I dropped down again in to a squat and took my maps back out of my pocket. I laid one out in front of him, liking the plastic covering the Army had put over the whole thing. I would be able to call fire in the rain without hiding inside my poncho to keep the maps dry. I outlined how I could use the longer range 155s until we were out of their range but then we'd be dependent on the Americal battery with their limited air-dropped ammo supplies. We'd have to move very quickly through blown apart jungle and then very slowly through areas not so blown up and probably loaded with booby traps. The mountains around us were little different from what we would likely face on the way into the A Shau and it was nearly impossible to move along their flanks unless a path already existed. The undergrowth was heavy in some places and then impenetrable in others. The 60mm mortars would be useless, as well as the recoilless rifles and M79s. Our travel was going to be an infantry exercise and we were going to take casualties.

"What about a truce?" I asked.

"Truce?" the Gunny replied.

"Yeah, this is going to be dicey for the next few days and nights," I said. "We've got no support to speak of on the ground, no air, limited artillery and the enemy knows where we're going and when we're coming. First and Fourth Platoons. A truce. I haven't even met anyone from Second and Third. Do we even have those two platoons?"

Fessman pulled up silently behind me as I waited for the Gunny to consider what I'd proposed. *Joy to the world, all the boys and girls, joy to the world, joy to you and me, joy to the fishes in the sea…* played ridiculously from his small shoulder-mounted radio. The rock and roll song somehow catching an edge of what the Gunny and I had been talking about. The Valley of No Joy.

"Second and Third COs are shake-and-bakes. Buck sergeants, corporals, whatever," the Gunny answered. "They're okay. Just waiting like everyone else. You've run in and around them but they don't say much. They're okay," he repeated.

"What are they waiting for?" I asked, but the Gunny was done talking on the subject. He got to his feet.

"We're going across and in like we are. There ain't no truce out here, not among them and not among us. We get hit hard then they'll fight hard but it has to be brought to them. Hill 110 wasn't our first. Let's hit the line now. The sun's up and it's never going to be behind us." The Gunny began breaking down his hooch and loading his pack. "You might call in some of that arty shit because there's no cover. We'll use two moving bases of fire with the M60s. The rest of us will spread out and use whatever cover is available and then regroup inside the tree line."

I joined my scout team. They'd broken my hooch down and packed my pack while I'd been talking to the Gunny. We moved wordlessly to the berm and I took out my Japanese glasses to survey the area one last time. The new map gave me insight as to what was beyond the tree line. The path we'd be using would snake around the next peak but it wouldn't be a climb. I reached for the already extended microphone and made my series of calls to the two Marine batteries. I would only call the American Division further along the way and try to use pinpoint fire instead of ammo-eating zone barrages.

Fessman's little radio belted out "Waltzing Matilda" as I ordered the fire. I had no idea what a billabong was or a jumbuck or a swagman was, but it didn't make any difference. The Australians were some rough and tough soldiers and the song made me feel like I might be one of them under the right conditions. The new me. The new me who didn't even know who the old me was. I got my pack on and made sure I was ready. The artillery coming in made everyone around flinch but not me. I wasn't afraid of artillery. I was afraid that I might live and then be looking over other people's shoulders like the Gunny had looked over mine.

thirty-one

THE SEVENTH DAY : FOURTH PART

I had no idea how the attack into the tree line on the other side of the Agent Orange clearing would go down. Once more, as with each day's move since I'd been in country, things just seemed to happen without a lot of verbal orders, command post meetings or formal preparations. In training, everything had been carefully choreographed in order to make sure no details were left out, or open questions, unanswered. The Marine Corp was known for being experts at the frontal attack. Their "fire and maneuver" method involved a squad of men taking off with the fire teams roughly splitting up behind the squad leader. The squad would leap-frog across the exposed area, with one fire team dropping down to lay covering fire for the fire team nearby that was up and moving forward. That moving fire team would then drop, the process repeating itself over and over again until the whole company was safely, or unsafely, across.

My scout team surrounded me, all wearing the heavy packs we used to transport everything. In combat situations, the main packs would usually be discarded until the fighting ended and they could be retrieved. For reasons the Gunny had not shared with me, that wasn't being done for this crossing, which could be damaging to everyone in the company, to say the least.

The Gunny reappeared, moving smoothly through the hardening mud toward my position. I noted once again the mild but cooling wind of higher altitude and the lack of mosquitoes. Possibly, without the war and combat, parts of Vietnam could be considered places of comfort and beauty, but I couldn't imagine this battle zone infested with hiking tourists and day campers. I squatted down and dumped my pack next to me. Noticing that my hands and arms looked vaguely whitish, I rubbed my left hand up and down my right forearm. The mix of junk on my skin felt like an oily lotion but smelled like a mix of gasoline, diesel fuel and rancid milk. Whatever was in the mix would probably kill me down the line, but I wasn't too worried about down the line.

"The defoliant combines with the repellent and turns a strange milky white," the Gunny said, dropping his own pack next to mine and lighting up a cigarette with his neat looking Zippo lighter. "Probably a bad mix. Up here you shouldn't use the repellent, not close to that Orange shit, anyway."

"What's our plan?" I asked, wishing I didn't have to ask but no longer embarrassed in asking.

The Gunny had accepted me into the company, although that meant little to First or Fourth Platoons, and he'd also convinced me that I could not function as a commander of anything. At least not until I knew more. Watching the Gunny smoke his cigarette and looking at the open area beyond where we had to go, I knew at that moment that if I hadn't done things exactly as I had so far, under his guidance, I would not be alive. I couldn't afford to reflect on what the company was supposed to be all about, or how it was run. I had to think about the next right thing to do to stay alive.

The Gunny finished his cigarette, taking one last long drag before tossing the remains into a nearby stand of bamboo. He looked like a real warrior I might have seen in one of those war movies back in the States, except he was way too dirty and his eyes looked like pools of flat black obsidian.

"We're going in right behind the initial squad approach First Platoon is making," the Gunny said, working his way back into his own heavy pack. "We're wearing full packs because we can't be moving back and forth in the open, not with the tunnels they've likely got running under this whole area."

"I thought we'd be in the back with Fourth Platoon," I said, since neither the Gunny nor I carried anything but Colt automatics, and those were all but useless in making a full frontal assault on anything or anybody.

"You can't lead from the rear in this," the Gunny said, looking me straight in the eyes, before softening his expression, "and I sure as hell don't want to be anywhere near Sugar Daddy when you start calling artillery."

"What about Willie Peter?" I asked.

"What about it?" the Gunny replied, getting ready to move.

"I can call in a battery of six up and down the tree line before we cross," I told him. "The burning phosphorous will still be burning in little spots all over there by the time we make it."

"Will it burn our guys, too?" the Gunny said, his expression serious as he weighed the odds.

"Some," I replied. "Not much, maybe a second degree patch here and there, but the effect will probably keep a lot of NVA heads down while we cross."

"I'm not sure that's such a great idea," the Gunny said. "That shit's like napalm. If the guys get some on them then they'll hold it against you."

"Really?" I replied, with a cold smile. "I wasn't too popular in training and my peer evaluations here seem pretty god-damned low, as well."

I held my hand out toward Fessman without looking, my eyes locked with the Gunny's own. The radio microphone filled my hand but I didn't move.

The Gunny shook his head almost imperceptibly, a look of resignation on his face.

I made the call back to Russ, making sure to fire the first round deep, or over where I thought it might land. At fifty meters in the air it would blossom so huge and bright it would be impossible to miss, even with the naked eye.

"Make the call," the Gunny breathed, after it was too late.

The radio speaker said "splash, over," and I moved with Fessman to the back side of the berm to observe. In spite of being beyond effective range, the round blew itself to bits fifty meters above where the path should take us through once we crossed over. And it was about five hundred meters over. I dropped four hundred and fired for effect. Battery of one, and then adjusted the fire left and right, moving up and down the tree line in three hundred meter increments. I needed no map or numbers. It was child's play.

I pressed the transmit button after the last smoking pile of rounds burned its way into a thick mound of bamboo, high trees and jungle cover. The entire tree line was a smoking mass of little burning fires, and the smoke clouds just kept getting bigger. A great white and gray mass seemed to be moving over the entire exposed area the company had to get over.

"Yes," I breathed into the open mic.

"Not bad, eh?" came back over the radio, Russ having heard my approval.

"Thanks, Russ," I said back, softly. "You just took some of the fire out of Troub City by putting some real fire into it, and the smoke would cover a battleship attack up here."

"Let's go," I said to the Gunny, handing the mic back to Fessman.

"A fucking smoke screen," the Gunny said. "Why didn't I think of that?"

The Gunny pulled something out of his utility top that had been hanging around his neck. My first thought, "dog tags," until he blew it. A whistle, of course. Everyone began to move along the line. Men I hadn't even known existed climbed over chunks of bracken and through stands of bamboo to move out into the open and then on into the cloud. I knew the phosphorous would burn for about another ten minutes and then the smoke would be gone, the wind making sure that any residual smoke left behind by small fires would be quickly scudded away.

I wanted to run across the open ground as quickly as possible, but instead I waited with the Gunny, counting on the fact that his superior knowledge and combat experience would allow him to pick just the right moment. I knew that time had come when the Gunny spoke a few words to Nguyen. Almost before I saw the Kit Carson scout rise to his feet, he'd taken off into the cloud. Nguyen's ease of movement through the jungle, his tough endurance and silent accommodation of everything around him, made me fear for any success of the United States in this war. The enemy was like Nguyen. Like a bunch of Nguyens: bright, tough, loyal, and dedicated, fighting in its own back yard.

This time there would be no hiding. I knew that right away. My pack had to weigh almost sixty pounds and that didn't include my automatic, full canteens, extra ammo, K-Bar bayonet, and everything else. Naked, I'd probably be down to about a hundred and thirty pounds. No loads in training ever approached what I carried now. There would be no running across the open space. There wouldn't even be firing. I could not hear a single shot of small arms fire come back out of the smoke cloud, AK or M16. Maybe the clever wily NVA soldiers were simply dug in and waiting until the company was fully committed, like the Japanese holding the inland mountains on some of those island campaigns during WWII.

I trudged behind the Gunny, unable to see anything or anybody else, although I was aware of Fessman, Stevens, and Zippo right behind me. I had no idea what the Gunny said to Nguyen, or what my native scout might be up to. That the Gunny knew some Vietnamese surprised me. I should probably be upset by being left out of almost every decision, no matter how big or small, but I wasn't. I knew the only way I'd manage to stay alive was by taking one step after another forward through the covering cloud of my own design. I heard two distinct M16 round bursts, maybe three rounds of fire in each burst, but there wasn't any way in the thick smoke to see if the rounds were tracers, or what they might have been fired at.

There were no other shots. It took less than ten minutes to reach the tree line. The smoke cleared as we approached the line of jungle not killed off or eaten away by the aerial spraying months earlier with Agent Orange. The many little fires burning everywhere seemed to be burning off the natural smoke from the phosphorus being broken open and exposed to air.

My eyes and lips began to burn. I moved toward an area with less smoke. Some Marines in front of me had stopped to cough, leaning on the butts of their M16s, the ends of the weapons' barrels sticking into the mud. I knew why they were coughing. The smoke from white phosphorus was not usually dangerous. The Navy used it for making smoke screens for its ships. But in very humid conditions the gas changed chemically from a rather inert smoke to something called phosphoric acid. I breathed the clear air deeply in and out and opened one of my canteens to swab my eyes and wash out my mouth. Mucus membranes were the most at risk. Nguyen came from nowhere, seemingly unaffected by the smoke, while Zippo, Stevens and Fessman followed my example with their own water supplies without my having to warn them about the exposure.

"No enemy?" I said to the assembled group, the Gunny nowhere to be seen.

"Nothing yet, I guess," Stevens said, between tossing handfuls of water into his open eyes.

I looked around at the clear area. The fires were quickly going out as the phosphorus burned itself out and the wet jungle plants, ferns and trees provided no tinder for any kind of fire. After looking around, the whole team acted as one and eased down to the fern covered mud floor of the jungle. Either the enemy was dug in and waiting, which began to seem unlikely, or they had run away from the artillery barrages, the Willie Peter quite possibly being the last fearful insult to drive them out.

The Gunny came out of the jungle by pushing aside some young bamboo shoots and emerging only a few feet away.

"Sent out scouts," he said, squatting down to begin making his habitual preparations for a cup of coffee. "We'll wait here until they get back. We're losing the light so might as well stay for the night. Doesn't look like they waited around to try to take us out, or maybe they're just laying up to come at us from a more defensible position."

I looked around. In training I would have spoken up, as there was no better place I could imagine to defend from than a thick tree line with nothing but dense jungle behind you — a jungle that you knew way better than the veins on the back of your hand.

"We're gonna need a medevac, anyway," the Gunny said, talking in a way as if he had to talk to somebody.

It wasn't like the Gunny at all. I looked around and could tell that Fessman and Stevens had picked up on his odd tone, too. Zippo obliviously worked to begin the clearing and building of a hooch.

"I had Pilson call it in," the Gunny went on. "He's over there helping Jurgens out. Seems somebody opened up in the smoke, thinking they were shooting at the enemy but hit Jurgens' radioman instead. He's in a pretty bad way so we've got to get him out of here."

Nobody said anything. Something in the back of my mind bothered me but I couldn't quite identify it.

"He'll be back in a little bit and we'll get on with command and make sure they know we're across," the Gunny said, sipping from his canteen cover every four or five words, or so. "Gulf Company will be coming up the trail in trace tomorrow so we've got to be out of here early. That means no resupply until we're a whole lot closer to the valley."

"Jurgens' radioman, hit?" I asked, trying to figure out how a man so close to the platoon commander could take some rounds of friendly fire when nobody could see anything, and there was no incoming fire.

The Gunny didn't answer, shakily taking out another cigarette to smoke with his coffee — also unusual. From what I'd learned in my first week with him, the Gunny had specific and succinct habits. I looked over at Fessman, wondering whether Sugar Daddy and the Fourth Platoon crossed with us or whether I should get ready to lay down a carpet of artillery fire on top of our former position. Fessman diddled with changing the battery in his radio, which I presumed he would have changed just before we went into combat, and not after. Stevens made his own coffee and Zippo worked away. None of my team would look at me, no matter how hard I stared from one to the other. Then I noted that they took great pains not to look at Nguyen, either. I climbed to my feet without warning.

"Gunny, got a second?" I said, beginning to walk down the tree line we'd just blown to hell. I made sure not to step back out into the open area, however. The Gunny followed me, taking several minutes to do so. He carried his cigarette between two fingers of his right hand and his canteen holder handle in the other.

Once we were out of hearing range I stopped and turned. "He missed," I said flatly.

"Who missed?" the Gunny asked, his tone just a bit too incredulous. "Missed who?" he followed up. When I didn't answer right away he got a bit confused about whether to smoke his cigarette or drink the coffee. I waited.

"Jurgens," I finally said, knowing he was going to admit nothing. "Nguyen missed Jurgens in the smoke and hit his radio operator."

The Gunny stood with his cigarette and canteen holder, both half way up to his mouth.

"Shit," he would have said, but nothing came out. I read his lips.

I waited and he waited, neither of us moving.

"We need the artillery," the Gunny finally said. "And we can't get lost. If we get lost in these fucking mountains we're dead. And who in hell can call Army artillery, anyway? I didn't even know they had artillery in that god damned valley."

I massaged my forehead with my right hand. With nothing else to be said, I began to walk away. But after only a few steps I had to stop. I didn't turn around to process the words coming from behind me. After a slight hesitation, I moved on back toward the area where the team worked on making our home for the night. I rolled the words I'd only caught vaguely around in my mind. They sounded like "de nada."

"Thanks," I said to the Gunny, my voice a whisper.

THE SEVENTH NIGHT

Crimson and clover, over and over... The song played from Fessman's tactically stupid, but achingly home-calling, radio. The song's lyrics just repeated with no actual meaning, like the days and nights of my life in Vietnam. Brother John came on after the song to introduce "Eight Days a Week" by the Beatles. I liked that song, although, until I got out in the bush, I'd never put much emphasis on listening to rock and roll. For some reason being amerced in the wet-heated jungle, waiting for some gruesome death that might come at any minute, made every song burn itself into my brain. I understood why the men played their radios all day long, and why Armed Forces Radio shut down at night. It was worth the risk to all of us to be able to listen during the day. And Headquarters knew we'd play the music all night, too, if we had the chance.

Two choppers came in before sunset. Whatever Pilson said when he called for the medevac must have mollified Marine Air Command (Vertical) because the birds landed without Huey Cobras to fly their usual support. Either that or word had gotten back that the Army would fly in support of Marines in trouble, when the higher ranking Marine chopper pilots would not.

The Hueys came down close to where my scout team had set up their hooches. As soon as I'd heard the first vibrations of the helicopter's blades, my brain tuned out the Beatles and homed in on the medevac landing. My left hand clutched my two letters home. I could not forget to get them aboard, again.

The lead chopper took three Marines on IVs. They looked like anonymous slugs, folded and crumpled down in their poncho covers. There should have only been one. With no updates since the shots in the smoke screen, I didn't know where the other two casualties had come from. The Gunny was nowhere to be seen. I moved toward the loading chopper, the door gunner swinging his M-60 from side to side like the approaching Marines might be the enemy. He wore an air helmet that looked like it had been poured around his cranium, with bulges for his ears. He also wore large sunglasses so dark I couldn't see his eyes. If the man was trying to look intimidating, he'd succeeded.

Macho man stood beside the open door in his usual pose. Parade rest combined with port arms, so he could best show off his Thompson. For the first time I noted that he carried no canteen, bayonet or any other clip or junk on his belt like the rest of us did. All the pockets of his utilities were pressed flat and obviously empty. The Thompson had one stick magazine loaded into it. Twenty rounds, I presumed. What could you do with twenty rounds when all of them came out together in one burst? Maybe he had more ammo inside the chopper, I thought, but then doubted it. Macho man held down an extremely dangerous job and had probably been shot at a whole lot more than I had. He was doing his thing and in doing it, proving he was at least as looney as I was. I gave him my letters home. He released one hand from his beloved Thompson and took the letters. Surprisingly, he accepted them very gently, and then carefully placed them inside one of his flat chest pockets.

I backed away far enough from the still turning blades of the chopper to hear Fessman's civilian radio behind me. *We gotta get out of this place...* squeaked out of the speaker. Probably the last song of the broadcast, I realized. Brother John's end-of-day humor.

The second chopper unloaded supplies by dumping the boxes and bags into the mud, unlike the careful placement and stacking the Army had provided earlier in the day. Rittenhouse scurried about after making sure the Marines going out were properly noted, recorded and whatever else he did to make sure the identities of dead and wounded were established and maintained. The chopper dumped five of the plastic water bottles. I made a note to try to get one for my second shower if at all possible. I knew I'd never get rid of the white oil patina that covered my skin without soap and water. The water couldn't be carried in jugs because of the distance we'd be covering the next day, which would be long and hard. It made sense to lighten the load.

The first chopper, the one with Macho Man and the wounded, took off. I moved over to the supply pile and gathered in some boxes of Ham and Lima's. For some reason Rittenhouse seemed intent on trying to inventory with his little notebook. What was that all about, I wondered. He didn't try to stop me but I could tell he was displeased about what I was doing. I shrugged. There was, no doubt, a set of rules I knew nothing about because nobody else was going through the supply pile.

Rittenhouse walked over to me and I got ready to take some heat for my behavior.

"Here," he said, pushing a cardboard box at me. It was a little larger than a C-Ration box. Even before I took it I knew it was a care package sent from the states. My hopes soared, although I knew I had not been there long enough to get a box from my wife. I read the name on the box, but it wasn't mine. I looked up into Rittenhouse's eyes in question.

"From the tough guy with the Thompson," Rittenhouse said, raising his voice to be heard over the rising whine of the departing Huey's rotor. "He said to give it to Junior, the guy with the shoe button eyes."

I took the box and backed up. I got the rest of my stuff together and moved to my hooch. I wasn't able to get inside my tent-raised poncho cover before being surrounded by my scout team and the Gunny.

"Care package from home?" the Gunny asked, his tone light and casual.

"Says Waldo Vanilli on the box," I said, reading the name written in cursive on a white label across the top.

"But he gave it to Rittenhouse for you," Fessman said, as if he'd been right there, which he hadn't. He added; "The guy with the shoe button eyes."

My shoulders slumped a little at the phrase. I changed the subject by tearing the weak cardboard apart with my hands. Chocolate chip cookies began to fall out. The box was loaded.

"Cookies from home," Stevens exclaimed as everyone grabbed for the breaking and falling pieces. Not one crumb hit the mud. I ended up with part of the torn box and two cookies. I knew I'd just learned another etiquette rule of combat: care packages from home get shared, even if they don't come from your home and aren't addressed to you.

Fessman sat nearby eating cookies and reading off a torn piece of flimsy cardboard that the cookies had come in. "Waldo," he read. "You think the box belonged to him, or maybe was supposed to go to someone else?

"Nah," Zippo said, "he looks like he's Italian with that Vanilli name and all. 'Sides, it's bad luck to give out packages from home where you can't find the guy. If he's dead, then what?"

It surprised me to hear so much come out of Zippo. Other than Nguyen, who never spoke at all, Zippo was the most silent of the team. But they both ate chocolate chip cookies just like the rest of us.

"What are shoe button eyes?" Fessman asked.

The group became silent as I thought about answering the question. I knew what Macho Man, or Waldo, meant, but didn't want to say it. He meant that my eyes looked like those sewed-on button eyes found on a teddy bear or in a plastic or ceramic doll's head. Dead eyes. Eyes that gave no expression at all.

"Blue eyes," I finally said. "My eyes have always been bright blue. I've heard the expression before but not in a long time." I didn't mention that I'd never heard the expression used on me, or to describe my eyes. I wish there had been a mirror in the sundry packs we got all the time. If I ever got to the rear area, I tucked away the thought to look at my own face in the mirror. My wife thought I had nice eyes. A lot of people thought I had nice eyes. I couldn't have lost my nice eyes in only a week's time! But I knew the thought of that happening wouldn't leave me until I found a mirror.

Once again, the scout team erected our hooches touching one another. The proximity of my team made me uncomfortable at the same time it made me feel somewhat accepted. The men around me in combat seemed to more resemble predator cats in their physical behavior than human beings. They moved sinuously like Nguyen, winding, slipping and sliding their way through the jungle. They came close to one another but did not touch. Captain Morgan, with the Americal unit, was the only man in Vietnam who had touched me except for the Gunny, and the touches of the Gunny had been much more predatory than friendly.

The Gunny came out of the undergrowth and plopped himself down on my poncho liner. He went to work making the fixings for his habitual Coca Cola coffee. The sun had set below the edge of the west facing mountain ridge, with darkness fast closing in upon us. No more transistor radio music played, and my usual fear of the night began to creep into my stomach and up and down my back. I reached for my canteen holder to extract my canteen and join the Gunny, but my hands started to shake again. Instead of having coffee, I sat with my knees up and massaged both of my thighs. The deep muscle movement would eventually stop the shaking while at the same time, hiding my fear.

Soon, I knew, the Gunny would leave to set up his own hooch and my hands would be good enough to write another letter home. My daughter would be two months old soon. She'd been born as the most beautiful little creature I'd ever seen. I'd never seen a beautiful baby before had been been shocked not to find some red-faced crying thing. There would be no news from home, but I could write about my lovely daughter instead of talking about what went on around me — certainly not that I was deathly afraid of the coming night.

"Not a soul and not a shot fired," the Gunny said into the rising steam. He dumped two green foil packets of the black powder into the water, using his right index finger to stir the near boiling mixture. Impressed, I found the Gunny tough as iron with hands as steady as those of a carefully moving robot.

"Not exactly," I replied, quickly regretting the comment. The Gunny had tried to keep me alive and I now owed him, even if the wrong Marine got shot.

"What do you think?" the Gunny asked, ignoring my snarky remark.

I felt more than saw Fessman's head bob up in surprise from behind him. Did the Gunny really ask me what I thought? I was as surprised as Fessman but didn't let on. I took a moment to think, wondering if the Gunny was asking me about things in general or about the fact that we'd crossed the open area unopposed. I assumed his question pertained to our tactical situation.

"They're out there and they're waiting," I said. I pulled out one of my new maps and spread it between us. With barely light enough to read, I took out my taped up "one-eyed flashlight", as Fessman called it, and turned it on.

"Here's our position," I said to the Gunny, pointing with my right index finger. "And here's the saddle nine thousand meters away. After we cross that depressed area" — I tapped my finger on it — "it's a straight climb through heavy timber to the lip of the A Shau ridge. The saddle's where they're setting up. I mean, if I were leading their forces, that's where I'd set up. Plenty of time to dig in, lay fire base positions, walk off registration distances and set up incoming artillery fire. By the time we hit the saddle we'll be under their fire capability." I stopped and looked at the Gunny. In the flickering light from the burning composition B and the slight beam of the flashlight, his eyes looked like black glittering onyx.

The Gunny took a few long seconds and a couple more swigs of his coffee before answering. "They teach you that shit back in Quantico?"

"No," I answered with no derision in my voice. "I learned it from Nguyen. It's the way he thinks so it's the way they think. Nguyen wouldn't have attacked where we were today. The gunships, air, artillery, and a world of reinforcements would have arrived here in no time at all. The NVA are not stupid. But at the saddle we'll have almost no support. They want to hurt us. The war is about hurting us, not just stopping us…when we're not busy hurting ourselves."

I waited again, noting thankfully that my hands stopped shaking, at least for the time being.

"What about your artillery just leveling the place, like you did with it right here and over at Hill 110?" the Gunny asked, peering down at my map.

"Firebase Cunningham can't use plunging fire," I pointed out, running my finger from one small peak to the saddle ten clicks or so away. "Their rounds won't cross the peak between us firing as cannons, and they don't have the range to point the barrels up like howitzers and fire at high angle."

"Great, just great," the Gunny said, shaking his head and then sipping more of his strong coffee. "So what do we do, General Patton?"

"We don't go," I answered without any delay.

"Don't go? Then how in hell do we get to the A Shau? This isn't Hill 110. We can't just report we're there, because everyone in the world knows damn well where we are and where we have to go."

"We go up," I said, after the Gunny wound down. "No matter how thick the trees and brush, we go up to the top and then follow that wooded ridge all the way to the valley."

"Just like that," the Gunny said, his tone one of exasperation. "That's a hell of a hump up that slope to start with, and then along that high ridge? That's it? That's your lieutenant-type shit solution?"

"No, it's not my solution," I replied, as calmly as I could. "It's from the 'Frozen Chosin'. It's what they did. The Chinese thought the Marines would go down into the valley and follow it all the way to the sea, but Chesty Puller didn't do that. He took the ridge and followed that down, killing about four Chinese divisions along the way. They won't expect us to do this and we'll have the high ground."

"I was in Korea," the Gunny said. "It was damned cold."

I said nothing, wondering what he would say and do.

"Won't work," the Gunny finally concluded. "Can't work. The men aren't going to like it. Hell, fucking Jurgens is dead set on killing you, and Sugar Daddy isn't far behind. Like they're going to do what they say and if it wasn't for the snakes, they'd probably be on their way right now."

"Snakes?" I whispered, wondering if I'd heard right. But I had to go on with selling the plan instead of asking. "Artillery at Cunningham can fire all day long along our right flank, the machine guns cover our left and you can say it's all your idea, like before."

"Like before," the Gunny breathed. "Chesty Puller? You sure that was his plan and that's what did it?"

The name had an almost magical aura around it. Somebody on the plane coming into Da Nang had said that Puller's son was serving as a lieutenant with a Marine unit out of An Hoa, too. I fervently hoped he was doing better than I was. I waited, the idea of snakes haunting my thoughts.

The Gunny hadn't sounded like he was kidding.

"If Puller used that then maybe we can, too," the Gunny finally said. "I'm going to call a powwow tonight and discuss it. Puller's got five Navy Crosses, you know."

I didn't care if Puller had eight medals of honor, and I wasn't at all sure how the fateful and famous retreat at the Chosin Reservoir had really been accomplished. I just knew that I needed something because if the company just hiked up the trail, it would arrive at the A Shau a shattered, mostly dead wreck. And I would be, no doubt, one of the shattered or dead along the way.

"Snakes?" I asked softly, while the Gunny tossed the remains of his coffee into the mud and got up to go assemble his own hooch. I turned to look at my own team in the almost dark background and saw Pilson chewing away. The cookies were gone, regretfully, but I'd put my two broken small ones in my breast pocket. I couldn't wait to consume them, even though I'd probably get maybe four bites combined.

"Fucking Bamboo Vipers," the Gunny said, replacing his canteen holder and inserting the canteen into the opening. "These NVA assholes probably brought them in by the bushel. They wrap them around the bamboo about head high. You can't see 'em. They're the same color as the bamboo shoots. When you walk close they strike. The poison goes straight to your heart if you get hit in the face. And that's it. The other casualties... they were from the vipers. They say you don't die but you want to. Took two morphine syrettes to sedate both of them. It's why your guys are all clustered around you. For protection. Nobody will be moving around tonight."

The Gunny started to walk off, Pilson getting up to follow behind.

"How in hell can I protect them from poisonous snakes?" I said to the Gunny's back.

"By getting bit instead of them," the Gunny replied, his voice fading in the distance growing between us.

Poisonous snakes in Vietnam. I'd never thought about it. The Basic School didn't have geographic training for snakes, and certainly nothing about the related flora or fauna of Vietnam. Were there other poisonous snakes in country? Did they crawl in with you at night like scorpions in the desert? I had no clue. I moved to my pack to write my letter home. If the Gunny put the plan into action and it worked, then the company would be at the edge of the A Shau by sundown of the following day. And that meant I could mail the letter on a resupply or medevac chopper, if I did not die from a snakebite in the night.

I took my flashlight and shone it around my little area. Maybe a deeper moat, even empty, might be better than what I had. I wondered if I should tell my wife about the snakes but quickly got that idea out of my head. I'd write about Captain Morga, and how cool the Army food had been and how they'd come in to resupply us because the Marine Air Wing wouldn't fly through the bad weather. It was a good story. It would be a good letter. I got my stationery out and went to work.

thirty-three

THE SEVENTH NIGHT : SECOND PART

I stayed in my clustered hooch into the dark hours, whiling away the time it would take for the NVA to begin their own H&I fires. The concept of H&I (harassing and interdicting fire) created back at Fort Sill, had been used in Vietnam for years without any proven success. Another questionable strategy involved making totally random artillery drops. Since friendly units set up in supposedly known locations every night, the idea was that artillery could be dropped on paths, roads, and intersections, limiting the enemy's night operations and keeping them off balance, or from moving comfortably anywhere. But there had never been any results of such fire doing anything other than making sure no allied forces moved very far in the dark either.

I also wanted to see if, even given the fear of snakes everyone seemed to share, Jurgens would send out a team to finally eliminate the lone officer problem standing in the unit's way. I thought about the snakes, of which I'd seen none. It defied logic to believe that a specialized band of Vietnamese troops caught, and then strategically released, violently poisonous snakes, but rumors in combat raged everywhere about everything. The Bamboo Vipers that struck the two men earlier in the day were called "two-step" snakes. Anyone struck would supposedly get only two steps before falling over dead. The fact that both Marines bitten had been loaded onto a medevac Huey seemed to have blown right by the gossiping members of my scout team. After reviewing all the body bags that had been flown out during my short stay in country, I figured the snake dangers might be a bit overblown compared to other, more deadly threats. But I was still left to wonder what other poisonous snakes inhabited the hills or the dreaded valley ahead.

Two letters to send home. I clutched my pocket. What if the resupply chopper in the morning didn't come in? How many letters would I get backed up? I hadn't thought to date them. I pulled the envelopes out and then turned on my one-eyed flashlight. Using my black government (cheap) ballpoint pen, I carefully put dates on the back of the envelopes so my wife would know which order they'd been written. I wondered if they went on the same chopper whether that meant they'd arrive on the same day at her door.

Just after I replaced the letters and put away my flashlight, Stevens pushed gently with one foot against my leaning elbow. I moved the few feet toward his prone figure. He was on Starlight scope duty. The only area he could see was through the thin bit of vegetation we had between us and the big open area we'd walked across without incident. The area behind our hooches backed right up to the jungle, with only a small buffer zone laboriously cut for protection from snakes coming to get us in the night. I was thankful for the slight wind and cool temperature, but any relief the weather provided at higher altitudes came at the price of reduced security. An enemy coming at us from the jungle side wouldn't be encountered before he arrived. And although it was unlikely that any NVA would be out on the mud surface of the open area, Stevens insisted on setting up the scope to cover it.

"Nine o'clock," Stevens whispered, leaning away so I could stick my head behind the scope.

I liked the scope. It seemed so high tech. The science behind it, the sleekly different nature of its construction and the feel of it when I held it gave me confidence. I looked through the single lens, my eye pushed into the rubber grommet sticking out of the viewing end. A round green world came into existence.

Moonlight streamed down that I hadn't really noticed above the scudding dark clouds. The scene through the scope looked brighter than day, and only two things moved across the mud surface. Jurgens, with one of his henchmen, or 'shake and bake' squad leaders. I could see the sheen from the Slavic slab sides of Jurgens face gleaming in the dark. The two Marines didn't look like the last group that had come very slowly and low under ponchos. Both men crawled along at a good clip, able to move relatively unencumbered and not vertical enough to stand out against the jungle backdrop in relief. Neither Jurgens nor the man accompanying him sported M16 rifles, and that obvious fact surprised me. The company was deployed in the middle of a vicious pit of enemy occupation, probably surrounded on three sides, and that was only if the far side of the clearing wasn't filled with NVA who'd filtered in after we'd crossed. Marines didn't spend any time anywhere in such an environment without arms. The two crawling figures stopped their forward progress at what I thought was about twenty meters distant.

"Hey, Gunny," Jurgens yelled in a suppressed voice, cupping both muddy hands over his mouth.

Zippo replied before I could adjust to the fact that Jurgens appeared to be wanting a visit with the Gunny instead of coming for me. "What's the password?" he hissed back toward the men from his unseen position a few yards away.

My mouth formed a wry humorless smile. Password? There was no password. There'd never been any discussion about a password. I kept my eye glued to the eyepiece of the Starlight scope.

"There's a password?" Jurgens' squad leader asked, his voice one of complete surprise.

"Are you nuts, or just an idiot?" Jurgens whispered to the man with him, grabbing him by the upper arm.

"This is Jurgens, from First Platoon," Jurgens said, again directing his quieted words toward where my scout team lay.

"Okay, that's the password, you can enter," Zippo replied, instantly.

"What word?" the Marine with Jurgens said, crawling forward.

I watched Jurgens shaking his head in frustration, as he followed the smaller Marine in front of him.

"Jurgens is the password," Zippo said.

I smiled again, knowing Zippo had his M16 locked, loaded, and aimed at both of the moving men.

"Jurgens can't be the password," the Marine whispered, finally approaching close enough that I could pull away from the scope. "Nobody would make that a password," he went on. "You're making that up."

The Gunny appeared from behind me, as I prepared to receive the men, my right hand naturally resting upon the heel of my .45, the click of the safety lever being moved down to the off position unheard over the noise being made by the men crawling forward. Just because the two men were not sporting M16 rifles didn't mean they were unarmed.

"What are you doing here?" the Gunny asked, suddenly, taking full control of a situation I was too slow to react to.

"We have to talk," Jurgens replied. "We're unarmed so no idiot will shoot us without us saying so much as a word."

The reference to killing the three men from his platoon earlier was obvious, as was the potential threat that went with it. Why Jurgens chose to make even the slightest reference to it made me wonder about his real motivation in coming here. I turned my flashlight on suddenly, making Stevens swear. The light, aimed at the downed knees of Jurgens and his squad leader, must have blanked out the phosphor screen of the scope, I realized. Good to know, though, that Stevens was still scoping out the open area even if the two men appeared to be the only ones coming. The scope would take a few minutes to reset, but only if I turned off the light.

"Turn it off," the Gunny instructed, his mouth only inches from my right ear.

I followed his order, my mission accomplished. I knew right where both men were. If I drew and fired it would only take two shots to disable and two more after moving forward to finish the job.

"Talk about what?" the Gunny asked. "We're going up the mountain in the morning and then along the ridge all the way to the A Shau just like Chesty did at the Frozen Chosin."

"It's about the two-steps," Jurgens said, his voice indicating uncertainty.

A Prick 25 radio hashed twice and then clicked twice more. The radio was very close behind us. I half-turned in time to hear Pilson whisper into the Gunny's ear.

"Battalion six actual, Gunny," he said, his voice low, while sticking the handset between the Gunny and me.

The Gunny looked at me, then took the mic and punched the button. "Six actual," he said, his eyes too dark for me to see, although I knew he was looking into my own while he was waiting for a reply. But he didn't reply, instead holding out the handset toward me.

I took the microphone in my hand. The battalion commander, Colonel Bennet himself, wanted to talk to me, by name. He'd bypassed the Gunny completely.

"Six actual," I said, proudly, so everyone near could hear me.

And then I listened. I listened to the battalion commander berate me for demonstrated incompetence in avoiding a direct order by not attacking Hill 110 and then lying about it. I looked around at the Marines in my company. I could not see any of their eyes, but everyone waited. The colonel went on about how I could expect a bad fitness report on my next rotational review and an immediate entry into the daily report for my poor conduct. After "six actual," I never got to say a word, much less ask about any officers who might be assigned to the unit or what orders the battalion had for the A Shau, or anything. And then the line went dead. The man had not even said "over." I held the handset in my hand. I knew that one day, if I lived, and that wasn't real likely, that I would laugh at being told I would get a bad review when I was frightened to death of being killed in any of a variety of ways every minute of what was left of my life.

"Yes, sir," I said into the dead microphone, "I'll get right on it. We should be at the edge of the valley by late in the day unless we run into contact. I'll tell the men about the support we'll be getting."

I handed the microphone back to Pilson without further comment, and brought my attention back around to my real world. Maybe, if I lived, one day I would meet the colonel in some private place back home. It would be a very short meeting.

"The two men were medevaced, I said to Jurgens," speaking before the Gunny could. "The snake bites are painful but not fatal," I lied. "Both men are doing fine at the First Med Station in Da Nang."

"Once we get off the beaten trail we're going to be in the forested shit, and that crap is going to be full of snakes," Jurgens said.

I didn't know what else to say. I'd invented what I could. My hand fell back atop my Colt. Killing the men might be the best solution to a number of problems. I thought about imagining they were the colonel and his major executive officer. The Gunny finally filled the silence that hung over us like a little thick cloud.

"Tell your men the truth about the vipers," the Gunny said. "If they get bitten they get a free ticket home after a bit of pain. And we've got plenty of morphine. They get to go home."

I turned my head to look at the Gunny in wonder. He'd picked up the phony ball I'd metaphorically thrown and run right down the field with it. His tone and command ability impressed me even though I knew it was all based on a lie.

"What about Sugar Daddy?" Jurgens asked, surprising me again. The inter-company rivalry or war, take your pick, was ever on top of the table and never to be overlooked or forgotten.

"They're not afraid of snakes," the Gunny informed him. "They're afraid of the enemy. They'll take the point and clear our way to the top."

The two Marines said nothing further, not even goodbye, and certainly not "yes, sir." And they didn't ask permission to be dismissed, as even field protocol required. They simply backed up and disappeared the way they'd come. I was sure that Stevens could see them in the scope but their departure wasn't important enough to bother watching.

Neither the Gunny nor I moved for a couple of minutes. I waited for him to ask me what the colonel had said but he didn't speak. Finally, I decided to say something.

"Sugar Daddy's men aren't afraid of snakes and they're going to take the point tomorrow?" I asked, my tone more one of wonder than disbelief.

The Gunny did not reply, but he didn't move away either.

"Let's have a cup," he said, moving to take his canteen out of its cover.

"Aren't you a bit concerned with the light the fire will cause?" I asked, determined to come back to the Fourth Platoon issue in a few minutes, since the Gunny wasn't crawling back to his own hooch right away.

"You weren't going to be able to keep the flashlight on," the Gunny said, softly, lighting some Composition B to heat his water. "The NVA are out there and I'm sure they'll be a pain in the ass but not right here and right now because we've got a pretty good perimeter and they're not going out into the open."

"I just wanted to place exactly where they were," I explained.

"People move in the dark and it's very subtle," he replied, in a tone that made it sound like he was talking to a child. "From the second you turned on the light and for a few minutes, we were both night blind. The trade-off wasn't worth it. You can do a better job at measuring risk when both of our lives may be on the line."

I knew he was right. I knew it by the time he got to his second sentence. I'd risked us both needlessly. There was little question where the men were in front of us. Their shapes were visible, even if their features weren't. I should not have needed confirmation of anything, and I'd given up advantage in getting it.

The Gunny's water boiled after only a few minutes. He mixed in the coffee and then began sipping, slowly and lightly.

"So he found out already," he said, between sips.

The Gunny had figured out the substance of the colonel's call without even being able to see my reaction while the man had been on the handset. I thought about the shitty, unjust and truly outrageous radio call.

"Why didn't he talk to you?" I asked, finally.

"He needs me," the Gunny replied.

"To do what?" I said, knowing I was not thinking anything through but still upset by the call from our commanding officer.

"To train the next officer they send," he replied.

"After me," I whispered, not wanting to give that answer.

"After you."

The night erupted in small arms fire. The Gunny tossed his coffee and crawled away. I reached for the artillery net handset that I knew would be there, sticking out in the dark. It was. It was time to use what night defensive fires we had available to beat the enemy back again.

thirty-four

THE EIGHTH DAY

Dawn would not come. Again. A slight change in the dead blackness of lower jungle life was the only clue that dawn was in the offing. I looked at my combat watch only to realize that I could barely read it anymore. I rubbed it to see the luminous hands better but, after fruitlessly drying it using toilet paper from my Sundries Pack, I gave up. The problem wasn't moisture or dirt. The problem was Agent Orange. Somehow the mix of repellent and retardant formed a substance that melted plastic. Everyone said both substances were harmless but how could a solution so powerful it melted plastic be anything but dangerous, I wondered. In my short time in country I'd come to find that the sun always rose at about ten after six in the morning and set at about twenty after six every night. From the artillery registration data, I knew the equator was almost exactly eleven hundred miles away. Sunrise and sunset would not change much throughout the year because of that short distance. My melted plastic watch told me it was a quarter after five, or zero five fifteen in military time. The night had been filled with small arms fire and some thundering artillery explosions. I'd called fire using Russ and the battery back at An Hoa. The company was beyond the effective range of the 105 rounds, but Russ had agreed to fire anyway, in spite of the rules of engagement that were supposed to govern the potentially suicidal results that could occur.

We were on the wrong side of the mountain to call in Army supporting fire from Cunningham. There was no sleep in the company area inside the perimeter, not with shells that screamed in only a few hundred feet in the air right above everyone's head at over a thousand miles per hour. In the thickness of jungle growth, a high explosive shell's circular error of probability (the area of terminal destructiveness) was less than fifty meters. Dropping shells down little more than fifty meters from our perimeter had done quite a bit to dampen the enthusiasm of NVA snipers, but it had also added an additional edge to everyone's fear, including my own. I knew the A Shau Valley was going to be a different deal altogether because I'd heard, all the way back at Fort Sill, about the supporting fires the NVA had covering that area. The Ho Chi Minh Trail ran curling back and forth across the river that flowed fitfully along the bottom of the valley. That trail was the North's lifeblood of supply and they weren't going to surrender it without expending every round and all the personnel they had.

The Gunny approached with Pilson, his radio operator, right behind him. He squatted and began his usual coffee preparations. Dawn was closer, I knew, because I could see the two of them. I moved to squat next to the Gunny. If the choppers came in at dawn, then there'd be no time for anything except distributing supplies and getting rid of any and all stuff that was not necessary for the forced march up the mountain and then along its snaking ridge to the A Shau's western lip.

I noted once again that there seemed to be no verbal "good mornings" or good anything else's in combat, at least not in the combat unit I was assigned. I hunkered down and lit my explosive fuel. The Gunny tossed me a packet of instant coffee from his never-ending supply. I never had any, but he seemed to be able to gather in every extra packet laying around, or he simply got it because he was the Gunny, and I was Junior.

"So, Fourth Platoon is going to take the point?" I said, as a statement and not really a question. "How in hell did you pull that off?"

The Gunny sipped, while Pilson looked away. From Pilson's expression I knew there was something wrong. I decided not to push the Gunny. I sipped my own coffee and waited.

"Nope," he finally said, his voice low and broken up from his saying the words in the middle of a coffee slurp.

"Last night—," I began, but he cut me off.

"That was last night. This is, or will soon be, today."

I shook my head in frustration, and with a complete lack of understanding. "Why in hell did you tell Jurgens that then?"

"To settle him down, confuse him, kick the problem down the road," the Gunny said, stringing the words together without comma delays. "Fourth will follow up like they always do, Chambers and will lead with the Second. Jurgens backs up Chambers with Evans, and the Third Reinforced, between those guys and the Fourth."

I understood what he was saying and it made sense, except for the direct and unsupportable lie to Jurgens. "What about the First and what you said?" I asked again, in a slightly different way.

"Sugar Daddy already paid the price, not that he or his Marines will see it that way," the Gunny said, looking out over the open area we'd come across so easily.

"Price?" I asked. "What price?"

"The tax," the Gunny replied. "Two dead knuckle-draggers while you were dumping shit all over the jungle. Didn't you hear the grenades?"

"Maybe the grenades were from the other side?" I said, knowing my logic was way out there. The sound of Chicom grenades was nothing like the real stuff, M33s made in America.

"Really?" the Gunny said, thick sarcasm in his voice. "Let's see, the enemy is out there, probably no closer than fifty meters from the perimeter. Sugar Daddy's lovely crew is down there close to the edge of the open area. Do the math."

I knew from my single day at Explosives Ordinance Disposal School that throwing a grenade seventy or eighty yards across flat bare land, much less heavily wooded jungle terrain, was near to impossible.

"Tracers don't show much in the jungle, either," the Gunny finished.

I mentioned nothing about how the idea of using the tracers had become his. While I'd been totally involved trying to direct inherently inaccurate artillery against an engaged enemy, the life and death racial war in my unit still raged on. I wondered how that internal war could possibly be resolved. The black Marines should have been distributed evenly through all the platoons long ago but somehow that had all become screwed up. Equally bizarre, the southern white Marines had apparently assembled in one platoon, as well. Would the internal war simply rage on, with all casualties blamed on the NVA, or would one side win over the other? It also seemed like not one other soul in the company had picked one side over the other. Including the Gunny. I noted that he'd called Fourth Platoon Marines "knuckle-draggers," but not referred to the First Platoon as the Crackers they certainly had to be. Had the Gunny really chosen after all, but remained outwardly neutral, waiting for a change in time and conditions?

Rittenhouse showed up with his clipboard in hand.

"Enemy fire?" he asked the Gunny, squatting down with only a nod toward me.

I didn't take offense. I had come to realize in my first week that everyone in the company was in a difficult position when it came to my presence and my role in the unit. My specialties were being accepted but my leadership was judged to be incompetent and unwanted. Indicating favor or deference to me could easily mean a sentence of silent death in the night for anyone showing it. Or quite possibly, a place at the point of the coming very dangerous move only hours away.

"Of course," the Gunny replied, finishing his coffee.

I knew that none of the dead would ever go out as being the result of friendly fire. A friendly fire report had to have the source and nobody in the company was going to allow anyone else to put them down as a source.

The distinctive *whup, whup, whup* of Huey helicopters could be heard faintly in the distance. I checked my melted watch. It was almost exactly six a.m. Not first light, but close enough. Everyone moved. Fessman stayed with me, as I headed the few yards it took to move through the bracken back to the open area where the choppers had to land. I crouched down, as the usual four choppers became visible, the two Cobra ships in front, skimming nose down and low, while the two utility 'slicks' followed a few hundred yards behind. There was no firing of any weapons I could hear, but I'd learned about that from the scout team. If there was going to be fire, then it would come while the choppers were on the ground. Moving helicopters were a whole lot harder to hit than most inexperienced people might think, and shooting directly at the heavily armed gunships was nearly suicidal, at any time.

The blade wash struck with its usual cyclonic velocity. I shielded my face and eyes. Little pieces of mulch and other debris impacted on every exposed part of my body. My left hand was inside my pocket, gripping the letters to be sent off to my wife. Macho Man leaped out of the lead chopper as its skids touched down. I knew his real name but couldn't remember it from atop the cookie box, if that had been his real name. He was just Macho Man, although I found his stoic and cat-like attention to me kind of neat. I wondered, as he took his strange semi-formal parade rest pose next to the Huey, if he knew I wasn't really the unit's commander at all. How much information got aboard the choppers, what with the fact that so few of them made contact with the ground, and when they did it was for only a few seconds or minutes. The homemade black bar on my helmet cover would have told him that I was an officer, although the Junior printed in magic marker under the bar would be in conflict with the officer designation.

A crew member unloaded the supplies, one box after another, like had been done before. There was no Army neatness and stacking, although I noted the Marine methodology allowed for the choppers to spend a lot less time exposed on the deck. I gave Macho Man my letters. He reverently stuck them in his own pocket, as before.

Four sharp cracks punched through the blade driven air. Cracks I instantly knew came from AK-47 rifles. Macho Man leaped aboard the Huey. I saw the far door gunner slump over his M-60. The near door gunner left his position to dive across the chopper to help the other man. I ran forward, and then out in front of the chopper, more to get out of the line of fire than make myself a target. I reasoned that the gooks were firing at the most valuable target and that wouldn't be me. I hit the mud on my chest, twenty-five yards in front of the wounded helicopter.

The two Cobra gunships swiveled in mid air and the swept over the far tree line, raking the jungle with rotary machine guns. First the rear Huey slick lifted from the mud quickly and began to pull backwards with its rear rotor almost touching down. Macho Man's chopper lifted straight up, but very slowly. I looked out across the open area to see if the gunships had suppressed the sniper fire, when I saw two figures rise up out of the ground less than half way across the open area.

I could see them clearly. I was surprised to note that they were both obviously female and wore the dark colored uniform jackets of the NVA. Both also wore floppy bush hats, not unlike those of many of the Marines in my company.

And then I realized why they were standing. They stood to be able to angle their assault rifles up. They were standing to get a better shot at the wounded chopper.

I leaped to my feet in one arched rush. I stood under the chopper's prop wash, turned sideways to the two women and pulled my .45 from its holster. I flipped the safety lever on the left side down automatically, the click unheard with all the noise raining down from the Huey. I brought the Colt up until my arm was straight out, my combat training in how to use the weapon totally forgotten. I reverted to the many times my Dad, on the Coast Guard Pistol Team, had prepared me to shoot the children's .45 course at the Camp Perry NRA nationals. I breathed in and out, knowing that the sights on the combat Colt had never been checked out by me or properly sighted in. As I focused my right eye on the post of the front sight through the now hazy square "V" of the rear sight, I saw the women about forty yards away. They were no longer raising their weapons. They were up and running for whatever reason, headed toward the far side of the clearing.

I got control of my breathing. Easy in and easier out. Once, twice, and then a third time, while the women ran. I decided to aim over the head of the woman on the right and hope for a center of mass shot on her torso. The gun at the end of my fully extended arm shook slightly, but my breathing remained true. At the end of my fourth exhalation the gun went off and blew back hard in my hand, bending my elbow slightly. I brought the Colt immediately back into battery, and aimed at the same place above the second running woman's back, glad she was running directly away and not at an angle. One more inhalation the then another slow release. The Colt went off a second time, seemingly all on its own.

I moved the automatic over toward the right in order to see what results I'd had but there was nothing to see. The women were gone, like they'd disappeared up into the air.

"Shit, I fucking missed," I said, now able to hear myself because the chopper was a good distance up and moving away fast. My ears were already ringing from the shock wave of the gun's explosions, but I knew that would die down over time.

I went to my hands and knees and crawled into the bracken, punching down on the safety lever to avoid an accidental discharge.

"You didn't miss, sir," Fessman said, holding my binoculars. "You hit them both I think, but the ground cover out there's too thick to show them."

I didn't believe him and grabbed the binoculars. I could see nothing but very brightly colored foliage everywhere.

"I don't think so," I said. "There'd be some movement, or something."

"There's no place for them to go, sir," Fessman continued, pointing out at nothing.

The gunships followed the slicks and all four choppers were gone in less than a minute. Silence, except for the mild wind of the mountain highlands made any sound at all. The sound of the wind blowing through the trees of the jungle was muted but kind of rough, not the smooth calming sound of the wind through the pines across the Virginian countryside had provided while I was in training.

All of a sudden I saw a spidery figure scrabbling outward across the surface of the open area, disappearing for a few seconds and then reappearing a few feet further way. The figure made it to the spider hole the women had hidden in and was lost to view.

"Who the hell is that?" I asked, bringing the binoculars back up, but finding nothing to see.

"Nguyen," Zippo said, coming forward to where I was, with Stevens at his side. "He's gone out to get your stuff."

"What stuff?" I asked, my eyes glued to the rubber grommets of the big Japanese binoculars, waiting for Nguyen to pop up or slither out of the spider hole.

After a few moments I saw him get back into the hole I'd never seen him leave, and then begin to work his way back across the stretch of defoliated Agent Orange countryside. I brought the lenses down when he got close.

Nguyen eased into the brush and spore-laden fern leaves the rest of us lay in and among. He pulled down the two rifles he'd slung to his right shoulder and a small curled up cloth package.

"They're yours," Stevens said, avoiding using the word sir, unlike Zippo and Fessman.

"What are mine?" I asked, nonplussed.

"Their possessions," he indicated, pointing.

I looked down, and noted the blood on the cloth. Nguyen had obviously torn one of the women's blouses apart to make the sack. For a second I lost my balance a bit, digging my fingers into the jungle growth and mud I was laying on to better ground me. A wave of nausea swept up from my stomach to my throat and then subsided. I swallowed, heavily.

"It's part of the rules of engagement," Fessman stated, like he was reading from some military manual. "Going all the way back to Grecian times, the combatant who kills another combatant in open fair combat gets the possessions of the one killed. We'll itemize and tag all this for you, then send it back to battalion, who'll itemize and send it to division. They'll keep it for you and either let you take it home or send it home in a box for you. Rittenhouse will take care of the paperwork."

I wanted to say "you're kidding me" or something that might let me in on the joke, but I knew in my heart that it was no joke. All three Marines of my scout team stared at me with flat expressions, waiting.

I wasn't going to have the stuff sent home. I never wanted to see it again. I didn't want it itemized and I wanted to get as far from it as possible.

"They'll probably confiscate the AKs, though," Zippo said.

"Can't take automatic weapons home."

I realized right away that there was some code that regulated this kind of thing, and it probably didn't happen very often that one Marine was exclusively identified as the killer of another individual enemy soldier. I felt I could not just say no and hurry back to my hooch.

"Who wants the stuff?" I asked.

"What?" Stevens said, his voice indicating real surprise.

"I'll trade you this stuff if one of you'll build my hooch every night," I offered, wondering if such a thing was allowed or acceptable.

"Jeez, sir," Zippo replied. "We'll all do it and split the pot."

I watched Stevens brow knot up for a few seconds, like maybe he should have gotten all of the spoils himself, but then he changed.

"You got it, sir," he said.

I didn't miss the sir and that word felt better at getting it out of him than it'd felt in hearing it in some time. I left the scout team to divide and claim the spoils in whatever way they did that and made my way back to my hooch, noting that it was the first time I could remember Fessman not being cloyingly attached to me like a baby in a tethered stroller.

I couldn't stop thinking about Nguyen, who'd risked his life once again for me, or at least to get what he thought might be mine. Macho Man, Fessman, Nguyen, and maybe Zippo were in my camp, inside my wire, as I'd heard other combat seasoned Marines say. Stevens and the Gunny were right there at the gate, while the rest of the company was, without a doubt, outside the wire.

I laid down in my hooch and wrote a letter to my wife, detailing the odd different cultural nature of Nguyen and his attachment for Americans, and me in specific, that didn't seem to make much sense. I wrote fast and with poor penmanship. When I was done I sealed the envelope and addressed it before refilling my 'letter home' pocket. Then I closed my eyes to think about the fact that I'd killed the first enemy soldiers I really knew to have been killed by me personally. It wasn't the same as calling artillery. I could see the women's eyes and barely emotional facial expressions when they'd been targeting the Huey.

I wondered how long the memory of their existence would remain with me before I forgot about them completely.

THE EIGHTH DAY : SECOND PART

I finished my letter home, the light of dawn sufficient to allow me to see the paper almost as well as the lousy black ink from my cheap government ballpoint. I had already decided earlier, if I lived, that I would be buying a watch that didn't have a plastic crystal, in case I ran into Agent Orange back in the world. I added a quality pen to my imaginary collection. The moisture always present, even up in the highlands, made every other letter of my writing almost indistinguishable. I called Fessman over, as he returned from dividing up the "spoils of war" he'd likely be sharing with the others.

"Rittenhouse won't send the papers," he complained, before handing me the artillery net handset.

"Why not?" I asked, in surprise, before accepting the mic.

"Because everyone says that the guy on the chopper with the Thompson shot those women."

"What?" was all I could say, my face no doubt a study in consternation.

"They said you could never have made those shots with a .45 automatic," Fessman said. "The range was too great and each woman took a hit in almost exactly the same spot. The Thompson would have made that pretty easy, since it fires so many rounds, and it's got a lot more range."

"Ah, you were right there Fessman, and you saw it all," I said, raising my voice a little.

"Yeah, I know, but there was a lot of noise and the guy from the chopper might have been firing from the back side of the Huey. He'd just lost one of his crew and all."

The Gunny came walking out of the brush nearby. I presumed he'd arrived to announce our coming move.

"Who told you Macho Man shot them?" I asked Fessman, still in shocked wonder.

"I did," the Gunny said, hunkering down to make another of the instant coffee preparations he was obviously addicted to.

I just looked at him in disbelief, unable to say anything.

"They were women," he said, getting his canteen out. "The men hate the female NVA worst of all because if one of us gets captured the women do the torturing, and they seem to enjoy it a whole lot. But they're women, so you'd eventually look bad for shooting them, in the unit's way of looking at things. Don't forget to reload your .45, since you seem to know how to handle the thing."

My hand slid down to the comforting butt of the Colt. The Gunny was right. I'd forgotten to reload, and that failure shook me more than the strangeness of once again giving whatever credit I got for anything to someone else. I pulled open one of the dual magazine carrier covers I had snapped to my belt, took out a spare magazine and exchanged it carefully with the half expended one. I'd left the single round in the chamber so I was loaded with that, and five more in the fresh magazine. I clicked the safety on and re-inserted the gun back into my holster.

The Gunny watched my every move, while sipping away from his canteen holder.

"Had to be sixty, maybe seventy yards," he said, as if he was talking to himself instead of me. "Didn't think a .45 would shoot that far, not accurately at least," he went on. "You got one of those expert badges in training, I'll bet."

"Yeah," I replied, taking my own canteen out. "I had enough points to make master though, when I was going to Camp Perry, but I was too young to be awarded any. Slow fire was my favorite. Ten minutes to fire ten rounds. With a good Colt I could put every round in the black, and quite a few in the X ring, at fifty yards."

"I guess calling artillery and map reading aren't your only skills," the Gunny said, after a moment, while he extinguished the little fire he'd built. The Gunny got up and headed for his hooch, not far away.

"Let's get ready to move out," he said, with Pilson running to catch up to him, after slinging his radio onto his back.

I leaned back onto my dry poncho cover, the microphone Fessman had passed to me still in my hand. I looked down at it, thinking. The only three guns I'd fired in my life were my Dad's .45, his accurized .22 Ruger and the M14 rifle I'd qualified with in training. The crummy worn .45 I'd been loaned at the Basic School I'd left in my locker until the shooting qualifications were over. I'd taken my Dad's worked over professional piece and shot the course to not only get my Expert Badge in pistol but clean the course with all bulls-eyes. My instructor there had been very surprised. I was sure he would have been equally surprised at my success in shooting the two women. I tried to feel something. I felt nothing. Shooting the women had been just like shooting the course. Breathe and squeeze. The horrid bunched together bloody blouse of the women's belongings hadn't been so easy, but I was dead set on forgetting that, just like the girl's faces.

I could use Russ and the battery fire, at maximum charge and elevation, to safely clear the way, or terrify the way, for the company to force march up the side of the mountain. It was a nothing mountain with no name, or even elevation listing on my map, so it wasn't likely to be defended. And for the first time in days we would not be on the gun target line.

I had Russ give me a couple of zone fires along the way on up to the summit, but I didn't complete the fire mission. I motioned for Stevens to approach, and then instructed him to go to the Gunny and the platoon commanders to let them know arty was going to be coming in.

I waited for Stevens to return from his mission, packing my stuff together and dumping what I could from what little pack material I had. The mountain was steep and the company was going to go up the slope hard and fast. There was no other way, and I and every Marine there was supposedly in shape and trained for just that kind of a challenge.

Fessman's little transistor radio suddenly blossomed alive. Brother John and his soothing voice from Nha Trang came out of the tinny little speaker like poured molasses. The first song of the day was by a group fittingly called Truth. And then the song began. *In the year twenty-five twenty-five, if man is still alive, if woman can survive…*

The song's lyrics had some strange bite to it and it was a bite from an unlikely glum future. I didn't care. Any future was fine by me.

When Stevens and Nguyen didn't return, and after waiting for what I thought was long enough, I executed the fire command with the battery, figuring anyone who hadn't got the word would figure it out when the shells screamed in so close to the ground. Less than two minutes later the usual "Shot, over" radio message came in, and in seconds the "Splash, over."

There was no screaming of shells overhead because the company was no longer under the gun target line. A crumping series of explosions indicated that the shells had landed. It took me a few seconds to figure out that Russ had decided to hit the peak before rolling another zone or two down the slope in our direction.

The Gunny and Stevens came back, Nguyen hanging back in the jungle growth, visible but not really. He reminded me sometimes of one of the jungle apes stalking Tarzan in the movies.

"Let's head out," the Gunny said, tossing some of what he was leaving behind into a small hole he'd dug with his E-tool folding shovel.

I shook my head, when he looked over in my direction. "Let's wait a few minutes."

The Gunny finished his work, threw his pack up and strapped himself in, before walking over to where I and my scout team stood waiting. His look was one of impatience and question.

"They're walking the shells down the slope toward us in a few minutes," I said.

Just as I mouthed the last word the first of the descending shells went off, and then the others, with the sound of explosions growing stronger as they came down the slope toward where we were. We all ducked down, including me, although I thought it unlikely that Russ would fire outside the safe distance I'd given him from the company's position. When it seemed like the last of the patterns was done I called in to Russ to make sure.

"See you on the flip side," Russ replied to my inquiry. No matter how good Americal was, I knew I was going to miss the rather sad care and concern Russ and the battery back in An Hoa had showered us with, even when the rules had to be stretched.

"What did you do with the stuff?" I asked Fessman, as I handed the microphone back to him.

"Stuff?" he replied, looking genuinely surprised.

"The girls' stuff," I whispered.

"Oh, we're dividing it up and sending it home, anyway. Screw Rittenhouse. There's some neat things in there. Wanna see?"

I shook my head, a shudder I was unable to conceal running through my whole body. Fessman looked at me funny, but said nothing further. I didn't tell him that everything we sent out of a combat zone was searched, and anything like those girls' effects would be tossed or confiscated, and likely sent somewhere else. I'd learned that fact aboard the airliner I'd come in on, although I wasn't sure whether there was any truth to it. Combat zones had their own rules, I was rapidly experiencing, and there was no training manual. Marines coming out of combat zones were so happy to leave they said nothing to the guys replacing them. My mind went back to that first night, when nobody would talk to me. I knew that if I got to the rear I would be the same way. What was the point in telling anybody coming into hell that he was coming into hell? No new person from the States would believe a word about what it was really like, and anybody who'd been there for a while wouldn't be asking any questions.

"Any more death from above coming in?" the Gunny asked, sticking his thumbs into his suspender straps and leaning forward.

I shook my head. In seconds everyone was moving, as if by a silent radio command I had no receiver for. We started in, the sun no doubt above the horizon but invisible to us because of our position behind the mountain. We slogged into the jungle growth between bamboo stands, every Marine aware of the vipers now known to inhabit them. The going was faster than I thought and it got faster still when the heavier trees overhead sheltered the jungle floor to the extent that little could grow under their sun-blocking umbrellas. I'd never humped a load as heavy as the load I carried, and the pace was starting to take its toll on me, even though I knew I was in tip top shape. I looked back and forth from Fessman on my left to Stevens and Zippo on my right. They were all chewing gum which didn't make any sense. There was Wrigley gum in the sundry packs but I'd not seen anybody chewing it since I'd been in-country.

"What are you chewing?" I finally asked Fessman.

"Betel Nuts," he said, smiling and showing teeth that seemed stained a bit red, as if he'd been drinking some Kool-Aid that was too strong. "Helps with the humping." He pushed a little folded packet of brown paper over toward me. I took it and opened the flaps. There were no nuts, just some twisted black vines.

"Try it. The mountain people use it all the time when they have to move fast with heavy loads," Stevens said.

I took a few strands and started chewing. I didn't like the idea of chewing something I knew nothing about, but the brutal forced march was beginning to exhaust me, and I didn't want to call a halt or show weakness. I refolded the package and handed it back. I chewed for a while and then swallowed what was left, but felt nothing.

"You didn't swallow them, did you?" Stevens said, stopping for the first time since we'd started the hike an hour earlier.

Before I could answer I threw up down my front. I didn't even know I'd thrown up until it was over, and I was a bit of a mess. Fessman moved to wipe me down with C-Ration toilet paper.

"What the hell?" I exclaimed, surprised that I felt no nausea.

"Your system overloaded and you had to get rid of that stuff," Zippo said. "Happens to me all the time. You get used to it."

We began the march again. I tried to clear my head but to no effect. It was like I was a bit detached from myself. Then I noticed that in my detachment I felt no pain and no exhaustion. In fact, I felt great, except for the fact that when I turned my head to look at anything or anybody it took about a half second for my eyes to catch up. I smiled over at Fessman, which I must not have done before, because his brows knitted into a deep frown.

"It'll wear off pretty quick," he said. "It's just the narcotics that help."

Narcotics? My brain spun for a second. I was on a death patrol in a combat zone surrounded by the enemy, and Marines that didn't particularly like me, and I was high as a kite. "Shit," was all I could think to say, striding ahead, hoping that I could wear the drug off by moving faster up the hill.

We reached the peak just before noon. There had not been one weapon fired, explosive ignited or booby trap tripped during our whole journey up the side of the hill. The company had already formed a perimeter roughly around the open ground on the very top. I looked at the torn open space. There was debris everywhere. The zone fire on the mountain top had created the open area.

I threw my pack down, opened it and pulled my poncho cover and liner out. Without saying anything to anyone I laid down on my stomach and passed out.

I came to with the sound of a huge nasty fly buzzing in my ears. I turned over and looked at my melted watch. I could make out the little hand and saw that it was nearing mid-afternoon. Apparently, we'd been on top of the mountain for two hours. I sat up and then looked up. There was no fly. Rotating around and around our position was a big piston-powered aircraft. I couldn't believe my eyes, as I got to my feet. The plane was mostly white with blue or black lettering on the side that read NAVY. I followed the plane around one full circuit, like I was standing at an aircraft show watching a WWII plane orbit the crowd.

"Flying dump truck," the Gunny said, who'd somehow come from somewhere I hadn't noticed. Fessman joined him, watching the plane too. My head was fuzzy. The Betel Nut still had a hold of me but not so badly.

"A-1 Skyraider," the Gunny said. He can stay up there all day and look at that payload. Sixteen five hundred pound bombs on those pylons, just waiting for some gooks to land on. That thing carries more ordnance than a B-17 did during the real war."

"How does he tell us from the enemy?" I said, shading my eyes, as the big noisy plane came low out of the sun.

"Like this," the Gunny said, with a laugh. He waved at the plane. An arm stuck out of the side of the Skyraider and waved back.

I couldn't believe it. It really was a like an air show back in the States.

"What about placing the bombs?" I asked. If we had air power, and it was there and accurate, only a few hundred yards up in the air, then the limited capability of Firebase Cunningham's artillery might be held in reserve instead of used up.

Pilson walked around the gunny and handed Fessman a black box, mostly concealed in a brown canvas rucksack. "AN 323," he said. "Frequency for support is on it. Frequency for fighters is on it. Frequency for B-52s, forget it."

Fessman took the new radio. I wondered about my training again. Nobody, not one soul, back at the Basic School had mentioned that air support could not be reached on the radios we had for just about everything else. I wondered what radio was necessary for Naval Gun Fire.

"Ask him how long he's going to be on station overhead, because we've already been here too long," I said, my head beginning to clear. Fear was rapidly replacing my earlier euphoria. We had to get along the ridge and head toward the A Shau immediately. The NVA had been fooled by our change in direction but they'd figure out what we were doing and make their own interdicting moves pretty quickly, I knew. Or I thought I knew. I shook my head again.

Fessman fiddled with the new radio. He spoke into the handset and then handed it to me. As opposed to the Prick 25 microphone, it was a small round black disk with a little white button on one side.

"His name is Cowboy," Fessman said.

"He told you his name?" I asked, taking the dainty little thing handset.

The Gunny pointed up, as the A-1 Skyraider was passing close overhead with its fat fuselage banking into a turn. Just under the big raised cockpit side window the letters "COWBOY" were written in bold, black paint.

"How fitting," I said, before keying the mic button.

"Cowboy, do you copy, over?" I asked.

"Five by five, Flash, over" a southern male voice said back. The 323 had a better speaker, I realized, because the pilot sounded almost human.

"Who's Flash?" I asked Fessman, before continuing.

"He's into Flash Gordon," Fessman whispered. "This is all Planet Mongo down here and the bad guys all work for Ming. You're Flash."

My shoulders slumped a slight bit. Was nothing real? Yet, I knew, it was all real. Deadly real. I didn't bother to ask how Cowboy had become Cowboy in a science fiction series that had no cowboys. Like it mattered.

"You can see us down here?" I asked, pushing the button and holding it so I could go on. "We're heading due east down the ridge until we get to the A Shau. Charlie's going to be coming up on our left flank, or he's already set up ahead of us. You can see us good enough to tell the difference from up there I presume."

"Roger that, Flash," Cowboy radioed back, dropping the 'over.' "You would be the little white apes wearing those funny green outfits sometimes referred to as Marines."

"Roger that, Cowboy," I replied, thinking fast, not caring what he called us as long as he stayed up above us so that the NVA would know he was there. His presence might give away our position but it didn't matter. It was going to be a race to the A Shau ridge I'd pinpointed on the map, and the loser was going to take some serious casualties.

"We're shoving off in a second down here," I said, tossing the little Oreo cookie of a microphone back to Fessman. I turned to Stevens.

"Got any more of that Betel Nut shit?"

THE EIGHTH DAY : THIRD PART

I stared up at the unlikely and ungainly monster of a loud propeller-driven airship. The Skyraider didn't look like it could even stay in the air, but there it was, orbiting dependably not more than three hundred feet up. The Gunny nodded toward the 323 radio, also looking like it was from WWII, and held out his hand. I gave him the handset. I could tell right away that the Gunny had never encountered Cowboy because he winced every time the pilot referred to him as Zarkov, the mad doctor from Flash Gordon. I preferred Flash to Junior, but stood without expression listening to the exchange. The Gunny instructed Cowboy to fly the ridge all along our direction of travel to see what he could see and then report back. The 323 apparently had even less range than the Prick 25 we used for command and artillery nets, so I presumed we would not be able to get reports when the plane was at a distance.

"Look, Cowboy, or whatever name and rank you really are, I'm the Gunnery Sergeant down here, not some character in a movie. This is real."

The Gunny handed Fessman the handset by tossing it to him in obvious disgust, but the communication from the disappearing airborne dump truck wasn't over.

"This isn't Cowboy," a voice said, sounding almost exactly like Cowboy's. "This is his NFO. I'm Jacko. You know, like in jack-o'-lantern."

The Gunny walked away without saying another word.

"Jacko's not from Flash Gordon," Fessman said to no one in particular while he stowed the 323 back into its canvas sack. He threw the heavy little bag over his left shoulder, since his M16 was strapped over his right. I wondered if Fessman ever shot the rifle because every time the company was under fire, he was so busy with the radio his gun had to be set aside.

The hump down the ridge was harder than if it had been a hump up from the valley floor. Night dew covered all the foliage brushed aside to hold position close up onto both sides of the ridge. Although the temperature wasn't what it had been in the lowlands, the dew soaked everyone's uniforms and made moving on the slanted mud covered with fern, bamboo and other jungle growth debris, difficult and exhausting. The first four hours down the ridge had started out okay, but from then on the forced march had become agonizing. Finally, the company stopped. No orders were issued. Everyone simply stopped and went to the earth wherever they were. I went down with them but not for long.

Distant voices began calling and I was up moving with Fessman before "arty up" came echoing down the line. Whatever stopped the company had been some kind of threat. In moments I had worked through all the downed men to reach a small group of Marines peering over a hedge of bushes just back from a clearing that lay at the apex of the ridge. I dumped my pack behind the Gunny and took out my Japanese binoculars. Nobody said anything as I covered the line of heavy jungle from one side to the other across the clearing. I saw nothing. There had been no explosions or gunfire of any kind as we'd worked our way down the mild decline of the ridge.

"What is it?" I said, still out of breath from the long hike.

I turned back toward Fessman, but unaccountably the handset I reached for wasn't there. Instead, Fessman knelt staring out toward the center of the clearing. I followed his gaze. A large tiger sat in the center of the clearing staring back at me. A very large tiger. I'd only seen tigers in the zoo. This tiger didn't look anything like a zoo tiger. Although it sat on its hind legs, its body language seemed aggressive and possessive. I brought my binoculars up to my eyes again. The tiger stared right into my lenses, his head filling my view.

"Unhappy tiger," I breathed out, causing the Gunny and the men around him to snicker.

"No shit," the Gunny replied.

"Nobody's shot him," I said, now fully aware that everyone was listening to me.

"Not a he," the Gunny said, while he and everyone else continued to stare at the beast. "If it was male it would have taken off long ago. Females are territorial and we're definitely in her territory. Probably got young nearby. She's not going anywhere."

"Still, nobody's shot her," I repeated, changing the animal's sex. "How come? And what do you want me to do, call in an artillery round? The clearing's too small and we're too close."

"Respect," the Gunny said. "Nobody's going to shoot her. We're in her jungle, not the other way around. We're going around her. I didn't bring you up to call in artillery. I brought you up because I thought you'd want to see this."

"We're going around her?" I asked, in surprise. These Marines who were killing each other every night and who would not think twice about pulling the trigger on any enemy that could harm them, were averse to killing a wild animal in the jungle? That hundreds of combat hardened men could come to that same conclusion and let the animal live, jolted me to the core. The tiger's situation and the company's decision was one of humanity, and that display of humanity in my now inhumane life jarred me badly.

"What do we do, split in half and go around both sides of the clearing?" I asked.

"Nope, she'll feel surrounded and threatened. We go around on the down south side where it's not so steep." The Gunny pointed down slope, in the direction we'd come up from.

I looked as far down the slope as I could through the trees and bracken. I knew we would be unable to receive fire from Firebase Cunningham because of the ridge in the way. We were beyond the range of high angle howitzer rounds fired in defilade, and we were now beyond even the furthest reach of the An Hoa battery.

All we had for supporting fires was the Cowboy and Jacko. Why they were up there in one lone Skyraider was unknown. To my knowledge, all combat planes flew with at least two planes in a squadron, or whatever they called it. But there he was and here we were, about to file down into unknown territory with no supporting fires at all because a tiger would not move. Even the small mortars we had would be of no use, along with the LAW anti-tank weapons and M79s. It was going to be hand-to-hand combat if the enemy lurked anywhere close below. Because of our outlandish move, however, it appeared that snakes and tigers might be bigger risks than booby traps or a well laid ambush. Chesty Puller had been right, if Chesty had been at all behind the most famous Marine Corps retreat in history. Do the unexpected. Adapt. I'd applied a historic solution to a problem that lacked any resemblance to anything in Marine or any other combat training.

The company filed down along the northern edge of the clearing, staying out of the thickest jungle, but giving the tiger plenty of room. The tiger watched us intently, turning its head to the side as we passed, but making no move to slink down or rotate her body.

I watched the animal closely. She was close enough in passing to read her expression, which appeared to be one of interest and curiosity rather than predatory. I wondered if she realized that the most dangerous predators on the planet were passing only a few yards away. Predators giving another predator a pass, probably because there's little to be gained by one predator killing another predator unless there's a territorial dispute. The clearing belonged to the tiger and automatically the Marine predators knew and respected that. I felt a bond with the company I'd not experienced at all since first arriving. We, and the tiger, were all the same in certain elemental behaviors. We all fought to survive and killed without compunction to accomplish that mission.

The company moved by in almost complete silence, the transistor radios turned off for the first time since I'd come down on that dark night a week ago. I stared one last time at the side and back of the big tiger's head, it's one ear turning one way and then another, the only sign that it was alive and fully alert. I knew I would remember the animal's visage for many years to come. And I also knew I could write something good home, about the fantastically strange creature and the honor of the men in leaving it as it was.

The pace of the march slowed a bit after the unlikely incident with the tiger. I could not get the animal out of my mind. It sat there in defiance of all logic and counter to everything I thought I knew about animals living in the wild. Stevens and Nguyen worked through the jungle on my left, with Zippo on my right. Fessman stayed only a few feet behind, ready with his handset at an instant's notice. I leaned over to Stevens and asked him if he would get Nguyen's opinion of what had happened with the tiger, since he was from the mountain region we were hiking through. They talked in whispers back and forth for a few minutes. I presumed there was some exotic native explanation for the tiger's behavior. Finally, they stopped talking. Stevens scratched his head but said nothing.

"Well?" I demanded.

"Tiger sick," he said, shrugging his shoulders.

I was dumbstruck. And then it all made sense. The animal was sitting up, making its last stand. It was not being proud and guarding its territory or its young. It was too sick to go on and waiting for the death that comes to most animals in the bush when they are no longer physically able to go on. They get eaten by bigger predators. Yet the image of the tiger's head, burned into my mind the way it was, would not change. I marched along, working my way through the bracken, going around trees while trying to keep the low-hanging branches from snapping back to hit Fessman. My mind remained on the tiger until it finally came to me why I'd so fixated on the beautiful predator. He was me. He was making the best he could of the inevitable death coming right at him. Just like me.

The distinctive droning sound of Cowboy coming back up the ridge penetrated down to the bottom of the jungle. At the same time, small arms fire came radiating up from the unseen valley below — the same one we'd hiked up to take the ridge route toward the A Shau. Explosions reverberated from far below. The company stopped as one in its tracks, every one of us going down for cover onto the bracken or thinly covered mud.

"Give me the 323," I ordered Fessman.

Cowboy was the only support we had, and he was close by. We couldn't identify the distant firing until the command net began to light up. The Gunny dropped at my side, with Pilson right next to him.

"Kilo Company is taking it right on the chin down in the valley," he said, listening to Pilson's radio.

"Shit," I replied softly. "That's my fault."

"How in hell can it be your fault?" the Gunny asked.

"The NVA were set up for us," I replied. "Kilo walked right into their ambush without knowing anything. We didn't call it in."

"They don't tell us shit back at battalion," the Gunny said. "How were we supposed to know? They tell us where to go but nothing about why, or who is going with us. I call the six actuals of the other companies but they don't know what the hell's going on either."

"Did you call them when we made our move this morning?"

"Nah, I'll admit that one," the Gunny said, grudgingly. "Kilo thought it was following us up a cleared trail. I should have picked that up. Not your fault. My fault."

I reached for the 323 handset and got Cowboy right away.

"What's going on down in the valley?"

"Flash, good to hear from you," Cowboy replied. "Coast is clear all the way to that Ah Shit Valley, but there's some disagreement going on just north of you. I'll give it over to Jacko and steer this here Sandy right on down to take a look see."

"Roger that," I answered, understanding that from up in the air the pilot and his partner had a lot better view of what might be going on than we did.

"Sandies are what they call those funny planes," Fessman whispered in my ear. "Sandy means like the sandy bottom of a tropical drink, you know, they fly so low and all."

I didn't believe a word of what Fessman told me but I also realized it didn't matter one bit.

"Can we support them in some way?" the Gunny said, as I handed Fessman the microphone and pulled out one of my new Army maps. I studied the map of our area, letting the topographical contour intervals convert to shape in my mind.

"What if we attack back down the mountain?" the Gunny said, sounding shaky about his conclusion for the first time since I'd arrived under his care more than a week ago.

I looked at the difficult jungle area closely and then sat back. "How fast can our company move in this shit?"

"If we drop packs and carry ammo and water only, then pretty damned fast. Why?

"Seven thousand meters, or seven clicks," I said. We can't attack down slope because we'll just run into Kilo's flank and have the same problems they're having. We have to go straight in the direction we're going and then veer north and arrive behind the saddle. The saddle's got to be where the NVA are set up," I concluded. "We take them in the rear."

Fessman, Stevens and Zippo laughed out loud until I looked at them. I didn't get the joke but I knew there must have been one.

"We have to do it fast though, before they figure out what we're up to. In less than an hour. Can it be done?" I said. "Either that or let them take the hit and lick their own wounds."

"I thought you felt it was your fault," the Gunny said.

"What's that got to do with it? What's that got to do with anything?" I said. Can it be done?"

The Gunny nodded. "I'll get to the platoon commanders right now." He and Pilson disappeared in seconds.

I reached for the 323 handset, knowing Fessman would know what I wanted and when. He did.

"This is Flash, over," I said, pushing the little white transmission button. Jacko came on.

I described how we needed the Sandy to revolve in a higher pattern over where the saddle sat across the path in the valley below. I had no idea about radio security so I didn't say what our plan was. I told them I needed an hour to get into position, and I needed them to have all their ordnance on board without expending any before we were ready.

"You boys going to go head to head with Ming down there, we're betting up here?" Jacko transmitted back.

Zippo had turned his personal transistor radio on and I recognized the song Brother John was playing. It was called "The Battle of New Orleans" and it had come out while I was in high school. *In 1814 we took a little trip…*

I held out the 323 handset toward Fessman. "Play the song into the microphone for them."

I stripped down to minimums on my belt. I kept one canteen, the K-Bar knife, the latest letter home to my wife, the loaded Colt, and two magazines of rounds. I'd been in Vietnam for eight days, killed five human beings personally and many more with artillery support, but I was going into real combat for the first time. When I was ready, I packed my stuff into a poncho covered pile, and then sat against it to await the Gunny's return. I realized that I was less afraid of what might be coming than of almost anything I'd experienced so far.

thirty-seven

THE EIGHTH NIGHT

The move was a long hard one. In training I'd literally run twenty miles with a forty-pound pack on my back carrying an M14 and wearing a full helmet and liner. I had none of those things going down the ridge, in hopes of coming in behind whatever units were set up to ambush and cut Kilo Company to ribbons. Without gear, I felt cleaner and light on my feet, but the drop in altitude made me regret leaving my steel pot behind. The repellent was held to the side of the helmet by Fessman's big rubber bands, and with my increasing perspiration and the rising heat, the mosquitoes were back. I knew they would be worse when we stopped to set in.

Moving through the jungle was nothing like a hard forced march in the Virginia hills. The mud, mixed with the undergrowth, made slipping and sliding part of the journey and sapped energy at every opportunity. By the time the company made it to where I thought we should turn and head north, I was beaten to near submission. As if hearing my unspoken plight, the company came to a halt. I reached for my single canteen and drained half of it down my throat. Fessman handed me a little plastic bottle of the repellent without my asking. I smiled one of my new plastic smiles back at him. I popped the malaria pill I'd forgotten in the morning, put my canteen back into its holder and then slathered the oily mess into the mixed mess of whitish agent orange and jungle dirt that my skin had turned into.

The Gunny came up through a bamboo thicket, prying two shoots apart and looking like a character on a Tarzan movie set. He squatted down but didn't go to work making his usual concoction of coffee. Instead he drank deeply from his own canteen.

"I'm presuming this is the place you had in mind to head on down," he said, when he was done drinking.

I passed Fessman's repellent back without answering. I pulled out the correct map and located our position. I didn't need my compass because I knew the ridge we hiked along ran almost directly east and west. Down the slope into the heavier growth was obviously north.

There was no way to see anything from where we were, and the Sandy had not returned with it's unlikely but seemingly dependable crew. Instead of reaching for the 323 microphone I went for the artillery net handset. Fessman interpreted what I was doing before I did it. I knew that the backside of the ridge we were on would prevent America's artillery battery from giving us supporting fire, but the ridge would not block an airburst.

After registering our real position with Firebase Cunningham because we'd be moving from it rather quickly, I asked for a single ranging round of Willy Peter to detonate two hundred meters in the air. I gave the coded grid coordinate for the middle of the saddle where the path intersected its open space, hoping that the toothpaste and shaving cream code words were used by the Army in this area, as well as by the Marine Corps. There was almost no delay before "Shot, over!" came from the radio's speaker. I peered downslope and upward. We were right on the gun target line again, and the range to Cunningham was pretty great. I knew the round would come in arcing low and therefore be a bit risky and dangerous. Right after the "splash" transmission a boom of distant sound radiated up from far down in the valley. I couldn't see the explosion because of the thick jungle growth.

Nguyen, predicting the arrival of the round, had climbed a nearby tree. He yelled from high above and pointed. Direction was all I needed. With direction back toward the saddle I knew where we were along the ridge and where we had to go. I glanced up at the Montagnard, coming down the tree trunk like he was more spider monkey than human. He let go of the tree from ten feet up, rolled and then jumped to his feet turning to face us while still in mid-air. An Olympic athlete could not have been more impressive. I stared, my eyes wide in amazement. His suppressed smile was almost invisible, but I caught it.

The Gunny hadn't bothered to take in all that was going on. He lay with his back against a fallen tree branch with his eyes closed. I knew I was not the only exhausted Marine on the ridge. I hunkered down next to him with my map.

"We're exactly here," I said, waiting for him to open is eyes.

"More of your artillery map reading magic," he said, barely opening one eye.

"We need to be here," I went on, pointing at a spot just back of the saddle area and almost directly north down the slope. I knew the company, after being part of the recent move, would be able to get into place in less than twenty minutes if it left right away. There must have been more urgency in my voice than I intended because the Gunny groaned.

"I'm twice your age, if not more," he said, closing the one eye again. "I'm twice the age of everyone else in this company."

"And that counts for exactly what?" I responded.

"Jeez, give the man a little bit of power..." the Gunny replied but opened his eyes and leaned forward to study the map. His eyes went all over the thing. I knew he wasn't good with maps merely by the way he viewed them. I put my finger back on the target area, and then ran it back and forth from where our location was to the target point.

"The sooner the better." I knew if we stayed where we were for any length of time the enemy would know, and it wouldn't take a tactical genius on the other side to figure out we were pulling a potential deadly flanking maneuver.

"We've got to be in before dark and we're running out of light," I said, looking up and around.

"We get there, set in behind where they think they might be, which is iffy," the Gunny said, pointing at the target area with his own index finger. "And then what? Call Kilo and have them do a frontal attack so the NVA is driven right into us?"

I hadn't been looking up and around because of the waning light. I'd heard the very distant but distinctive drone of the Skyraider. Cowboy and Jacko were coming back, as promised. We had to get down in the valley and set in before the plane had to go home, wherever home was for it. We were seriously running out of light for the air crew to see the battlefield by.

"Nope," I replied to the Gunny. "Kilo's on the far side of the saddle. They know Kilo's there because they've been shooting at them. We pressure the back of the near side. The NVA is caught in the middle. They can only go north or south to escape and they can only do that quickly, the same way we did back when we had the other open area. They'll have to expose themselves on the open ground of the saddle."

"Why do I get the feeling that there's something more?" the Gunny said, taking another drink of water from his canteen. He got to his feet and stretched his arms and shoulders before he spoke. "*Di di mao*," he said, raising his voice to everyone around.

I looked at Fessman in question.

"Means 'let's go'... sort of..." he replied, with his usual smile.

The mix of Vietnamese and French was befuddling, but the expressions I was beginning to learn were also indelible. Once heard, the strange words would lay there unused and unknown until someone said the expression again, and at that point understanding what it meant was instant.

The company moved after a very brief discussion, wherein the Gunny related that he'd let the platoon commanders know that the company was to flow down the slope in size, break into platoons and then squads. From there it would form itself into a single thick line of automatic weapons and machine guns, set to absorb the NVA troops when they were forced to back down from their likely ambush at the saddle.

When the company was on the move again, this time even faster than before, I wondered about the circumstantial evidence I'd used to come up with the plan. If we succeeded in hitting the NVA hard, not getting hit hard ourselves, the Gunny would no doubt get the credit. If the operation was a complete failure and we took any casualties at all, then the whole thing would drop on me.

"Cowboy," I transmitted, using the 323 handset, my heavy breathing making my words hard to understand. The pace of our approach down the mountainside resembled a loping run. Although the growth had increased, the natural trails around the trees and bamboo stands became more pronounced and easier to negotiate. Darkness was fast descending. I could no longer see the illuminated numbers through my melted watch face.

"Jacko back at you," came over the radio. "Cowboy's indisposed using these infernal instrument things."

I told Jacko my plan. I could hear the Skyraider orbiting overhead, but I could also hear the growing roll and then staccato fire of automatic and semi-automatic weapons in the distance. The dark, the Skyraider, the NVA and the saddle were all about to collide and I realized there was no predicting what might happen. What if the enemy troops were set in too far back? That would put them behind the company. What if there was nobody there at all, although the chances of that were pretty slim given that live fire could be heard coming up the slope while we talked.

"We're gonna lay down some CBUs for you, so don't go walking around or sunbathing out there in that open area when we're gone. Some of that shit blows up later on. We'll orbit up here for now. We can see the saddle area and some of the dispute going on over that resort property right now. When you want us to come zooming down just use the code words 'Dale Arden.'"

"CBUs?" I whispered to Fessman, handing the handset back to him.

"Cluster bomb somethings," Fessman replied.

My scout team had dropped all the way to the rear of the company by the time we stopped. I laid down on the flat cushioning surfaces of a fallen bamboo stand with Fessman on my left and Stevens, Zippo, and Nguyen lining up along my right. The Gunny appeared, barely visible, in the low light. I slapped at mosquitoes before turning and squatting down with him.

"Fire one round of white phosphorus like before and Kilo will open up," the Gunny said. "That will drive the NVA in front of us back. Then we'll open up and they'll run out into the open."

I sat listening to the battle plan. It made no sense. Professor Henor, my ROTC instructor, had once taught a class on combat tactics. "Never shoot at your own men, unless you are all dead anyway," he'd said. I wasn't about to be behind the NVA taking Kilo's fire if I could help it.

"No," I said, as forcefully as I could.

"We open up. Kilo doesn't fire at all. The NVA react by moving back onto the edge of the open area. Cowboy comes zooming down and drops cluster shit all over them. Let Kilo pick off the survivors. The survivors will head down slope but we don't have time to set up anything for them as a reception party."

"We could use the combined fire," the Gunny said grudgingly after a few seconds.

"Our fire will be plunging down and almost none of it will get over where Kilo's at," I argued. "If Kilo opens up they'll be shooting straight through this brush and we're going to take plenty of hits. Screw the NVA. Let's take care of our own."

"You're the company commander, Junior," the Gunny said, a subliminal anger laying there deep between the words. "We're out of time. Call the damned fire. I'll tell the guys to open up."

Fessman held the arty handset out. I called for the round to be put down on the same target as before. I then used the 323 to call Cowboy. Jacko indicated that they would be on target in five minutes and make a single run, releasing sixteen five hundred pounders and plenty of 20 millimeter cannon fire. The Willie Peter came in less than a minute later and the company opened up with so much tracer fire it looked like there was a moving bridge of fire extended out between the strung out company position and the thicket lining the back of the saddle's open area. The cluster bombs sounded like huge popcorn kernels exploding, sometimes one or two and sometimes ten or twenty of them. I had my Colt out and I tried to see into the Stygian blackness in front of me. What if the NVA plunged backward instead of forward? They would run right over or through us, killing us as they went. My terror returned.

The sounds of combat deafened my ears and the brilliant bursts of light overloaded the rods and cones in my eyes. I realized I was blind, and then I could not hear. But I did feel the roar of the amazing night-flying Skyraider going by. It must have only been a few feet off the earth to transmit its deep propeller drone right into the ground. I felt the explosions and then the second roar of the plane's 20 millimeter cannons swept by. I tried to talk to Fessman but nothing would come out of my throat. Fessman's lips moved but there was no sound. I'd forgotten to make field earplugs. Minutes passed and everything began to die down. The plane was gone, there were no more tracers and my hearing came back, although the ringing in both ears would be a long time in passing.

The Gunny was back. My night vision had not returned enough to see him. He grabbed my upper arm and squeezed to let me know he was there.

"Is it over?" I asked. "What happened? Did they run? Was there anybody there? Did we hit anybody?" My questions flew out, one after another, my adrenalin running so high that I felt the hairs sticking out on the back of my neck and on my forearms.

"Don't know. There was a whole lot of movement. Get the damned Starlight scope online just in case, not to mention it'd be a great time to get rid of the asshole lieutenant causing all this trouble. Nobody's moving until first light. At least we'll have the saddle to get medevac and supply."

Medevac, I wondered, but had no time to ask, as the Gunny was gone as suddenly as he'd appeared. I, my team and the company would have to lay in among the fronds and mud all night, waiting for dawn, before we could start hiking back to get our packs. I was more worried about how the Marines in my company would feel if they'd done all that work for nothing than I was of anyone coming in the night to kill me. If medevac was coming, then we'd taken casualties.

My scattered mind tried to reassemble itself into some sort of rational condition. Was that it? A whole battle? Just horrid loud sounds and flashes in the night? My left hand reached down to massage the single tiger letter that wasn't written and not there yet. I didn't have to massage the right pocket. I knew the morphine was there.

thirty-eight

THE EIGHTH NIGHT : SECOND PART

Relief flooded through me. It was over. I'd survived another of what my team called "fire fights." There was no way to adjust to the change from combat to whatever this was. It was still dark. My ears still rang. But with my night vision returning, I could vaguely see a moon above the ever-present clouds. There was no rain or mist. Just the quiet after the raging sounds of screaming combat with tracers, bullets and explosions blasting the air everywhere. I hadn't lain in the muck watching for movement, or looking for an enemy who might be attacking at any second. I'd lain face-down like that very first night, my eyes squeezed shut and my face buried in jungle debris and mud. But it was over. I got to my feet and unkinked my shoulders, hips, and knees.

The scout unit formed around me, Fessman standing at my side and Zippo moving around absently trying to clear his ears by sticking his fingers in them and shaking his head. I looked up, wondering how to spend a night in the bush with nothing. I'd left all of my stuff back up on the ridge. I wasn't at all ready, physically or mentally, to be struck by a fast-moving freight train of a Marine Gunnery Sergeant. I flew through the air, the Gunny's shoulder buried in my right side as he dug his boots into the cloying muck. The weight of his body drove me down hard onto a bed of fern fronds and rough-edged branches. I couldn't breathe. I couldn't breathe even when he sat back and stared down at me, his anger all but paralyzing. Holding my sides I waited, panicked that I would never get my breath back.

"You dumb fucking new guy asshole," the Gunny hissed at me, his face coming down to only inches above my own. "This is the same goddamned move you pulled when I saw you get off that chopper. I knew you were bad news then and you're bad news now. You think this is over? Nine or eighteen holes and we all turn in our clubs and get showered up for the drive home?"

My chest heaved and I got in one sucking breath. It was enough to stay conscious to hear the Gunny go on.

"We're not fighting gooks, VC, or the wooden soldiers in some toy movie. We're engaged with the North Vietnamese Army and there's no quit in these assholes. I wish they were Marines of mine, for fuck's sake."

The Gunny jerked back and up, bouncing to his feet. I noted that the whole scout team was back to being buried as deep as they could get in the mud, more to avoid the wrath of the Gunny than in fear of the enemy.

"That battery might not be able to do much for us, but they can sure as hell give us some illumination for what's coming," the Gunny said. "Get us some light and get the mud cleaned out of your weapon. This fucking night is a long way from over."

"Sorry, Gunny," I whispered hoarsely, finally getting my breath back but still trembling slightly at the likelihood that the enemy was nearby.

"They got hit hard," the Gunny said. "When they get hit hard they counter attack, so get ready and get the god-damned place lit up."

I rolled over and reached out for where I thought Fessman had to be close by. He was there. The handset was in my muddy fingers. I still held my .45 in the other but it was a black mass I couldn't really see. I clicked it on safety and jammed the muddy thing into my holster.

"Fire mission, over," I called, hoping Fessman had the frequency right and that the Army battery would recognize who was calling and not require all the registration crap again. I knew Illumination rounds were the most restricted fire missions because of where the uncontrollable canisters might fall.

I oriented myself. I didn't want to take out my map because the little pencil of light might give away our position. I took a few seconds to think and try to approximate our position. We'd come pall mall down the slope, heading directly north about two thousand meters, maybe a bit more. We were not on the gun target line anymore so it didn't matter where the canisters holding the little burning parachute loads might land.

I asked for an adjustment to the last round I'd called in. I moved the round two hundred meters right, which would be correct from where we were the last time I'd called in. Two hundred meters should be close to the edge of the clearing but it was anybody's guess in the dark. The Starlight scope was useless amid the dense foliage and nobody was going to head into the open area in the dark.

The round came bursting above the jungle, completely visible in all of its amazing Technicolor splendor. The explosion went off, and then the white phosphorus draped down like the tines of a giant umbrella. The night sparkled with the sound of the round going off, booming seconds after it exploded.

I called for illumination up and down the edge of the clearing, figuring it was about a thousand meters from one end of the saddle to the other. One round every minute every hundred meters. The shells started coming in and Kilo company opened up from far in the distance. I hugged the mud, pressing myself into it, the sounds of distant small arms different than it had been. I realized that Kilo was firing directly at us, but the rounds were impacting the thick jungle between the company and the clearing. Most of them. The sounds were sharp cracks instead of what I had become used to. The few rounds that got through were enough. They sounded like fast moving slivers in the night. No ricochets from the movies. Just hyper-fast flying and invisible snakes going by above my head. I realized then that the illumination rounds had not been for our company. They were to illuminate the open area so Kilo could see the working, withdrawing, or reforming enemy before they could get under proper cover and concealment again. I hoped fervently that Kilo was killing them all.

And then I remembered my Colt. I pulled it out and checked it as carefully as I could. The muzzle was jammed with mud. How the hell was I supposed to clear that? My little finger would barely fit into the very end of the barrel. I could not field strip the weapon in the dark. There was only one thing to do. I removed the magazine and stuck it into my pocket to keep it clean, and then ejected the round from the chamber. The slide stayed back, held by the detent snapping up for just that purpose. I took out my pen and began pushing it through the barrel from the tip. A minute later I thought the thing was probably clear enough. I put the extra round in my mouth and swirled it around. It tasted awful. I pulled it out, spit deeply, and took out the magazine. I pushed the wet round into the top of the magazine, reinserted it into the butt, chambered the round, and clicked the safety on.

A running shape appeared before me. I didn't recognize what or who it was although I saw the faint light gleaming off a pair of shiny rimmed glasses. I drew the gun smoothly and aimed the Colt .45 at his center of mass, and pulled the trigger. Nothing. I tried pulling harder but the shape disappeared. I heard shots nearby but concentrated my attention on the gun. I realized that the gun was on safe. I clicked the safety off and thought glumly about the apparition that had appeared before me. If it had been the enemy, and who else could it have been, then I was more than lucky to be alive. If I'd been killed, I wondered if anyone would have taken a few seconds to figure out that I'd been killed because I was too dumb to click my own safety off.

I waited. My scout team, nearby, waited with me. The illumination rounds continued until ten had been delivered, the whirring of the canisters eerie in the night. There would be a sudden pop, and then the whirring would start and run for a few seconds until a thud indicated that the forty-pound metal container had hit the mud. I yearned for daylight or a Starlight scope I could wear like a pair of glasses. Waiting in the dark for the enemy to come was painstakingly awful — second by second, minute by minute, with only the mild wind sweeping the tops of the trees to pass the time or make any sound.

After what seemed like hours the Gunny found me. How he knew how to get around in the mess of night combat, jungle and cloying mud was beyond me. I could read a map like there was no tomorrow but I had no idea where I really was in the company.

"We've got to form a perimeter for the night," the Gunny said in a low voice. "They're done. Kilo ripped them a new asshole. They'll be back, though, and they know right where we are. We can't stay in a line with our tits and asses hanging out all over the place."

The Gunny was right. I couldn't believe how slow my mind was working. The Gunny had told me on that first day, after the first night, that I'd be able to function, but nobody would listen to what I said. I now understood. I was caught seconds behind the real world cascading in front of me. I had to somehow catch up. Perimeter. Dig in. Night defensive fires. Ammo check. Commo check. I knew that without the Gunny I'd have laid there all night, waiting for the comfort of a coming dawn that had every chance of never coming.

I got to my feet but stayed hunched over. I followed Stevens with Fessman just behind me, as usual. After twenty yards of bulling through heavy brush it became easier going. Stevens ran into the Gunny's back and then I ran into Steven's back. Fessman was quicker and stopped in time.

"Here," the Gunny said. "Just hunker down. We took some casualties and the docs are hauling one over. He's hit bad. Take a look at him. I'm going to check the line."

The Gunny was gone for several minutes before a group of men came out of the brush nearby. I realized I had no protection at all except the .45 still gripped so tightly in my right hand that my whole arm ached.

I forced my hand to relax a bit. My whole body seemed to sag with the arm as it relaxed. My holster, filled with dirt, would have to do. I plunged the Colt .45 into it, feeling the squish of it adjusting to whatever muck was pushed into the leather with it. If Jurgens or Sugar Daddy were coming in this night, then I was a dead man for sure, and my Colt .45 wasn't going to change anything. I squatted down from fatigue, my body a mess of pain. My side hurt like hell where the Gunny had struck. My legs ached from the forced march and I could not get rid of the hand shake that had come back. At least it was night, I thought, and nobody can see the shaking. I massaged some nearby branches instead of my hurting thighs.

Two corpsmen laid out a poncho. The poncho contained a Marine. One of the corpsmen knelt down on his knees beside me.

"No chance, sir. Won't be a medevac until dawn and this is a zero life situation."

I stared into the corpsman's eyes but he said nothing further. After a few more seconds he got up to leave. "Might want these," he said. "The kid got him, but then the grenade went off. Spoils of war, if you want to record them."

I accepted the bandana of goods, reminded of the woman's face looking up at the chopper and the bloody mess of her stuff right afterward. I handed the goods to Fessman and approached the Marine. I knelt beside him on the poncho liner before realizing he wasn't all there. Half his body was gone. He had no legs or anything legs might attach to. I looked up to try to catch the attention of the corpsmen but they were gone. The Marine had to be dead.

"Who are you?" a raspy voice asked.

I sucked in my breath. The words had come from the body.

"Ah, I'm ah, Junior," I blurted out, wanting to curse myself for saying the word.

"The crazy man," the voice said. I leaned down toward the Marine's face to listen more closely, and not look at his lower body.

"Can you fix me up, crazy man?" he said. "Can you put me back together like Humpty Dumpty?"

I didn't know what to say. "What's your name?" I got out in desperation.

"Alfonso, Lance Corporal," he said. "But they call me Alfie."

A moaning sound came low from Alfie's throat. I waited half a minute for him to say something more. "The pain," he gasped out. "So bad." Another long moan.

I didn't think about anything. All thoughts of waiting the night through with Alfie disappeared from my mind. I eased my right hand from the butt of the Colt down to the outer pocket of my right leg. As if on its own, my hand pulled the morphine packet out and joined my other hand in getting the syrettes unfolded and revealed. I was more watching myself work than thinking anything through.

Alfie started to talk again, so I waited, kneeling and patient, my own pains forgotten as I listened to the story of the boy's life. How his mother, father, and cocker spaniel dog were waiting for him to come home a war hero. He was from a farm in California. A wave of pain overwhelmed him for a few seconds before he went on. He played the piano and was so happy the wounds had not hurt his hands. I waited for the next excruciating wave of pain to come over him, while carefully removing four syrettes from the pack, feeling each one to get it right.

When Alfie stopped moaning again I squeezed the first into the muscles under his right arm. And then I just kept going, the boy recovered again, and then continued his story about how hard it was to do farming chores and go to school at the same time. The fourth syrette was in and yet the boy talked on. I stopped listening to him, instead drawing myself closer until I was lying beside him and hugging him with my head buried in his neck.

"Thanks, Junior," he said, his voice very faint. After a few more breaths he went still.

I backed away and sat with my butt flat in the mud, looking at what I could see of the boy's unmoving body in the mud. I looked around but there was nobody there. For only the second time Fessman was gone too. I was alone. With the boy. I moved to wrap the remaining supply of morphine up and tuck it back into my special pocket. I wondered, if I got back to the Basic School, if I could tell them that a short course in teaching what I'd just experienced might be in order, but then I gave that thought up. I was never going back to the Basic School and I knew it.

I rose to my feet and moved to the little open area where the Gunny had led us. My team sat in a circle, smoking cigarettes. Fessman handed one up to me and I took it.

"Is he gone yet?" he asked.

I slid down next to him, inhaling the cigarette without coughing for the first time. I handed it back to him. "Yeah," I said.

Fessman handed me the little bag of personal stuff taken from the NVA soldier he'd killed before the soldier killed him. I slowly unwrapped it, wondering what the enemy carried with them. I didn't get far before a pair of glasses fell to the mud. I plucked them up and examined them. Pointed gold rims gleamed out.

"Oh, Christ," I said, feeling like I'd been hit in the chest, and then the head, with a brick.

"What?" Fessman asked, with a tone of concern in his voice.

I couldn't say anything. I couldn't tell the truth and I couldn't think of a lie. I'd killed Alfie when I'd failed to get the safety off my .45. The soldier had moved by and then tossed the grenade at the kid. Then I'd killed Alfie for a second time with the morphine. I looked around at my team in the dark, ignoring the mosquitoes that were biting me in the face and on the backs of my hands. I could feel nothing, and I could never tell a living soul about killing Alfie twice.

thirty-nine

THE NINTH DAY

The rest of the night passed in mud, a penetrating mist returning to add some sort of cutting liquid thinner to the blood being sucked in by the feeding mosquitoes. As I lay in my semi-comatose state replacing real sleep, I couldn't hear any more firing. There were no more explosions that I was aware of.

I didn't need an alarm clock because I was always conscious, but never truly conscious. I could move if I had to, or was called upon to move, but I chose not to. I counted for the dawn to come. One, one thousand, and on up to the hundreds, finally keeping track of thousands with the fingers of both hands. Seconds to live. Light was life, if only I could get there, or the world could get there around me and take me along with it. When there was enough light to see my hands, I unwound them from their counting positions and stretched. There was enough light to stop the counting and push back the blackness of night and fear.

I stood and looked around me, my boots sunk inches deep in the mud. I pulled one up a bit and it broke loose with a faint sucking sound. It wasn't the kind of mud that stuck in inch deep patches to the soles, like mud back home would do. This mud was more like a wet putty that let my feet go after a delay, just so they'd know they were working through mud and not on solid ground.

Nothing moved, but I couldn't see very far. Slight movement could be seen if I held myself very still. The mist collected on the edges of the leaves and ferns around me. Slowly the mist came together on the surfaces to form drops. The drops ran to the centers of the vegetation and slipped off to fall to the mud. The surfaces of the plants and tree leaves lightly rebounded and slightly bobbed from losing the water's weight, and there was my movement.

The Gunny came for me before the dawn. My scout team rose up to form around me, as the Gunny and Pilson squished through the mud and then squatted down next to my wet poncho cover.

"Cup of coffee?" the Gunny asked, not bothering to wait while he went through the process of making his own.

I wondered why Pilson never prepared anything for himself. Fessman was a Mormon and didn't drink coffee, Stevens didn't like instant stuff, and Zippo was an unknown. What Nguyen drank in the morning was anybody's guess. For all I knew the man was nuclear powered because I'd never seen him eat or drink anything. But I was only entering my ninth day. I lit my own explosives and waited with my canteen cup of water over the small but powerful little fire. I was proud of the fact that my hands were not shaking. It was light, and I could function in the light.

"Seven," the Gunny said, without adding more.

"Kilo?" I asked, using the alpha-numeric letter for "K," meaning "killed."

"Roger that," the Gunny answered.

"How?" I asked, befuddled. As far as I knew the company had fired into the bushes until it was nearly out of ammo. Then Kilo Company had fired into the other side of the bushes from across the saddle and inflicted more damage on the enemy thought to be there.

"The one," the Gunny said, stopping for a few seconds. "Then the other six who didn't get down when Kilo opened up."

"Friendly fire?" I said, in shock. "All friendly fire?"

"The six? Yeah, kinda think so, unless the gooks are using 16s."

"Kilo Company Commander wants to come over for a pow wow," the Gunny said. "He sent over a runner. Be here at dawn. So will supply and medevac so it should be a regular cluster fuck."

"Their resupply, or our own?" I asked, concerned about getting all the way back to our own supplies we'd dumped to make the forced march down to save Kilo. Our ammo had to be very low and probably everything else, as well. Plus, we'd be crippled in not having packs to put things in from the resupply stockpile until we recovered our stuff.

"They had five wounded, so the medevac's all theirs. Our bags will go out on the slick."

"All that shit we went through, and they only took five wounded?" I said in near disgust. "We lost seven Marines!" Where my anger had come from, now directed at Kilo about not having as many dead as we had, I couldn't figure out. But anger was the first emotion I'd been able to dredge up since landing in the shit.

"Not the way to think, Junior," the Gunny said. "Your action saved their ass, after your action put them in the shit in the first place.

We never told them we were diverting from the plan so they walked right into what was waiting for us."

I knew the Gunny used the nickname to make a point. If I was going to act like a Junior he was going to call me that, or so I presumed. I also knew that he'd used the word 'we' in stating that Kilo had not been informed. Once again I was getting little credit and a good load of blame. I delayed a few seconds by drinking some of my scalding hot coffee.

"When?" I asked, hoping the subject would change without my asking for the change.

"There's enough light for a body count so I imagine any time now," the Gunny said, lighting a cigarette to go with his coffee. He looked over at the bush we'd fired into so enthusiastically the night before, or at least most of the company had fired into. He held out the cigarette.

I looked at the narrow white cylinder. I didn't smoke, or hadn't until I'd come to the 'Nam. I knew though that the Gunny wasn't holding out a cigarette. He was holding out a peace pipe. I took it, puffed, didn't cough, and then returned it. I blew the smoke out slowly. It did nothing for me except make my throat a bit hoarse and my mouth taste even worse than it did. I grimaced slightly and then swallowed. My toothpaste was back up the mountain in my pack.

The bushes were wedged aside by a Marine smoking his own cigarette, his 16 slung over one shoulder and an M79 over the other. Across his chest were two bandoliers filled with the big grenade-thrower rounds. The image in my mind, of another Tarzan book cover, was broken when another Marine stepped through the opening, followed by a few more men.

The Gunny came to his feet quickly, leaving his canteen holder sitting next to his little fire on the mud.

"Captain, this is the CO," the Gunny said, waving one hand down to me in a strange form of introduction.

The captain's cleanliness was the first thing I took in. He wore the uniform utilities as they were meant to be worn, and one of the useless flak jackets on top of it. His helmet had the proper two bars on its cover.

I sat on my helmet in the mud. I didn't get to my feet because I didn't know how to present myself after the surprise of being introduced so abruptly.

The Captain squatted down next to me. "Mertz," he said, "John, Captain, out of the Point. What's your date of rank?"

A "Pointer" from the academy. I'd only met two before, both back in Quantico. I looked for his West Point gold ring but didn't see it. Maybe it was too valuable to wear in combat.

"I don't know," I replied, hesitantly.

"You don't know your date of rank?" he asked, in obvious surprise. "When did you get promoted to Captain? We need to establish who's senior to who. What's your serial number, then?"

I gave him my seven-digit number, a number no Marine ever forgets.

"That's too new," the Captain replied, his forehead screwed up in thought. "That number wouldn't have been issued until very recently."

"Yeah, about six months ago," I replied, getting the idea where the conversation was going.

The Captain stood up, almost coming to a position of attention. "Jesus H. Christ, you're a second lieutenant," he said, making the word "second" sound like an expletive.

I would have smiled up at him if I smiled anymore. "Yes, I believe that's right, unless they gave me a combat promotion I'm unaware of."

"Jesus H. Christ. You're that second lieutenant, and there aren't any other officers to call a meeting of the CP. You're *that* company."

I got to my feet slowly, watching the Gunny back up a bit. I pulled my helmet out of the mud and brushed it off as best I could. Next to the West Point Captain I looked worse than a street bum staggering up after a night of drinking cheap rum. I put the filthy helmet on my filthy head.

"Actually, they call me Junior," I said, with a smile as wide as it was fake.

"You call your commanding officer Junior?" the Captain said, turning his head to face the Gunny.

"Ah, no, sir," the Gunny gasped out, not expecting the question or the Captain's fierce turn of direction. "I mean, yes, sir, or no, sir, or…" the Gunny got out before giving up and going silent.

"What's your MOS, Lieutenant?" the Captain asked, turning his attention back to me.

"Oh-eight-oh-two," I replied, leaving off the sir. For some reason not calling him sir made me identify with my own company better.

"We don't have an Artillery Forward Observer," he said, as if I should somehow volunteer for the vacant job.

"I don't have any platoon commanders," I replied.

"Not my problem," Captain Mertz said, two more Marines coming out of the bush behind him. They both wore helmets with one black bar on them, but no nickname printed underneath their bars.

I nodded at the two Lieutenants but they only stared back, making no move to join their CO or engage in the conversation.

"You're to take your company and proceed up the trail to the lip of the A Shau," the captain ordered, as if reading from a written directive. "Once there, you are to hold and wait for further orders. I lost some good men because you failed to stay on this path so let's not go there again."

"Seven," I said, my voice going lower and quieter.

"Seven what?" he replied, leaning in closer to hear me.

"Seven dead this last night, this last action," I said, my voice a whisper, the new found anger coming over me and combining with the dead flat analytical expectation of combat and death.

"Jesus H. Christ," the captain replied. "How in hell did you manage to lose seven men? I doubt we got that many of the enemy when our body count is done."

"We're going to hike back up to the position we left to get down and break the back of that ambush that was waiting for you," I said, my voice low and without any emotion. "Then we're going to come back down here to lead you into the Valley of No Return. You send your body count back in to battalion with our compliments, and wait until we return."

I watched emotions scroll across the Captains face. I waited, my right hand falling to the butt of my .45, the Colt sending a shiver of support back up through my arm. I knew I could not click off the safety without anyone hearing, so I left it on, knowing my thumb was on it and ready, however. The Captain suddenly turned to confer with the two officers who'd appeared behind him earlier. They talked for several seconds.

Captain Mertz spun around suddenly, but I made no move. I got no sense of physical danger from him, but I knew by instinct he was dangerous mentally. Dangerously out of place for his own survival and mine.

"Yes, you are ordered to take the point," Captain Mertz declared. "Kilo Company will wait until you return to organize the resupply and medevac. My radioman will coordinate to get us a side frequency so you can receive orders outside the combat command net."

I nodded, but said nothing.

"You're dismissed," the captain ordered.

"Ah, you're inside our perimeter," I responded, raising one eyebrow and shrugging my shoulders.

"Of course," the captain said, recovering himself. "Do you need anything?"

My eyes locked with the Gunny's. He was standing just off the Captain's shoulder. The Gunny shook his head, ever so slightly. I noted Nguyen just behind the Gunny but buried deep in the brush. I blinked once. He blinked back.

I held out my left wrist. "I could use a new watch. The face on this one melted from the defoliant back there."

The captain peered down, the two officers behind him frowning at me over his back, their frowns obvious expressions of anger for something I didn't understand.

The captain showed his own wrist. "This is a Rolex. The face is made out of a thin sheet of clear sapphire. Hardness factor is seven. Harder than steel. Pick one up at the base PX when you get to the rear area next time." He leaned forward, bringing his arm down. "Don't let them call you Junior, or any of that. They don't have to call you sir in combat, but they should at least refer to you as Lieutenant."

I looked the Captain in the eyes and suddenly felt old. I'd been in Vietnam for less than nine days but I felt like I'd been there for years. The Captain was not in my Vietnam. He was someplace else, and he might live, although probably not. There was nothing to be learned or expected from him that would benefit my survival or that of my men. There was no point in talking any further to him, so I merely turned and walked away.

When I got to my poncho Fessman appeared, another radio operator who I presumed was the Captain's knelt on the poncho edge next to him. I turned away while they whispered their radio jargon to one another. Suddenly they stopped talking. The mist had gone away and the air was warmer down at the lower altitude, and there was an uncommon clarity to it that made it more comfortable. It was clear enough to hear Fessman whisper to the other radioman.

"Whatever you do, don't tell him your grid position on the map."

Minutes later the sound of choppers could be heard in the distance. A lot of choppers, which was comforting because it meant that Huey Cobras would accompany the slicks. Not as good as having a Skyraider overhead all day, but good for as long as they were able to stay on station. The hike ahead would be almost fourteen miles round trip, only to arrive right back where we started, and then to make off before nightfall on up to the edge of the A Shau Valley.

forty

THE NINTH DAY : SECOND PART

The West Pointer Captain Mertz's plan to wait for resupply and take credit for the kills, along with any wounded NVA left behind, made logical sense. Neither I, nor any of the Marines in the company, gave a tinker's damn about who got credited for anything, or who was decorated for it, either. I was concerned, however, about what condition our equipment would be in when we returned to our position back up on the mountain ridge. I tried to convince myself that it wouldn't be a problem, at least with respect to whatever was left of the supplies when Kilo got done going through them. If our belongings were gone, then resupply would at least make up for some of what was lost. Our dead were another matter, left on the ground and stacked like black plastic cord-wood for the Huey pickup.

We began the hard hike back by going straight into the climb. It would be a gently-angled climb until we made the turn west to the much higher ground where we'd left most of our gear. The Marines took the forced march in silence, except for the tinny blare of the small transistor radios. Brother John came on to announce what he called an "appropriate song" to start the morning. It was called "White Rabbit." The lyrics played and I listened. Brother John was right. The song was all about Alice in Wonderland and Alice falling down that proverbial rabbit hole. *When logic and proportion have fallen sloppy dead, and the White Knight is talking backwards, and the Red Queen's off with her head, remember what the dormouse said: feed your head, feed your head.* I walked fast, agreeing with Brother John at the same time I tried to get enough traction to avoid slipping backwards with each step. In training I'd learned the art of the forced march the Marine Corps was famous for. No running. Running burned energy four times faster than walking, even really vigorous walking. Fast, long-legged strides were what was required. Once into the gait of it, great distances could be covered rapidly without expending too much energy.

I stopped moving and went to one knee. The second song of Brother John's set drove me down, breathing hard. It was "Alfie." The night before, and time with Lance Corporal Alfie, came crashing in. I'd managed to put those events into a separate compartment and set them aside for later, but now they hit me hard.

"Sir?" Fessman asked.

I got up unsteadily, knowing I could not say a word to anyone in the company. They all had to know about Alfie, but I knew if I showed weakness I would very quickly become more prey-like than I already was. And I could not fall back. The training in Quantico had been valuable in teaching that. There, on long unbelievably demanding marches, if a candidate fell back he was placed on a gurney to be hauled by selected Marines along for that purpose, on the same march. A demerit was assigned for falling out of the unit, no matter what the reason. Three demerits and an officer candidate was shipped to Camp Lejeune to become an enlisted recruit. I watched the backs of the men of the rest of the company moving in front of me. I could see them disappearing through the foliage. Falling back on the field of combat would result in no demerits. It would result in death. I moved, forcing my feet to plunge down into the jungle growth and mud. I pushed with my legs, one after another, catching up with the rear guard of Marines, working at it so hard that the physical exertion made remembered thoughts of Alfie almost impossible. Then the song was gone and the surfaced horror with it. I gained on the men and began passing one after another. My place in the unit was any place I chose it to be, unless the Gunny himself told me otherwise.

The company made it to the ridge, and then turned without stopping or discussion to work up the miles along the ridge, retracing the forced march down the day before. There was nothing but muscle searing and bone aching work to be done. The Marines were built and trained to perform such hard work without complaint. The march took four hours, or so I calculated by a returned sun. The temperature dropped and a slight wind came out to celebrate the arrival at our former position. The company stopped just before reaching the exact point where all the packs and other loads had been left.

"Arty up," came down the line, the words passed quietly from one man to another.

I moved forward, knowing that I would encounter the Gunny before long. As expected, he lay crouched behind some sort of overhanging tree, peering through the foliage at what seemed to be nothing.

"You got those binoculars on you?" he asked, as I went down to my knees next to him.

"No," I answered. "Left them there with my stuff. Why?"

The Gunny pointed straight ahead. I focused my eyes and finally saw what looked like a light brown cloth-covered helmet — a Vietnamese helmet with its flattened rice farmer look. The helmet sat atop a short stake. The cloth had a gold star centered pin, set into a small shiny red background.

"Shit," I whispered, "they found our stuff. I was afraid of that. Now we have nothing."

"Well, not really," the Gunny said. "Look deeper to where we left everything."

I stared beyond the helmet, gently moving atop the stick. As my eyes focused in I saw packs and equipment. It all looked untouched, in a rather shabby way. Maybe it had been gone through, but it was too far away to tell.

"They were here," I said, my tone one of question. "They were here but didn't take our stuff, and then put up that helmet to let us know they were here."

"What do you think about that?" the Gunny asked.

I looked over at him with surprise. The Gunny didn't usually ask my advice unless it was about our position or artillery related.

"Booby trapped?" I replied.

"Why the helmet alerting us then?" the Gunny said. "Why bother to let us know they were here and found our stuff? Doesn't make any sense."

"How do we make sure?" I asked, with no idea about the disarming of booby traps. Explosive ordnance training at Quantico had consisted of throwing one grenade and then blowing up some blocks of Composition B. That was it. At Fort Sill if anything blew up in the battery you didn't want to be around for it.

"Nguyen," the Gunny said, quietly.

"Send him out like an FNG?" I asked in amazement, keeping my voice low as well. "I don't think he'll go."

I turned to look around but didn't have to look far. My scout team was right behind me, having come forward when I was called. Stevens spoke softly and rapidly to Nguyen, and then stopped to listen.

"No booby traps," Stevens said, after a few seconds. "That's a sapper regiment helmet. Nguyen says they left it out of respect."

"That's a new one," the Gunny said, getting to his feet. "Tell Nguyen to go on over there and make certain."

"No," Stevens said. "I'll go. I believe him."

Stevens walked toward the roughly hidden piles of stuff we'd left behind. I got up and went with him. I didn't trust Stevens fully, but my trust, for whatever strange reason, was nearly complete in Nguyen.

It took only seconds of pawing around to discover that there were no booby traps and it appeared that everyone's things, although roughed up a bit and strewn about, seemed to have nothing missing from them.

"Un-fucking-believeable," the Gunny kept saying, over and over. "Respect my ass. These clever gook assholes have something up their sleeves."

"What would they respect us for, if that's really it?" I said to Stevens.

"Don't know," he replied. "Nguyen's not saying or doesn't know either. I don't understand a lot of what he says, but he thinks you are somehow special. Maybe it's the tracers or the artillery or how we fooled everyone, even our own battalion, in coming up here. Maybe he thinks it's good for us to have you so we'll lose."

"Here, you can have this while you contemplate your greatness and their respect," the Gunny said with a laugh, reaching out to spin the sapper helmet into the mud at my feet. "We need to have a command post meeting now, like we did before Hill 110."

I moved to my things and assembled what I had, vowing to never leave my binoculars behind again, no matter how heavy they were. Zippo had hauled the Starlight scope all the way to the saddle and back because it was on the list of things that could never be surrendered to the enemy. The binoculars were a whole lot smaller and lighter. I thought about what the Gunny said and grew ever more uncomfortable.

The CP meeting was some sort of sham, mostly because the shake-and-bake platoon leaders were mostly a sham, as was I, as company commander. Hill 110 had been a direct disobedience of orders I would never be comfortable with. Why had the Gunny used it in reference to the de facto leaders of the company getting together? I decided to say nothing. After a few minutes, almost the entire company had recovered all of its stuff. There was not one complaint about anything having been taken by an enemy that should have stolen or destroyed it all, and certainly, barring that, not have left everything behind untouched. Once again there was something seriously wrong with what was going on, and I had no training or experience about how to evaluate, or do anything with, this bizarre information.

The Gunny squatted next to his stuff in a small clearing nearby, with Pilson as attached and close by as Fessman was to me. Sugar Daddy and Jurgens arrived at the same time as the other two platoon leaders. I waited a few minutes before walking over, trying to assume some of Captain Mertz's air of authority and command. I realized my mistake in delaying, immediately. The circle of supposed leaders had closed before I got there. And nobody moved to accommodate my arrival. I stood just uncomfortably outside the circle, with Fessman at my side.

"Nice trophy," Sugar Daddy said, pointing at the sapper helmet I'd stupidly not discarded after picking it up.

Everyone laughed quietly for a bit. I handed the helmet to Fessman and waited through the expressed mirth from my place outside the circle.

"What are we doing?" Jurgens said, in his usual aggressive and forceful manner.

The Gunny stared at Jurgens, and then each other man at the meeting, except me, before speaking. "The apparent orders, issued by Mertz in Kilo, are for us to return to the scene of last night's battle and then lead the way up the trail into the A Shau."

"Shit," Sugar Daddy said, lighting up a cigarette.

"What are we doing?" Jurgens asked again, this time losing a bit of his aggressive tone, probably because of the Gunny's glare.

All of the Marines present had glanced at me when the mention of the previous night's battle had come up. There would be no sharing of the blame for the losses, I understood. I knew nighttime would be problematic again, and hoped that the Starlight scope had weathered the rough march up and down the mountain.

"We're going with Junior's plan instead," the Gunny said.

My mouth fell open. My plan? What plan? I had no plan. Barring any word from battalion on the command net, the orders of Captain Mertz should be followed, or so I assumed. I waited without saying anything, enduring the looks of everyone around the circle, once again.

"Ah, what was that plan again?" Sugar Daddy asked the Gunny, blowing smoke out as he said it. The smell of the smoke was not from tobacco, however.

I frowned, but continued to take the meeting in without saying anything. I remained expressionless as possible, even though I knew Sugar Daddy had blown the marijuana smoke directly at me for effect.

"The plan to get off the trail and get our asses up this mountain. Chesty Puller's plan," the Gunny reminded them. "Then we were to move forcefully down this ridge until we hit the lip of the A Shau, catching the NVA off guard and getting us through without casualties."

"I thought that was your plan?" Jurgens said.

The Gunny glanced once at me with a slight frown before continuing. "I don't know where you got that idea. It was Junior's plan all along and it's not a bad one."

"We took eight dead for casualties," Sugar Daddy said. "Was it his idea to go pull Kilo's fat out of the fire, too? And what about resupply? We're low on water and almost out of ammo. Junior's helmet there would seem to indicate that there's a whole regiment running around on this mountain and it ain't ours. What of them?"

"Lieutenant?" the Gunny stated, more than asked.

I was stunned again. Somehow, I'd instantly gone from Junior to lieutenant. I stared into the Gunny's eyes and thought furiously. And then I had it. The Gunny was stuck with the question Sugar Daddy posed, and probably realized that no plan was going to work without artillery support and some decent map work, which meant my cooperation. He knew I was mad as hell about Hill 110. I read a question mark in his expression and knew what that was, too. Would I go against Captain Mertz and his quasi-legal orders? Mertz wasn't in our chain of command and therefore did not have to be obeyed. But he was a real captain and real commander while I was an undetermined junior something-or-other.

I leaned down and took the sapper's helmet from Fessman's hand. "If that sapper regiment is waiting somewhere up here, then they're waiting between us and the saddle. Resupply was at the saddle. They'll know we need resupply because they looked at our stuff. The trail to the A Shau extends up from the saddle and they know we're headed there, and whatever NVA unit was down there last night took a bashing and will need recovery. Our orders from battalion are to get to the A Shau and await further orders. How we do that is our affair."

I tossed the helmet through the air. It landed at the Gunny's feet.

The Gunny jerked back, but only a few inches. He didn't touch the helmet or look up at me.

"So what do we do?" Jurgens asked, for the third time. "I don't like doing anything Junior tells us to do. We lost a ton of good men last night on his say so."

I looked at the platoon leaders of Second and Third platoons but neither man said a word. The silent platoons, I thought. Were they the workhorse platoons manning the perimeter and facing up the trails with point men? I wondered in my own silence. The things I didn't know about my own company could fill volumes.

"We stay on the ridge and head for the A Shau," the Gunny ordered. "We exercise fire control and save ammo if we get hit. The top of the edges of the valley are pretty clear so resupply should be there in the morning if we can make it and set in before night falls. If he's...." and there the Gunny stopped for a few seconds. "If things go right then the NVA won't ever know we slipped by and Kilo can make its own way up to the A Shau."

A moment of silence fell over the group.

"Good plan, Gunny," Sugar Daddy said, finishing his reefer and then putting it out in the mud at his feet, glancing once in my direction for effect.

I gave him nothing back, looking at the Gunny and waiting for him to adjourn the impromptu meeting.

"Alright, head 'em up and move 'em out," the Gunny said, imitating foreman Gil Favor from the Rawhide television series.

Jurgens got up abruptly and walked over to me. My hand went to my .45 casually, so as not to alert the bigger and older sergeant.

"Just because you took care of Alfie like that don't get you off the hook for the other seven," he said in a whisper.

We stared into each other's eyes for a few seconds. I wondered why both he and Sugar Daddy directed so many deadly threats my way. I fully intended to kill both of them when the time was right, and I was not about to threaten either man. Why would I ever want to warn them of what was coming? It made no sense I could understand for either of them to threaten me. When Jurgens and his small retinue moved off, I waved Fessman to me.

"Forget the frequency Mertz gave you," I told him. "If the six actual comes up on the command net and orders us to the saddle that's one thing. If he doesn't, then we're not talking to Kilo until we get to the A Shau."

"Aye aye, sir," Fessman said with a smile.

I moved to my stuff to get ready to make the hump to the A Shau. It was past mid-day and the hump would be another tough one with full packs, even though it would all be down slope. I sat down and unlaced my boots. I hadn't had my boots off in five days. My socks weren't identifiable as socks anymore, but I rolled them up and put them in an outside pocket anyway. I put on a thick pair of white socks and laced the boots up tightly. When I stood up I felt unaccountably like a new man. I joined the scout team, approaching Stevens from the rear.

"Why did Nguyen say the sappers respect us?" I asked, not satisfied with the sergeant's earlier laconic response.

Stevens waved Nguyen to him. They spoke back and forth for a couple of minutes. Stevens turned back toward me while Nguyen stared over his right shoulder. Suddenly, the native Vietnamese moved forward and pointed down at my right wrist.

I looked at the elephant hair bracelet he'd given me earlier.

"Respect," Nguyen said, very softly, in English.

"They're Montagnards, sir," Stevens said, "like him. They don't think like we do. They're pretty weird because you've made an impression on him and them somehow or another. He said they're not waiting because they know they'll see you again."

I looked into Nguyen's eyes but the man's dark orbs didn't give me anything back. I blinked and then he blinked, just like the times I saw him disguised in the bush. The man was inscrutable. The Montagnards were inscrutable. The Vietnamese were inscrutable. Even my fellow Marines were almost impossible to understand. Somehow, taking out Alfie was credited as a good thing while the seven Marines who'd died was a bad thing, for me, even though they were all veterans who should have damn well known to keep their heads and asses down when there was live fire about to begin. And then there was the Gunny's responsibility, which didn't seem to really exist. It was all on me.

I began the move down the mountain and on into the afternoon. The short rest reinvigorated the company and knowing that they did not have to go back to the saddle where we'd lost so many. The company wouldn't have taken the point for anyone or anything. With this revitalized energy the company moved faster than it had in rushing to the rescue of Kilo Company. I brought up my usual place near the rear, thinking about how I did not want the respect of the enemy, nor the hatred of my Marines. I didn't want anything except to get through the afternoon and then endure another night.

Zippo passed me on the right. He was wearing the sapper helmet like it was his own. When I exchanged glances with him he grinned. I could not help grinning back, not because he looked ridiculous, which he did, but because I knew he needed me, too.

forty-one

THE NINTH DAY : THIRD PART

When the company came to a slowing halt, I was more than ready to rest. The straps of my pack burned where they pressed down over the narrower suspender straps that held up my web belt. We'd made it back close to where the company had veered north and gone to the aid of Kilo Company the day before. I stripped off the pack and collapsed to the jungle floor. I checked my canteens but both were empty. Fessman pushed his own toward me, and I accepted it willingly. I drank down about a third of the warmly awful, but so welcome, liquid before giving it back. I looked around. Even though we were moving downward along the ridge we were still high enough for the temperature to be cool, the wind slight and the mosquitoes limited to occasional bites not important enough to warrant slathering on the nasty oil repellent.

My scout team rested only a few feet away. I leaned over to ask Stevens about the sapper regimental helmet affair. Zippo had discarded it when others around him had taken to calling him a black gook.

"I thought the Montagnards were on our side," I said, motioning for him to put the question to Nguyen. It took almost a full minute for Stevens to counsel with the Kit Carson Scout and reply.

"They are advisors to the sappers, as he is an advisor to us," Stevens said. "They don't call themselves Montagnards. That was the French. They call themselves the Moi. Nguyen is Jarai Moi and the advisors to the sappers are Mnong Moi."

"Why do some choose the NVA instead of us?"

"They help so that their villages will not be burned and their people killed," Stevens said, without counseling with Nguyen this time.

"We don't burn their villages, I don't think," I replied. "Why does Nguyen work with us?'

"His village was already burned."

I looked over at the Moi scout. He stared back at me with his usual expressionless eyes. I knew if I blinked that he would too, though. I turned back to Stevens. "His family?"

"Gone."

"Shit," I said, softly, wondering what it was like to lose your whole family while you're gone somewhere trying to do the right thing and take care of them, too.

In the back of my mind, in spite of the loyalty I felt from the strange man, I wondered just how much communication he had with other Moi around. The sappers would have had to hear about us, and me specifically, from someone, if that was really the point of the symbol.

"Arty up," came whispering in from around me.

"Shit," I said, wondering whether the Gunny needed artillery, which seemed unlikely because there had been no small arms firing or explosions of any kind. I began crawling along the jungle floor. I thought of snakes for the first time in three days. I found it kind of funny that I'd been too afraid of other things to be afraid of snakes, or maybe that was as it should be because the lack of them seemed to indicate that any snakes around were smart enough to stay high in the trees or underground.

I felt more than heard Fessman behind me, since my own noisy progress over the moist but solid ground kept me from hearing anything else. I found the Gunny thanks to many silently pointing fingers. This time I'd brought my binoculars, as the jungle near the edge of the ridge was more open and I hoped to be able to look out over whatever valley lay beyond it to the south toward, the American artillery fire-base.

The Gunny turned as I approached, holding an index finger over his mouth and pointing down to the south.

"There's somebody out there," he whispered. "And then there's that..." He pointed downhill in the direction of our travel.

I couldn't see anything in either direction. "What?" I finally asked in frustration, keeping my voice as low as his.

"I don't know who's there," the Gunny said, pressing his head down behind a small pile of leafy bracken. "I just know that these Marines have been doing this for a while and they're pretty good about knowing such things."

I pulled out my binoculars and scanned the area down to the south. We were about a quarter of a mile, I guessed, from where we'd turned to head toward Kilo the day before. There was nothing. I swept down toward the second area the Gunny had pointed out. I silently cursed the stupid individual focusing of the eyepieces on the Japanese binoculars. Each had to be adjusted for distance individually whenever focus was needed. Regular combat lenses had one lever to quickly make that adjustment on both lenses, not to mention meter scales to approximate distance. I finally got the focus right and saw what concerned the Gunny, and helped bring the company to a halt. Two Marines lay next to a dark spot. Just beyond the spot a bamboo reinforced slat of leaf-weaved matting leaned up against the trunk of one of the larger trees. Without the Gunny saying a word, I knew I was looking at the entrance to my first tunnel. At Quantico they had created a field of tunnels to train enlisted Marines how to find and fight the enemy below, or destroy underground supplies. The Marines who went down in the holes were called "tunnel rats."

I put my binoculars down. "Okay to check it out?" I asked the Gunny, "or have you already sent in the tunnel rats?"

Both Fessman and Pilson snickered right after I made the comment. I caught their laugh but didn't understand.

The Gunny got to his feet, and then started moving low toward the hole in the ground guarded by the two Marines. I followed with Fessman and Pilson bringing up the rear.

"I'm more worried about what's out there rather than down in this hole," he said over his shoulder as he crouched low.

I laid on my chest looking down into the hole, surprised by it's size. The round hole would have barely fit my body. If I crawled down into it, my shoulders would be pressing up against each side. The tunnels at the Marine Base stateside had been square, plenty big and dug into hard ground. I pointed my flashlight into the hole. It went down for about four feet before veering off in the direction of the company's travel. I could not imagine a less welcome place to climb into. I stared for a moment more before deciding that I would never enter such a place if I could possibly help it. I noted that the cover of the tunnel appeared flimsy, but with cross-slatted bamboo strengtheners, it would probably hold the weight of a man stepping on its surface.

"Tunnel rats?" I asked again, still staring down.

"We don't have any," the Gunny said, accepting a green cloth-wrapped package from another Marine. "Nobody in this unit is dumb enough to go down into one of these tunnels. We find them all the time. The A Shau's supposed to be full of them, but I don't exactly remember."

I realized the Gunny was priming several pounds of Composition B at my side. I eased back.

He glanced up at me. "You can write the words 'tunnel rat' on each package if you want."

Fessman and Pilson laughed again, this time not so secretly.

"So, we blow them in place," I said, thinking about the ramifications. "We never find out where the tunnels go, and what's down there?"

"Got a better idea?" The Gunny asked with a smile, while he worked away.

"But the explosives will only affect a small part of whatever the complex below really is," I replied, not having a better idea.

"How about some of that concrete piercing arty shit you were dumping around before?" the Gunny said, getting to his feet and beginning to walk backward while unwinding a thin set of wires from a small spool.

I got up and moved with him. "The canopy," I said, pointing upward. "The concrete-piercing will trigger in the tops of the trees and then detonate before hitting the jungle floor. The fuses are that delicate, even though the rounds themselves are called concrete-piercing."

The Gunny squatted down behind a tree trunk and prepared a small metal box for transmitting the electric signal.

"Ah, the others you're worried about, won't this let them know exactly where we are?" I asked.

"Now that's funny, Junior," the Gunny laughed, stopping to light a cigarette. "We're out here playing rock and roll across the jungle, and some huge regiment passed by and left a helmet dangling on a stick to let us know how much they respect us. And the enemy doesn't know where we are? You're killing me here." The Gunny blew some smoke, but didn't direct it my way like Sugar Daddy had.

I took off my helmet and liner to scratch my head and think. There was really nothing to be said about how badly we'd had to let our position be known in coming to Kilo's defense. If we'd all been killed, no one would have ever known about the company's good intentions.

"Fire in the hole," Gunny suddenly yelled out, dodging behind the tree trunk and twisting the little lever on the box.

The shock wave of the blast rocked my head and body back. I swallowed a few times to clear my ears. Bits of jungle and mud rained down for almost half a minute before subsiding.

The Gunny grinned while he pulled in and wound what was left of the wire back around the little box. I put my helmet back on and prepared for what was ahead, although I didn't know what was ahead other than the fact that we were either already in, or just short of arriving in, what everyone called Indian Country. And that was all bad.

"Who do you think is out there?" I asked, when the Gunny finished with his explosives task.

"Well, if it's those sapper guys, and there's a regiment of them, then we're dead as door nails no matter what we do. What do you think?"

I looked out in the direction we were traveling and then down where we'd gone before. And then it came to me. They were out there alright, but it wasn't the sappers, if the sappers even existed.

"It's the remnants," I said. "When we hit them down at the saddle, and then Kilo followed up, they took unexpected and big casualties. This part of the tunnel complex is probably part of it. They didn't move down the mountain afterward. No, they followed us and now here we are. They weren't expecting us to go get our stuff and come back because they didn't know we left it there in the first place. Now, they're waiting again for us to pass by on our new path to the A Shau."

"Jesus, Junior, if I didn't know you were green as a pea pod and been here for nine days I'd think you were a gook. You think like a gook. Hell, you're about as tall as a gook."

"Thanks for the vote of confidence," I replied, as acidly as I could.

"So what do we do now?" the Gunny asked. "We're damn near out of ammo, food, water, and you name it. If we pass on by where they probably are waiting, then we get blasted. If we try to attack them first, we get blasted for sure."

"What's the edge look like?" I said.

"What edge?" the Gunny said, taking a last drag of his cigarette before putting it out in the jungle debris at our feet.

"The edge of the mountain over here to the south," I replied, pointing to my right. "The contours are pretty compressed on my map but if we've got any margin at all then I can use Cunningham to our advantage." I pulled out my map and unfolded it to show him.

"Can we try that in English?" The Gunny said, his tone one of frustrated impatience. He deliberately looked away from my map.

I refolded the map and put it in my morphine pocket, wondering when I'd get a chance to write to my wife again. I could write about finding my first tunnel and what it was like, leaving off the rest, of course. "Come on, let's just move a couple of hundred meters south and check it out."

We walked past the tunnel entrance, which was a large smoking crater after the blast. I wondered how far down a surface explosion caused damage. If the tunnels were angled and blocked with anything at all then the shock wave would do little, beyond barely penetrating dirt cave-in stuff. It took only a few minutes for the Gunny and my scout team to arrive at the edge of the mountain ridge, although ridge turned out to be the wrong word. The edge of mountain wasn't an edge at all, except for a cliff that dropped about six feet down. After that the side of mountain went down into a relatively shallow valley in flat steps, each about twenty feet long protruding from the side of the rock and dirt.

The Gunny studied the land around and below us as we stood on the top edge of cliff. The view wasn't stunning but it was pretty beautiful. The sun was low overhead but not close to setting, and the wind had picked up to make the warming air pleasant instead of cloying and miserable, as it always was in the lowlands.

"We can go one level down and just walk right by them if we keep our heads down," the Gunny said, with one hand rubbing his chin.

I shook my head. "They've got Chicom radio crap and maybe even Prick 25s by now. If anyone spots us down there moving right along, they'll attack and simply shoot down at us until we're done, given that we can barely shoot back. Sitting ducks is the expression, I think."

"So?" the Gunny asked.

"So, we climb down right here and move until we get about a thousand meters further along. That's about where we detoured and headed for Kilo. Then we climb back up and set in right near the edge. We let them know we're there. They'll wait until the sun goes down and attack. When they attack we'll quickly climb back down again. I'll call in an artillery strike using variable time fuses. Should work like bug spray. The rounds will impact on top of the mountain while we're covered completely by the lip of rock."

"Shit," the Gunny breathed out. "Variable time, like in radar-timed?"

"Yeah," I replied. "The gunners can set the fuses to go off from thirty to three hundred meters off the ground. The little radar waves will go right through the jungle and play back from the jungle floor. We can have them set for about a hundred meters. The shrapnel will spray down at about twenty-four thousand feet per second. Wonderful stuff."

"I'm sure," the Gunny said, sounding anything but sure. "Sounds a little bit complicated to me."

"Well, it's a plan," I offered. "I can't think of anything else right off the bat. Maybe you can."

"Might as well try it," the Gunny said, and then walked back into the jungle without saying another word.

"What do we do, sir?" Fessman asked.

"Let's just hunker down here to wait and see," I said. "I don't imagine there's going to be another CP meeting."

We waited, resting next to the side of the cliff. It took about fifteen minutes for the company to begin pouring over the length of the edge that was visible. I watched in surprise. I had not seen the full company since I'd been in country, only bits and pieces. Watching over two hundred men in full gear ease over and then drop down to the ground below was impressive. I felt more confidence in my plan although the idea that a scheme like I'd just dreamed up might prove so wrong that all of us could get killed nagged at the back of my mind. Would the company stop after a thousand meters? Would Cunningham have a supply of VT fuses on hand? Would the battery even be able to fire them, or fire enough rounds to make a difference?

When the company was over I moved to the edge, tossed my pack down and then climbed. The rocks were mossy but not too slippery. I let myself fall the last four feet, or so, onto the soft plant covered soil. It took less than half an hour, following the company lead, before we stopped to climb back up like everyone else.

Once back in the jungle, but not far from the cliff's edge, we settled in to await nightfall. The Gunny joined us a few minutes later. Fessman had turned his little radio off, like the rest of the men, as we'd been making our way along in the defilade. He turned it on and immediately Brother John introduced Smokey Robinson singing "Tracks of My Tears."

"The life of the party, right," the Gunny said, lighting another cigarette. "Because I tell a joke or two," he continued, after letting some smoke out. "Either this is going to work or there's not gonna be much of a party."

forty-two

THE NINTH NIGHT

I lay prone on the jungle mat of fallen leaves, fronds, and smaller branches. I couldn't tell how deep the mass under me was, although back at the hole we'd blown earlier, the jungle floor mat seemed like it was almost a foot thick. It was better than the mud. We had to be ready to retreat back over the lip of the cliff at the right time so I'd placed my full pack between my head and the likely direction of the enemy, not that the pack would stop anything more powerful than a Daisy air rifle BB. I realized it might also give away my position, even though it was green. It was the wrong green. There was no right green in the jungle of Vietnam. Everything that was supposed to be there blended in. The Bamboo Vipers were yellow but they blended invisibly. The only thing that didn't blend in was Marines. I wondered if our faulty ability to blend in was responsible for the high casualties we took. There was no way to tell how we really stacked up against the NVA. We made up their casualties to please a demanding command structure. Our own casualties were evident every day by counting the wounded going out on medevac and the body bags, but then the friendly fire dead weren't listed as being from friendly fire. Were those Marine dead from such friendly fire really the result of that, or was Vietnam simply killing them in a different way?

The longer we waited, the more questionable my plan became. If we'd simply run down along the cliff, we might have avoided detection and be sitting at the A Shau Landing Zone by nightfall. Instead, we weren't going anywhere for the rest of the light, and on into the dark. There had been no contact from Kilo when we'd failed to show up. The Gunny said, before he moved up and down the line to make sure everyone was attentive and waiting instead of asleep at the switch, that Kilo wouldn't really care whether we showed up or not as long as they got our resupply and added it to their own.

"What time should we expect to get hit?" Stevens asked me. I knew he was speaking for my whole scout team. I made believe I could read the time on my watch, although I couldn't see through the damaged crystal anymore. I would have smiled at that point, thinking about enjoying the new Rolex I could buy when I got to the rear, but all I felt was smoldering anger at the stupidity of it all.

"Eight," I said, presuming it was about five o'clock. "About three hours from now, although they could wait until just before dawn. They like that just before dawn shit."

I looked up and could see that the team was buying it. I didn't have a clue about the time, or what time we'd get hit, if we got hit at all. There were so many ways for me to come out of the whole thing looking like an idiot or, at the worst, not come out at all. I knew I was feeling anxiety and deep fatigue at the same time. If I could only call Cunningham to find out if they had the fuses and the rounds I needed, I'd feel a whole lot better. But I couldn't do that. I suspected the NVA were lying in wait only a few hundred meters away and if they had Prick 25s, they'd be able to hear our communication. If they heard us begging for ammo, we'd be dead very quickly.

"It's Sunday," Fessman announced. "Maybe they won't come on Sunday."

"It's Sunday?" I replied in complete surprise. I had lost all consciousness of time when it came to days of the week. I knew it was the ninth of the month because I was on my ninth day and I'd come in on the first day of the month. Maybe the mythical Mertz Rolex would have the day of the week as part of its expensive movement, I thought.

"Are you Catholic?" Zippo suddenly asked me, the others looking at him expectantly when he said the words.

"Well, yes, although I'm not a great one," I answered, wondering why he was asking that particular question. I felt he was serious about something. I couldn't just blow him off, although I wanted to. Officers were supposed to remain aloof and remote from the members of enlisted ranks to preserve command ability. My shoulders slumped to the bracken beneath me. All I wanted to do was lie and rest. Everything ached. And, for the second or third time since my arrival in country, I didn't really want to be a Marine Officer anymore.

Fessman waited without replying. He stared at me, and then blinked like Nguyen when he was buried in the bush.

"What is it?" I asked softly, trying to keep the exasperation out of my voice.

"We wondered if you'd say something," Fessman stammered back. "You know, like a priest or something. We're going to get attacked and we don't have any ammunition, and its Sunday, so we thought…"

I looked at the three of them. Nguyen hung back, remaining just beyond the rest, in his normal place. I glanced at him, but got nothing back from his flat expression and obsidian eyes.

"He's Catholic, too," Stevens said motioning toward the Montagnard, having watched me closely while I was looking at Nguyen.

The last Catholic mass I'd been to was in Virginia to get married. My wife had insisted on the full mass because her Catholic parents attended. The priest at Quantico would not marry us because my wife was pregnant, even though we had both gone to all Catholic schools all the way up through college. I'd heard about a Catholic priest in Fredericksburg, though. It was said he'd marry anybody for two hundred bucks and a bottle of Jamison whiskey. I'd gotten hold of a bottle of the whiskey, but could only raise a hundred dollars in cash. After four shots of the Jamison though, Father O'Brien agreed to do the wedding.

"Just a few words," Fessman said.

The request came out of nowhere. I thought about the fact that I didn't know any services or the words to go along with them. I'd been an altar boy, so I knew responses to the priests in Latin. I didn't think Latin would work.

"Okay," I said, lifting my torso up on my elbows. The team gathered around, even Nguyen coming in to hang just outside our small circle. I looked around to make sure we were far enough away for any regular Marines so I would not appear even more idiotic than they already thought me to be.

I told them about what I knew of Paul in the Bible. How he'd gone through all kinds of misery and tribulations not believing in the Lord but finally, when he'd come to his knees and seen the light, his life turned around and he found safety and peace, and the calling to serve the Lord the rest of his life. I didn't mention Paul being beheaded by Nero because that small detail hadn't been documented in the Bible anyway. I finished the little "service" by reciting one of the few poems I knew by heart. It was called "Footsteps in the Sand" and I'd always loved it. The last words came out of my mouth in a whisper: "My precious, precious child. I love you, and would never, ever, leave you during your trials and testings. When you saw only one set of footprints, it was then that I carried you."

I made the sign of the cross, keeping my expression blank, like Nguyen's. My lack of a solid belief in a supreme being didn't bother me, but I knew it would bother them if they knew it. We were all very likely to get killed. It was pretty obvious, just in doing any counting of the daily death toll. I couldn't save myself, much less any of them, except maybe for the shortest periods of time. I'd been stringing those short periods together like the sewn patches on blankets put together in old grandmothers' quilting bees, but the end result could not be put off forever. I knew those "footprints in the sand" weren't there because God wasn't there. "Footsteps" was a great poem, but reality was right in front of us, and if we lived through what was in front of us, then the A Shau awaited, to claim those of us who had survived.

The Gunny crawled up next to me, with Pilson at his side. I noted that Pilson pulled the big heavy Prick 25 off his back and used it as a barrier between his head and the likely position of the enemy. The Prick 25 radio body would stop about as much as my pack, which meant almost nothing, but I liked his gesture, so similar to my own. The company's position along the lip of the cliff was not a defensible one, without actually going over the edge, and even then the distance down precluded having secure cover to fight from, even if ammunition had been more plentiful.

"Are they out there, or not?" the Gunny asked, keeping his voice low, looking straight ahead instead of at me.

"What about air-dropping in a pallet of ammo and water?" I asked back, ignoring the question both he and I knew had no answer.

The Gunny turned his head to look over at me. "If they aren't there, then an emergency air drop would make all the sense in the world. If they're out there, and we think they're out there, then the first sign of a resupply-loaded slick will cause them to attack. In which case we're dead."

"I'll get some coffee," the Gunny said, after a few silent moments. "I've got water," he finished, somehow knowing I was dry. He went to work getting some stuff out of his pack.

We hunched low together near the lip of the cliff. I noted that some of the company were already over the edge, setting stones atop one another to form a step up from the eight-foot face. The light was beginning to wane, causing the Gunny's lit ammo to form a small glowing bulb under his canteen holder.

"Will anybody see them?" I asked him, working on getting my own water hot.

The Gunny glanced over the edge and saw the Marines silently working away. "Everything's a trade-off," he replied, mixing his coffee powder into his boiling water with the end of his K-Bar. He handed me a packet.

"When it gets dark, should I call in the mission whether they hit us or not?" I asked him, bringing my water to a boil. "We could all jump down to the ledge and run like hell toward the A Shau."

The Gunny sipped his coffee, making a slurping sound like he always did, but he didn't answer.

"Well?" I finally inquired, impatiently.

"And here I thought you had it all planned out," the Gunny finally said, his voice so expressionless that I couldn't tell whether he was entirely serious or not.

I wanted to share my angst about whether the American battery would be able or willing to support us, but I couldn't because it didn't make any difference. If I called in fire too early, I might stop the enemy from attacking if I was able to hit their exact position, which was unlikely. If I called fire in early I might also exhaust the limited rounds stored at the battery, if I was going to get that fire at all. If I waited until we were being attacked, then I'd have the NVA exposed and pinpointed up and down the line. Our return small arms fire would probably be enough to hold them off for a bit, given the company was so oversupplied with M-60 machine guns, and then I could make the artillery effective enough to allow us to head out east toward the A Shau without fear we'd be taken out along the way. I was about to sip my coffee when my hands started shaking again. I put the cup holder down. My hands went to my thighs and I massaged them deeply.

"Long day," the Gunny noted, observing my movements.

I was almost sure the Gunny did know about the shakes, but I knew it was wise to keep my little secret as long as I could. There was nothing to be gained by showing weakness, even though the Gunny knew I was anything but strong command material.

"We wait until they hit us," I said, sounding as confident as I could. "It's likely they're coming back to the tunnel complex we found further back, or something like that. Obviously we're in their way and also a target of opportunity that they can't ignore, plus they're probably really pissed that they lost so many men."

"See, you're learning," the Gunny said in his best aged and wise voice. "We wait, which is always hard, and then we hit them where it hurts again. Unfortunately, the prize is the A Shau and that kind of sucks. But we'll deal with that tomorrow."

I stopped massaging my thighs and picked up my canteen holder by its big U-shaped handle. No shaking. It was either the massaging or the seeming confidence the Gunny exuded. I drank some coffee and then set the holder down next to the tiny dying embers of the Gunny's Composition B fire. I pulled some paper and an envelope from my pack and went to work writing a letter home. I described the mythical tunnel complex I knew had to be underground if the NVA unit we were about to come into contact with was coming back to it. I left out the enemy attacking part. To explain how I knew what was down there, I made Fessman into a tunnel rat when he was not operating my radio. Fessman was way too big, even at his young age, to fit inside one of the poorly dug tunnels but she would not know that. If we made it to the A Shau and then got resupply and medevac to come down in the morning, then my letter would go out. I paused in my writing. I could not remember how many letters I'd written. I should be on my ninth or maybe tenth but I'd been backed up in getting them out.

I lay behind my pack and next to my letter, which was too moist because we couldn't take out our hooch-building material without giving away our positions when the fighting got close, if it got close. I could start numbering the letters going out, but then I'd possibly be letting my wife know that I could not remember. "Why can't he remember," might be a phrase she could not explain or get over. I wrote on about the cliff and the kind of rock making up the mountains of the highlands. I also wrote about the Montagnards thinking I might be okay. I didn't mention that it might be the enemy thinking I was okay. How could I explain that to anyone?

The light was fast disappearing by the time I finished my letter. I made a few notes for myself and then pulled out my map. I reviewed the number I would use for the registration round, which I'd call in using a Willie Peter round, just in case. I worked to formulate where our own unit would be registered so I would not be limited on how close I could call the fire. Even as "danger close" fire mission could not be fired within two hundred meters of the company's imaginary perimeter. I needed a real imaginary registration position because we might need some rounds to fall a helluva lot closer than two hundred meters.

That wasn't a problem. The problem was that I had to have our position firmly in mind for adjusting fire. From where Cunningham was located, and firing up and down the line along the ridge, I would be adjusting using left and right instead of up or down. If I screwed up about the lie of where we were then friendly losses, quite possibly with me among them, would be substantial. VT fuses were brutally murderous and completely careless when it came to who got taken out under their umbrella of death.

The night set in. The wind died down and there was no rain or mist. The moon came out just north of due east. It was near full, although it wasn't high enough early on to see that. The clue was in the amount of light that penetrated the jungle and beamed down on the visible valley behind us.

"Starlight scope," I whispered to Fessman, who slithered away to find Zippo.

Although the double canopy jungle we were in was fairly dense, there were patches through the bracken and tree trunks that extended out thirty meters or more in the direction I suspected the NVA regulars would be coming from. For the first time in many nights, I felt no fear from either First Platoon or Fourth. The company's differences were temporarily put to rest until the bigger threat could be dealt with.

Zippo appeared, crawling on his hands and knees. He said nothing, although I could see big white teeth exposed by his big smile. He unloaded the scope and went to work setting it up. He'd brought his own pack to rest the barrel across.

"It's good, sir," he said. "You want to see?"

I didn't answer right away, instead leaning over toward Fessman.

"Nudge Stevens," I ordered, not raising my voice. "All of us are going to spell one another in looking through this thing."

Stevens came out of the murky darkness seconds later, with Nguyen at his side.

"Focus that thing on the end of one of the open areas," I told Zippo. "We'll scan from open area to open area as long as it takes."

"What are we looking for?" Stevens asked, as Zippo worked to focus.

"Footsteps in the sand," I replied, in a whisper.

forty-three

THE NINTH NIGHT : SECOND PART

I waited, my body spread face down and flat on the jungle floor. It would have been a time of rest and relaxation if an attack by unknown numbers of wily, capable, and well-armed opponents weren't also waiting somewhere out in the night. Counting breaths and numbers to hold back the terror of the night wouldn't come. Staring ahead into the dark, a useless task, could not be avoided.

Every U.S. Marine is trained for guard duty, even officers. Guard duty is conducted continuously by the Corps all over the world. All U.S. Embassies and consulates are guarded by Marines, as well as many military bases and commands of military services not Marine related. Marines guard the White House. The applied science and art of guarding involves two conflicting actions. Total vigilance and total boredom. Total vigilance is impossible to accomplish while total boredom is impossible to avoid, at times. Waiting for an attack that might not come should not have been boring, but it was, like guard duty, although with an element of terrifying fear that was indescribable. And there was nothing to do in a darkness that had to be maintained as near to being complete as possible, in spite of a blooming full moon behind us. No flashlights or lighting of cigarettes.

The company wasn't a total loss or mess, I realized, because there was almost no sound coming from anyone or anything, as the massed company was one. That silent exhibition took training and experience. There was no clearing of weapon actions, clicks of lighters, flashes of light, or anything else to give away our position, even though everyone knew the enemy had to know exactly where we were and the fact that we were stationary out ahead of them in the night. It was unlikely the NVA knew we were low on ammunition, however, because American units were so vastly over-supplied compared to Vietnamese forces.

I'd mentioned semi-auto to the Gunny, but I didn't know if he'd carried the idea down the line. M16 rifles could be fired on full auto or semi-auto, depending upon where a small selector on the lower left of the firearm's receiver was placed. All combat troops and Marines were known to favor full auto, but ammunition was low. Semi-auto was more controllable and wasted a whole lot less ammunition.

I didn't know the actual state of our ammunition supply, but I knew the Gunny would not be worried unless that amount was critical. I figured that my plan was probably acceptable to him because it involved the most sparing use of small arms fire, if everything went according to the way I hoped it would. Since I didn't have any idea of what the ammunition situation really was, and no effective way to find out, there was no point in going on about fire control any further. Either there was enough to hold the enemy back when they attacked or there wasn't. I'd also learned that individual Marines don't necessarily do what you want them to do when they are alone in the night.

It was too dark to see my map unless I turned on the tiny-holed lens of my taped up flashlight, so I did the best I could to recall our ridge position in my mind. The registration grid for my initial ranging round could be worked back and forth across the ridge, as I planned, with full battery fire. I hadn't planned for the other option, however. If we ran out of small arms ammo, and were overrun, then bringing the VT fire down along the cliff position we ourselves occupied would be required. I decided that that suicidal plan was really no solution at all, but I couldn't stop thinking about it. Finally, I went through the process of designing that alternate plan as well, since I had nothing else to do with the slow-moving time. Would I have a better chance of living if the place was swept by shrapnel up and down the cliff, or if at night I might be missed by an enemy working from downed Marine to downed Marine, shooting everyone they found in the head? The artillery "ultimate solution" began to seem more and more like it was the best course of action if we could not stop the NVA long enough to blow the hell out of them. If the artillery fired at all. My worry made me physically uneasy. I crouched to rub my thighs and try to get rid of the shaking. I'd need my hands to call the battery with the handset. No matter what I thought or tried, however, I couldn't stop fidgeting and moving around on the jungle floor.

"Sir, you're making too much noise," Zippo whispered over to me, his right eye glued to the rubber grommet of the Starlight scope.

"Too much noise to see by?" I whispered back.

Zippo sighed loudly and I was immediately sorry for commenting. But I couldn't stop moving around a bit either. I wasn't built for combat and I knew it. I was a mess, mentally and physically, but all I could do was hide that fact as best I could. Whatever narrow chance I had for survival was dependent upon not becoming more prey-like than I already was.

The Gunny came in out of the night, climbing up and over the edge of the cliff rather than working through the jungle along its upper lip.

"Anything out there?" he asked, keeping his voice almost too low for me to hear. I leaned close to his prone figure. I sensed Pilson nearby but couldn't see him. I realized that my shakes were gone again. I wondered if it was the Gunny's presence or the fact that exercising my hands had been effective again. I hoped it was the exercise.

"Not yet," I murmured back. If movement had been spotted there would have been no need for the Gunny's question or my answer, I knew. The Gunny was nervous too.

"What's the ammo situation?" I asked, more to make conversation than because my knowledge might make any difference. The die was just about cast, as far as I saw it, and making slight changes wasn't gong to affect the outcome. The Gunny remained silent, so I changed the subject.

"If we moved quietly down the ridge in the dark that might just work," I said.

"They fight at night, not us," the Gunny replied, his voice having more timber but still remaining low. "And then there's the moon."

I looked over my shoulder. I saw Pilson's head sticking up over the edge of the cliff, illuminated from behind by the full moon. I felt like a complete idiot. The Gunny could not be more correct. We were hunkered down at night, and even though we had the Starlight scope the night belonged to the Vietnamese. If the company moved through the moonlit night through the NVA controlled jungle it would probably not last long.

"Maybe it would be best if you climbed down over the edge and waited there," the Gunny said.

"I've got to see the first round in order to adjust fire," I replied, "and I've got to be up here to be able to tell when it's the best time to call fire for effect." I looked over at him, and waited for a few seconds for him to answer. When he didn't, I added, "If they're out there."

"They're out there, but they know how to wait for just the right time to strike," the Gunny said, cupping one hand over his mouth to light a cigarette which he shouldn't have been lighting. "They know we have to be beat to shit, and we are. Some of the guys are probably asleep right now. They would know that, too. When they hit, you call in the artillery and then get over the edge as fast as you can. The only way out of here, if the arty doesn't stop them, is straight down, going from ledge to ledge, but that's presuming one of the ledges isn't a forty footer, or so."

I thought about trying to go down that side of the mountain into whatever unknown valley was below and I cringed. There were no good options if Cunningham and the Army didn't come through according to my plan. I'd gambled everything for everyone on a plan that had been created out of nothing at all. There was little evidence for anything I'd based it on, except the deadly enemy was very real and probably more deadly than I even wanted to think about. They'd taken heavy casualties from our company, and that of Kilo. They'd be in no mood to spare anyone.

I turned to look over the moonlit valley behind me. The fact that it was a gentle valley at all was barely visible, thanks to the limited light the full moon radiated down. The moon was high in the sky and would not set until near dawn. I examined the orb closely and discovered that it was not full at all. It was close to being full, but instead was something I knew to be called a gibbous moon. I wasn't sure exactly what that term meant but I was comforted in knowing the word.

The shelf of outcrop just below where I lay was filling with Marines. There was no doubt that when the NVA attacked, the shelf would be a safer place to be, protected by the abrupt cliff of solid volcanic rock. I couldn't make out the features of any individuals. The light was too low and diffuse.

"Zippo, take a scan up and down the shelf behind us," I whispered, nudging the big man.

Zippo shifted about, making barely audible complaining sounds, but finally complied. "What we looking for?" he asked, examining the area up and down the line. I moved to position myself next to him.

"Let me have a look," I said, gently assuming control of the bulky black cylinder. It took me less than ten seconds to identify Jurgens among the Marines setting up along the shelf behind us. I pushed the instrument back toward Zippo.

"Go back to checking out the open areas," I ordered, keeping my voice from breaking with an effort.

I tried to relax as best I could. I had the enemy in front of me and First Platoon directly to my rear. I'd managed somehow to be put right between two forces that had every reason to kill me at the earliest convenience. I knew Jurgens had to know about the plan. He had to know that the artillery was the key to making the plan, and thereby his own survival, the key. That meant he and his men would not shoot me in the back prior to calling the artillery barrage. It would be afterward, if I lived through the NVA attack. I grew more frightened. How had I trapped myself into such a position so easily? The Gunny was next to me in the same position, but not likely any kind of target for Jurgens and his men. Did the Gunny know?

I motioned toward Fessman. He immediately held out the artillery handset but I waved it away. "Stevens," I whispered. In seconds Stevens plopped himself down between Fessman and me. He said nothing.

"The NVA are in front of us and Jurgens has set up behind us with First Platoon," I whispered low, my lips close to his right ear. I knew the situation placed the whole scout team right in the middle of a crossfire, not just me. If the enemy opened up on us, and then First Platoon did the same, there was no way any of us would survive the exchange. The company being low on ammunition was not going to save us.

"What am I supposed to do?" Stevens asked, his voice rising a bit as he began to realize the precariousness of his own position.

"Leave the Starlight scope and the radio," I ordered, after a few seconds to complete a Plan B. "Take Fessman, Zippo, and Nguyen down the line fifty meters or so. I can use the scope and radio myself."

"What are you going to do, sir?" Stevens asked.

I felt the first tiny warmth inside myself that I'd felt in days. Stevens had surprisingly referred to me as sir. I thought furiously about my options. I had nowhere to go. I didn't even know where Sugar Daddy's platoon was, but it certainly wouldn't be any better to be in front of them. The topography I'd so carefully chosen to survive the company was being turned into a death trap for me personally. I thought of telling the Gunny about my fears but decided that was out of the question. If he knew already, then it didn't matter. If he didn't know, what was he supposed to do, go beg Jurgens to get behind somebody else? That solution could not be made to fly either.

"All I've got is the artillery," I said to myself, and then realized I was answering Stevens' question. I didn't go on to mention that I might well have nothing at all, because I had not called to see if I could get the artillery support I now had to have whether the enemy attacked or not.

There was no time to lose, as Stevens gathered the scout team together to fill them in. I pulled loose the straps holding my rolled up poncho cover to my pack. I pulled the cover up over my head, took the map from my morphine pocket and turned on my flashlight. To pull off Plan B I was going to need precision. I could not use my original registration point for the first ranging round. And I needed nearby grid targets for subsequent fire. My brain, operating at flank speed and cold panicked efficiency, committed the grid coordinates and code words to memory automatically, and so accurately that I knew I did not have to check my data. If I was wrong about our position, or what I was about to call in, then I was dead, and my calculating brain knew it.

I clicked the flashlight off and came out from under the poncho.

"They're not coming," Stevens said, confronting me in the moonlight.

"Who's not coming?" I replied stupidly, my mind still on the numbers.

"They refuse to leave you."

"Ah, that wasn't a request Sergeant Stevens, that was an order," I replied flatly, while re-rolling my poncho and getting it back onto my pack.

"They're not going," Stevens replied, as if he hadn't heard me.

Fessman was down next to Stevens and he still had the radio on. Zippo was staring through the Starlight scope, just like before. Nguyen had slithered in close like he was waiting for some news in a language he didn't comprehend.

My shoulders slumped again. Why in hell had the Basic School trainers neglected to tell new officers, about to go into combat, what to do if their men would not obey orders. The Marine Corps was not supposed to be organized that way.

"Problem, Junior?" the Gunny asked, having moved a bit closer, probably because of all the conversation.

"No Gunny," I said, determined not to share any weakness at such a critical time.

The Gunny retreated to light another cigarette, the glow each time he pulled on it lighting up his face like a small red lantern, and quite possibly visible to a lurking enemy.

"Why?" I hissed, turning back to Stevens.

"Fessman says you can't operate the radio alone because the frequency is different and it's too dark to see the knobs. Zippo says you can't look through the scope and do the radio thing at the same time. Nguyen won't say why he's staying. He just is."

"What about you?" I asked.

"I'm not crazy," he replied. "I'm going."

I sensed a tightness in the boy's voice. I knew he didn't want to go but was being driven by the same forces fighting to keep me alive.

"That's the smart move," I told him. "But get maybe a hundred meters down there if you can. This could turn very ugly, and very bloody back here."

Stevens pulled on his pack, and then strapped his M16 to his right shoulder.

"What are you going to do, sir?" he said, calling me sir for the second time.

"Chicken," I said, rather absently, turning slowly to look out over the silvery valley behind me. "I'm going to play a game of chicken."

Stevens was gone in seconds. I turned to the remaining members of my team, knowing Nguyen could not understand me because his interpreter was gone. I didn't know whether to thank the remaining team members or be furious with them. I wondered how many more days I'd have to spend in Vietnam before anyone would obey an order from me simply because I gave it.

We waited, and then waited some more. The Starlight scope should have been called the Moonlight scope I realized, after a few hours. The light of the gibbous moon made the machine perform so well that it was like looking through the lens at the brightness of day, except the day was all green. Zippo spotted the first anomaly on his own.

"The bushes are moving, sir," he said softly.

"Bushes don't move on their own," I replied, moving to look into the grommet.

"These are," he replied, before backing up a foot or two to wait.

I stared through the scope until my eye fully focused. Zippo was right, I realized. Many of the bushes in the open area were moving. Some would move and stop, and then others would do so.

"Fire and maneuver, without the fire part," I whispered. "They're coming," I said, a bit louder.

"You sure?" the Gunny asked, moving over to look through the scope.

I backed up, and then held my hand out toward Fessman. I pushed the transmit button, said a brief prayer in my head, and then gave my pre-established radio code. The battery came right back.,

"Fire Mission, over," I said, feeling deep relief.

The Army officer on the other end repeated the words, and then reported that the battery had four tubes active. I let out another sigh of relief. Although Cunningham Firebase had two guns down they could give me a battery of four without difficulty. I could live with that. We might all live with that.

I called in the first round of Willie Peter, to explode a hundred meters in the air, but I didn't register it at the pre-established position I'd chosen earlier. I knew I wasn't going to have any trouble seeing where it would go off. I simply turned around and looked out over the valley behind me, when the words "Shot, over" came through the Prick 25 speaker. The Gunny looked over at me strangely, after pulling himself away from the Starlight scope.

"What?" he began, but was interrupted with "Splash, over" coming from the radio.

The round went off about three hundred meters from our position, but over the valley behind us, instead of over the enemy position to our front. The light show it provided glowed down on the Marines strewn behind us along the shelf below the cliff. I could see the Marines below all looking at one another, and out at the showering phosphorus.

"Left two hundred, Hotel Echo, repeat," I ordered into the microphone, asking for a high explosive round.

Seconds later the next round came in, but it was anything other than a load of white phosphorus burning up in the atmosphere high in the distant night. It was forty-seven pounds of high explosive going off at a position against the slope of the mountain only a hundred yards away. The shock wave shook the trees around and blew debris blasted from the mountainside undergrowth all around us.

I flinched and ducked, along with everyone else.

I raised my voice, holding the handset firm, I yelled out, "Left one hundred," and then I stopped. I didn't push the handset transmit button this time. I waited.

The line of Marines below wasn't a line anymore. It was a bunch of clumps of departing Marines, running up and down the shelf for all they were worth.

"What the hell?" the Gunny said, but staying low, as small arms fire was beginning to come from where the enemy was attacking.

"Withdraw everyone Gunny, and get them over the edge," I said. "In thirty seconds I'm calling in full battery fire and it'll take about a minute more of adjusting and flight travel time. Anybody up top is going to be full of holes."

I brought in the first round of white phosphorus, as planned, adjusting from the last high explosive round I'd called in nearby instead of starting anew. The round came in perfect, and also initiated a full scale attack by the NVA. It took only a few seconds to get the first battery of four of VT rounds on target. I rolled off the cliff and onto the shelf with the Gunny and my scout team. There was nobody else there. The first four rounds came in as ordered, off to my left. I began walking more battery fire across and down the ridge. The rounds were so close that, even down below the lip of the cliff, my ears were starting to ring. I had forgotten to put tissue in my ears. I did six batteries of four and then swept six more across the plateau above. I heard screaming from above, before my hearing went almost entirely.

The Gunny came to my side minutes later.

"That was something," he said, almost yelling into my face to be heard. "Screw the night, let's get the hell out of here now. They had to take one hell of a bashing. Let's not wait for them to regroup."

He didn't wait for my confirmation. I strapped on my pack. Stevens rejoined us from below, as we prepared to leave.

"That went pretty well, sir," he said, his tone one of sheepishness.

Nguyen leaned close, as if to check on me.

"Thank God for the United States Army," I said to him.

Nguyen nodded, as if he understood.

We followed the Gunny down the shelf of rock and wild grass, moving into the night I feared so badly, but behind First and Fourth Platoons, and with a deadly enemy torn and tattered apart on our left flank. The moon was going down and at some point I knew the sun would have to be coming up. The A Shau awaited us in the morning, as if placed out there as a bleak macabre gift, given in return by a heartless god, for the carnage I'd strewn across the top of the ridge.

forty-four

THE TENTH DAY

The shelf running just down from, and alongside the top of, the mountain's descending ridge eventually played out. The company once more trudged through the jungle under a barely seen double canopy of heavy brush, bamboo stands, hanging vines and cutting saw grass with umbrella-like layers of tree foliage. The moon glowed distantly above, hardly visible through the mess of foliage and flora.

My body and mind were run through with deep fatigue. If I had been hunting alone, headed back to my car or truck in the real world, I knew I'd drop my pack and belt and leave them behind, intent only on making it back to safety. But I was bound for the A Shau Valley and if any, even one, of the reports I'd heard about it were true, then it was one of the ugliest and most perilous destinations on the planet for a human being to go and attempt to survive. When I'd read Dante's *Inferno* in college, I'd laughed at the old English language descriptions of gargoyles, devils, and demons. What I'd never felt was the reality of a fear so deep that it was powerful enough to drive back the brutal fatigue, and even reason itself.

"Not so bad…it's not so bad," I whispered to myself, thankful that I could hear myself again following the hours-old artillery barrage I'd brought down further up the mountain.

"Sir?" Fessman said, scurrying up from behind like an eight-year-old kid trying to take care of his dad.

"Nothing," I said, making sure there was no bite in my tone.

My armpits hurt from the old, layered sweat, dried and re-wet in my utility blouse. My crotch hurt the same way. I was covered in old oils and mud, and we were coming down out of the cooler air accompanied by slight, but oh-so-welcome, winds. The mosquitoes were back, although not in force. I'd had no food or water all night long and what passed for rest up on the plateau, waiting to be attacked, could not be defined as rest at all, no matter how it might have looked. Every time I thought of myself as a miserable mess, I knew I was soon to become more of a miserable mess just by thinking about it.

The Gunny appeared in front of me, easing back, probably to see if I and the scout team were still there. The Gunny was herding his chicks along, I knew, which just added to the feeling, or lack of one, that I'd ever command anything in the 'Nam.

"Do we have flank security out on the left?" I asked him. Small patrols of Marines were supposed to be extended out from the main unit along the line of travel of any moving combat unit.

"Right," the Gunny said, across a few feet of passing jungle, as we moved. "Nobody's going out there. This isn't the open wooded and pastoral Virginia land of your training. Nobody's going out there to die."

I looked behind us, realizing right then that there was no rear security either. If the angry half-mangled enemy had sent out a party to attack the rear of the company while we traveled toward the A Shau Valley, the place they had to know we were going, then I and my scout team would become the first very vulnerable targets of their attack. I wondered how it was possible to put into practice any of the principles learned in training, principles there because of bitterly hard-learned lessons of the past, if the Marines could not be ordered or commanded. If survival considerations were only applied to the present instant, then what of the future, even the near future? I determined that I would attempt to not only make future moves in a different place deeper inside the company, but would find a way to make sure that flank security was always out. Without flank security, warning of an impending attack, the entire company could be totally wiped out.

"Probably less than an hour out," the Gunny said, before moving ahead to check on the rest of his flock, or so I thought.

My spirits began to lift as I moved, the waning light of the partial full moon fading to be replaced by an invisible dawn diffusion of light coming from up ahead. We were heading due east into the rising sun, toward a dead end that would be defined by the lip of the river cut A Shau chasm.

"The A Shau can't be as bad as this," I murmured to myself, only to draw another inquiring "Sir?" from Fessman.

The mosquitoes loved perspiration. They had no problem biting my face and hands while I moved. I pulled my repellent out of my helmet rubber band and "cleaned" my face and neck with the awful stuff. I looked at over-burdened Zippo, lumbering along not far from me. He didn't use the repellent. He slathered on the mud from under our feet. He claimed it worked better, but he looked like some creature from the

Black Lagoon movie. Whatever discomfort I got from wearing the utility blouse in the heat was returned in some comfort by the fact that the mosquitoes couldn't bite through the tough cotton of its manufacture.

Dawn was breaking by the time we reached the natural edge of the jungle. A clearing extended out from that broken line all the way to the edge of a great cliff. The Gunny set up the company's first security perimeter since we'd left the position up on the mountain. I was relieved. I'd already learned how hard-bitten tough the Vietnamese enemy was, and I didn't doubt at all the capability of its leadership or ability of NVA units to take hard hits. The company had only escaped taking heavy casualties by pulling bizarre and unexpected moves, and getting some perfectly fired artillery. How long that might be continued was anybody's guess.

I shed my pack near the tree line, and threw down my poncho before walking over to the lip of the cliff to stand next to the Gunny.

"Holy shit," I breathed out.

"Looks are deceiving," the Gunny replied, cupping his hand to light a cigarette against the light wind rising up over the edge.

"Holy shit," I said again, the scene so stunningly beautiful that I couldn't think of anything else to say. I'd been raised in Hawaii and, because of my father's Coast Guard position, I'd traveled to all of the islands. There were some beautiful valleys on those islands but I'd never stood at the top of one of them and looked down the expanse of the whole thing at one time. The river below was a brown and blue ribbon, glinting occasionally as the water shifted and moved. The walls of the great gently sloping sides of the valley were covered in green growth of all kinds and hues. There were little canyons feeding into the main canyon in many places, and heaving round-topped mountains rose up from different points along the valley's entire length.

"Resupply is going to roll in," the Gunny said. "It's a weird run because command said our mission to enter the valley will be on the chopper. Usually they just tell us. What shitty crap do they have up their sleeves this time?"

"It looks empty down there," I said, having nothing to add about the coming resupply drop.

"B-52s have dumped hundreds of thousands of pounds of bombs down into that," the Gunny said, blowing smoke out to let the wind sweep it back over our heads. "You see any evidence?"

I ran my eyes slowly up and down the valley, and then did it again, even slower. "There's no evidence at all," I answered, shaking my head.

"The A Shau eats everything that enters," the Gunny said, snapping the butt of his cigarette into the air. Unlike the smoke, the butt went up, out, and then plunged down, like it'd been grabbed by a small invisible hand.

" A Shau is a dead valley predator and it wants more dead for company, except mosquitoes, snakes, and crocodiles."

The Gunny turned and walked back toward where the company was setting up to receive the hoped and prayed for resupply chopper.

"Crocodiles?" I whispered into the wind.

"Crocodiles?" Fessman repeated, from just behind me.

I didn't know there were crocodiles in Vietnam, but I didn't want to let Fessman know that so I let it go. Each day in the 'Nam was like getting a barely passing grade in some arcane and painful college course.

"If you gaze long into the abyss, the abyss gazes back at you." I quoted from some philosopher I'd read somewhere.

There was a delay of a few seconds before Fessman replied. "What's an abyss?"

I felt the throbbing beat of distant helicopter blades working their way toward us. Even at a great distance, I could already tell that there was more than one chopper, and that one of them was a big CH-46 or 47. The welcome resupply was about to come in. I pulled myself away from the gorgeous vista and hurried toward my stuff, to secure it from the hundred-mile-an-hour winds that would blast out from under the big chopper when it landed.

For the first time since I'd landed in-country there were no body bags stacked and waiting for the chopper, and I smiled a very faint smile of pride. The giant twin-rotor helicopter came gliding in, moving a lot faster than it seemed. Two Huey Cobras flew shotgun, the crews obviously enjoying diving down into the valley and then screaming upward to veer in low and fast over the landing zone. Debris flew about, as the CH-47 flight engineer set his crew to work running boxes and other gear down the rear ramp that had flopped down on the hard lichen-covered rock surface below. The twin rotors kept spinning at high speed. The process of unloading only took a few minutes. At the end of that time three Marines in rear area utilities, including flak jackets, walked down the ramp before ducking down as the monster chopper spooled up and lifted from the flat surface at the top of the cliff. In seconds all the choppers, plunging down into the valley, were just fast-fading blade-slapping echoes.

I stared at the three men, my eyes going wide. The first real smile of my tour began to stretch its way across my face. The black bars on the Marine's helmets were clearly visible. A captain and two lieutenants. The company was getting real officers. I didn't move. The Gunny came out of nowhere, strode past me, and went out to greet the new officers. I heard Captain Casey and First Lieutenants Billings and Keating introduce themselves. The Gunny pointed back to where I stood, still gaping, with Fessman, Stevens, Zippo, and Nguyen lined up next to me.

The three officers walked toward me. I inhaled deeply. I didn't know what to say. Would they want the company's condition explained, or knowledge about the night's countering of the NVA attack or even the state of our supplies?

"You'd be Junior," Captain Casey said, his face hard and his tone even harder. The first lieutenants formed up behind Casey, spreading out slightly, like fighter planes supporting the leader of a combat squadron. I noted the Gunny slowly backing away, until he disappeared from my focus.

"Yes, sir," I replied, almost coming to attention, but not quite.

Casey turned his attention to the scout team. "You'd be Sergeant Stevens, I'm told. Stand at ease, Sergeant. You're now my Scout Sergeant, with your little assistant there." The captain pointed toward Nguyen, before turning back to me. "You can keep the radio man, Junior. The Gunny won't need one anymore so I'll take his. And you," he pointed toward Zippo, "you'll be heading for one of the platoons just as soon as we take care of this racial thing." The Captain scowled at me again. "How in hell you managed to get a race war going in this company, Junior, is the kind of stuff that'll be written up for future training commands."

The captain pointed at me with his right index finger extended.

"Yes, sir," I replied, nearly struck dumb, my mind having gone blank as he finished the last few words about the problems with First and Fourth platoons.

"We need to talk," Captain Casey said, approaching to within a few feet of me. I had to lean back a bit to look up at him. I was a little less than five-nine, which put him at about six-foot-three, or maybe a touch more, I calculated. He wore the new jungle utilities and boots I'd only hoped to one day acquire, as did his supporting lieutenants. "Step this way," he ordered, and then walked back toward the edge of the cliff.

I had already assumed that my place was to say nothing. I walked next to the captain, knowing I wasn't going to be asked any questions. I was going to be told what to do. That was the way it was supposed to be in the command structure of a regular Marine unit. There were no excuses. You did what you were ordered to do or paid the price.

When we came to the edge of the abyss he stopped and turned, staring deeply into my eyes. He said nothing, instead pulling a pack of Camel cigarettes from his blouse pocket and a small box of C-Ration matches. I waited, glancing surreptitiously down the face of the cliff. I figured it was about four hundred feet down to the forest bracken below. It was not a survivable fall. I looked back at the Captain and figured he probably weighed about two-twenty, or so.

"You fucked up your first, and probably only, command, Junior," he said, facing out over the vastness of the valley below. "Now we're going to run this company by the book. You disobeyed a direct order to take Hill 110. You refused a direct order from Captain Mertz by ignoring it, and you've used up about a quarter of all the artillery supplies in the whole damned area, plus calling in the Army to do Marine Corps work. How can I say this? You haven't even had a decent kill ratio. Your company has more casualties than all the other companies of the battalion put together."

"Yes, sir," I said, not knowing what else to say. The captain inhaled and blew out smoke three more times, before going on.

"Finally, this whole war is being fought using the rules of engagement. Have you ever even heard of the rules of engagement?"

"I heard that there's a copy of them on a special podium in Division Headquarters," I replied. "I think I saw them there on my first night." Unlike the Captain, I kept my voice flat and emotionless. I looked at our relative positions on the lip of the crevasse. I was just to the left and a little behind him. I knew I could handle his two-twenty fairly deftly. I looked back toward where I'd tossed my stuff and saw almost the whole company making believe it wasn't watching the show at the edge of the cliff. What would happen to the company if Casey took a fall?

"You're now the forward observer," the Captain said, turning to face me. "And that's all you are. You can have your radio operator to reach the artillery net, but you don't fire a single round without my pre-approval and you don't fire on anything or anybody I don't order you to, and that sure as hell includes our own men. Am I understood?"

"Yes, sir," I replied, wondering how many times I'd said the only words I'd spoken to the man, and how many times I'd have to say them again.

"You're dismissed," the captain said, but I didn't walk away because he kept talking. "I'm going to separate and blend in the blacks with the whites in all the platoons before nightfall. The two problem platoon commanders, the shake-and-bakes, are reduced to squad leaders or even fire team leaders if their new commanders so choose."

I stood waiting, again not knowing what to do or say.

"Any questions?" Captain Casey said, although he didn't say the words like they were a question, or that he welcomed any.

"How do you know what's going on in the company, sir?" I asked, truly befuddled. The radio contact with battalion command was extremely slight, and controlled up until now by the Gunny.

"The daily reports, of course," the captain snorted. "Rittenhouse has filed very accurate and detailed reports on all of this crap."

I was stunned to silence, once more.

"You're dismissed… again," the captain said, with a wave of his hand, which had to mean he really meant it this time, I guessed.

I walked over to my gear, which had been blown about ten feet by the chopper's down draft. I gathered my stuff together, aware that Zippo and Stevens were getting their own together. I didn't know what to say to them so I just made believe I was working away setting up my own hooch. When I looked up both men were gone. I felt an ache inside me I could not quite place. Fessman built his own little hooch next to mine, placing it closer, like he'd done when he was afraid of the snakes. Nguyen sat on one edge of his laid down poncho in his tight cross-legged pose that only natives could pull off for any extended period of time. I wondered if he'd gotten the word that he wasn't my Kit Carson scout anymore.

I finished building my hooch by myself. I laid out my poncho cover like it was a little flat porch. I was thankful that the ground was not wet mud for a change. For some reason, possibly because of the wind coming up over the edge of the cliff, the mosquitoes were all but gone. I could not see where the Captain and his two First Lieutenants had gone off to bivouac, and I didn't much care either. It was daytime, but the company wasn't going anywhere without some kind of rest. Fessman hauled in a big plastic bottle of water and a load of my ham and lima beans. I had water but was no longer thirsty. I had food but was no longer hungry. And I could rest but I could not rest. I sat with my legs up and knees spread, with my elbows lying on my knees. Fessman's transistor radio played some blues piece — *... sittin' here resting my bones, and this loneliness won't leave me alone, two thousand miles I roam just to make this dock my home...* — while I stared out over the beauty of the A Shau stretching out below.

The Gunny came striding through the bush behind me, and then sat down on the other edge of my poncho liner. He immediately went to work making a canteen holder of coffee. He tossed a packet of the instant stuff at my feet. Fessman appeared next to him with a holder filled with some of the new fresh water. I didn't really want coffee, but I wasn't going to interrupt whatever was going on. I began to make a cup for myself, using the Gunny's flaming explosive chunk when he was done with it.

"Rittenhouse," I said, softly.

"Yeah, I heard," the Gunny replied. "That's a problem that'll be taken care of posthaste."

I knew then that the Gunny hadn't thought about the potential of daily reports going back to command and the necessity of making sure of what was in them before they went off. It wasn't the Gunny who'd filed the reports. I tried not to show my relief.

"The three knights of the orient look real good," the Gunny said, between sips of his too hot coffee.

I checked out the Gunny's gear, taking a sip of my own coffee. He looked a bit more tattered than I did, if that was possible.

"Nice boots," I commented.

"What size do you wear?" the Gunny replied.

I laughed out loud for the first time since arriving in Vietnam.

"Jurgens and Sugar Daddy want to see you," the Gunny said, after he stopped laughing himself.

"You're kidding," I said, with a sigh. "Now what? Are those guys ever going to lighten up, or do I have to climb into a body bag to make that happen?"

The Gunny lit another cigarette instead of answering right away. I waited. In only a few minutes I'd lost my whole scout team, been reduced to even less of an officer than I'd been before, and then blamed for every misstep of the company, past and present. On top of that, it was all on paper back at battalion, not that it mattered much with my lousy prospects for continuing to live.

"There was an old Chinese general who once said that the enemy of my enemy is my friend," the Gunny said, blowing a big cloud of smoke out toward the lip of the A Shau.

I drank my coffee with my right hand. My left started to shake a bit so I reached down to massage my thigh with it. I felt the letter inside the pocket. I'd forgotten to send my letter home when resupply lifted off. For the second time. I looked out over the beauty of the A Shau and became afraid again. I was afraid that Vietnam was claiming me. Slowly, ever so slowly, back home was being pried loose from me like one narrow board after another in the disassembly of an old farm house floor.

forty-five

THE TENTH DAY : SECOND PART

I went to work on my stuff, just outside the exposed rock area where the choppers had come in. The area wasn't that large, having hardly the footprint of an average small home back in the real world. The jungle that sprung up right near its edge looked like it could have been put together by a Hollywood set-building team. The Gunny finished his coffee and headed back into the bracken. I presumed he was going to talk to Jurgens and Sugar Daddy. I couldn't think of anyone I would like to see less of, but then the three officers getting their stuff together at the edge of the stone landing zone came into focus. Rittenhouse was taking notes among them, and the supplies, while some of the company Marines were going through them.

Fessman caught my attention with a small wave of one hand that he held down near his waist. I frowned, thinking he might be ready to shove the radio handset at me. From behind him stepped Nguyen, who stopped and seemed to be waiting for something.

"What does he want?" I asked Fessman.

"Oh, well, it seems that the new officers don't want him as a scout," Fessman said, squatting down while he talked.

Nguyen squatted with him, both men looking me straight in the eyes.

"They don't trust indigenous gooks, or so Stevens said," Fessman whispered, as if there was someone around to hear or care if they did hear.

"So, I have my scout team back," I said with a big sigh. I didn't mention that my scout team was one seventeen-year-old kid and a local Montagnard that didn't speak English.

"How are we supposed to talk to him?" I asked, in exasperation, knowing Fessman would not be able to answer the question, but letting my frustration force me to ask it anyway.

"Sign language," Fessman said, with a big smile. He turned to Nguyen and made an okay sign with his right hand, and then pointed at me. Nguyen held up one finger before closing his fist again.

"He says you are number one," Fessman said, laughing, before pointing out to where the new officers were having Stevens build their hooches. Stevens was hunting around trying to find some way to put pegs into the hard stone.

Nguyen flashed ten fingers up very briefly. I didn't need Fessman to translate the hand sign. Number one was the best in pidgin Vietnamese — and number ten the worst. I knew some of Nguyen's differential analysis was based on the fact that I'd already survived for ten days and the other guys were FNGs. Some, but probably not all.

Stevens looked back at us and beckoned with one arm. Nguyen took off at a trot. He knelt by Steven's side, and then got up and loped back.

Nguyen went to work brushing the jungle cover from atop the ever present, but mostly dried up mud beneath. He drew two small circles far apart. He connected them with a line forming a long arc. Then he put a big "X" next to one circle, and pointed out where the officers were getting set up.

I looked out at them and then back at the diagram. While I was thinking, the back of my mind marveled at the officers bringing full canvas shelter-halves to the bush. Shelter-halves were like partial tents, but weighed about three times more than the simple structures we generally made using ponchos. I knew it was unlikely that they planned to carry the equipment themselves when the company had to move.

Suddenly, I stood up.

"Shit, I got it," I said to Fessman, looking down at Nguyen with even more respect. "We've got to get away from here. Come on, we're moving deeper into the bush. I don't give a shit about the perimeter or the enemy that might be there." I began to quickly gather my things.

The Gunny showed up, stepping out of the jungle like he'd been close by all along, or been called.

"What's going on?" he asked, staring out at the supply pile being worked over, and the new officers standing around and looking out into the A Shau valley.

"Registration point," I said, throwing my stuffed pack over my right shoulder and carrying my binoculars in my free hand. "The landing zone is pre-registered for range. Stevens and Nguyen spotted the marks on the stone."

"That's gotta be for mortars," the Gunny said, "but we don't have any infantry around here, at least not that we know of. It's quiet as a church, except for a bit of wind, and that valley is good six miles across, maybe more. We're out of range of their stuff."

"Out of range for the 105s. Howitzers have way less range than cannons. The NVA have 122mm long guns," I replied, beginning to work my way into the denser part of jungle. "Those things reach out to seventeen, sometimes eighteen miles. That lovely open area of rock is registered and everyone in the world can see us. The only reason we got away with the resupply is because they didn't know we were coming, but they sure as hell know now."

"Junior," the Gunny said to my departing back.

I stopped, and waited.

"Aren't you going to tell them?" he asked.

"I'm not in the command structure," I said, not turning to face him. "I'm staff. Forward observer. That's it."

"We can't just leave them out there like that," he replied.

"A man's got to do what he thinks is best," I said, wondering about whether the Gunny was right. But, was it my responsibility to warn Rittenhouse and the new officers? I knew in my bones that Stevens was out of there, too. The wily scout knew how to weasel his way out of danger, rather than confronting it directly though. He'd probably figure it out. There was always the chance that the NVA wouldn't fire on the location, as well.

"You can't kill officers just because you don't like them, Junior," the Gunny said, his voice low.

I finally turned, lowering my pack to the jungle mat at my feet. I looked the Gunny straight in the eyes.

"What am I, the example? You didn't kill me because you didn't like me, so I shouldn't do that either?" I asked.

"I still don't like you," the Gunny said, and I knew from his expression he meant it.

"What do you want of me, Gunny?" I asked, my shoulders slumping. "You want me to order you to go tell them that they're as ignorant as they are?"

"You're an officer, when it's all said and done," he replied, his eyes unblinking. "They're officers, like you, except they haven't been lucky enough to run the table for ten days."

The Gunny hiked off, his own pack bobbing behind him. He didn't head back out to the exposed area. I knew he was leaving it to me, and I resented him deeply for that. I was only a commander when the shittiest jobs had to be done, and only an officer if it meant someone had to be blamed for something.

"Come on, Fessman," I ordered, letting go of my pack and heading back. "I'm not doing this one alone, but there's no reason for Nguyen to risk his ass. Sign him somehow to stay here."

Fessman held one hand up to Nguyen, with his two smallest fingers bent while spreading the other three. Nguyen sat down atop my pack to wait. I walked toward the landing zone, wondering why I was complimented by the Montagnard sitting on my stuff, and also wondering how Fessman knew so much about hand signs, and Nguyen, too.

We got within five ten feet of the group before anyone noticed us. Rittenhouse looked over one shoulder from the supply pile, and said "Sir" when he noted my approach. I looked the young man in the eyes, feeling strangely detached. It was like I was in chemistry class looking at an interesting specimen, except none of those had been alive. He looked away, and then back. I bent my head a bit to one side in examining him from top to bottom, my expression turning to one of question. Who was this boy and why was he in my life?

Rittenhouse backed up four or five paces but I didn't move.

"What is it Junior?" Captain Casey asked.

"You're making camp on an artillery registration point," I indicated, pointing at the strange carvings on a chunk of nearby stone. "The 122mm rounds from NVA guns can reach out all the way from Laos, across this valley. The mark means that they've fired on this position many times before and know exactly where it is."

"I know what a registration point is, lieutenant," Casey replied, his tone one of irritation. "I don't know why any of this should be of concern to you."

I took a long deep and slow breath. "It's not really, except I know artillery, and, with Rittenhouse being killed with you, I'll have to write the letters home about how you died."

"You know, Junior, you have a real smart mouth." Casey said, glaring at me. "What Basic class were you in, and who in hell was your battalion commander back there?"

I just looked at all three of the officers and waited. Rittenhouse seemed frozen in place next to the supplies, his pencil not moving on his upraised clip board.

After a few seconds of the sound being the wind coming up over the edge of the cliff the captain spoke again.

"There may be some merit to the registration thing," the captain agreed, after conferring for a few seconds with his two lieutenants. "We'll move over to the edge of the LZ."

"The company's moving half a click inland and setting up a perimeter," I replied. "You may want to be inside it when darkness comes." I turned to go.

"The company moves when I order it to move, Junior," Captain Casey said, his voice going hard again.

"I understand, sir, and you have that right," I replied, knowing I was going to walk away in a few seconds no matter what else was said. Any inbound artillery would not announce itself. No ranging rounds were needed in firing on a pre-registered target, and the rounds would be traveling beyond the speed of sound.

They might even already be in the air, I realized uncomfortably. I looked beyond the clumped officers, and out over the valley, as if I might be able to see something coming in. "You're aware, of course, since you've obviously been briefed, how the officers who served before me died."

The captain pointed down at my left hand, where my binoculars dangled.

"Let me have those," he ordered, holding out his hand.

I reluctantly handed the Japanese instrument over. My need for them, as long as we remained up on the ridge high on the wall of the valley, would be greater than it had ever been if I had to call in artillery support.

"You're dismissed," Captain Casey said, turning back to stare out through the binoculars over the wide expanse of the valley to its other side.

I left the four of them standing there. I'd followed the Gunny's advice, against my better judgment, and felt no better about having warned them, even as minimally as I had. I walked fast, almost breaking into a run. I passed one stack of boxed ammunition, mostly gone through, and the other of C-Ration cases and water bottles. I hefted a box of C-Rations from the stack Rittenhouse had been accounting for.

"Put that on my account, Corporal," I yelled over my shoulder to where Rittenhouse had retreated from the center of the landing zone. "Put it down with the rest of the stuff we'll go over later."

I moved away from the area as fast as I could, with the heavy case of C-Rations on my shoulder. I didn't know what circular error probable was for a Soviet 122mm round, but a slew of them coming in would have to take out anyone alive. There was no cover on the open rock area.

By the time I rejoined Fessman and Nguyen, my hooch was up and waiting. I plopped the extra box of rations down next to Fessman's poncho liner. I noted the company forming and setting in around us, all of them moving deeper into the jungle. Our position, about a thousand meters in form the lip of the ridge should be sufficient unless the NVA had a competent forward observer with a decent radio lurking nearby. I was fast discovering, however, that trained forward observers were about as rare in the field as decent company grade officers were serving in the chain of command.

I laid on my poncho liner and tried to rest before taking some of my ratty stationary from my pack and beginning a second letter home. The beauty of the A Shau Valley was the substance of the body of the letter, and I didn't have to lie about that at all. Completing that task, I went about setting up defensive fires on the west side of the perimeter, in case the night was active with NVA troops coming from that direction. I knew their commanders would be suffering from the two past run-ins they'd had with our company and Kilo.

Fessman leaned near, his too-close hooch almost touching my own. "Where'd you leave the binoculars?"

"The new C.O. is keeping them for me," I replied, not looking up from my map, while continuing to make small notations with my grease pencil on its plastic covered surface.

The Gunny forced his way noisily through the foliage and squatted down to make coffee, not far from where my left boot stuck out from where I lay on one side trying to work with the map and marker. I only looked up when two more Marines came straggling along behind him. I sat up and put away my map very quickly, and then turned to face the men with both hands free.

The two Marines were Jurgens and Sugar Daddy, but neither looked like either man had looked before. Jurgens' face was a study in saddened worry and Sugar Daddy looked entirely different without his flattened bush hat and purple sun glasses. Neither man had brought along bigger enlisted men to serve as protection or for intimidation. They were so non-threatening that my hand did not automatically fall to sit atop the butt of my Colt. Both men scrunched down by the Gunny, who was busy heating his water.

Suddenly two more Marines appeared from behind Fessman. It was Stevens and Zippo. They stood uneasily at the radioman's side.

"Aren't you supposed to be with the C.O.?" I asked, looking upward to Stevens. I was putting off the coming confrontation with the two former platoon commanders and I knew it.

"He said to go scout something, so we're scouting this location," Steven replied, as both men settled down to squatting positions.

"What do they want?" I asked the Gunny, who was working on sipping at his coffee with one hand and smoking a cigarette with the other.

"What do you think?" the Gunny said, not looking at me or the two former commanders.

"I'm not the C.O. here, but then they know that," I said, although my curiosity was piqued.

"So what is it?"

"What do we do?" Jurgens broke in.

I noted that he didn't use the name Junior in talking to me, plus the tone of his voice was actually almost polite.

"What do I get?" I asked, almost enjoying myself, not really expecting an answer.

Jurgens and Sugar Daddy looked at one another for a few seconds, and then both looked at the Gunny, as did I.

"They've been to the A Shau before," the Gunny said. "A number of times, like me."

"Yes, I've heard," was all I could think to respond.

"We're going to get hit tonight," Jurgens said, his voice quiet and low. "They're going to hit us from the west on the ground while the arty shit comes pouring into the landing zone in the east. We got nowhere to go except maybe down into the broken valleys on both sides, and they've probably mined those years back."

"Why would they hit us tonight?" I asked.

"Ask your 'yard' over there," Sugar Daddy said, pointing at Nguyen, who squatted just beyond our circle. Nguyen allowed no expression to cross his facial features. I looked at him, and he blinked.

"Okay, so we know that," I agreed, part of my mind already beginning to design a plan to handle the expected attack.

"You're right in the middle here," Jurgens pointed out. "When they hit, you'll be among the first to go down."

I looked at the man, wondering why he'd terrified me for so many days and nights. He didn't look terrifying. He looked like a tough kid on a high school playground, which he was not long from being on.

"So, for this warning you want something," I stated, flatly. "What in hell am I supposed to do?"

"The Gunny said you did that Chesty trick," Jurgens said, looking down at nothing in front of him. "We need a trick like that to get through, and we want to be the leaders of our platoons again. Breaking up the platoons won't work. The guys won't do it, and there'll be nobody to fight the NVA tonight."

I massaged both thighs with my hands. They weren't shaking but I didn't want to take a chance of showing weakness in front of the two dangerous predators. My left hand clutched my two letters home and my right the deadly morphine packet. I had to come up with something but I had nothing. I was now more of a nobody officer in the company than I had been before. With Rittenhouse writing the daily report, added on to by the three real officers, I was likely to end up in Leavenworth if I somehow lived through my tour. I thought of the magnificent cliff I'd stood next to once again and how far down the cliff face extended. A kernel of inspiration ignited in my brain, fanning itself into a fire, the more focus I gave it.

"Okay, here's what you get back," I said, clearing the bracken in front of me until I had a small section of flat mud to work on. I smoothed it with my hands, and then reached in my pocket for my cheap government pen. I didn't click it to allow the point to be exposed.

"First, you two go back to your platoons and ignore the captain's orders," I instructed. "Run your platoons just like before. If the new lieutenants show up, you ignore them. You're good at doing that to new officers. What are they going to do, make you go down into the A Shau?" I thought about the rest of my developing plan for a moment.

"Well, what about the attack?" the Gunny asked, as if reading from my special script.

"We'll use the King Kamehameha plan," I said, quickly leaning forward and making a drawing on the mud in front of me. I drew an elongated oval around the landing zone, then a rectangular box running back and forth across the swell of mountain edge we were currently on. Finally, I drew arrows running outside and back and forth from and to the rectangle, reserving one giant arrow for the incoming sweep of the NVA that would attack from the jungle toward the landing zone.

"Soon to be King Kamehameha used this to capture Oahu and become the King of the Hawaiian Islands. He had his troops make believe that they were trapped between his bigger enemy and a giant cliff edge. The enemy thought they had him. But in the daytime Kamehameha allowed his forces to sneak away to each side and when the enemy attacked right up the center of where they thought his forces were, Kamehameha had his men drive them over the edge of the cliff."

I looked up and pulled back from my diagram with obvious enthusiasm.

"Pushed them over the cliff?" the Gunny asked, skeptically. "The NVA have AK-47s, not spears."

"Oh that," I said. "Their artillery's going to open up and then walk itself right into where they think we are. But we'll be holding them there from the sides. We'll force them right into their own artillery barrage since it's not likely they have a forward observer with a radio that'll reach out that far. Finally, we come in right behind them with our own artillery. It's perfect."

I waited as everyone present sat thinking. I had no idea of when or even if the NVA would use their artillery. I also had no idea about whether we would be attacked from the exposed western flank located at our front. Finally, it was a complete toss up about how the new officers would react to being told to go screw themselves. That last part forced a grim smile out of me.

"You heard the man," the Gunny instructed, rising to his feet and snapping his cigarette into the bush. "Junior has a plan."

In seconds the only Marines left at my hooch opening were Fessman, Nguyen, and the Gunny.

"Get the hooches moved," I ordered Fessman. "We want to be a bit down that northern slope before the fun begins."

Fessman went to work, while the Gunny finished cleaning out his canteen holder.

"What were you thinking there, when you smiled?" he asked me, quietly. "About Rittenhouse?"

I didn't answer his question, as there was no point. My mind was already on the other problem I knew I was going to have before sundown. Captain Casey wasn't going to like implementing any plan that wasn't his own, and his two officer lackeys might become difficult to deal with. "Flank security. Part of the price is that these two clowns send out patrols to find out what's down there, where we have to go," I said. "If it's mined, we have to know."

"They're not going to like that," the Gunny replied. "Who are they supposed to send?"

"FNGs, of course," I said, flinching inside, but not letting the Gunny know.

"And what was that Kamehameha shit?" the Gunny came back. "Does he even exist, and if he did, then did he really do that?

"The place is called the Pali," I replied. "He existed. What he did up at that pass is anybody's guess."

"Again," the Gunny whispered, before moving back into the jungle.

I sat on my poncho cover and reflected on the simple fact that I was in the rotten position of having to hope that the enemy hit us.

forty-six

THE TENTH DAY : THIRD PART

I lay in my hooch, dug into the side of the hill through the effort of using Fessman's entrenching tool. The hill was too slanted to lay against without a step being carved into its side. Fessman was just down from me, while Stevens and Zippo were over to my right. How the scouts had managed to get away from being under the direct eyeballs of the new officers I had no idea, and I wasn't going to ask. I felt a depth of rotten care toward the new officers. Rotten because I knew I would trade their survival for my own in a heartbeat.

I knew that was not right. Not just very few months before I'd gone through Basic School with men just like them. I'd liked them better back then. A lot better than they'd liked me. I smirked at the thought. At least I didn't have that problem now. But I knew there was going to be trouble from them, and more trouble from Jurgens and Sugar Daddy. Men like them did not take coming to anyone like a mafia godfather, with their hats almost literally in their hands. There would be a price, and it would be one I could not want or be able to afford. I realized, shifting around on my poncho uncomfortably, that I didn't want to kill them. But I did want to kill them. Not kill them exactly. Just make them gone away to somewhere else. I didn't care where.

I took out my pen and doodled on the back of my map. I liked my Kamehameha plan. It was simple. I knew the 122s would come in at some point. The enemy battery had to be holding its fire, waiting for the tattered outfit we'd tangled with before to get ready for their attack. Again. So that part of the plan should work, depending on timing, which I had no control over. There had to be some guy on the other lip of the valley staring through his own lenses at our position, waiting. He'd walk the artillery fire inland once he confirmed that the battery was dead on target with the registration point. That part was simple logic, unless the hard scrabble band of Vietnamese was too beaten to counter-attack. If I was a laughing man anymore, I would have laughed. The NVA were tough as French snails, and about as prolific too. They were everywhere. They'd come. My own use of Cunningham Firebase to drop rounds behind the attacking force was simple too.

Cunningham had proven its worth. If they had about sixty High Explosive rounds laying around, then bringing the fire down and walking it into the rear of the attacking force would be child's play, with my guidance. That left only where the NVA could go. And that was my weak point in the plan. They could only come down the slopes in either one direction or the other, or both. If the company was properly set up, with two lines of machine gun arrangements, then it would be a slaughter house if the NVA advanced down either side. If the Marines in the company believed me enough to be really on guard and ready. If the blacks and whites, and god knew whatever else we had, could get their shit together long enough to act like a real Marine company. I knew how unlikely that eventuality might be. I could only do so much, though. I laid down, with the backs of my hands crossed over my forehead. The sun was penetrating through the double canopy of trees but there was still a little wind making its way through the bracken close to the ground. The wind held the mosquitoes off and provided some cooling.

"Sir," Zippo whispered from near my right shoulder, just as I heard footsteps squishing through the jungle muck near my feet. I sat up and rubbed my face to clear my head. One of the first lieutenant's stood, like he was some sort of Civil War statue, one hand behind him at parade rest and the other holding out my binoculars.

"The captain says these are junk and would like the real ones," the lieutenant said, before tossing the binoculars into the mud near the left edge of my poncho liner. I retrieved the binoculars and tried to brush the mud from the lenses, before setting then down to pay attention to the man in front of me.

"Jappo specials that don't focus properly, the captain says."

"We don't have any real ones," I replied, wanting to defend my Japanese binoculars, but figuring it wasn't worth it.

I could see the man's name, printed in black over his left breast. "Keating," it said, in big, black letters printed in bold. Against the bright green, gold, and brown of his new utility blouse the name looked like a perfect aiming point. I thought about being at a distance and holding the front sight of my .45 just above the line of letters. Perfect.

"What's going on with the company?" Keating asked, looking around nervously. "Why is everyone down here and not up on the high ground. You don't look like Marines," he said outward in a loud voice. "You look like a load of tacos stuck into the side of a hill."

Fessman started to laugh, and than tried to stifle his giggles with a fake coughing fit when Keating glared over at him.

"Yes, sir," I replied.

"I'm a first lieutenant, Keating replied, instantly. "You don't call me sir."

I just stared up at him, wondering what he would do if I said "Yes, asshole." I shook my head. "Never give warning" was becoming an applied mantra in almost every situation I was living through.

"We're going to get hit on the high ground tonight, Mr. Keating," I said, as patiently as I could. "The company's set in on both sides of the high ground because the landing zone is going to be alive with enemy cannon fire walking itself west while I'm going to be bringing in artillery east behind the NVA and driving them into their own falling rounds. Or our own. They can take their pick."

"But the command post is encamped on that high ground," Keating said, showing a bit of fear in his eyes.

"That's probably a bad idea," I replied, and then waited.

"You know all this because you're Svengali, or what?" Keating demanded, getting control of himself by becoming aggressive.

"Is he an officer?" I asked, innocently.

"Who?" Keating said, his voice almost cracking.

"Svengali," I said patiently. But I didn't give him a chance to answer because I was bone tired and didn't want to banter further.

"The captain wants to see you," Keating said.

I stretched and clasped my hands behind my head.

"Ask him when he wants to come down and see me," I replied.

"I don't know who you think you are or who you think you're dealing with," Keating fumed. "Casey's going to chew you up and spit you out when I tell him what you said."

I breathed deeply in and out a few times and closed my eyes, hoping the irritating lieutenant would be gone when I reopened them. But he wasn't.

"At least I know where I am, Keating," I said, softly. "I'm about four hundred meters from the edge of the A Shau Valley. Marines who've gone in there call it the Valley of No Return. The reason it's called the Valley of No Return is because the man who goes in is not the one who comes out. Tonight you're going to experience your first full contact combat. You don't seem afraid, and that's to your credit. Tomorrow morning I'll come find you and if you're not huddled in a puddle of terror then it'll be because you're dead."

Keating stood wavering a bit in front of me, maybe from the slight wind I thought. He didn't say anything but he didn't leave either.

"You're not in Kansas anymore, Dorothy, so trot on back and inform Casey that he needs to haul ass off of the high ground if wants to avoid getting a Purple Heart and being bagged up in the morning. Seeing me is the least of his problems."

I closed my eyes again and wished the lieutenant gone. Keating waited for a full minute before moving. "Thanks for the advice," he whispered out in such a tone of sincerity that my eyes snapped open. And then he was gone.

"Shit," I said to myself. I didn't want to feel sorry for the man, or worse yet, like him. But his last comment made him sound like a twelve-year-old, and a twelve-year-old in trouble. His tone had taken me backward ten days in an instant.

I wasn't the Gunny. I had no time or inclination to teach an FNG officer on how to survive under conditions I wasn't really doing very well surviving in either, except on a wing and a prayer. Besides, Keating was too tall, too good looking and too much of what passed for a real Marine officer, while I was none of those things. I didn't think much of myself for thinking that, either.

"That was pretty tough, sir," Fessman said, from down below me.

I knew he was right but there was no response I could come up with that made sense.

I sat up again. I knew I was not going to be able to avoid the captain for long. Even though we were all tired, down to our very cores, I had to get cleaned up. We had extra water, and if we were headed down into what I'd seen of the A Shau it wasn't likely we would get resupplied for some time.

"Zippo, get a bottle of water," I ordered, getting to my feet after scrounging inside my pack for a crummy little bar of white surgical soap. I stripped down a bit away from where I was dug into the hill, making sure the five gallons of water poured over my head would not run into anyone else's hooch. Zippo was perfect, being big and strong enough to hold the bottle firm in the air, even while I took a few moments to lather up. When it was done, I looked at my miserable combat gear. The only good thing about it was that it blended in with everything around me.

I dressed, wearing the same socks for the third day and night. I was trying to get three days to a pair because when I was done the socks were too. If you washed your governmental issue socks in Vietnam, you had nothing but filmy threads left when you were done. I laced up my boots and felt a whole lot better, until I saw the safari headed my way.

An entourage appeared out of the bush, with the three new officers in the lead. All three carried M-16s, which I thought uncommon, but certainly allowed if they wanted to add that weight and bulk to their loads. Except they didn't have any loads. There were five enlisted Marines carrying all of their stuff. No matter how I felt about their near childish naïve behavior so far, I had to admit that they had enough leadership ability to at least get some of the company to do their bidding.

The three approached, with Pilson just behind the C.O., and felt nearly as much trepidation as I had when the door opened in the back of the armored personnel carrier ten days ago. I stayed where I was, thinking about how trepidation wasn't nearly as bad as the terror I was accustomed to. I realized that I didn't know where the Gunny was and that bothered me a bit. I'd seen him earlier, carrying a whole box of the mosquito repellent. I presumed that the nasty little monsters would be much worse an affliction down in the valley. The men started digging into the side of the hill nearby. I let my breath out slowly, as it came to me. The officers were coming down to stay where I was.

Pilson dropped his radio and went to work digging his own clam shell hole into the side of the mountain. I watched him work, liking the fact that, for the first time I'd been dropped out of the sky, the company was actually digging in. Underground was protection from so much, including the RPGs the enemy would have any stray rounds from either artillery battery. He didn't make much headway before the captain stepped close and talked to him. Pilson put down his entrenching tool, strapped on his radio and headed in my direction. That he put on his radio first, before traveling only a few yards impressed me. I realized that a lot of the Marines in the company had learned and applied good survival skills and practical field experience.

"The captain wants to see you, sir," he said, almost apologetically.

"I can see him over there from right here," I replied, knowing I was being adolescent and irritating.

Pilson looked down at me, and waited.

"Jesus Christ," I whispered, more to myself than Pilson, wondering if I wasn't bringing the wrath of God down to join the wrath of

Vietnam that had landed on my shoulders. I got up and put on my wet utility blouse I was trying to dry a bit. I'd washed as much mud off it as possible without more water and real detergent. I buttoned up and walked the ten-yard distance. The captain was sitting cross-legged on his poncho liner. I wanted to tell him to layer his poncho cover under it to avoid the liner getting wet for the night ahead but I didn't.

"Forward observer, reporting in, sir," I said, standing in front of him, and trying not to look like what I really was. In Basic School they had a phrase for what I had to look like. It was called a "soup sandwich."

"That's right, lieutenant," Captain Casey said, his tone flat and commanding. "You're not the company commander anymore. Certainly not when it comes to planning to respond to an impending enemy attack. What's this Kamehameha crap I'm hearing about?" He pulled the section of map I'd drawn the outline of the plan upon. I'd given it to the Gunny so he could inform the platoon leaders. "I've been to Kaneohe Marine Base on Oahu. I know about Kamehameha. What is this crap?" he finished, tapping his right index finger on the map laying over his thigh.

I looked up into the trees over my right shoulder. The sun had already set over the ridge so the light was beginning to die. I understood why the two lieutenants were back with Casey. They'd been sent packing by the existing platoon leaders and none of the three of them knew what to do about that, although they'd exercised good judgment in leaving.

"They're going to hit us tonight and they'll probably bring their own artillery fire onto that open area near the edge of the cliff," I said, as plain and simple as I could sound. "The Kamehameha plan is to draw them into the kill zone on the map there, and then slam the door behind them shut with our artillery."

"I don't want you calling in that Army artillery shit," the captain said. "It looks bad in the reports. Use our own artillery."

"Yes, sir," I replied, wondering whether the captain had any knowledge of the codes used by the Marine and Army batteries to direct fire. My answer was given betting he didn't. It was useless trying to explain that at the end of the An Hoa battery's maximum range the rounds could land anywhere within a thousand-meter diameter circle, or worse, of where they were targeted. We were in a situation where each Marine perimeter was only two hundred meters from the middle of the kill zone. There would not be any play available for inaccurate rounds.

"This will be the command post for our time here," Casey said, looking around him, "and I want you in the CP unless I tell you otherwise." He aimed his last sentence directly at me.

"If you want my advice, sir…" I began, wondering if he'd cut me off, but he didn't, so I went on, "…you'll stay inside your hole here from now until the sun comes up in the morning. The Marines will shoot anything that moves in the night, the artillery will be impossible to judge where it is, and the enemy is going to be a bit bloodthirsty too. I have to adjust the artillery so I can't go underground like I'd love to."

Casey turned and began talking to the two lieutenants that huddled right behind him. Pilson looked at me, and slowly shook his head without showing any expression on his face.

"This is all bullshit," Captain Casey said, pointing at me instead of the map. You expect the 'kill zone,' as you call, it to be perfectly rectangular?"

My mouth dropped open in amazement. The rectangle I'd drawn was a representation of an approximate area. Such representations had been used in every military text I'd ever read or studied. I realized that there was very little to say.

"Yes, sir," I replied, wondering if the captain would see that as saying as dumb as what he'd said.

"Whatever, carry on," Casey said, waving one hand at me, and then tossing the piece of map down on the poncho liner next to him.

I noted then that all three officers had removed their boots, placing each pair neatly next to him.

"Ah, you took off your boots?" I asked, in more wonder. We never took our boots off in combat unless it was to change socks, and then we put them back on as fast as we could. There was no way to move along the jungle floor without boots. The bracken would cut regular skin to shreds in seconds.

"The Gunny said to air them out and dry them every chance we get," Keating said, from his position off to the left of Captain Casey's.

Once again, I was speechless. The Gunny had told them that? I struggled, attempting to understand. Why would the Gunny say that when every one of us out in the bush knew that night or day we might have to move fast and far in an instant's notice?

I wanted to ask for the map plan back but realized I didn't really need it. The combat company was amazing in that no five paragraph orders were needed to let everyone know what they were supposed to do, and when. They just somehow got the word and knew. Since we'd been engaged with the NVA, I also noted that our casualties had gone down.

"Anything else, sir," I said, wanting to salute but knowing that might be over the top in expressing my disdain.

"Carry on," the captain said, not looking at me while waving one had as if to dismiss some sort of menial servant. The Marines digging the holes for the officers looked up at the same time but I looked away, not wanting to reveal anything of my feelings. I walked away into the bush and headed up the slope, hoping to run into the Gunny without having to ask around to see where he was.

Fessman, Nguyen, Stevens, and Zippo trailed along with me, like no new officers had ever been sent in to command the company. The Gunny was not far from the more open area of trees and sporadic brush that comprised the top of the slope the company was divided down on each side of.

The Gunny looked back at our approach, then turned to await our arrival.

"I hear you've got a command post now," he said, without a trace of a smile.

"Rittenhouse," I replied, getting right to the point.

"Wondered when you'd get around to him," the Gunny said, waving at someone I couldn't see near the top of the ridge. "We don't have a replacement, you know, if you're thinking about…well, you know…" his voice trailed away into silence.

I squatted down to wait. Fessman handed the binoculars to me with a clean sock he'd scrounged from somewhere.

"Thought you'd want to clean these yourself," he said, with a smile.

The Gunny joined us, going to work brewing a canteen holder of coffee.

I began wetting the sock from some of the moist leaves flapping around us in the light breeze. I noted the lack of mosquitoes that would return with a vengeance once the waning sun was gone and the breeze died out. I slowly massaged all the little pockets of mud out of the lenses, finally rubbing the outside of the worn outer coating clean.

Rittenhouse came through the jungle alone, carrying his clipboard, with a pencil stuck behind one ear on his bare head. He looked like a young clerk working at some stateside factory.

"You wanted to see me?" he asked.

"Do you have a daily form you use or do you just write something out in freehand?" I asked back, noting his complete lack of anything but a 'can-do' attitude.

"Of course we have a form," he replied, slipping a sheet of paper out from some others on his clipboard.

I took the sheet and examined it. It was a piece of paper to be filled in, accounting for supplies, with KIA and WIA blank blocks for Marine and enemy casualties. There was one blank space, near the bottom of the form that was titled "Miscellaneous."

I frowned at the blank document, before handing it back. "And so how did the new crew discover that I was the evil genius behind all the company's problems?"

"I don't know," Rittenhouse replied, looking a little perplexed. "I just fill in the blanks and use the miscellaneous box to let battalion know what's going on as best I can."

"So, how did my name come up?" I asked, beginning to wonder about the whole reporting process and who was being told what by whom.

"I never used your name," Rittenhouse said. "The company commander is responsible for everything. You were the company commander, or so the Gunny said. Before that it was him."

I looked over at the Gunny. He shrugged, his face a puzzled mix of frowning wrinkles and a smile.

"The miscellaneous box," I said. "Do you have to put anything in it?"

"I suppose not," Rittenhouse replied.

"Then leave it blank and make sure the Gunny or I see it every damned day before it goes on a chopper. And if those guys want to see it then make sure we see it after them," I followed, pointing back to where the command post was being erected.

I sat checking out my binoculars after the boy-clerk was gone. It wasn't Rittenhouse I realized. It was the war, Vietnam, the situation, and a whole load of bad communication and piss poor leadership at all levels. I had no doubt that the name "Junior" had come to Casey and his lieutenants from the daily report, but Rittenhouse also had a point. Just who in hell's fault was anything? Was I at fault if the whole Kamehameha Plan went into the toilet and we suffered heavy casualties? If it all came off as planned, then we'd simply move down into the A Shau in the morning. There would be no reward. If it went wrong, many of us would die and it would all be my fault. I stared at a bug sitting on a leaf through the right lens of my "Jappo" binoculars. The bug didn't know what was coming in the night and enjoyed a state of being at fault for nothing, no matter what happened in that night. I would not have that luxury.

Brother John came through with his last radio broadcast of the day. No homilies, no preaching, and no smarmy talk about going home. Just Jay and the Americans singing about *this magic moment … forever till the end of time …*

addendum

Thirty Days Has September: The First Ten Days was written over a period of three months, with the chapters published online day by day until it was done. Comments were accepted from the thousands of readers who read the regular episodes of the novel being offered. You can read those comments at *www.JamesStrauss.com*.

A selection of those comments are detailed here in this addendum because of the heartfelt nature in which they were offered. The author could not help but respond to each and every of the thousands of comments because of the poignant manner in which they were written and freely offered.

Ron Johnson

The comment section is almost like a reception party, with you as the host — and a very good one. Much is shared in common at the gathering here with those among you, and even with those of us that stayed behind, but with you now. The camaraderie is excellent. Then I realize the sobering fact of just how personal this all really is to many with you here, but especially to yourself. It is reflected in your explanations of Gunny, Sugar Daddy, Jurgens, and the Captain *etc.* and how each touched you personally by their actions. The making of this epic tale involved the blood, sweat and tears of your whole company, and then the historical approach to your documentation in writing it to share with us. I can't thank you enough, but by the prayer that when the reception is through, and we all return to our own thoughts, that a great warmth of comfort may be appreciated by you from the fires ignited here in our breasts. Thank you, James. S/F.

Comments from John Conway
12-23-2016
I invariably attempt to compose my comment immediately after reading the segment for the first time. I invariably fail. My emotions are raw. My thoughts totally jumbled.

I try to write, and it's gibberish. I can't even recognize it as my own writing. I feel within me the panic set in that would accompany your head-long rush down that hill. Soldiers throughout history cause their own stampede as their backwards motion turns into a flight that undoes all thought but escape. Whatever is back there can't be as bad as what's coming. Yet you stop. "My terror was back. I realized I was blind, and then I could not hear. The sounds of combat deafened my ears." Not only required to curb your own doubts, but to argue your not-even-confident plan to the Gunny, and accepting the "damned if I do and fucked if I don't" reality. The bald fact that you can, and do, recall these events with such clarity is testimony to the ferocity of the flame that burned them into your brain. You should never have to explain or apologize why that brain is imprinted with the scars of war.

12-28-16

I have come to look forward to reading the comments almost as much as reading your narrative. To say you've struck a collective nerve would be bordering on the trite, but it's a fact nonetheless. I see no "fools or simple vicarious adventure-seeking creatures" in this line up of commenters. (And your well thought-out replies reflect that.) You've given voice to a genre of reluctant remembers, all of similar vintage, who applaud your efforts and your accomplishments. It's an analogy only the farm bred will get, but when you're digging manure and the pitchfork finally hits the concrete under the compacted shit, you know you're making headway. Write on, Strauss, we've got your six.

01-19-17

"I celebrated at being alive, unaware of any responsibilities I might have or communications I should consider." And that encapsulates the entirety of the previous 24 hours of self-doubt, fear, uncertainty, and second-guessing of the "new leadership" of the company. The "what ifs" evaporated. The NVA did what you guessed they would. The Army arty did what you expected them to do. Your own Marines did more than you dared to hope they would. And you,

Strauss, self-deprecating, sleep deprived, exhausted Lieutenant of Marines, made it happen. Deal with it.

Comments from SFC. Robert Ecklund, Army (Ret.)
02-22-2017
Afternoon, Jim. Yes, love it. Let the story be told raw and
deep, There is deep truth in what you are reveling as you
write it raw…..Like the unhealed wounds that still fester
from then till today, Yes reality deep raw and ugly Yes,
From one magnificent bastard of the dark to another,
Keep the story coming raw…… I am waiting on your
book, I will buy it, But two things, Yes, The response's
as they come in now, and the raw story before editing,
should be added, especially the responses from those who
saw it in the reality of then.

I find it funny, The discussions of time travel, and I have
come to the conclusion that it would be impossible, For
like a Map those points in time are fixed and in flow of
time and space they are fixed to the past to be learned
from, I do believe that God made that so, Yes so we could
never go back to wreak justifiable vengeance on those who
would abuse our youth so venially, The Dwyer's Stewart's
Casey's, Jergen's….. Yes if time travel was possible we
would have a time world of blood feud that would make
the worst of any historical feud look like a dance after the
Friday night football game.

Yes, I sit and read, and My now screams with suggestions
and knowledge that cannot be transmitted back to a person, That My military career taught me to mentor, con-
serve, and protect, Yes, I have put together a good map
with the information in the story, Yes flying slicks gives
me a highpoint overview of the world of shit the A Shau
Valley is in the coordinate in time and space is for a young
Second LT. I can see two other FSB that could bring fire,
one to your direct east, FSB Bradley a Army FSB, and one
to the WSW of Cunningham, LZ Erskine, Yet due to what
ever it appears that you were not informed of their exis-

tence for what ever reason ... ... Yes the stupidity of inter service rivalry, and the Fog of War, Yes, I want to badly to have a way of getting that information to the Fighting Bastard Junior because I am suppose to take care of my men first, last, and only when Murphy queers the play, say good by, rest, you have done your time min hell.... Yes, My Crew Chief .... My CWO II ... My Platoon Sargent .... selves and Now my Old Bastard are screaming all of our hope and knowledge and prayers for a LT. Named Junior, a Magnificent Bastard of the Dark ... ... Lost ion time .... Thankfully still alive to tell the story, Yes, That is why I believe in God, Because this is his plan for you, to tell Your story and Help other Heal, and Heal Yourself Junior, SIR! LT. Strauss.

01-16-2017

Man, you bring back so many memories, Yes Flying every day unless the bird was down for maintenance, Dealing with dickheads who didn't realize how far up their fourth point of contact their heads were, and that it could get them killed, Yes that captain who they dumped on you so he could check His next career box for advancement, He reminds me of one we received into my flight platoon for career development, I was lucky, I survived the my day fly with Him, My sister bird 298 didn't, He wouldn't listen about flying the same route, You didn't ever go to the same LZ the same flight route twice, If a single bird flight, It was either low level as you could get, balls to the wall, or 1000 feet or above, in and out, to do log and resupply to the grunts, He was hogging all the stick time he could, well His HU4PC, cost him, the problem is it took 4 other men with him.

Comments from Walter McKinley

01-09-2017

The use of " fresh" 2nd Lts. as scapegoats in the Army existed in Korea also. By no means as deadly as the Nam but the same career killer. The RTT Platoon, Co. B, 304th Sig. Bat. 8th Army Support Command was a rather rowdy bunch that needed a bit of a kick in the discipline area. No "good" Lts. were available because no one cared. A new CO brought a plan. First was the ROTC 2nd. Lt. that we chewed up and spit out. We didn't know that that action allowed the CO to get his man in, a 1st. Lt. with a love for the Orient grown in the Nam. He survived an extended tour there, came to our little paradise and chewed us up and spit us out like pistachio hulls. That you've survived so far in this must be like you said, Artillery, that your Gunny was in survival mode only must be testament to previous command. I've not heard of a Gunny taking any kind of shit from anyone, you were well, and truly screwed before you started

12-13-2016
I wonder how many civilians even think about aiming at and killing an individual. Heats of the battle, shooting to keep "them" down, that sort of thing, we all think that. The personal touch of what you did is a whole other thing. I chambered one round and switched my M-14 to "fire", pointed it at one man's chest one time and STILL wonder.

Comment from Suzanne Ward
03-04-217
I'm following your story with my husband, Ron. As a Vietnam vet, he understands the situation in ways I never could. Thank you for sharing such a compelling account of this experience. It has created, for us, a way to talk about it, and a way for me to understand what he went through, and how it still impacts him. Thank you for expressing what so many have lived and felt. You're creating a vehicle for important dialogue.

Here's a conversation between a reader and me. You can see many more conversations like this at *www.JamesStrauss.com.*

Molly Dalrymple Miller
My fear is that you are not going to be able to keep up with the demand of this book. I'm the wife of a Vietnam Vet.

I'm not sure if he will read it because he still suffers from his tour. But I'd love to have it and have the chance to read it myself !! Thank you so much for sharing this story of a tour in hell !

James Strauss
Thank you so very much for that thought Molly. It's my surprise and pleasure that so many real vets have taken to like they have. I didn't think I'd have much credibility in telling the story because I thought it was so rare. But it turns out it wasn't. Lots of guys were seeing and living through versions of the same...

Molly Dalrymple Miller
Consider it a blessing to a lot of them. You are helping them cope with something they otherwise might not ever be able to !! Thank you again and God Bless !

The Next Installment of the Trilogy

Thirty Days Has September

THE NEXT TEN DAYS

Stay alert! Watch your six!

www.JamesStrauss.com
for updates and more!

James Strauss

Down
In
The
Valley

An Arch Patton Thriller

"If you temporarily want to escape your mundane world, have a great adventure, and safely re-enter your own reality, this book is for you."

www.JamesStrauss.com